Camp Resurrection

A Novel

Joerg Mueller

Copyright © 2021 Joerg Mueller
All rights reserved
First Edition

NEWMAN SPRINGS PUBLISHING
320 Broad Street
Red Bank, NJ 07701

First originally published by Newman Springs Publishing 2021

ISBN 978-1-63692-656-8 (Paperback)
ISBN 978-1-63692-657-5 (Digital)

Printed in the United States of America

December 21, 2019

I'D BE AMISS if I didn't thank several of the people who were of tremendous help and invaluable morale booster while I was writing this book.

First and foremost, thank you to Mira Garin, a graduate of Brandeis University, whom I haven't seen in well over twenty years. It was Mira's glowing review of my manuscript that pushed me and *Camp Resurrection* over the finish line. Without Mira's encouraging review, this book would still linger among millions of useless bytes inside my computer.

And then there are Kaitlynne and Kassondra, my two incredibly gifted granddaughters whose enthusiasm designing the cover illustration for this book was contagious, infecting everyone around *Camp Resurrection* with their passion.

And lastly, but certainly not least, a great big thanks to my wonderful wife who put up with my highs and lows, and my more than occasional bouts of bitching while I was trying to find the right words.

Thank you, all of you.

Prologue

DAVID NATHANIEL KOERTNER was born at 8:20 PM on May 25, 2048. According to Amelia Swenson, one of the nurses on duty that night in Manhattan's St. Luke's Hospital, David was a beautiful baby, whose light blue eyes, cherubic face, and light blond fuzz transcended his bloody afterbirth and set him apart from the other babies in the maternity ward. Nurse Swenson was quoted as saying, "Mark my word, this little boy is destined for greatness."

On August 25, 2048, three months after his birth, David Koertner underwent government-mandated DNA testing at Downstate Medical Center in accordance with the Future Crimes Prevention Act of 2023. David's genetic makeup was found to be defective and a statistical analysis predicted that he would commit felony crimes during the first forty years of his life. He was convicted and sentenced to life imprisonment without parole at Camp Resurrection, a federal maximum security facility in Upstate New York.

Immediately following his conviction, David was placed in the custody of the Federal marshal's office and processed. His parents were ordered to submit to psychiatric counseling to help them cope with loss of their only child. After attending one session, during which they were informed that they would not be allowed to have any contact with David, they both committed suicide.

*****

Camp Resurrection is a three-hundred-thousand-acre detention complex in an area formerly known as Catskill State Park, a mountainous and heavily wooded region approximately eighty miles north of New York City. Fifteen years in the making, Resurrection was thought to be an ideal place to isolate socially unacceptable children and let them mature into adults without exposing them to the pressures and temptations of modern America. Resurrection did not resemble a conventional prison. The towns and villages of the area had been recycled into a community infrastructure. There were group homes, hospitals, schools, and administrative buildings. There were restaurants and ball fields and recreational halls. There was also the Wall, a half-mile wide strip of denuded no-man's land that ran along the perimeter of the camp. And there was a total information blackout. Resurrection was a closed society in which history books had been rewritten and where knowledge of the outside world was punishable by death.

*****

On June 1, 2048, David Nathaniel Koertner was processed at Checkpoint K-1, one of four official entry points into Camp Resurrection. He was examined by Dr. Liu Xiang and given a clean bill of health. David was immunized, deloused, prescribed 500 milligrams daily of Libidex-M, a male sex hormone retardant. He was outfitted with three sets of Resurrection Rags, green cotton infant clothing, which identified him as a Quadrant 1 resident, and placed under the supervision of House Mother Mathilda Quog, a fifty-five-year-old ex-nurse at the Poughkeepsie House of Detention. Quadrant 1, originally known as the city of Kingston, had an ample supply of schools and hospitals and was considered ideal to house and treat the camp's youngest residents.

The screaming and red-faced baby Koertner was transported to a semi-private room in Greenkill House, a group home on State Street. Thirty-five minutes later, he was assigned to room 311, bed A, where he would remain indefinitely. His roommate was Justin Frederikson, who had been classified as a maximum security inmate due to his IQ of 169.

Chapter 1

"You what? Are you out of your mind?" Cecilia Austin stared at her daughter with incredulous disbelief, then made an about face and stalked into the hallway.

And so Dawn Austin, a shy and introverted twenty-eight-year-old Barnard graduate, found herself alone in her living room, painfully aware of her mother's abrupt departure. Seventeen floors below, traffic snaked along Manhattan's Riverside Drive in a monsoon-like downpour. Beyond, Riverside Park was a ribbon of sodden green separating a stream of brake lights from the leaden waters of the Hudson. Suffocating clouds blanketed the distant lights of New Jersey.

It was a miserable night. A depressing night on which Dawn couldn't find comfort in the cozy cocoon of the small but posh two-bedroom apartment she shared with her mother. Everything about the place was usually so soothing. The glowing embers in the fireplace, one of only three in the entire building that had been restored to working order at great expense. The gleaming cherry-wood mantle that held a collection of family photographs, three generations of Austins, most of which Dawn had never met but all of whom she loved. Mom had made sure that the Austin family history was a living part of Dawn's life. Ever since her toddler days, Mom had kept the family history alive, reminiscing about relatives while they cuddled on the cushy living room couch. Stories which made the past come to life with accounts of her grandparents who'd arrived at JFK airport more than sixty-one years ago, carrying one suitcase and life-long memories of Ireland. Stories about Aunt Sylvia whose eccentricities knew no bounds but who had been shrewd enough to amass a small fortune in the bull market of '14 through '21 while a member of an investment club of likeminded spinsters. And of course, countless stories of her father, whom she'd known for only sixteen years but who had, according to Mom, swept her off her feet on the eve of a long-planned wedding to another man, someone who Mom now described as a stuffed shirt, a pompous ass, and an unabashed womanizer.

Dawn let her eyes move along the gallery of relatives, wondering how they would have reacted to her decision to enlist as a psychiatrist in a prison. Dad wouldn't have objected, she knew. And Aunt Sylvia would definitely have encouraged her. But the others? Dawn couldn't imagine the rest of the stern relatives approving of a member of the Austin clan going to work at a dreadful place like Camp Resurrection. Studying their collective faces, she could well imagine their reactions, seeing their disapproving frowns, even downright shock. Imagine, they'd say, an Austin, one of their own, a woman in the prime of her life, living and working in a camp for genetic misfits. It was a fate worse than death.

Dawn frowned at the photographs. Dad gave her an encouraging smile. Sure, he was concerned. She could tell by his furrowed brow and the probing look in his brown eyes, but his smile said, *It's your life and nobody can live it for you.* She turned to Aunt Sylvia's photo and immediately recognized the determination in her eyes. *You show 'em what us Austins are made of.* Well, two out of eight wasn't bad, Dawn thought and dismissed the rest of the clan.

Mom was harder to dismiss, though. She wanted her mother's approval more than anyone else's. Mothers were supposed to encourage their daughters, not hold them back. But that was exactly what mother was doing with her misguided maternal instincts. And although there was nothing Mom could do to change her mind, her adamant reaction hurt. When would she accept the fact that her daughter had grown up? Mom of all people should realize that gangly pre-teener Dawn had grown into gangly psychiatrist Dawn, courtesy of Mom's money and Barnard College.

With a defiant *so there* lodged in her brain, Dawn nevertheless felt familiar twinges of self-doubt nudging aside her fragile confidence. And once she got into this blue funk nothing helped but a good, old-fashioned little-girl cry and Mom's reassuring voice telling here that everything would be okay. Not even Dad telling her that she was a big girl now and that big girls have to stand on their own two feet and that making mistakes was okay because that's how little girls became big girls. Even Aunt Sylvia's nod of approval, with a twinkle in her eye that said *Go get 'em, girl*, couldn't make her feel better. All of which convinced Dawn that maybe, just maybe, she was still Mom's little girl after all.

Sure, she could think of plenty of reasons why a smart, young woman like her should pursue a safe career counseling angst-ridden patients. How else could she make two-hundred dollars a pop helping her rich patients come to terms with their psychotic phobias in the comfort of a leather couch. And wasn't that what it was all about, making money? And if she could make someone feel better in the process, great. So why should she run off to some Upstate prison and waste her time on a bunch of genetic misfits who neither wanted nor deserved her help?

Why? Because she was as guilt-ridden and psychotic as those she had vowed to help. Because of an event that was still etched vividly in her mind twelve years after it had happened. So maybe she wasn't quite the idealistic woman she wanted to be, so what?

Self-examination wasn't her strongpoint though because it often led to admitting one's weaknesses. And so, utterly confused and frustrated, Dawn did the next best thing. She slouched into her favorite wing chair and started crying, which brought Mom rushing back into the living room. Dawn avoided her eyes with an embarrassed smile.

"Sorry, Mom. I didn't mean to scare you."

"Can we talk about it?"

"Oh, Mom, please don't nag," Dawn pleaded. "It's too late. I'm signed, sealed, and almost delivered. So what do you say we make peace and you buy me dinner in my favorite Chinese restaurant. It'll probably be my last hot-and-sour soup for a couple of years."

*****

Signed, sealed, and *almost delivered* turned into *delivered* at 1700 hours on Tuesday evening. Funny, Dawn mused as she walked into the Times Square recruiting station, I'm already thinking like I'm in the military, referring to her appointment as 1600 hours. Also reminding her that she was now government property were more tangible signs. The Times Square office, which only three days ago had made her feel like a grown-up who was making a grown-up decision, looked, for lack of a better description, military. It reeked of bureaucracy. It was drab and dehumanizing and desensitizing, a place where her previous life ceased to exist. If its intent was to make recruits feel insignificant, the office was a smashing success.

Shoulder-high partitions separated the space into five cubicles, each crammed with a metal desk, filing cabinet, and two uncomfortable chairs. Substituting for ambiance were numerous flags: Stars and Stripes, the New York state and city flags, and of course the official Camp Resurrection banner. Framed by this colorful display of patriotism were portraits of uniformed men with stern expressions. Below the ceiling hung a stale mustiness that irritated Austin's throat and made her eyes tear.

Apparently not many New Yorkers had read the ad in the Barnard journal that had attracted Dawn's interest. She was the only civilian in the office. Still, she was subjected to standard bureaucratic red tape. She signed in, took a number, and sat on a wooden bench for ten minutes before her name was called. Dawn used the wait to compose herself. By the time lieutenant Bradenton escorted her into one of the cubicles, her jitters had all but disappeared.

Bradenton was a short and stocky man with a buzz-cut, piercing brown eyes, and an annoying habit of clearing his throat. In his late fifties, his skin was taut, his voice strident, and his mannerisms those of a gung-ho DI. He brushed an imaginary speck of dust from his starched shirt and pointed in the direction of the only visitor's chair in the cubicle.

"Have a seat, Austin."

Bradenton excused himself and returned a minute later, carrying a soft-cover booklet, several pre-printed forms, and what looked like a hotel laundry bag. He placed the items on the desk and arranging them as if building a symbolic wall between himself and Dawn.

They sat facing each other for what seemed an eternity before he spoke. When he did, he pointed at the articles piled on the desk.

"This," he said, "is what we refer to as the Resurrection Bible. The first section explains everything about Camp Resurrection, its purpose, its social structure, and so on. The second section deals with your particular function in the camp. It explains your job, your rights and responsibilities, how your performance will be measured, in short the rules and regulations associated with your particular job classification. The next section deals with such general issues as Camp etiquette, the moral values we expect from you, permissible social interaction between Camp employees and inmates, a description of typical staff living quarters, and suggested personal behavior. In other words, it spells out how you're expected to conduct your personal life as well as the environment you can expect to live in."

He smiled dryly. "There's a reason we call it the Resurrection Bible. We expect you to follow it and the rules it outlines religiously. Understood?"

Dawn nodded. She still hadn't said a word.

"Good. But just in case you don't, there's an appendix dealing with infractions and the consequences, your rights to appeal any disciplinary actions, etc. You should also know that as an enlistee in Resurrection, you fall under the jurisdiction of the New York State Department of Corrections. Their judiciary is structured similar to the Military's. Major infractions may therefore lead to court-martials by a Resurrection Tribunal. I suggest that if you have any questions about what's I permissible and what's not, ask before you do. Understood?"

"Yes, sir." Dawn had the ridiculous notion that she should snap to attention but Bradenton had already turned his attention to the second stack on the desk.

"This is a standard medical release form." He slid the paper to Dawn's side of the desk. "When you arrive at Resurrection, you'll be medically re-certified. You'll need to fast for twelve hours prior to your appointment. Also refrain from having sex during a twenty-four-hour period before the exam. Any questions?"

"Yes, I just…"

"Is that a problem, the sex part?" Bradenton asked sarcastically.

"No, of course not."

"Because if it is you're in for a heap of disappointments for the next three years."

Dawn blushed and thought better of giving Bradenton a piece of her mind. *Drop it*, she thought, *you'd better get used to it*.

"Look," Bradenton softened his tone. "It's not a big deal and we're doing it for your own protection as well as ours. We just have to make sure that if there's anything wrong with you, you're not bringing it into Resurrection. You see, because of the virtual isolation our inmates live in there are a number of modern-day diseases like AIDS that have never made their way into the camp. We're not about to jeopardize our medical paradise because one of recruits is infected. Okay?"

Dawn nodded.

"You are to report to Resurrection City's main gate at 0800 hours on Monday, the seventeenth. If you need a ride, there's a bus that leaves from this office at 0400. No reservations required. Just make sure you bring no more than one suitcase and only those articles permitted in Camp. You'll find a list of permissible items in section one of your Bible.

"After your medical examination, you'll be transported to Boot Camp at 0100 sharp. That'll give you plenty of time to have a bite to eat in the cafeteria. Please don't wander off, though. Any contact with inmates is prohibited until you've been issued your permanent ID card."

Bradenton picked up the next form on the desk. "Here's our confidentiality agreement. Believe it or not, this may be the most important document of all. The people who run Resurrection are pretty damn touchy about keeping certain things confidential and I can't say I blame them. Basically you're sworn to secrecy at all times about everything. So keep your mouth shut. If you're not sure if something is confidential, assume that it is."

Bradenton picked up the last paper. "And finally, here is a copy of your enlistment certificate."

"And this?" Austin pointed at the plastic bag.

Bradenton reached for it and slid it to Austin. "It's your uniform. You don't have to wear it until you get to Camp although most recruits prefer to put it on before they make the trip upstate. It seems to help them make the transition from civilian life."

Austin peeked inside the bag.

Bradenton allowed himself a rare smile. "It's not the latest Paris fashion," he said, "but it's sturdy and well-made. You'll be issued another set in Camp."

"Is that it?" Austin asked. The entire process had lasted less than ten minutes.

"What else did you expect?"

"Well, I guess I expected to get oriented," she said. "I mean, that's what this was supposed to be, wasn't it? Orientation."

Bradenton didn't look pleased. "Okay, Austin. What do I have to do to get you thoroughly oriented? I wouldn't want one of our people to be disoriented so early in her career."

"Well, I'd like to get some insight on the workings of the Camp and its residents. Just so I can be prepared when I get there."

"You'll have plenty of time to get prepared once you're in Boot Camp. And there's really nothing you need to know that you won't find in your Bible."

He was about to dismiss her but changed his mind. "Let me give you some free advice," he said. "You just referred to the people in Resurrection as residents, and that's the politically correct way to call them. But what they really are, are inmates. They just don't know it. I know it and you know it. So watch your back. It may someday save your life."

He stood and Dawn jumped to her feet. But instead of shaking hands he gave her a quick salute. "Dismissed, Private."

*****

Dawn didn't know what she had expected, but this wasn't it. Her session with Bradenton had been brief, impersonal, and above all, intimidating. Equally as intimidating were the possessions she was now lugging home on the A train. One shapeless uniform tailored of green khaki and one-hundred-fifty-six pages that spelled out her life for the next three years.

As the subway wound its way beneath Manhattan's Upper West side and she was jostled by the usual rush-hour crowd, she steeled herself for what Mom would have to say. And suddenly Dawn realized the wisdom of what Bradenton had told her about wearing her new uniform. But it wasn't just the fact that it would ease the transition. Putting on that uniform was a symbolic gesture, an act that made her enlistment irrevocable and set her apart from fellow New Yorkers.

*****

Mom wasn't home yet. A message on the machine said that she had to work late and wouldn't be home for dinner so why don't you call for some take-out. But Dawn wasn't particularly hungry. She dropped her belongings next to the bed and avoided them for the next hour as if they were contaminated with bubonic plague. Instead she rummaged through the refrigerator and opened a Budweiser, something she hardly ever did. She gulped the full twelve ounces in less than a minute. Straight from the can too. Very unladylike, and very un-Dawn-like. But this wasn't the same old Dawn, she told herself. This was Counselor Austin, woman of responsibility and authority, Resurrection psychiatrist, little girl grown up, standing on her own two feet.

And so Dawn slipped into her next life, trying to act worthy of her new position. Trouble was, she didn't really know what that entailed. So she bit the bullet and trotted into the bedroom to get her copy of the Bible. She even considered putting on her uniform. That would really get Mom, wouldn't it? She reconsidered quickly. Why antagonize Mom? And the drab uniform was probably even less flattering than she remembered and the last thing she needed right now was to look like a girl scout on a field trip who got herself separated from her troop.

She opened the Bible and randomly flipped through its crisp pages until a chapter explaining her living quarters caught her eye.

Staff accommodations are based upon occupant's rank. Use index on page 58 to determine which room classification applies to you.

Dawn flipped to page 58, located her accommodation category, and found her job code. *You are entitled to a single-occupancy suite of no more than 210 square feet, located on the ground floor of the group home you are assigned to. Your suite will be outfitted with a twin-sized bed, nightstand, writing desk, desk chair, and one occasional chair. A private bathroom adjoins your suite and will be equipped with a water-saving toilet, single-sink vanity, and stall shower.*

Thanks for small favors, Dawn said, thinking wistfully of her whirlpool tub. And while you're at it, you might as well say goodbye to your comfy, queen-size bed and down comforter and the wall of books. Not to mention the convenience of a doorman and a concierge. But it got worse.

For your personal entertainment, your suite will be equipped with a single-channel television set and an AM radio, which can receive all stations between frequencies 550 and 1100. You may also borrow books and periodicals from your local Resurrection library.

Dawn flipped through a few pages until the text caught her attention. *A word about security. In order to foster a climate of trust, staff quarters are to be kept unlocked at all times. Security is provided by closed-circuit surveillance cameras, which will be monitored twenty-four hours a day by same-sex security staff. In addition, a panic button is located next to your bed and in the bathroom. In the unlikely event that you should need immediate assistance, use them. Remember, safety comes first.*

A few pages later, she found what she considered a demeaning piece of advice. *Use common sense and remember that you are a model of authority and moral virtue. Never act in a suggestive or seductive manner, even if it appears innocent to you. Such behavior may invite unacceptable behavior by the inmates, the consequences of which could be severe. Never invite an inmate into your suite after curfew. It is a punishable offense for both you and the inmate.*

Enough of this. Dawn flipped to the first page. *Welcome!* It read. *Welcome to a challenging and rewarding career in America's premier rehabilitation institution. Camp Resurrection is a place unlike any other in the United States of America. It is a model penal institution that has made breakthrough strides in the complex effort of modifying criminal behavior for the good of all humankind. Our methods are revolutionary yet simple. We welcome the youngest criminals with open arms, raise them in strict isolation from society at large, and use the most advanced behavior modification techniques to re-engineer their defective minds.*

In order for you to become an integral part of Resurrection, it is important that you understand its concepts. This chapter is therefore intended to familiarize you with our world, the rules we live by, and the treatment we administer. You may think it presumptuous to refer to a prison camp as "our world," but that is exactly what it is. Inmates are admitted to Resurrection at a very young age, usually before their first birthday. That is also the last time they are referred to as inmates or prisoners. From the moment they are admitted, they become residents. They have no concept of family life. Parental roles are filled by camp workers. In short, the traditional role of family runs counter to the concepts of Resurrection. Here, everyone is family. Everyone is loved and treated equally. The words mother and father are meaningless, and while residents are familiar with those words, they are only used for the animal kingdom. Horses and dogs and cows have mothers and fathers, but not our residents. They have merely brothers and sisters.

We go to great lengths to protect our insular society. The world of Resurrection ends at its containment perimeter, beyond which the known world ceases to exist. Our residents think of anything outside Resurrection the same way people think of life outside the universe. Everyone knows that there are countless galaxies in outer space but they are a vast unknown. It is our job to insure that our residents feel similarly. This obviously requires re-educating the mind and suppressing curiosity.

Resurrection's social structure works in many ways to reinforce these goals. It begins with the concept of communal living. Residents live in group homes, usually twenty to thirty residents per home. They share semi-private bedrooms with roommates that have been selected based on genetic compatibility. Each home has common living quarters and bathrooms. Strategically placed communal buildings are used as recreational facilities, cafeterias, and so-called quiet rooms which are reserved for inward reflection and worship.

What you will not find are locked doors. Locks are superfluous in a communal society and tend to reinforce segregation or class systems. Additionally, a locked door provides an unhealthy environment in which residents could be tempted to express antisocial behavior. You will also find that the door to your suite cannot be locked. This too has been done to eliminate segregation and make residents think of you as their equal. Rest assured that in the forty years of Resurrection's history there has never been a single case of a staff member being robbed, attacked, or molested.

A word about nomenclature. Residents start life in Resurrection as Disciples. They proceed through school, are taught a trade, and perform meaningful and satisfying jobs. Most will remain Disciples for the remainder of their lives. A small minority who have responded well to treatment and demonstrated extraordinary promise are promoted to the rank of Apostle, an elite status among residents and one that may eventually lead to release into society. Apostles are assigned to administrative, scientific, and teaching positions. They also enjoy private suites and are allowed greater interaction with camp staff as explained in chapter 17.

As is the case with residents, camp staff members are assigned appropriate job titles. Prison guards are Guardians. Teachers are Sages. Doctors are Healers. Psychiatrists and behavior modification professionals are referred to as Counselors. Top administrators are called Benefactors. If this sounds righteous and self-serving, it has stood the test of time. You will find that the social structure and naming conventions have gone a long way to preserve our virtual garden of Eden.

You will also find that this garden of Eden bears a remarkable likeness to life in small-town America during the mid-1950s. The top rated shows on WRES, the camp's only television station, are Brother Knows Best, The Sister Reed Show, and Ted Mack's Disciple Hour. News shows are not generally aired, nor are documentaries dealing with inappropriate or confidential subject matter. Religious shows are permitted but all references to particular denominations have been edited out.

Printed materials are readily available via many libraries throughout Resurrection as well as the Resurrection Sentinel, our daily newspaper. Residents are encouraged to read at all times.

Private telephones are not permitted. Public telephones are located in many communal areas. They are provided free of charge but are restricted to service within Resurrection and monitored at all times. Transcripts of...

Dawn put down the Resurrection Bible. Words spun in her head and disillusionment nudged aside her dedication to heal. How the hell was she going to work in this Disneyland for the criminally insane? Had Mom been right all along? No, she told herself. She'd just have to find a way to work within their rules. Besides, it couldn't be as bad as they made it sound. Fighting back self-doubt, Dawn picked up the Bible again and flipped through more pages, hoping to find something encouraging. And she did when she spotted a chapter describing how she'd be working one-on-one with her case.

Upon arrival you will be issued temporary residency documents, examined, and transported to Resurrection University. There you will be trained to deal with the unique requirements of your new job. After graduation you will be assigned to work one-on-one with a Disciple, whose progress is your sole responsibility. You will remain with your assigned case until he or she is deemed rehabilitated by an administrative panel. Should your tour of duty end prior to that event, Camp administrators reserve the right to extend your enlistment period by up to three twelve-month terms.

While you are on active duty, you will be free to socialize with other Camp employees and take advantage of all staff facilities. You are also entitled to two weeks furlough per year, which you may spend at one of Resurrection's two resort facilities. You will, however, be restricted to Resurrection property. Under no circumstances are you to leave Resurrection or have contact with any person outside the Camp. While you are on active duty you will also be subject to a camp-wide information blackout.

You will find that these restrictions may inconvenience you at times. Rest assured that they are necessary for the wellbeing of our population and the furtherance of Resurrection's guiding principle: breaking down barriers between staff and Disciples and building the trust without which Resurrection cannot function.

Once again, the Camp's administrators welcome you and hope that your tour of duty will be fruitful and beneficial for all.

Dawn placed the Bible on her bed. So far everything she'd read made Resurrection look like an alien world shrouded in religious propaganda, similar to cult camps of yore. All that emphasis on secrecy gave her goosebumps. They apparently didn't even trust the people who worked for them. But what the hell. She wasn't planning any grand vacations, and besides Mom, there really wasn't anyone she kept in touch with. And sooner or later she'd find someone in Resurrection with whom to bond. So it probably wouldn't be so bad after all.

Convinced that the rest of the intro would be the same mix of religious fervor and self-congratulatory drivel, she flipped ahead to what Bradenton had referred to as Camp etiquette. According to what he'd told her, this section would explain such items as moral values, permissible social interaction between Camp employees and inmates, and suggested personal behavior. What she read made her heart sink. *For obvious reasons, any pictures, photographs, wall hangings, and other items of decorative nature are subject to review by authorities and may be confiscated if found to be of objectionable nature. Printed, audio, or visual materials of any kind are strictly prohibited. As a rule of thumb, you will not be permitted to keep any articles other than those intended to promote physical wellness or personal hygiene. If you can live without it, don't bring it. All confiscated materials will be returned to enlistee's home address at enlistee's expense.*

Convinced that sooner or later she'd come across something encouraging, Dawn kept reading. *This place is so surreal*, Dawn thought. *It really is a Disneyland for the criminally insane. Imagine living in a theme park and believing that's all there is to the world? Don't these people even know that they're living inside a wall?*

She was quick to answer her own question. "No, of course not. Not if they're brainwashed and drugged up." But she knew full well that the alternative, conventional prisons with locked cells and barbed wire fencing, was a far worse fate than living in a place like

Resurrection. The next paragraph reassured her even more. It listed literally hundreds of clubs and organizations that were available to the inmates. There were athletic organizations for virtually every known sport. There were chess clubs that held annual tournaments, a debate club, Bible classes, music instructions, a performing arts society which put on shows and concerts, libraries, workshops, and on and on and on.

She breathed a bit easier. Until she picked up the book once more and continued reading. As soon as she did, her misgivings were back.

To reiterate, in order to maintain an insular society, Resurrection enforces a strict information blackout of the outside world. As mentioned previously, you will not find radio or television coverage of news events. The camp's own radio and television station restricts news coverage to Resurrection itself, while entertainment programming usually consists of 1950s and 1960s vintage situation comedies. The Resurrection Sentinel is the only newspaper permitted in camp. Each of Resurrection's five libraries have extensive collections, encompassing children's books, theological works, classics, mythology, and some scientific publications. Works of fiction are censored for content, with particular emphasis on violence, sexual situations, and depictions of any of the ills that plague modern society.

"Christ, this is worse than *Fahrenheit 451*," Dawn told herself. "How can these prisoners ever get released into society if they're kept in the dark?"

Everything she read rebelled against her psychiatric training. Her dark mood became oppressive. She put down the Resurrection Bible and tried to regain her earlier enthusiasm. Usually one to find reasons for optimism even during the darkest moments, description of life in Resurrection was a lot to swallow. She was tempted to close the light but knew that sleep would be elusive.

"Might as well get all the bad news out of the way all at once," she said out loud and picked up where she had left off. *It is important to remember that your job is to reinforce Resurrection's life style at all costs. You must be enthusiastic, fair-minded, and committed to the Camp's principles. You are expected to serve as a role model at all times. Above all, you must remember that you are no longer a civilian. During your term at the Camp you are subject to Resurrection's laws. Failure to comply may result in dishonorable discharge or court-martial. You can find a complete list of "dos" and "don'ts" in chapter 18, but here are some common sense tips. Observe the camp-wide curfew of 10:00 PM. If you have a demonstrated need to be away from your quarters after curfew, you must obtain a permit from the Camp administrator and must be accompanied by a guard at all times. Wear your uniform whenever you are in contact with inmates, regardless of the hour of day. Avoid revealing or provocative clothing even when in your own quarters. Do not socialize with any inmate, even in the interest of rehabilitation.*

"Oh well, there goes my social life," Dawn grimaced. Not that it was anything to write home about, but with a ten o'clock curfew and her decidedly asexual uniform she might as well forget about dating for the next two years. Throw in Spartan living quarters, grueling work hours, minimal pay, and doing household chores she wouldn't think of doing at home, she'd be happy to crawl into bed by ten.

"I suppose they're trying to make me look and act just like one of the inmates…oops, Disciples I mean. Maybe by the time my tour is up I'll believe in their Land of OZ myself." Dawn allowed herself a brief chuckle before she flipped to the next page.

A word of caution, Never forget that all inmates are subject to ongoing behavior modification, psychiatric counseling, as well as medical treatment. Many have developed chemical dependencies. Some suffer from a variety of mental illnesses. All have genetic deficiencies which make them potentially violent. Every one of them has been convicted by the New York State supreme court as a potential felon. Their ingenuous and childlike behavior is a veneer that covers their predisposition to commit violent crimes.

Never underestimate any of them. Never do or say anything inflammatory. Avoid close physical contact. Report all suspicious behavior to your supervisor at once. Failure to comply will result in disciplinary action.

Dawn shrugged her shoulders, closed the book, and turned off the bedside lamp. Wide awake, she whispered, "I hope I'll get my own life back before it's too late."

An hour later she was still crying.

Chapter 2

"Hi, David, ready for Retooling?"

Doc Brauner greeted me with a warm smile and a firm handshake, trying to put me at ease. He led me past a row of waiting Disciples and ushered me into his private office. I'd been in Doc Brauner's private domain many times before, but despite my familiarity with the small, cramped space I was apprehensive. The once-a-month ritual, officially known as Physical and Spiritual Maintenance, always had that effect on me.

Come to think of it, no one in Resurrection liked going through the mandatory one-hour procedure that was meant to keep your body primed and your mind pure. The physical part of it wasn't bad, just the ordinary stuff where they hook you up to all kinds of equipment and look at every bodily function from your heart beat to brain waves. But the spiritual portion was a different story. It was ominous, even sinister. They put you to sleep and you had no idea what they found out while they were snooping around in your brain. It was like going to confession without knowing what you confessed to. You only remembered that it started with Brauner giving you an injection. Then, within a few seconds you drifted into a deep sleep. By the time you woke up the treatment room was empty. Only a hint of Brauner's cologne reminded you that he had just dissected your mind. I don't think I had any secrets, but if I did Brauner knew them even if I didn't.

That secrecy surrounding the Spiritual Maintenance portion was probably what bothered me the most. Not knowing what transpired during the sixty minute session, was unnerving. I suspected that something important had happened while I was asleep on one of the paper-covered examination tables. I had dim recollections of Doc Brauner's droning monotone while he talked to me. Somehow I knew that I answered his every question, even volunteered answers. When it was over I felt a tiny sting in the crook of my arm where Brauner had injected me, a Mozart piano concerto floated in the air, and a glass of chilled orange juice sat on a metal bedside table.

Although it was a relief knowing that all my sins had been forgiven and that my newborn purity of soul would help me serve my fellow disciples for another month, I couldn't help but think that I had a right to know what it was I needed forgiveness for. Maybe if I knew I wouldn't have sinned in the first place. But then, who was I to question anything? I was only a Disciple. *Rejoice in the blessings of Camp Resurrection.*

In a way I was one of the lucky ones though. I didn't think I had much to worry about because I did my best to use each day to better myself. Unfortunately not all Disciples felt that way. Like my roomie for example. Justin wasn't bad. Far from it. He had a heart of gold and I loved him like a brother, but he asked too many questions that he wasn't supposed to. Lately he'd been talking incessantly about *The Outside,* a subject that was taboo in Resurrection. We all knew there had to be something outside our world, but the thought was so inconceivable, so scary…

Justin had become obsessed with the subject, and I was really concerned that he'd wind up in a heap of trouble. *Borderline subversive* is what Brauner had labeled him. *Inquisitive to the point of being a danger to himself.* And those were the kinder comments that hung over Justin's head. Others called him a Judas, and some even said he should be shipped to *The House.*

Merely thinking of *The House* was intimidating. I'd never seen the place myself; none of us ever had. But we all knew it existed, about fifty miles west of Resurrection City, surrounded by hundreds of mountainous, uninhabited acres. The fact that I didn't know anyone who'd ever seen *The House* in person made it all the more ominous. We only talked about the place in hushed whispers, as though it was a living, breathing creature and speaking about it would bring us bad luck. It was best to keep your mouth shut and your nose clean.

Whenever *The House* was in the back of my mind I wondered if I ever talked about it with Brauner during Retooling. Which brought me full circle to Retooling, which awaited me in less than two hours. And to Justin, whom I was increasingly worried about.

I've shared room 311 with him all my life, through good times and bad. I've laughed at his pranks, cried for him when he didn't make the cut as Apostle candidate, and argued with him when he called me Brauner's pet flunky. Justin was as much a part of my life as breathing and eating and sleeping. Now, as I was laying in Doc Brauner's *Retooling* room, waiting for my session to begin, recollections of this morning's events were typical of why I worried about Justin.

"Hey Justin," I called.

There was no answer.

I squinted into bright early-morning sunlight, rolled over on my side, and stared at his empty bunk. Crumpled-up sheets lay in disarray at the foot of the bed. A misshapen lumpy pillow was propped against the metal headboard. But Justin's Resurrection rags, his Camp-issued Jeans, green cotton shirt, baggy white shorts, and green tube socks, which he usually left strewn between his bed and closet, were missing. And so was Justin.

"Oh shit," I said under my breath. "Where the hell is he now?" I knew he could be in a million different places. He could have a perfectly good reason for not being in his bunk. But I knew Justin. And I knew that Justin being AWOL was trouble with a capital T.

Five minutes later he bounced into the room, twitching with excitement and a broad grin on his face. He let himself fall on his bunk and turned to me. "Hey Davey, guess what?"

"What?" I was in no mood for playing one of his stupid games and my voice showed it.

"Gee, you don't have to sound so pissy," he said, still smiling. "I have some news that'll blow your idea of Resurrection being a Paradise to smithereens. I just…"

I held up my hands to stop him in midsentence. "Stop it, Justin. I don't want to hear any more talk about *The Outside*. Enough. Don't you realize that you're gonna be in a shitload of trouble if you keep that blasphemous talk up. Brauner's gonna ship you to *The House*."

Justin wasn't fazed by my sudden outburst. "Just listen, Davey."

I shook my head vehemently. "NO. I'm not going to listen. As a matter of fact I'm going to talk to Brauner about an idea I've had. I'm going to suggest that you're reassigned to work on the Sentinel with me. You could do research on some of the articles I have to write. You'd be good at that, going out in the field, interviewing Disciples, digging up little tidbits. You have the right kind of personality, an easy charm, a charisma that disarms people and makes them open up. And we both know how you love to dig up dirt. That way I can keep an eye on you and keep you out of trouble."

Justin looked stunned. "You think Brauner would go it? He asked.

"Why not. He himself said that I needed help. And he's got the pull to make anything happen."

Justin nodded. "Yeah, he does. But do you think the little fag would trust me?"

I nodded. "I'm sure I can talk him into it."

Justin had turned quiet. He was obviously interested, weighing the pros and cons. Then his face lit up. "I'd be a real reporter, huh? I could go out and snoop without getting into trouble? Ask a lot of questions? Get at the truth?"

"Yeah, exactly." I said with resignation.

A smile flickered across Justin's face. He stuck out his hand. "Shake, partner." We shook. Justin with excitement, me with trepidation. He must have noticed my expression and said, "Don't worry, Davey. I'm not going to get you in trouble. But I will get to the truth. Even if they kill me for it."

"No one is going to kill you," I said with forced cheerfulness. "Not in Resurrection. And now, what's that exciting news that'll blow me to smithereens?"

Justin turned solemn and stony faced. "You know Josh?"

"You mean Josh Brannigan?" Brannigan was a twenty-eight-year-old Disciple who lived in Ulster Hall. I had just interviewed him last week. He was an all-around nice guy, a hell of an athlete who'd made the Resurrection All Star football team three years in a row. And he wasn't just a typical jock. Unlike a lot of those muscle-bound jerks Josh was quiet and hard-working. A real role model. "What about him?"

"He's dead. The poor sonofabitch was stabbed to death night."

Chapter 3

AN EMBOSSED NAMEPLATE mounted eye-level next to the door read *Bruno B. Brauner, MD*. From behind the door, visible through a two foot square opaque glass panel that had been reinforced with wire-mesh, the soft glow of a desk lamp threw a muted puddle of light into a narrow hallway. It was the only light in the deserted corridor that ran the length of Terwilliger House's ground floor. At eight o'clock in the evening the official Psychiatric Evaluation and Behavior Control headquarters of Camp Resurrection had been locked up for two hours. Bruno Brauner was the only person still in the building.

After concluding his last examination of the day he had dead-bolted his office door and engaged the privacy chain for added security. That had been more than an hour ago, minutes after Rachel Firestein, his administrative assistant, had left for the day. Brauner had used the time since her departure to sort through the day's events, trying to come to grips with a potential problem he hadn't anticipated. It had taken him a full sixty minutes to convince himself that he didn't have anything to worry about. And even if he did, there was very little he could do. Therefore, he concluded, the best thing to do was to do nothing.

Now Brauner was hunched over his desk, a disarray of papers staring at him. An overflowing ashtray reminded him that he had smoked way too many cigarettes during the last hour. Next to the ashtray sat a half filled coffee mug, which Brauner hadn't touched since his last appointment, David Koertner, had left. Next to the mug stood a water glass that was coated with the pungent remnants of his second three-ounce shot of Wild Turkey, Brauner's unofficial early-evening nightcap.

Nearing sixty-nine years of age and continuously abusing his body with Bourbon, Brauner was in deteriorating physical condition. He was overweight, his waist having grown half an inch a year during his last five years, and had a wheezing cough that racked his chest for twenty minutes each morning and wouldn't quit until he coughed up a mouthful of phlegm. He attributed the deterioration of his physical condition and appearance to the normal aging process. But lately the deterioration had accelerated. His face, once cadaverous looking and characterized by prominent cheekbones and a large nose, had filled out and was perpetually flushed. He found it harder to breathe. His energy levels had dropped off sharply and he now required short catnaps in the afternoon. His reflexes had slowed at an alarming rate and he found it increasingly difficult to drive a car, having had several near mishaps when he wasn't able to brake in time. Simultaneously his receding hairline had lost its battle against baldness more than two years prior. He now had a tonsure of closely cropped gray hair, trimming it whenever wispy white curls threatened to give him the appearance of a disheveled drunkard. But to Brauner's dismay, his near baldness had not spread to his face. Grey stubble covered his cheeks and chin by early afternoon despite a daily 8:00 AM shaving ritual, which always started with whipping up a foamy solution with his late father's bristle-hair brush and stropping his treasured straight razor. Brauner held on to the archaic razor even though shaving with it had become a difficult chore, based in part on the changing contour of his face and his aging skin which had lost its elasticity over the years. Despite occasional nicks and perpetual rashes, he always concluded the ritual by splashing after-shave lotion on his face and inspecting himself in a magnifying mirror until the burning ceased.

He had bought the magnifying mirror at the same time he had purchased a new pair of reading glasses. His watery blue eyes could no longer detect the tiny white stubble beneath his lower lip or focus on standard size print. The day he couldn't read the Resurrection Sentinel, the camp's weekly newspaper, without the aid of a magnifying glass, Brauner had reluctantly put his physical needs above vanity and bought the glasses at the local commissary. For a while he had considered wearing a monocle, thinking that a single lens held in place by nothing more than ocular muscles would lend him an air of old-time disciplinarian, but had given up on the idea in favor of the convenience of wire-rimmed frames. It was his jowls however, two increasingly prominent folds of flab that framed his once strong jaw line and had lately become the source of ridicule by his patients, that bothered Brauner the most. He had always been self-conscious to a fault. Hence the tendency to wear his hair short and shave every morning, even on days when he didn't have to be in the office.

He loathed slovenliness, which he attributed to a breakdown of old-world values. Brauner knew it was preferable to look like an old-time authoritarian rather than wear Jeans and sports shirts, sans ties, as his younger colleagues did. Their casual attire was a betrayal of his upbringing, and Brauner wanted no part of it. He stubbornly held on to his three-piece suits, white cotton shirts with plastic collar stays, and subdued navy-blue ties. His suits had been let out three times during the previous five years. The lapels were wider than fashion dictated. The material was threadbare and shiny. Yet he scoffed at remarks that he looked like a twentieth-century pretender to the throne of a third-rate European monarchy. Let them call him the king of Resurrection. Let them laugh and snicker behind his back. Let him be the butt of their jokes. Brauner preferred to stand out as a symbol of old-world dignity. More importantly, all the ridicule in the world meant nothing because he had the ultimate weapon on his side, power.

Brauner inhaled the remaining fumes of Wild Turkey and squinted at the wall clock. He'd wasted enough time already this evening. Paranoid about being spied on, he turned up the radio's volume until Beethoven's Eroica boomed from the speakers and no one could hear him. Next he shuffled to the door and double-checked the deadbolt, then drew the blackout shades. He considered another shot of Wild Turkey but abandoned the thought reluctantly. Instead he locked up the bottle in his filing cabinet and rinsed his glass thoroughly.

Brauner crossed back to his desk and knelt next to the chair. He genuflected and bowed his head, his scalp reflecting the glow of the desk lamp. He shut his eyes and began an incantation with impassioned fervor. "All powerful father, give me the wisdom and strength to remain your faithful and obedient servant. Forgive me my transgressions, for I have failed thee miserably once again. I have not yet rid myself of the demon bourbon and as a result my judgement has been clouded at times. But I have never once wavered in my commitment to thee."

The words came easier now that he had admitted his sins. "And I have not wavered in my commitment to preserve Resurrection as your kingdom. All preparations have been completed with magnificent results. I think you will be pleased. Within a month, *He* will be placed in the hands of a counselor who will test his resolve and guide him during his difficult transition. He will see the boundaries of Resurrection. He will learn of the outside world and reject its evil ways. He will become our greatest Apostle."

Brauner's voice turned an octave shriller as he continued. His chest rose and fell with mounting excitement. But despite his feverish pitch not a soul could hear him above Eroica's thundering climax. "He is ready. Before long you will welcome David Nathaniel Koertner into your army. Hail to thee, father."

Brauner pulled himself up, holding on to the desktop to steady himself. Despite aching knees and his lower back screaming with pulsing spasms, he felt renewed. Once back on his feet, he hurried on stiff legs to the filing cabinet. He selected the top drawer, but the rollers resisted him. Infuriated by the drawer's obstinate disobedience, he yanked hard until it budged open. Standing on tiptoes Brauner peered inside the drawer and selected one of the folders that were crammed tightly into folding hangers. Again he yanked, increasingly annoyed that an inanimate object should give him this much trouble, and pulled the folder free. *D.N. Koertner*, and in smaller letters beneath the name, *Final Recommendation*, stared at him. His hands quivered with anticipation and he nearly dropped the folder, catching it at the last moment and wedged it between his chest and right arm.

Eroica was over. It was almost nine o'clock. He'd have to hurry so as not to arouse undue suspicion. Rachel Firestein, who was a dreadful snoop and who he suspected to be Axton's mole, had already asked him in a most undiplomatic manner what he was doing locked in his office every night while all the other staffers relaxed in the *Apostle's Lounge*, sipping drinks and discussing the day's events. He had smiled politely at his secretary, detesting her arched eyebrows, pointed nose, and pinched lips, and told her in the most jovial voice he could muster *Just wrapping up the day's loose ends, Rachel. When you get to be my age, you know, everything takes a little longer.* Then he had winked at her in a conspiratorial manner but had merely succeeded in looking lewd, and smiled again despite the distaste he felt for the woman.

He hurried back to his desk and swept a mountain of papers aside to make room for the Koertner file. He stared at it, transfixed by the gravity of the moment, his hands folded prayer-like. Then he took a deep breath and flipped to the first page. His eyes scanned across the paper, drinking in the familiar words, and he allowed himself a triumphant smile. Page after page glided past him, each filling him with satisfaction and heady accomplishment. Yes. He had done his job well. David was ready. Except for the final detail of course.

Brauner reached the last page and stared at the only blank section in the report. He uncapped his fountain pen, another treasured memento left to him by his father, and wrote in intricate script, applying varying degrees of pressure to the pen and thus visually emphasizing the importance of specific words. He wrote haltingly at first, careful to choose the right words, searching for descriptive adjectives to stress a particular phrase or de-emphasize another, all the while striking a delicate balance between a psychiatrist's professional evaluation and a priest's impassioned plea to his flock. Soon the words formed in his mind quicker than he could write them, and he forced himself to slow down his thoughts so he wouldn't lose them before committing them to paper. Fifteen minutes later, satisfied with the results, he blew on the paper to dry the ink, a habit he had developed when the pen had been willed to him. Brauner knew that the act was completely symbolic. The ink had long since dried, but he knew that authors of old used to do the very same thing and enjoyed imitating them. His act of self-indulgence was the perfect ending. With the day's work behind him, Brauner read his recommendation out loud.

It is the unanimous recommendation of the Psychiatric Board of Camp Resurrection that David Nathaniel Koertner is elevated to Apostlehood at this year's meeting of the Judgement Day committee. Our recommendation is based on scientific data which is fully documented in appendix A. Methods of evaluation included DNA analysis, medical examinations, psychiatric evaluations, Most importantly were Koertner's positive reaction and unshakable commitment to Resurrection's tenets during stress-inducing virtual reality sessions. In accordance with Camp Resurrection's guidelines, results of the aforementioned categories were assigned weights and served as the basis of computer projections. As is customary, three separate statistical models were run with the following results: Mr. Koertner scored 100% when the best-case scenario was used, 95.47%, when the most likely scenario was used, and 91.76% when the worst-case scenario was used. Given a margin of error of +/- .0005 basis points, Mr. Koertner has scored well above the required minimums. In fact, his total score is the highest in Resurrection's history.

As is typical of all inmates who have undergone years of behavior modification and sexual inhibitors, Mr. Koertner has developed severe emotional retardation and chemical dependencies. He cannot function without Resurrection's rigidly structured support system or continued use of medication. These conditions are usually not reversible but Mr. Koertner has shown that he is an exceptional candidate for transition into the final phase of behavior modification and intellectual engineering. He is well equipped to handle the rigorous demands of future assignments.

His emotional negativity factor, measuring malice, prejudice, and greed are the lowest ever recorded in Resurrection. Mr. Koertner's knowledge of the outside world will be infused in massive doses during intensive psychiatric sessions with an outside counselor. This will help to de-emphasize his association with and reliance on the Camp's own doctors. Monthly dosages of Pro-Cerebrexx will be administered and adjusted as needed, and he will be weaned off Libidex-x as to decrease his reliance on that drug. It is expected that Mr. Koertner will exhibit symptoms of adolescence within three months of treatment and transition into nor-

mal adulthood within six months. It is estimated that at that time he will be able to receive and interpret sensory impulses at the level of a genius. Concurrent with his increased mental capacity, his reaction to emotional stress will be diminished. Consistent with the final objective, Mr. Koertner's ability to perform his duties will therefore be based on facts, not emotion.

Mr. Koertner's transition will commence as soon as his psychiatrist. Dr. Dawn Austin, bas completed Resurrection's induction requirements. Transition treatment is expected to last up to six months. At that time, Mr. Koertner will be made aware of his new responsibilities.

In the unlikely event that Mr. Koertner does not respond to treatment, as determined by this board no later than twelve months from the date of this recommendation, Mr. Koertner will be cancelled. Bruno B. Brauner.

Brauner wrung his hands with pleasure, knowing that failure was out of the question. Never before had he seen a more suitable candidate than David. It wasn't just the computer results, the myriad of statistical models, or the psychiatric evaluations, all of which had yielded high marks during David's thirty-two years in Resurrection. Neither was Brauner's conviction based on the steady upward curve of several success-probability projections, which had caught Brauner's attention years ago. More than anything scientific, it was Brauner's gut that told him he finally had a winner.

He scanned his recommendation into Camp Resurrection's central computer system and filed the original in the filing cabinet, one drawer above his Wild Turkey. Then he raised the blackout shade and peered through the window. A three-quarter moon hung in a cloudless sky and splashed Albany Avenue with pale light. As usual at this late hour, neither pedestrians nor motorists could be seen. Devoid of life, Albany Avenue and the row of stone houses facing it reminded Brauner of another place, another time. The image was disturbing, and he armed himself with quick shot of Sour Mash before venturing outside.

Euphoric yet still paranoid about keeping his late-evening whereabouts secret, he attempted to disengage the privacy chain without making undue noise. It resisted his fumbling fingers and he mumbled under his breath, *Get a hold of yourself, you bumbling fool. Nothing will go wrong.* His hands steadier, he slid back the privacy chain, flicked the light switch, and released the deadbolt. He twisted the doorknob and tugged the door ajar.

Facing him, standing on the other side of the threshold and bent over at the waist as though his ear had been pressed against the door, was the shadowy outline of a man. Brauner sucked in a deep breath and flicked the light back on, feeling tendrils of panic crawl along his spine.

"Hi, Dr. Brauner," the man grinned and straightened up. "I didn't know you were still in the office."

Brauner took another deep breath and wiped a trickle of sweat from his forehead. "Hello Justin. What are you doing here?"

Chapter 4

"WELCOME TO RESURRECTION, Private Austin. Do you have any other luggage besides this?"

Border Guard Pulsifer, a squat, middle-aged man with military style buzz-cut and acne-disfigured face placed Dawn's induction certificate next to her Coach suitcase, a going away present from mother. He tapped it with a wooden pointer.

Dawn shook her head, becoming irritated with the man's arrogance.

"Open it please."

She did as told, fitting the key into the lock.

"We will hold that for you," he said curtly as she dropped the key into her purse. "You'll find that in Resurrection there is no need for keys."

"But..."

"Please empty the contents on the table."

Again his pointer tapped, this time because she hadn't obeyed his order quickly enough. Dawn fought back anger and unpacked her meager belongings.

"Your purse also."

She dumped the contents of her purse unceremoniously unto the table.

"Thank you, Private."

She watched dumbfounded as Officer Pulsifer painstakingly inspected and segregated her belongings into two piles. The entire process took less than five minutes, after which Pulsifer filled out a legal-sized form letter. He handed her the completed document.

"Sign here, please. The items I've checked off are prohibited and will be returned to your home address by ground carrier. You may pack the rest of your belongings and proceed to gate 'C' where a bus will take you to Boot Camp."

Dawn was stunned as Pulsifer began placing a small mountain of her belongings into a cardboard box. *This is absurd,* she thought, as she watched a number of innocent looking personal articles disappear inside Pulsifer's carton. *Totally absurd,* she thought again, and said aloud "This is absurd."

"Private Austin, if you have any objections you may state so in writing to Colonel Axton."

"I don't understand. What's wrong with this stuff? Here, take a look. It's nothing but…"

"Fill out this protest form and send it Colonel Axton. Now move along please. You're holding up the line."

With those parting words the last of her objectionable items were gone and she made her way through gate "C." Left behind were her cell phone (all communications devices were prohibited), her makeup kit (promoting vanity), her lacy black panties and brassiere (articles of moral turpitude), her keys, and various other sundry articles. Also left behind were her dignity and self-esteem.

*****

Following a bad beginning at the hands of Guard Pulsifer, things turned progressively worse. At the completion of her first week in Boot Camp, a run-down onetime resort complex thirty miles north of Resurrection City, Dawn Austin regretted her decision to enlist in the face of Lieutenant Bradenton's warnings. Although she wasn't quite sure what galvanized her disillusion, a continuous sense of depression and hopelessness had replaced her usual level-headedness. Sergeant Ritter, a seasoned and pragmatic instructor who had been assigned to Dawn's class, downplayed her malaise as a normal reaction that plagued most recruits. He blamed it on a combination of homesickness and what he called the *Wall Syndrome,* an unfamiliarity of living within the confines of a prison. But Dawn knew instinctively that there was more to it than that.

She could excuse her humbling treatment at the hands of Pulsifer as a normal reaction of a pampered young woman who found herself thrust into a quasi-military environment. She could overlook her living quarters, which she considered far worse than some of the halfway houses where she'd done volunteer work. The saving grace was a private suite that awaited her after graduation.

What she couldn't come to grips with was a numbing hypocrisy that pervaded every nook and cranny of boot camp. Despite the do-good, pseudo-religious zeal of her instructors, she suspected they were narrow-minded and self-serving posturers who didn't give a damn about anyone, least of all the inmates. Compounding her misgivings was an intuition, almost a clairvoyant feeling, that absolutely nothing in Resurrection was real. She felt as though she had entered a surreal world. And although this world was neither particularly frightening nor depressing, it filled her with hopelessness. If she felt this way, Dawn reasoned, how must the inmates feel?

Dawn had always prided herself on being straightforward and honest. She decided to confront Ritter with her misgivings after her first week in Boot Camp. The other recruits had already filed out of the classroom, eager to get back to their quarters and enjoy two days of relaxation. Dawn fidgeted in her seat, not quite sure how to approach Ritter, when he raised his head and asked her pointblank, "Something wrong, Private Austin?"

His brusque question caught her off-guard and she started to blink her eyes at once. "Well, yes." She hesitated and cleared her throat while Ritter waited for her answer. She could tell from the drum roll of his fingers against the desk that he was getting impatient. She continued, "Not wrong, sir. But something is bothering me, and I'd like to discuss it with you."

"Well, go on, Private. Discuss."

"It's this place. It…"

He interrupted her with a sarcastic smile. "It gives you the creeps?"

"Well, I wouldn't put it quite that way, but, now that you say it, yes. It does."

He stepped off the podium and walked to a window that faced a large meadow fringed by trees. In the distance, mountains thrust into a leaden sky. Ritter pointed toward the meadow.

"Private, I want you to take a good long look out of this window. Do you see the meadow out there? You know, every Monday morning, when the maintenance crew mows, you can smell the grass clippings all over boot camp. There isn't a smell in the world that can compare to it. And those trees at the edge of the meadow, they're over one hundred years old. Century old maples and willows. In the fall the colors are glorious. As a matter of fact, in the fall the mountains are glorious. Every shade of red and orange and yellow that you could imagine. And still there is some green among the foliage. That willow over there for instance remains green long after most of the other trees have lost their leaves. Then when autumn is over you would think that this place looks dreary for the next five months. Quite the opposite, Private Austin. There is a special beauty here in the dead of winter. It turns into a stark landscape, cold and forbidding, but quite beautiful with an ethereal quality. You see, the snow doesn't melt like it does downstate, it just gets deeper with each snowfall. And it never turns slushy and gray the way it does in the city. It remains like a virginal blanket, not unlike a downy featherbed protecting the earth from bitter cold winds and long nights. And when Spring finally arrives, a million flowers burst into the most incredible bloom you have ever witnessed. Wildflowers become an unending kaleidoscope of colors, subtle nuances and brilliant shades, nurtured by Spring rains and a gently warming sun."

"Why are you telling me this, sir?"

"Can you think of a more beautiful setting, Private? Take a hard look. Use your imagination if you must. Then compare it to the Manhattan House of Detention, that brick bastion of criminal justice that towers twenty stories above the slums of Lower Manhattan. Maybe you don't know, but that place is home to ten times as many rats and roaches as it is to prisoners and more than twenty inmates commit suicide every week. Here on the other hand, we haven't had a suicide in over a year."

He turned from the window and stared into her eyes. "And on your way to your room tonight, take a look at some of our group homes. Go inside and take a firsthand look at how at how our Disciples live. Look at the doors. You won't find any locks on them. And the windows. No bars anywhere. Then come back and tell me that you think Resurrection gives you the creeps."

"Sir, I agree with everything you said. It is beautiful here. But that's not the problem."

His voice turned harsh. "Then what is the problem, Private?'

"I don't know," Dawn admitted and threw up her hands. "That's just it, I don't know. I can't put it in words, but there's something different here. Different and frightening. Oh, just forget it, sir."

She rose to her feet when Ritter stopped her. "You're quite right, Private. Camp Resurrection is different. No matter how beautiful the setting may be, no matter how much freedom we give our inmates, it's still a prison. And all of our prisoners are like children, innocent and ingenuous. They haven't been given the chance to learn hatred and bias like the rest of us. We're teaching them to live in peace and harmony. We teach them love. Maybe that's what you feel. Maybe a crime-free society is something you're not used to."

Dawn gathered her books and turned to leave. "I'm sure you're right, sir. I'm sure I'm not used to your virtual Garden of Eden." She walked past rows of desks and empty chairs, painfully aware of his eyes on her back. "Thank you so much, sir. Thank you for setting my mind at ease."

*****

Dawn told herself that Ritter was correct. It was easy to forget the real purpose of Camp Resurrection when the setting was so contradictory. A prison without visible bars. Thirty thousand inmates living without crime. Guards that looked like forest rangers. More doctors and nurses and teachers and psychiatrists per capita than could be found in a typical American town.

Her cheerlessness gave way to optimism. It lasted until she readied herself for bed in Cryder Hall, a dormitory style room she shared with nine other recruits for the duration of boot camp. Still wearing her uniform, she brushed her teeth and combed her hair. In a fit of childish abandon she stuck out her tongue, screwed up her face like a wrinkled prune, hunched forward and scratched her sides. Her 'Dawn the Monkey' pose, which she'd perfected over the years after seeing Natalie Wood try it in *Miracle On Thirty-fourth Street* had never failed to cheer her up. Today she cringed. The Dawn of old, that idealistic and comfortably familiar person was gone. In her place a new depressed, cynical, and draconian Dawn stared back at her from the mirror.

Her olive green uniform, consisting of military-style cotton blouse with epaulets and breast pockets, ankle-length skirt, white tube socks, and work boots, minimized whatever traces of femininity she had. The uniform's only saving grace was that it hid her legs, which were blessed with a long-distance runner's calf and thigh muscles rather than the shapely curves of a model. Without makeup, her face looked pale and drawn. Lack of sleep had left dark smudges beneath dull eyes. An ugly pimple bloomed in the corner of her mouth.

"They've succeeded," she said gloomily. "They've taken an ugly duckling and made her even uglier." No man would give her a second look now, even if she were the last woman on earth.

That however was nothing she needed to worry about. Although she hadn't expected an active social life, she hadn't counted on spending her next two years in monastic isolation. But that appeared to be her fate. Contact with inmates was forbidden outside therapy sessions unless prior approval had been obtained. Camp employees didn't offer any relief either. Guards were generally aloof. They didn't like psychiatrists and regarded her as a necessary evil. To them she was a nerdy egghead who meddled in affairs she knew nothing about. The Camp's professional employees were cliquish and reluctant to be associated with a "rookie," perpetuating a plebe class system they once endured themselves. That left her classmates, ninety eight young men and women who would soon be dispersed across three hundred thousand acres.

Neither did she have any time to socialize. Pre-sunrise bugle calls and 10:00 PM curfews framed a grueling work day which left her too exhausted to think of anything but sleep. The few moments of free time she had were spent studying, keeping her quarters clean, and making sure that her uniform was freshly laundered, ironed, and ready for inspection.

Each week Dawn earned an additional "stripe." Not a stripe actually, but rather a cross which she had to sew on her jacket. On this, her first Friday night, she stitched her first cross to the flap of her breast pocket. She stared at her bare breast pockets and epaulets, reminding her that she still had three weeks of Boot Camp to endure. She crawled into bed, drew the covers to her chin, and cried.

But none of this, not the *Wall Syndrome*, not the perceived hypocrisy, not her unflattering uniform rivaled the chilling effect next Monday's class had on her. After taking a hasty last sip of morning coffee, Dawn picked up her briefcase and hurried out of dorm room 3A. Dodging a rush of other recruits, she weaved her way along the hall, down two flights of stairs, and took a shortcut through the sports complex. She cut across an overgrown tennis court and hurried along the swimming pool which had been abandoned five years ago and was filled with ankle-deep brackish water. She zigzagged across the picnic area, through a stand of pines, and arrived at Matthew Hall a minute later. In her previous life Dawn had always romanticized about the halls of higher education, convinced that they reeked of academia, of books and chalk, and that one could smell knowledge in the mortar and brick. Matthew Hall smelled merely old and musty.

Five minutes into class Ritter addressed her with his usual sarcasm. "If you don't mind, Private Austin, would you please grace us with your presence. I can see you. I recognize your face. Now if you could get your mind to join your body, maybe we can get started. We have a lot of material to cover today."

As Dawn had feared, her Friday afternoon confrontation with Ritter seemed to have been a mistake as he picked on her. She snapped to attention and looked up self-consciously.

"Thank you." A round of sniggles accompanied Ritter's reprimand. "As I recall, we reviewed Resurrection's social structure last Friday. Does anyone have any questions?"

There was no show of hands.

"Then we'll go straight to the meat of why you're here. During the next three weeks you'll learn how to live with our Disciples. If I do my job well, you'll recognize them for what they are. Not the innocent, sweet men and women they appear to be, but dangerous and potentially violent criminals. The hardest lesson for all of you to learn is that you're dealing with the proverbial wolves in sheep's clothing. Make no mistake, they are outcasts from society. It'll be your job to remake them, to shape their minds, to play God if you will. You, and only you will have the power to convert them into lambs."

Blind sheep would be more appropriate, Dawn mused.

"The best way to prepare you for your work is to throw you to the wolves in the form of real-life, unrehearsed confrontations with some of our Disciples. I think you'll be surprised at what you'll experience. Do I have any volunteers?"

Again there was no show of hands. Dawn surveyed the sea of faces around her, all of them apprehensive, each trying to look occupied with one thing or another, none of them much older than she. Ninety eight men and women, none willing to be God. Not even for a day.

"All right then. Private Austin, will you do us the honor and join me on the podium?"

Shit, she mumbled under her breath. She picked up her textbook and notes, and squeezed her nearly six foot frame out of her old-fashioned school chair.

"You won't need those." Ritter's words stopped her in her tracks and she dropped her book on the desk. "This will be completely ad-lib. Even the slightest hint that you have prepared yourself for the encounter, such as carrying a textbook, will be counter-productive."

Ritter held out his hand and helped her up the podium, a ten by ten foot elevated platform at the head of the class. A sweep of his hand pointed to one of two chairs.

"Have a seat please."

He let her sit in silence for a few seconds, waiting for stage fright to set in. The class watched with eager anticipation for their first encounter with one of *Them*. The normal hushed murmur died. Ninety eight pairs of eyes were glued on Dawn.

"The important thing to remember," Ritter finally went on, "is that there is nothing you can learn from a textbook to prepare you for an encounter with a Disciple. The only weapons at your disposal are quick thinking, a healthy respect for your opponent, and a thick skin."

"Is that what they are, opponents?" Dawn surprised herself with her question.

"Oh yes, certainly. At least until you have transformed them. What they ultimately become is up to you." He rewarded her with an oily smile. "If you're good, and lucky, you might even mold one of them in your image."

"Isn't that a bit presumptuous?" A disembodied voice at the back of the class wanted to know.

"Perhaps. But unless you're cocky enough to assume the role of God you're dead meat. And remember. Thick skin. Disciples are like children, no matter how old they are. They possess the candid ingenuousness of children, along with the inherent cruelty children bring to the table. Never forget that politeness is a learned trait, as is obedience. Our children never had a father figure or role model. The veneer of civility found in adults hasn't hardened on these men and women. They're as delicate as egg shells and crack just as easily. So while you have to be firm and authoritative, don't squeeze too hard or you'll have egg on your face."

"Not to mention a dead chick," Dawn added sarcastically.

"Quite true," Ritter said with equal sarcasm. "But you can always make an omelet."

Dawn cringed at Ritter's tasteless remark, realizing that it was exactly this kind of callous attitude that made Resurrection so depressing. She felt a confluence of hatred and fear, feelings she seldom experienced. This otherwise unimposing middle-aged instructor frightened her. There was nothing about his looks to justify her fears. He was bland, strictly average looking, neither handsome nor ugly, with no unusual features or characteristics that set him apart from ordinary men. If she were introduced to him at a party, she wouldn't remember him the next day. Indeed, although she had seen him every day for a week now, she wasn't sure of the color of his eyes or even his hair. If it weren't for his uniform, a black cotton outfit of pleated baggy pants that disappeared inside ankle-high combat boots, a waist-length jacket with epaulets, breast pockets and two flapped pockets on each arm, a red silk ascot fluffed beneath his chin, and a red beret cocked roguishly at a twenty degree angle and emblazoned with a silver cross, she'd be hard put to pick him out of a crowd. But his voice revealed the true Ritter, unemotional, dispassionate, and sarcastic.

Ritter disappeared momentarily into an anteroom to her left, then walked quickly back to the podium, leading a young man to the empty seat by her side. "I'd like you to welcome Disciple Ezekiel Vandeman. Ezekiel, please take a bow."

The young man bent stiffly at the waist. Dawn was fascinated. He was the first Disciple she had met face to face. Tall and lean, with the brutish good looks of a movie star, fierce blue eyes, and a shock of light brown hair, Ezekiel looked nothing at all what she had expected one of *Them* to look like.

"You may sit down now Ezekiel," Ritter said with a rare resonance of tenderness, as though speaking to a son. "I'd like you to meet Private Austin. She is new here. She doesn't know very much about our home. Will you help her?"

*****

Within minutes Dawn Austin forgot that she was sitting in front of ninety eight recruits. Long gone was her nervous twitching. She didn't know that she was in Matthew Hall and that minutes earlier she had been too frightened to think clearly. This, after all, was why she had enlisted. Helping him. Helping hundreds of others like him. Suddenly the notion of playing God wasn't quite as preposterous. She relaxed. *You can do this*, she told herself. *Just be yourself. All you have to do is touch his heart.*

The very next moment she was blindsided.

"Why do you hate me?"

Spoken with the honesty of a child, accompanied by intense probing of his eyes, the question left her speechless.

"Why…? I, I don't hate you. What makes you think I do?"

"Aren't you here to take me away from my friends and family?"

"Of course not," she protested, but knew she sounded unconvincing. *Quick thinking* she remembered Ritter telling her. *What did Ezekiel mean? Something was terribly wrong. What was this stuff about taking him away from friends and family?* "I want to help you and teach you. To get you ready in case you ever do want to leave."

"Leave for where?"

More quick thinking. *All they know is Resurrection*, she told herself. *They don't know about any other place.* Shit. How could she be so stupid? She glanced at Ritter for help but his face was a blank slate. Help came from an unexpected source.

"And what if I don't want to?" Ezekiel asked. Apparently he had already forgotten his first question.

A wave of relief flooded through Dawn. "I don't know the answer to that, Ezekiel. I don't have all the answers, you know. But I want to make sure that you learn enough to make a decision, whatever that decision might be."

She sensed that she had told him the right thing. His intensity softened and he smiled. He extended his hand. Instinct again told her to shake his.

"Okay. I believe you. That you don't hate me, I mean. We're friends then?"

"Yes, we're friends. If you'll let me be your friend." She squeezed his hand.

His smile broadened.

"Okay. You can be my friend. Even though I have plenty of friends already."

*****

The class watched with breathless attention. Ritter had faded into the background, having taken a seat off to the side. The musty odor of Matthew Hall turned into heady perfume as her excitement mounted. It was finally happening. She and him. Now it was all up to her.

But when Ezekiel spoke again his eyes clouded over. "I have a lot to learn, don't I?"

"I suppose. It all depends on how much you know already. But I can help you."

"Will you teach me about the *Outside*?"

Ezekiel's question left her stunned. *So he does know*, she thought. She started to panic, frantically trying to think of what to say. *Hadn't everyone told her…?* She searched for Ritter again, hoping for help. Again he didn't offer any.

Ezekiel grew restless. "Well, will you? I heard that it can be dangerous outside. That there are many bad people there."

"Yes. I'm afraid you're right."

"Then why should I go there?"

"Because…" She paused and leaned forward, was compelled to put her hands on his and look into his eyes. It was important that she'd win his trust. She knew instinctively that it had come down to one critical moment and that she had to make the most of it. If she blew it, there might not be another. Ritter's prophetic warning rang in her ears… *Be firm and authoritative, don't squeeze too hard or you'll have egg on your face.* "Because the most important thing in the world is being allowed to make you own decisions. Freedom to think for yourself."

He looked somewhat perplexed by her answer. "Freedom to do anything I want?"

"Most anything."

"Most? I don't understand."

"What I mean is that you can do anything you want as long as it's legal."

He nodded and his eyes lit up with understanding. "Oh sure, now I understand. I know all about that. We have plenty of rules right here in camp. As long as I follow them I can do anything I want to. But if I don't…" His voice trailed off.

"And if you don't? Go on, Ezekiel. Tell me what happens if you don't follow the rules."

He grinned sheepishly. "Sorry, but that's one of the rules. I can't tell you what happens if I don't."

"Not even to a friend?" She had a feeling she shouldn't push him. He might break.

"Especially not to a friend. Because then my friend will get into trouble too."

"Okay. I understand that." She didn't argue, deciding to back off and changed the subject. "How old are you?"

"Twenty nine and thirty one" he answered immediately.

"Huh? Which is it? Twenty nine or thirty one?"

"Both. I've been in Resurrection for twenty-nine years. I was too young to remember the first two years of my life but they don't really count. So I guess that makes me twenty nine."

"That's a really long time. Did you ever wonder why you've been here all these years?"

"No no no no." He waved his forefinger in front of her. "That's a no no. I can't tell you that. Why are you trying to trick me? I thought you were my friend."

"I am." She was frustrated. Speaking to this grown man with the mind of a child was exhausting. She needed time to think, time to anticipate his answers. She could use a break. She let down her guard. And was totally unprepared for what happens next.

"Can I touch your breasts?"

She froze with shock. "No. Of course not." The words sounded harsher than she had intended and Ezekiel withdrew into a shell immediately. Knowing that she was in danger of losing him she added quickly, "It's just not right to do something like that."

"Is it against the rules?"

Dawn felt like a trapped animal. She had promised herself not to lie. "Not legal rules. Personal rules," she added, trying desperately not to hurt him.

"You mean it's okay to do it, unless the other person doesn't want you to?"

She nodded softly.

He turned from her and lowered his eyes. "I guess that means you don't want me to."

Dawn bit her lower lip and held her breath. Then, her fingers trembling, she reached for Ezekiel's hands and placed them on her breasts. At first she felt nothing but shame. She squeezed her eyes shut and held her breath. It was the hardest thing she'd ever done in her life. She tried to convince herself that Ezekiel's intimacy was only a clinical experiment but failed miserably. Tears welled in her eyes. Her cheeks reddened. Humiliated in front of the class, her shame turned to anger. How could Ritter have allowed this to have happened?

Ezekiel's fingers pressed into her, exploring, pinching. Then they were gone. She opened her eyes and looked at him through a veil of tears.

"Thank you. Thank you for letting me be your friend."

*****

Matthew Hall was deserted. Ninety-eight recruits had filtered out fifteen minutes earlier, leaving Dawn alone with her anger and shame. She had remained on the podium, sitting cross-legged. She had lost all track of time. Inch by inch, late-afternoon shadows crept across Matthew Hall's wooden floor. Dust motes danced in the remaining beams of light that slanted through the windows.

She jumped when she heard approaching footsteps. Ritter made his to the platform and took the seat next to her.

"Congratulations, Private. You passed your first test." For once his voice wasn't sarcastic.

"You could have warned me," Dawn said.

"About what?" he asked. "About the kind of questions he asked? About him wanting to know about the outside? Or maybe that he wanted to touch your breasts?"

"Yes," Dawn whispered. "Yes to all of that."

Ritter cleared his throat. "Let's get something straight. I told you all along that Disciples are children," he said. "Remember the word I used? Ingenuous. What did you expect?"

"Not this."

"The trick is never to expect anything but the unexpected," Ritter explained. "Let me give you some free advice. Forget the textbooks. As a matter of fact, you can forget everything you learn in Boot Camp, including what I try to teach. Except for what I'm telling you now. Our Disciples may be childlike, but never underestimate them. And never forget that they are adults. They share the one quality that sets us humans apart from more primitive species, an indomitable thirst for knowledge. It'll be your job to channel that thirst in the right direction. You alone can answer their questions because the answers are different for each Disciple. But one common thread binds all Disciples in our population: Resurrection and the mysterious world outside their three-hundred-thousand-acre homeland. Sometimes they even wonder about breasts."

Dawn blushed at his words. To her surprise, he put his hand on hers reassuringly. "There's no reason, no need to be embarrassed, Private. Sex is an age-old human instinct. Put it out of your mind. The important thing to remember is that you became his friend. You didn't wind up with egg on your face."

"That may be so," Dawn said. "But I don't understand something. Resurrection is the most contradictory place I've ever seen. These people, these Disciples, they know and yet they don't. You want them to learn and yet you don't want them to learn too much. Where do I draw the line? What am I trying to achieve?"

Ritter shrugged his shoulders. "You better ask Doc Brauner that question."

Chapter 5

"I know I'm rushing things, but I don't have a choice. I know damn well what the risks are but I also know what'll happen if we wait any longer. You'll have to trust me on this," Brauner shouted into the phone. Usually a person who kept his emotions under control, he bristled with anger.

The events of the last few days had been so unnerving that he'd doubled his medicinal consumption of Wild Turkey, which in turn had left him in a constant foul mood. This morning's run-in with Xavier Axton was the straw that broke the camel's back. Brauner was infuriated with the autocratic chief of Security and Violence Control. The man was an imbecile who didn't give a damn about anything other than running Resurrection as though it were his personal fiefdom. *Well, I've had it. Up to here,* he thought and touched his Adams apple.

Brauner's anger bubbled over. "As far as I'm concerned it's outside your sphere of authority. I'll take your comments under advisement but you're not going to change my mind. Have a good day." He slammed the phone into the cradle and regretted his impulsive outbreak immediately. Getting on Axton's wrong side was not a smart thing to do.

Brauner reluctantly pushed aside his Wild Turkey and sprang into action. Damage control was utmost in his mind. He stormed into the outer office. Rachel Firestein was on the phone. From the sound of her conversation it was a private call. Along the far wall all four chairs were occupied by this afternoon's Retooling appointments. Each of them stopped talking as soon as they saw Brauner.

Rachel Firestein did likewise, ending her conversation with a quick "I gotta go."

With five pairs of eyes observing him, Brauner forced a cheerful smile and nodded at the four waiting Disciples. Then he directed his attention at Firestein.

"Rachel, sorry to bother you, but something's come up. I need to cancel all appointments for the rest of the day. Would you please reschedule these gentlemen? And then ask David Koertner to stop by, will you please?"

He turned, then made an about face. "Oh, and get Ritter on the phone for me. Page him if you have to. And one last thing. See if Colonel Axton is available for dinner tonight. Around seven at the Lounge. My treat, and tell him there's something rather important I'd like to discuss with him."

Again he turned, and again he stopped short of the inner office door. "And when you're done why don't you take the rest of the day off. I'll be busy and I'm sure you can use the time. Good afternoon, Rachel."

He returned to his office and let the door close behind him.

Ten minutes later Brauner was in a much better mood. David would be here in twenty minutes. Xavier was *thrilled to have dinner with him* as Rachel had quoted the Colonel as saying. When the phone rang a moment later it was Ritter. The conversation with the instructor was cordial and brief. Ritter didn't anticipate problems. The usually taciturn man had been uncharacteristically enthusiastic, even praising Brauner for his foresight and promising his full cooperation. Now Brauner could relax in anticipation of David's arrival.

*****

I arrived at Terwilliger House five minutes late. By the time Miss Firestein's order to be at Btauner's office ASAP had made its way from Greenville's official phone to my room, more than ten minutes had already ticked off the clock. When I arrived, Brauner ushered me immediately into his private office. He was subdued to the point of impoliteness, which made me feel more apprehensive than I had already been. Being summoned by Brauner was out of the ordinary. Finding him alone in the office, without patients in the waiting room and no Miss Firestein presiding behind her desk was equally extraordinary. Having a usually cordial Brauner greet me with monosyllables was an ominous sign.

At his invitation I took a seat in one of two leather armchairs that faced his overflowing desk and waited for bad news. I didn't have to wait long.

"David," Brauner started gravely. "I have become aware of some alarming news. What's even more disturbing is that you seem to be in the thick of it. You do know what I am referring to, don't you?"

I shook my head.

"David, David, please," Brauner intoned. "Please don't make things worse than they already are. You know you can trust me. Why then this sudden change? It's not like you."

The seriousness of his opening remarks scared me. I thought frantically of what I'd done wrong but drew a blank. "Dr. Brauner," I ventured, unsure of myself, "I really don't know what you're talking about."

Brauner shook his head sadly. I couldn't remember ever seeing him this disconsolate. He took a seat next to me and stared into space. His silence proved to be worse that his accusations. I wanted to reassure him that whatever it was he blamed me for wasn't true, but couldn't think of a word to say.

Brauner finally broke the silence. "It's not one thing, but several," he said. "Any one by itself wouldn't have troubled me. At first I didn't put two and two together. It was something I noticed last week during Retooling that first tipped me off. It took me a while, but when I ran your test results through the analyzer I realized what I had failed to see."

The expression *blood running cold* came to mind. That's exactly how I felt sitting next to Brauner. I shivered, hoping that he wouldn't mistake my sudden panic for an admission of guilt.

"Doc," I stumbled over the words. "I'm sure I can explain everything if you'll just tell me what this is all about."

"It's Justin Frederikson. I caught him snooping in my office. When I confronted him he turned insolent. *I just came to pick up a prescription* he said. *Remember? You prescribed it yourself*"

"Oh, is that it?" I exclaimed, feeling relieved. "You know Justin, He's always snooping around, looking for conspiracies."

"Which is exactly why you should never have given him a job at *The Sentinel*. That was extremely poor judgement on your part. And why didn't you tell me about it."

Shit. I had completely forgotten. "It must have slipped my mind," I said. "I'm sorry about that. I…"

"Apology not accepted," Brauner cut me off. "But that's not all of it. He started to spout his ridiculous drivel, He claimed Josh Brannigan was murdered and asked me what I knew about it. He practically accused me of complicity in this imaginary crime."

"I don't know what that has to do with me," I protested. All I…"

"Don't make up any excuses." Brauner interrupted. His voice rang with anger. "You know what Justin is like. As I said, it was extremely poor judgement on your part to give him a job that legitimizes his constant illegal snooping and spouting conspiracy theories. There's a reason he was assigned to janitorial duty at the library. He can't be trusted. His falsehoods are of the vilest and most dangerous kind. Don't you see, David, he's a subversive who should have been treated for severe mental disorders a long time ago. The only reason he hasn't been admitted to *The House* is because of you. I thought your steadying influence would be beneficial to him. Instead you stab me in the back and offer him a position that makes it easier for him to spread his dangerous his rumors."

"Sir, I didn't stab you in the back. I just wanted to help Justin. That's why I wanted him to work with me in the first place. I thought if I could spend more time with him and give him an opportunity to see Resurrection's goodness he might become a better Disciple."

"Aha," Brauner cried triumphantly. So you did notice how dangerously twisted Justin's mind has become?"

I protested lamely. "I wouldn't call him dangerously twisted, sir. I just thought his inquisitiveness might be potentially damaging."

Brauner's face was a mass of skepticism. "Are you sure that's all it was, trying to help him? You know, I said before that I wanted you to be a steadying influence on him. It never occurred to me that in the process he could become an unsteadying influence on you. Those things happen occasionally. Maybe a bit of Justin rubbed off on you in the process. That could also explain the abnormality I've noticed in last week's Retooling analysis."

I was instantly on the defensive. "What abnormality?" I demanded.

My reaction did nothing to soften Brauner's dark mood. He went on, "It could be nothing. We've had spikes before. You scored in the eighty-nine percentile on one of the Emotional Simulation Models, which indicates that your ability to judge could be diminished by emotions."

I was confused. Whenever Brauner talked about this kind of stuff he lost me the second he started. I had no idea what an Emotional Simulation Model was. "Sir, I'm not real sure what all this means. All I know is that I was trying to help Justin."

Brauner chose his words carefully, finally striking a conciliatory tone. "Let's assume that I believe you David." His voice turned even softer. "And you see the danger in the rumors he spreads?" Brauner added.

I nodded quietly, averting his eyes.

"Okay. Then you'd do anything to help him, wouldn't you?"

"Yes, sir."

"Even if it caused you pain?"

"I…I guess so." I wasn't sure where Brauner's questions were leading.

"You see, David, helping those we love comes at a price. It means making unselfish decisions, sometimes even painful decisions. Resurrection works in mysterious ways. It is not up to us to question, but only to serve. If you want to serve, you too must be willing to endure pain. Do you think you can do that?"

I nodded again, feeling like a kid who's been caught with his fingers in the cookie jar.

Brauner studied me for a long moment, doubt creasing his brow. "I hope I haven't made a terrible mistake, David. I trusted you. Can I still trust you?"

I nodded silently.

"Good night, David. Don't disappoint me again,"

With that I was dismissed.

*****

I found Justin in Room 311 when I returned half an hour later. The radio was turned to WREN. Humming along to Rosemary Clooney's *Come On-A My House* Justin looked as content as I'd seen him in years. Seeing him sprawled on his bunk, eyes closed, fingers tapping to the music, I felt a sudden surge of anger. I'd just been put through the ringer and he, the cause of my troubles, lay in bed like he didn't have a care in the world.

I didn't say hello. He was the last person in the world I wanted to talk to. If I said just one word I'd blow up and say something I'd regret. I grabbed a chair, dragged it noisily across the floor, and sat at my desk.

"Oh Hi, Dave. What's up?" Justin greeted me cheerfully.

"Nothing's up," I barked.

"Jeez, you don't have to bite my head off. Where've you been, anyhow?"

"With Brauner," I said.

"That explains it," Justin grinned. "What's the old bastard up to now?"

"He's not the one who's up to anything. You 'are."

"Huh?" Justin pushed off the bed and came to my side. "What're you talking about?"

"Oh come on, will you. You know damn well what I'm talking about. What the hell were you doing snooping around his office? And why the hell did you tell him it was my fault? I never sent you there and you know it."

Justin's eyes glazed over with surprise. "Huh?" he said again.

"Is that all you can say, *Huh?* Why didn't you say *Huh* when Brauner caught you?"

"Look, I don't know why he's blaming you. Your name never came up. I told him Rachel Firestein called and told me to pick up my new prescription. Which is exactly what I did. You can check with her if you don't believe me. And while I was there I figured…"

"You figured what?" I interrupted him. "You figured you'd break into his office? Are you out of your fucking mind? Now Brauner's pissed off at me for giving you the job at the Sentinel and I'm in deep shit."

"Whoa, hold on a minute, will you. I didn't try to break into his office. I just wanted to listen to what the old fart was doing in his office when everyone was gone. And by the way, I never told him about the job on the Sentinel. You must have told him yourself. And speaking of that job, you can shove it. I quit."

With that Justin stalked out of the room and slammed the door behind.

Still furious at him, I yelled "Fuck you," at the empty walls and let myself fall on the bed. A minute later a troubling thought came to me. How the hell did Brauner know that I had hired Justin? I'd forgotten to tell him, and Justin said he never… Who told him? The more I asked myself the more troubled I became. I turned on my side, shut the light, and stared at inky blackness.

"Retooling," I said to myself. "I must have told him during Retooling."

Chapter 6

I HATED MONITOR Patrol. Brauner had pushed the job on me a couple of months ago. *It's about time you took on more responsibilities,* he'd said. I was in no position to argue with him.

Most Disciples thought I was lucky. As far as they were concerned being a room monitor was a cushy job. They were probably right. The job came with a couple of bennies that were hard to come by. For one, Monitors didn't have curfew since it was their job to go around town and make sure everyone else was in their room by ten. Then there were Lounge privileges. As a Monitor I could go to the Apostles Lounge whenever I felt like it. The couple of times I'd gone there I'd really enjoyed myself, especially the time when Guardian Schroeder had bought me a Johnny Walker Black. The scotch gave me a pleasant buzz but the real high was eavesdropping on the Guardians who sometimes came to the lounge to hobnob with the hoi polloi. Listening to their juicy gossip was like being in reporter-heaven.

Of course there was a downside to the job. The other Disciples didn't trust me anymore. They automatically assumed that anybody who had been picked to check up on them was almost as bad as a Guardian and nobody trusted Guardians a whole lot. Except that as far as the Guardians were concerned I was still a Disciple, so they didn't trust me a lot either. When I told Brauner about my dilemma he shrugged it off as learning to live with responsibility. To me it meant being an outsider.

To Brauner's credit he had started me off with an easy schedule. I was assigned to the uptown Stockade District, a warren of crooked, narrow streets and stone houses that dated back three hundred years.

Most of them had been turned into Resurrection's administrative buildings. With only two group homes on my tour, Brunjes House and Shuyler Manor, both located on Albany Avenue, it made for a relatively quick shift. There were fewer rooms to check, fewer heads to count, fewer excuses to listen to, and fewer bribes to turn down when I caught someone breaking curfew.

A light drizzle had started to fall, bringing patches of dense fog as the heat of the last few weeks retreated grudgingly before a cold front that had pushed south. Tattered fingers of moonlight filtered through occasional breaks in the clouds, making the walk along Albany Avenue's cracked sidewalks treacherous. All streetlights had been turned off after curfew in an effort to conserve energy. The aging generators at Ulster Power Plant One and the dangerously low water levels of the Ashokan reservoir had combined to create an energy crisis in Resurrection. Brownouts and blackouts were common lately, and all nonessential services were curtailed. Even radio and television broadcasts of WREN, Resurrection's Entertainment and News station, signed off the air by eight o'clock at night. That didn't matter a whole lot to me since I hardly ever listened to the radio and the group TV was on the fritz, but I wished they'd turn the streetlights back on. Making my way towards Brunjes House with nothing but a flashlight powered by a dying battery made for slow progress.

Fortunately it had been a smooth night so far. After making my rounds through uptown with nothing more dangerous to report than a pack of stray dogs rummaging through overturned garbage pails near the old Senate House, I headed towards Albany Avenue and Brunjes House.

The two-story building lay in darkness. I was tempted to skip bed check. It seemed a waste of time to check twenty rooms and forty beds, especially since Brunjes was one of Resurrection's most elite group homes with large, airy rooms that were comfortably furnished and reserved for the most trusted Disciples. Nobody ever broke curfew in this place. But I was worried about breaking the rules. *Remember, David. We know. We know everything* Brauner had warned me when he made me room monitor. My sixth sense told me that he wasn't bluffing. Last night's confrontation with Justin confirmed it.

The outer door creaked open and I found myself in a spacious center hall that soared twenty-two feet to the roof. On either side of the hall marble stairs curved upward to a second-story landing and an interior balcony that circled the stairwell. An enormous pewter chandelier, holding two tiers of twenty candles each, had long since outlived its usefulness and was almost relegated to the garbage dump when two Disciples had lighted the candles and nearly set Brunjes House on fire.

Fanning out in either direction from the center hall, a wide corridor led to ten rooms on each side of the front door. The counselor's suite was straight ahead, and a communal bathroom to my right. Wall sconces were placed between each of the rooms, but they too were merely decorative. Their candles had been removed the morning after Brunjes House's near brush with fire. I could have used them dearly tonight.

I played my flashlight along the hall. Its yellow glow dimmed, sputtered off, then on again even dimmer, before it died completely.

"Fuck." Hoping to make sure that everyone knew I was making my rounds, I cursed out loud. Through an open doorway to my left a high-pitched falsetto voice mimicked me "Fuck fuck fuck fuck."

I ignored it and made my way along the hall. I'd been here often enough to know every square inch of Brunjes, including the many spots where the carpeting was worn and patched and could be treacherous. One cautious step at a time, keeping my arms extended to feel for opened doors, I inched along.

Everyone was accounted for in room 101. I made my way to the next door. Room 102 was okay too. And so was room 103. Again the same with 104.

Then a faint noise, the sound of shuffling footsteps and creaking floorboards, caught my attention. I froze and held my breath. Inky blackness made it impossible to see. I listened but the sound was gone. Convinced that my imagination had played tricks on me, I resumed inching forward. But the momentary interruption had made me lose my bearings and I banged against an opened door that led to room 105.

And then I heard it again. The same sounds, growing more perceptible with each second, as though someone were sneaking from the far end of the corridor towards the entrance foyer. Someone was in the hall with me. Someone who was trying to sneak out of Brunjes. Someone who didn't know I was waiting between him and the front door.

The easy thing would have been to disregard whoever was there, go on with my rounds, and let well enough alone. And that's exactly what I was going to do. Until the muffled steps stopped and I got a whiff of peppermint breath so close to my face that I didn't have a choice. I lunged in the direction of the intruder. My hand tightened around an arm. I yanked as hard as I could but lost my grip as he pulled back. I heard what sounded like fabric tearing and lunged again. The rest was a blur. We struggled silently for a couple of seconds and my flashlight dropped to the floor. It landed on the carpet with a dull thud before it was kicked out of reach by the stranger. By now I was afraid for my own safety and flailed wildly, hitting air. Then I got lucky. My right fist made hard contact. On impact a fiery sting spread across my knuckles. At the same time I heard a grunt, followed by a sharp intake of breath. I didn't know where my blow had landed but I knew I had hurt him. Thrilled with my success I let my guard down for the briefest of moments. It was a costly mistake. I heard another grunt, then a knee crashed into my groin. The pain was immediate and excruciating. It spread through my lower body like red-hot lava and sent me sprawling to the floor. I rolled on my side and crawled on all fours until I reached an opened door. I gasped for air, tasting bile in my throat, and still the pain wouldn't go away.

Less than a minute had elapsed between landing my lucky punch and going down to ignominious defeat. During that time there'd been another rush of air, this time as the front door was opened. When I looked up I saw the outline of a man disappear north along Albany Avenue.

I wanted to cry. Not from pain, which had ebbed to numbness, but from shame. *What kind of Monitor are you?* I told myself. And how could I tell Brauner that I'd failed miserably? Not just Brauner but to Axton too. Unless of course I didn't say anything.

I reached for a doorknob and pulled myself to my feet, holding on to steady my legs. Slowly I caught my breath. By now my pain was tolerable but my humiliating shame was obsessive. The more I thought about it, the more I was convinced that I should keep my mouth shut. Nobody would have to know. Especially not Brauner.

Coming to that conclusion calmed my frayed nerves. I took a deep breath, then another, and waited for my hands to stop shaking. I flexed my right hand several times. Nothing was broken. I even had the presence of mind to crawl along the floor until I located my flashlight, which I tucked securely into my belt. With my psyche back under control and my body apparently undamaged, I climbed to the second floor.

I hadn't reached the upstairs landing when I got spooked again. This time it wasn't anything I heard. This time it was a premonition. And that was far more frightening than approaching footsteps.

I shrugged it off. *Stupid fool. Pull yourself together and stop shaking like a leaf. Nothing else is going to happen tonight. This is Brunjes and nothing bad ever happens here, especially not twice in the same night.*

I agreed with myself and felt better.

The door to 201 stood open and I stuck my head inside the room. "Henry?"

"Here."

"Charles?"

"Here."

The door to room 202 was closed. I tugged at it and it swung open easily.

"Walter?"

"Here."

"Ezekiel?"

No answer.

"Ezekiel? You there?"

There was no answer.

The blackout curtain was drawn. The room's interior was blacker than black except for a sliver of light that fell across bunk

202B. I moved towards Ezekiel's bunk. "C'mon Ezekiel. Stop the shit. I'm not in the mood."

I shook the bed and shouted "Ezekiel?"

Ezekiel was face down on the bed. His left arm was pinned beneath his stomach. His right arm was at an awkward angle, palm up, and resisted me when I pushed it. It was the first time in my I'd touched a corpse.

Chapter 7

JUST WHEN IT seemed that graduation day would never arrive, it was Friday, September 15, and the Resurrection City fairgrounds had been groomed for the special occasion. The grandstand sparkled under a fresh coat of paint. The expansive meadow was freshly mowed. Twenty-thousand squares of newly lain sod contrasted with the dark-green, weed-choked carpet of old grass. Resurrection banners hung listlessly in a gray sky.

The grandstand had filled early with dignitaries, most notable among them Senator Kerr who had traveled north from his home on Long Island to witness first-hand what his constituents had paid for. Resurrection's drum and bugle corps warmed up at the north end of the large grassy area that usually hosted milking contests, sheep shearing tournaments, and tents displaying hand-made artifacts by Resurrection's most gifted artisans.

Inside the dignitary's box, flanking Senator Kerr and his wife Salome, who's career as a lap dancer in New York nightclubs had ended abruptly when she married the senator who was thirty one years her senior, were General Amadeus II, Dr. Bruno Brauner, Chief of Security Colonel Xavier Axton, and Alderman Bradislav Stokowski.

The general, a classical music aficionado whose given name was Armand Fingerhut before he changed it to that of his idol, was Resurrection's ranking military officer. For the occasion Amadeus was in full dress uniform, proudly displaying the medal of valor he won during the campaign against Montana secessionists. A sheathed sword dangled ceremoniously from his leather belt, and his three-star general's cap couldn't hide his distinctive shock of red hair. At the age of sixty-seven, although no longer the Marine Corp's iron-willed leader who struck terror in the hearts of subordinates, he was still an imposing figure, his six-foot five-inch frame towering over the other dignitaries. In contrast to the general's military splendor, Brauner looked more out of place than usual. His customary blue three-piece suit, red silk tie, and wire-rimmed glasses lent him an air of faded elegance and gave him the appearance of a onetime English schoolmaster. Brauner didn't mind being overshadowed however. On the contrary. He felt more comfortable assuming the role of unimportant civilian. He knew he had intelligence and the unflinching loyalty of an elite group of apostles on his side. And he had his prescription pad, a powerful ally in Resurrection.

The last of the triumvirate was Alderman Bradislav Stokowski. At the age of forty-two he was the youngest of the Camp's leaders and was its appointed financial watchdog. A career politician, Stokowski had blended legal training at Harvard Law School with a passion for capitalist entrepreneurship to become a wealthy business man whose campaign contributions were instrumental in getting his appointment to Resurrection. Stokowski was the stereotypical CEO, a hard-driving, energy-charged workaholic who enjoyed confrontations and was convinced that the meek shall inherit nothing. It had often been remarked that Stokowski's energy level was so high that the air crackled when he walked into a meeting. That however was an understatement. The air didn't just crackle; it arced whenever the Alderman made an appearance. And he never *walked* into a meeting. He strode. With purpose and self-confidence that bordered on abrasive arrogance. Similarly, his dress code was an extension of his personality. Expensive Italian designer suits and white pima cotton shirt. Always white and always starched. He never wore his jacket. Today it was slung across his lap. The top button of his shirt was undone, his silk tie loosened, and his sleeves were rolled up to mid-forearm. Stokowski was ready for action. He leaned forward in his seat, his fingers drumming impatiently against his thigh, and raised his lips to the general's ear. "Damn it, General. Can't you do something to get this show on the road? I don't have all day to waist on these snot-nosed recruits."

The recruits were seated on metal folding chairs facing the grandstand. Dawn Austin sat surrounded by ninety-eight classmates, mired in forty-fifth place in her graduating class. Despite her initial enthusiasm and considerable mental toughness, the past four weeks had transformed her from dreamer to skeptic. No longer the Pollyanna who had walked into the Duffy Square recruiting station six weeks ago, and not yet a hard-nosed soldier on the side of God and country, Dawn simply felt let down and soiled. She still wanted to help her Disciples, but the sheen had rubbed off her halo. One too many encounters with Ritter, one too many failed attempts to get inside the mind of a Disciple, and one too many sleepless nights in her dorm left her as disillusioned as the rest of her class. By now being a counselor was just a job. Looking ahead to her future was depressing; twenty-four months of hard work with nothing more to show for than sixty-thousand dollars, a letter of thanks from Governor Fitzpatrick, and thirty-eight college credits she didn't need in the first place.

The band struck up a medley of stirring military marches and religious hymns, followed by the camp's anthem *To thee I pledge my life, Oh Resurrection.* Snare drums and Glockenspiels competed with bugles and fifes. Two-hundred goose-stepping Guardians marched across the meadow, dipped their flags as they passed the reviewing stand, and took their position alongside the recruits.

Speech after speech thundered from the loudspeakers and at last the moment arrived. As the last speech faded into a dreary September sky ninety-nine caps were tossed ceremoniously into the damp air. The roar of a twenty-one gun salute pierced the cheers of the crowd and dissipated inside clouds of gunpowder. Dawn Austin had earned her last cross.

She followed the line of recruits. They snaked their way past the reviewing stand. She saluted General Amadeus II. He shook her hand vigorously, smiled at her, and saluted in return. Brauner didn't warrant a salute, merely a handshake. He studied her with intense interest and nodded with approval. Before letting go of her hand he pulled Dawn toward him and whispered into her ear "We need to talk about your first assignment, a fellow named David Koertner." With that he let go of her hand.

Stokowski was the last to congratulate her. He hardly paid attention to her and withdrew his hand at her touch. His nose wrinkled in a clear indication of distaste. She shuffled past him and the rest of the spectators in search of Sergeant Ritter to pick up her case folder and the keys to Greenkill House, her home for the next two years. She could hardly believe that boot camp was finished and she would finally have her own room. To her surprise, the long awaited moment was bitter-sweet. Dormitory life had thrust her into a society of like-minded recruits. Despite lack of comfort and privacy she hadn't been lonely. She could only imagine how lonely she would be in her own suite. The prospect of solitude deepened her disillusionment.

Equally as depressing was mother's uncharacteristic lack of attention. Mother had never been at a loss for words, usually striking a *I told you so* tone, and had never hesitated to chastise Dawn when she needed chastising.

So why the hell hadn't mother criticized her for letting Ezekiel touch her breasts in front of the whole class. It was the kind of thing she normally would have pounced on, and Dawn had been reluctant to mention it in her last letter. *I guess she's really pissed that I joined up before she could talk me out of it*, Dawn told herself and shrugged her shoulders. *Mothers! They bitch when you try to do the right thing and they don't bitch when you expect them to.*

*****

"Permission denied."

"But why? Why can't I have a phone in my room? You already confiscated my cell phone but this is different. All I'm asking for is one of your internal lines. You know yourself that I won't be able to make any outside calls with it, so what's the problem? If it's the money I'll pay for it myself." Dawn was furious. She wanted to pound her fist on Ritter's desk but stopped herself in the nick of time. Having an all-out, little-girl hissy-fit, the kind of foot-stomping, crying, I'm-holding-my-breath-till-I-faint temper tantrum that used to drive mother up the wall wouldn't work with Ritter. He'd only throw her out of the office.

"Private Austin, you better get something straight," Ritter explained with more than a trace of irritation. "This isn't a summer camp for little rich kids. If you wanted all the creature comforts of home you should have volunteered for the Y. This is a confinement area with very special requirements. And we have rules for these special requirements. Not having a phone in your room is one of those rules. Do you understand me?"

Dawn wasn't ready to give up just yet. "But what if there's an emergency? What if I have a heart attack or slip in the shower and break a leg? What'll I do if someone breaks into my room?"

Ritter wasn't fazed by her arguments. "Are you quite finished?"

Not being able to think of any other calamities, she nodded.

"Good. I was worried you had an exotic affliction, like epilepsy and were worried about choking on your tongue. But just in case something does happen, which I'm sure won't since you seem to be a healthy young woman, all you have to do is to push the panic-button in your room. As a matter of fact, you have two of them, one right next to your bed and another in the bathroom. Just touch the thing and I guarantee an emergency response team will be at your door in less than three minutes. It's quicker than a phone and it doesn't need to be installed."

Arguing with Ritter was as frustrating as it was useless. The man had an answer for everything. Dawn therefore shifted gears, trying a new approach. She was, after all, a psychiatry major and if there ever was a perfect time to put her education to practical use, this was it. "Okay, sir. I buy that. And believe me, I don't want to be a pain, but all you've told me is why I don't *need* a phone and not why I'm not allowed to have one. All you keep telling me is that it's against the rules. That's the only explanation I ever get, rules, rules, rules. Don't you think it's about time someone explained them to me, like why particular rules exists rather than using them as catchall excuses? The way I see it, sooner or later one of the Disciples is going to ask me the same question, and then what do I do? I can't just give them the same pat answer. If they're going to trust me, I have to explain things to them without sounding like a prison guard. How can I expect them to follow the rules if I don't understand them myself?"

She gave Ritter a demure smile. He didn't bite. But he didn't dismiss her either. With a deep sigh and a shrug of his shoulders he went on to explain. "It's really very simple, Private. All Disciples, and Apostles for that matter, are conditioned to accept rules unconditionally. It's a part of everyday life for them like breathing and sleeping. For the most part they have no idea that they're prisoners or what they've done. The nature of their potential crimes are sealed in justice department files. Even I don't have access to them. As far as they're concerned Resurrection is the end-all and be-all. They know nothing but their own insular society. A society, I might add, that has worked remarkably well for longer than you've been alive. You may think that your education qualifies you to pass judgement on us, but you need a lot more than textbooks to earn that right. You need years and years of experience. You need to roll up your sleeves and get your hands dirty and live side by side with these prisoners. So try doing your job without bitching and maybe, just maybe, you'll be allowed to remain in Resurrection long enough to earn our respect. Right now you're not doing yourself any favors. All you're doing is making a pain in the ass out of yourself and nobody likes a pain in the ass. Least of all me."

If Ritter thought that his lecture would end the conversation, he was wrong. Austin, despite being painfully shy, had a stubborn streak, especially when she knew she was right. And this time she was right. "If that's so, what about Ezekiel. He knows there's more to the world than Resurrection."

Ritter lowered his eyes. "If you remember, I didn't say that all Disciples are ignorant of where they are or why they're here. I said for the most part. Ezekiel is one of those rare cases who have an inkling. He will be dealt with in an appropriate manner."

"Which is?"

Ritter looked like he was about to walk out on her. To her surprise he continued, although in a menacing tone that she found intimidating. "Austin, if you were still a recruit I'd tell you to go to hell. But you're a full-fledged counselor now, so I'll indulge your meddlesome curiosity. Ezekiel's case is rare but not unprecedented and we have guidelines on how to deal with these rare occurrences. First, we segregate them from the rest of the inmate population. That way they can do no further harm. Then we make a case by case decision. Either we sentence them to solitary confinement, or we promote them to Apostlehood, which will qualify them for parole and eventual release into society."

"And where does Ezekiel fit in?" Dawn asked, recalling the young man's brutish good looks and ingenuous mind.

"I'm afraid I don't know the answer," Ritter replied. "But I'd guess that he's got as good a chance as anybody of being paroled. He's a candidate for Apostlehood next year anyhow and he's always kept his nose clean."

Dawn kept pushing. "If you don't know, then who would? And who makes that decision?"

"Technically it's Resurrection's board of governors, but in reality they only rubber stamp Doc Brauner's decision. And since you'll be working for him starting tomorrow morning you should probably direct the rest of your questions to him. He's much better qualified to give you correct answers."

For a split-second Dawn saw a flash of fatigue in Ritter's eyes. She was wearing him down, and that gave her renewed reasons to keep talking to him. "Sir, with all due respect, it's not necessarily the correct answer I'm looking for but the truth."

"Austin, with all due respect, this line of questioning is over. I'll be more than happy to assist you in any way I can as long as you confine your questions to matters of Resurrection's policies, your rights and privileges, or your duties."

"As long as we don't talk about telephones, right?" she scoffed, realizing that she had struck out with Ritter.

"Exactly. I think we've beaten that issue to death."

"I don't think so," Dawn protested. "You still haven't told me why."

"I thought the answer was obvious."

"Indulge me. I'm a slow learner."

Ritter silently counted to ten before answering. "I think you're well aware of why we need to keep knowledge of the outside world at bay. Anything else would destroy what we're trying to accomplish here. A phone is an unacceptable security risk, even if it is restricted. But there's another reason."

Ritter motioned for Austin to take a seat. He poured himself a cup of coffee and stirred in a teaspoon of sugar before glancing in Austin's direction. "Would you like a cup? I can see we're going to be here a while."

Austin declined.

"As you wish. All right, let's see if I can satisfy your curiosity. You're going to keep bugging me anyhow, so I might as well get it out of the way. Your job is to evaluate Disciples' readiness for parole and then to transition them mentally for eventual return to society. A cornerstone of your success is trust. Unless these people trust you, they'll never open up to you, and unless they open up to you, you'll never know if they're ready for parole. The only way you can do that is to be one of them as much as possible, and that includes your living quarters. It's bad enough that you have a private room. It's even worse that yours is the only room with a private bathroom. Having a telephone in your suite would compound the problem. It would reinforce the fact that you are an outsider. It'll scream privilege. Therefore no phone."

Ritter's explanation sounded so contrived that Dawn couldn't help but laugh. "That's ridiculous, sir. It's contrary to every psychiatric principle. You win someone's trust by…"

The look on Ritter's face told Austin that psychiatry was a sore subject with him. No longer sarcastic, he showed cold contempt. "Austin, I deal with facts, not abstracts. Save your psycho-babble for the Disciples, it doesn't work with me. The last time I took one of those damn ink blot tests I failed miserably. All I saw were ink blots, period. Nothing interpretive, nothing imaginative, nothing subjective. I don't analyze my dreams. I don't subconsciously hate my mother and blame her for every little hang-up. If everybody was like me, every psychiatrist in the world would be unemployed. As far as I'm concerned, having shrinks in Resurrection is a total waste of tax payers' money. But if the board wants them, then the board'll get them. That's one of the rules. And by the way, it's one of the rules I don't like. Just like not having a phone is one of the rules you don't like. Of course you may always appeal to Colonel Axton."

"Who's he?"

"Colonel Axton is Chief of Security and Violence Control. His department is also in charge of all appeals and grievances, including personal requests like yours."

Ritter opened his desk drawer and flung a pre-printed form letter at her. "All you have to do is fill out this application and state your grievance. It will be reviewed and, if approved by the review board, will be presented to Colonel Axton."

"And who is on the review board?"

"I am, Austin," he smiled. "Would you like the form?"

She shook her head. If ever there was a case of catch-22, this was it. She was frustrated and angry but wasn't about to let her emotions get the better of her. Ritter had been plain enough, calling her a pain in the ass. Being labeled a troublemaker would only make a difficult job impossible, especially when she had to deal with thick-headed bureaucrats like Ritter. And she was sure there were hundreds of Ritters in Resurrection. So bite your tongue, swallow your pride, and bide your time, she told herself. Instead of telling him what she thought of him and his goddamn rules, she slid the form back into Ritter's hands, smiled sweetly, and said a simple "Thank you, Sergeant. I won't be needing this after all."

"I thought so. Is that it then?" Ritter eyed a stack of papers on his desk, obviously eager to get rid of her.

Against her better judgement Dawn remained standing in front of Ritter. He was visibly annoyed by now and snapped "I can tell you're not done with me yet, Private. Make it snappy, I don't have time for any more nonsense."

Hoping to look as demure as possible, she lowered her eyes and, with a small voice, continued. "Almost, sir. You've been more than kind but I have one more question, if you'll allow me."

"Yes, yes. What is it?" He tapped the stack of papers impatiently.

"I understand what you've told me. I don't necessarily agree with it but I understand. I also know that this, how can I put it, this virtual unreality you're imposing on the inmates includes radio and

TV. For instance, I know all about news blackouts and TV shows that have been censored and doctored up to make the whole world a sugar-coated version of *Father Knows Best.* But…"

"I don't like phrases like censored and doctored up," Ritter snapped. "They have such a sinister connotation. I like to think of it as filtering out inappropriate materials."

"Whatever. And what would you consider inappropriate."

"Any news that might have a negative impact."

"Such as sex? They must know something about sex. Everybody does. Ezekiel certainly did."

Ritter looked uncomfortable. "That's your opinion, not mine. I think he was merely curious, that's all. Why, did you find the incident sexual?"

It was Dawn's turn to feel uncomfortable. She went on haltingly, "Look, you can't deny that he knew at least something about sex. He was interested. How can you expect thousands of men and women…"

"I think this has gone far enough," Ritter jumped in before she could finish.

"…living together without having a sex issue," Dawn went on despite Ritter's interruption.

"I'm not at liberty to discuss that, Austin."

"More rules?"

"Yes, exactly. More rules. And now, if you don't mind…" His tone was a clear indication of dismissal.

"Of course. And thank you for your time, sir."

*****

That night, before the lights in Greenkill House had been turned off by the Resurrection Power Authority, Dawn Austin surveyed her room. Her new world was a ten foot by twelve foot Spartan room on the ground floor. It had a window facing State Street, the only door in the building equipped with a lock sans key, and the relative comfort of newly installed wall to wall green carpeting. A metal frame twin bed was placed alongside the far wall. A night table holding a digital clock radio and an ash tray stood next to the bed. Below the window was a petite wooden desk equipped with a high-intensity desk lamp and a blotter. An office chair on casters, a metal filing cabinet, a three drawer dresser, and an incongruous wing chair completed the furnishings, leaving barely enough room to walk without bumping into furniture.

Decorator touches were sparse and of a style she thought of as *Salvation Army*. Olive green curtains covered the window. Olive green sheets and blankets adorned the bed. Green paint, the color of pea soup, coated the walls. Green everywhere. Dawn hated green.

A framed color poster above the bed depicted Resurrection's triumvirate, the General, the Doctor, and the Politician. The trio stood side by side in front of a wood-paneled wall, right hands placed over their hearts, smiling benignly, flanked by the American and Resurrection flags. If not for the chill she felt at seeing this assemblage of absolute power, she would have burst into laughter. She leaned into the poster to decipher a handwritten scribble at the bottom of the photograph. It read *If this is Resurrection I'd rather stay in hell. JM March 2077.*

A calendar was pinned to the door, reminding her that she was about to spend the next twenty-four months in Suite 1. The thought of living for two years in a place the color of pea soup made her stomach queasy and she yearned for the noisy, chaotic life in her dorm. But to her surprise the bathroom, though tiny, was a refreshing change from the rest of her suite. It wasn't green, but outfitted with oatmeal colored tiles, white fixtures and white towels. Against this unexpected sea of brightness, only the toilet paper contrasted. It was sand-colored to match its sandpaper coarseness and was manufactured from 100 percent recycled paper.

"I guess I better develop thick skin in a hurry," Dawn quipped and dropped her suitcase on the bed. She spent the next five minutes unpacking, folding, and putting her meager belongings away. Her clothes fit into two chest drawers. A prohibitively expensive Angora sweater which mother had bought as a going-away present shared the top drawer with a pair of leather gloves, earmuffs, a ski cap, and her nearly empty pocketbook. The lower drawer held her Resurrection-issued intimates (after looking at her new bra, panties, slip, nightgowns, all of them anything but intimate, all faded green, and all manufactured in Resurrection of undeterminable fabric she wanted to cry), as well as five pairs of balled up socks. Ten wire hangers dangled in the closet, but all she needed were eight. Only the shoe-rack was filled by the time she was done: a pair of hiking boots, knee-length rubberized snow boots, the clunkiest combat boots she had ever seen, and her own Adidas walking shoes. The desk had two small drawers, but thanks to Guard Pulsifer, she had nothing to stow in them.

Continuing into the bathroom, she unwrapped the 'personal hygienic kit' that had been part of her graduation package. Hermetically sealed inside a see-through plastic casing were two toothbrushes, a deodorant stick, a three-pack of glycerin soap, unscented shaving cream, a safety razor, one chapstick, and a first-aid kit. Not a drop of perfume, no lipstick or mascara or anything remotely associated with makeup could be found. This time, she did cry, a short-lived hickuppy self-indulgence of misery.

It had never taken her less time to settle in, but she never had fewer belongings. With nothing left to unpack and not yet ready to call it a day, she nestled in the wing chair and opened a text book she had been given in Boot Camp. *The Face of Crime In Today's Society*, a thoroughly boring but mandatory reading assignment rang as hollow and cliché-ridden as one of Ritter's lectures. The author, despite years of study and training, had obviously never spent time in Resurrection. She closed the book, dropped it on the floor, and reached for the case folder Ritter had handed her earlier, hoping to find it more interesting than the textbook.

She was immediately mesmerized by it, anticipating tomorrow morning's session with David Koertner gave her goose bumps. Forgotten were disillusionment and disappointments. A familiar tingle was back in her spine. No matter how uncomfortable her quarters were, regardless of the red tape that would frustrate her every inch of the way, despite all the setbacks she was sure to run into, tomorrow promised to be an exciting beginning. Tomorrow she'd meet her very own Disciple and, God willing, shape him into an Apostle. Tomorrow she will meet David Nathaniel Koertner.

*****

The lights were out. The blackout curtain was drawn. Above her head she heard floorboards creaking under someone's feet. The footfalls faded and total stillness assailed her. She was not used to such quiet. At home there had always been one sound or another to distract her. Garbage trucks rattling outside her apartment window. The upstairs neighbor practicing piano. An endless stream of sirens. Her neighbor's apartment door slamming shut. Telemarketers calling. Mozart or Vivaldi or Brahms on the CD player. Max barking, Mother chastising. Mother vacuuming. Max barking some more. Door bells ringing. Hairdryers whining. Dishwashers clanging. A constant, delicious assault on her ears. In its place Resurrection's silence was suffocating.

She needed a quick fix of background noise and turned on the radio to help her fall asleep. She rolled on her side and twiddled with the tuner. At first she heard only static and remembered Ritter's comments about all frequencies except one being jammed. She turned the dial until WREN came in loud and clear.

"…has become the pride and joy of Resurrection City. The ten-year-old last night won the national spelling bee, taking just fifteen seconds to correctly spell *Xerophthalmia*."

Dawn, who had no inkling what that word meant, was duly impressed, especially when the ten-year-old gave a precise medical explanation of the dangers of vitamin A deficiency to the announcer. *They're a curious breed*, she told herself, much more contradictory than she had expected. Maybe Ritter was right. Maybe conventional approaches didn't work with unconventional patients.

Dawn continued to listen as the news switched to the next story. "In the world of sports, the Mt. Tremper Pirates defeated the Resurrection City Bombers by a score of three to one in the deciding seventh game of the world series. Resurrection City, who was the overwhelming favorite, went down to defeat when its star pitcher, Josh Brannigan, was unable to play due to other commitments."

Something she had said earlier that day stuck in her mind. "Virtual unreality." She had hit it right on the head. Walt Disney himself couldn't have created a theme park to rival Resurrection in its ability to fool the mind. Even she found it difficult to differentiate between reality and trickery. Considering she had only been in camp for two months, and that those two months had been spent in the harsh reality of boot camp, how could she expect Disciples to doubt Resurrection's totality?

"And now WREN proudly presents Masterpiece Radio. This evening's featured performance is the enduring classic Rip Van Winkle. In this week's episode, find out how Rip…"

Shit. Double Shit." Dawn turned off the radio and rolled on her side. "I wonder what'll happen when Rip finally wakes up and finds out that he's living in the middle of a prison."

*****

Dawn Austin felt an icy chill. She jolted upright from a shallow sleep and stared wide-eyed into blackness around her. Her skin felt clammy. Her throat was dry. Her heartbeat pounded in her temples. Her nerves were on razor's edge.

"Hello? Anybody there?" The words were a croak, afraid to leave her mouth.

She swung her legs over the side of the bed and turned on the desk lamp. The sudden movement sent the room spinning like a runaway merry-go-round. Closing her eyes to fight her vertigo attack, she pressed her palms against her temples. She didn't know how long she sat on the edge of her bed but didn't think it was more than a few seconds. When she opened her eyes gingerly the room's mad whirling had stopped but her heart raced as fast as before. Her perspiration was drying and she felt that same icy chill that had jolted her awake. She was wired to the point of sensory overload, feeling a million goosebumps break out on her skin. And she knew intuitively what had spun her out of control. She wasn't alone. Someone was out there, watching her.

Christ, what the hell is happening? This isn't just a dream. It can't be, it's too real. Someone's here, staring, watching.

She pulled a robe around her shoulders and made her way to the door. She twisted the knob and pulled. The door opened instantly, but with a creak. If anyone had entered the room she definitely would have heard the noise. She stepped to the window and tried to lift the lower pane. It obeyed grudgingly, a few inches at a time, then refused to budge. No one could have entered that way. Doubting herself she walked back to the bed and crawled under the covers.

Staring at the inky blackness, alone with her terror, she waited for sunrise to rescue her.

Chapter 8

"It's from a car accident."

"I...I'm...I'm not sure what you mean." Without knowing why, I had a feeling that I should be embarrassed.

"This," Dawn Austin explained matter of fact, her index finger tracing the faint outline of a scar that ran from the inside corner of her right eye to her mouth. "I was sixteen years old when it happened."

I followed the path of her finger, hypnotized by its slow progress across her cheek. "I'm sorry, I didn't mean to stare. I was just..." Stinging heat rose in my cheeks. I knew my ears had turned deep red.

"It's okay." A quick smile curled her lips. "It always happens when I meet someone for the first time. No need to apologize."

Dawn Austin sat in Brauner's leather chair at the far end of his small, cluttered office, facing me across a wooden desktop covered end to end with a chaotic disarray of medical journals, computer printouts and an overflowing ashtray. At the first sign of my embarrassment she jumped up, trying to ease the awkward moment, and came to my side.

"It's nice to finally meet you, David. I'm Dawn Austin." She held out her hand and I scrambled to my feet. "I believe Dr. Brauner told you about me?"

Her hand was cold to the touch even though the office was oppressively hot. A typical Indian Summer day had blanketed Resurrection City. The window air-conditioner wheezed and sputtered clammy air but did nothing to cool the room.

"Oh, sure. You're my new counselor," I stammered. "Nice to meet you too. And I really didn't mean to..."

"I told you it's okay," she interrupted me at once. "Yes, I'm your new counselor, although that's a tall order. Counselor implies that I have all the answers and that I can give you advice."

"But isn't that what you're here for?"

"Eventually, yes. But there's so much I have to learn first. About Resurrection City, about you. About your friends. So what do you say you help me learn the ropes around here. That way I won't be a complete dummy. And I'll try to answer whatever questions you have. Hopefully by the time we're done I won't get lost around Resurrection City and you won't get lost wherever it is Dr. Brauner wants you to be. Deal?"

"Sure."

She extended her hand a second time and we shook.

"Good. Let's get started then. Why don't you…" She interrupted herself and motioned with her head in the direction of Brauner's inner office. "By the way, did Dr. Brauner tell you why I have been assigned to your case? Why me instead of him all of a sudden."

I shook my head.

"Okay, let me explain. He thought it was time for you to gain a new perspective, that you could learn things from me that he couldn't teach you. Not that I know more than he does, but I've had different experiences, a different perspective on life. In fact, I've led a totally different life than him. Different than anyone in Resurrection. He would like me to share those experiences with you. Does that make any sense to you?"

"I guess so."

"I know I have some pretty big shoes to fill. I also know that if I'm going to succeed I have to earn your respect and trust first. The only way I can do that is to be completely honest with you. So if you ever think that I'm not being straight with you you'll have to let me know. Okay?"

"Okay."

"It works both ways though. So if I think you're not being straight with me I'll let you know too. Still okay with that?"

I nodded, liking her no-nonsense style. It was refreshing. More to-the-point than Brauner had been. It also made me feel as if I'd known this skinny, somewhat exotic looking woman for years. "Yeah, I think so."

"Good. I'll tell you what, David. Instead of me acting like the big-shot counselor I'm supposed to be, why don't you fire away. Ask me anything you want. I'm willing to share all of my secrets with you. Except for what I used to write in my diary." She smiled briefly. "That's privileged information and for girls only."

"Sure. But I'm not really sure where to start. And I don't want to embarrass you."

"If you do I won't answer. But just in case, how's this for an easy out? If you see me hem and haw and turning red you'll know I'm embarrassed. And then instead of me telling you to mind your own business you'll just change the subject. That way you'll let me off the hook and neither of us will feel bad."

For a counselor, she sure was different. Not like Doc Brauner, who always acted like a proper gentleman. And she sure looked like no counselor I'd ever met, and certainly not like any woman I had ever seen. Resurrection's women looked healthy, with tanned complexions and some meat on their bones. In comparison, Austin was tall and skinny, bony actually, with shoulder length black hair and large brown eyes that made her face look pastier than it actually was. And she balanced the strangest kind of glasses on the tip of her nose, with small elliptical lenses that were all wrong for her large brown eyes. No wonder she squinted above her glasses whenever she wanted to get a good look at me.

"Is anything wrong, David?" she asked when she saw me stare. "You look kind of odd, like you've just seen a ghost."

"Oh no," I said. "It's just your glasses. They're so…so different."

She laughed. "I don't know about different but they sure were expensive. Genuine Yves St. Laurent. But enough about my glasses. What do you want to know about me? For starters, what if I tell you how I got my name?"

Happy that she had given me an out I nodded quickly. "Please do. I've never met anyone named Dawn. It's kind of an odd name." Again I turned red and added "Not that there's anything wrong with it. I think it's a nice name. It's just different."

Austin agreed. "Thanks. I kind of like it myself. Originally my parents wanted to name me Rebecca. But I was born at six-thirty-seven in the morning, the exact moment the sun rose that day, and my mother decided on Dawn at the spur of the moment."

"I'm glad. I like Dawn better than Rebecca."

"Thank you, David. Anyhow, little baby Dawn grew into a typical teenager and young adult. Nothing exciting in my life, I'm afraid. So let's skip the next twenty-seven years, which brings yours truly smack into your life. I'm a board-certified psychiatrist, courtesy of Barnard College and mom's money. In my spare time I like to read and watch old movies. I'm afraid this is my first fulltime job and you're my first patient. I guess that makes me a rookie. Now that you know how inexperienced I am, are you still willing to trust me?"

"I don't see why not. Experience has nothing to do with being good."

"I'm glad you feel that way. It's settled then, and I'll try to live up to your faith in me." Much more relaxed after confessing how little experience she had, Austin crossed the office and scrunched into Brauner's chair. Looking lost in the big leather chair and a bit intimidated by the disarray of papers in front of her, she pushed her glasses up the bridge of her nose, took a deep breath, and said with a dreamy voice, "Wow. I can't believe it. It's finally happening. I'm so nervous I'm forgetting everything I learned in school." She cleared her throat. "Sorry David. Just bear with me, okay?"

As much as I liked her, I was getting a little apprehensive. I thought I was the one who was supposed to be nervous and not her. I understood what she had said, about new perspectives and all that stuff, but if she was this nervous it probably wouldn't work. Unless of course this was what Brauner had intended all along. Maybe she was just another test I had to pass. Maybe I should be more proactive?

"Sure, take your time, Private Austin."

"Call me Dawn, okay?"

I hesitated. "I don't know. Dr. Brauner is real old-fashioned when it comes to things like that," I said. "He always insists on proper etiquette. I don't want to be disrespectful."

"I'm sure he wouldn't mind. And you would actually do me a favor."

"Okay, Dawn." This unlikely looking counselor, this young woman who looked so vulnerable and nervous, had a way of getting what she wanted just by being nice. I fell into easy conversation with her, hoping to learn more about her.

"Okay, fire away. She smiled. You must have a million questions."

"You said you went to Bernard. What's that?"

"Barnard," she corrected me. "Oh boy. I'm just beginning to see how much you have to learn. Do you have a couple of years?"

She didn't expect an answer, nor did she wait for one. As she spoke she became more animated. Gradually her eyes filled with excitement and her voice became passionate. "It's a school on Manhattan's Upper West side. One of the best schools in the country."

She stopped when she saw my blank look. "Sorry David. Let's start at the beginning. I lived out there," she swept her right arm in the direction of the window. "Way out there. Outside of Resurrection. I'm one of *Them*. Isn't that what you call us?"

It felt like an explosion in my head. I was in total shock. And scared. Why was this happening? Why was Doc Brauner doing this to me? All my life I had only talked about *The Outside* in whispers. Even thinking about *Them* was dangerous. And now this woman, my new counselor,… Everything I've ever learned, everything I believed in suddenly collided in my head. I felt dizzy. Damn you, Brauner!

"I'm sorry, David." Austin was at my side in a second and put her hand on my shoulder. "I should have realized what a shock this must be to you. I wasn't thinking. I guess Dr. Brauner didn't tell you a whole lot about me, did he?"

I shook my head without saying a word.

Austin returned to Doc Brauner's leather chair. She cleared her throat and, after a few seconds of searching for the right words, resumed in a very low voice. "Maybe it's best this way. There really is no good way to tell you about the outside world. I just hope you won't suffer from information overload." She cleared her throat again and continued in the same low voice, as though she was speaking to a child, "You see, I was born in…"

For the next ten minutes her voice filled the room while I sat in stunned silence. She talked about New York, one of the largest cities in the world, approximately a hundred miles south of Resurrection. She spoke of the millions of people there, so many that they had to live in tall houses, hundreds and hundreds of people in one building. She told me of other countries and languages and war and crimes and diseases and on and on until I couldn't take it any longer.

I held up my hands. "Stop, Private Austin, okay, please stop."

She smiled gently, lovingly. "I'm sorry, David. I know it's a lot to digest."

Before she could go on, I put up my hands again to stop her. I knew our conversation was headed into even more dangerous territory. This whole thing smacked of Justin's wild ideas of people and places outside Resurrection, and that was a definite no no.

Private Austin seemed concerned by my renewed refusal to listen. She blinked a couple of times. "What is it? What's wrong, David."

"I don't think I should hear any more of this."

"Why not. It's what Dr. Brauner wants."

"I don't believe you. He would never…especially about the *Outside,* about *Them.*"

Dawn gave me an understanding smile. "It's okay, David. As I told you, he's the one who suggested, even insisted, that you learn everything. He felt that you were psychologically mature enough to handle it."

I wasn't so sure that I was.

"Believe me," she went on. "You can ask him yourself. The only thing he said was that you shouldn't repeat anything we're talking about. Think of it as doctor-patient confidentiality. Do you know what that means?"

"Sure. Doc Brauner insists on it every time I go to Retooling." Now that I was almost convinced that it was okay with Doc Brauner I began to relax. I was still confused by this sudden outpouring of information, but I was more relaxed.

"It's settled then. So hold on to your hat, David. Here comes your first lesson about the life and times of Dawn Austin. Like I said,

I used to live in a place called Manhattan, which is kind of a vertical city with lots and lots of tall buildings. Some of them are so tall that more than a thousand people live in them."

"That can't be much fun."

"Well, it's different from Resurrection City," she admitted. "And you're right. Sometimes it's not much fun. Especially when the elevator is broken…" She stopped herself again and shook her head apologetically. "Sorry. I'll try to explain as much as I can, okay? Let's see how I can explain about elevators. An elevator is like a small room that moves up and down from floor to floor, so that if you have to go to the thirty-ninth floor for instance, which is where I lived, you don't have to climb the stairs for hours."

I nodded as though it all made perfect sense but it really didn't.

"When the elevator works it takes me up to my apartment in less than a minute. And when I look out of my window I can see for miles. Way down below is the Hudson river."

My eyes lit up with recognition. "The same river that's up here right outside Resurrection City?"

"Yes David. But it's a lot wider in Manhattan because that's where the river ends. It empties into New York Bay and the Atlantic ocean."

Although interesting, I soon tired of her geography lesson. After all, I knew all about the Hudson. But I did want to hear more about the house she lived in. "This house where you live, tell me more about that."

"Like I said, it's on the thirty-ninth floor and faces west, overlooking the river. It has two bedrooms and two bathrooms. I live there with my mother."

"That's odd."

"What is odd?"

"That you live with your mother. Here in Resurrection with live with our brothers and sisters. They're out friends. We never see our mothers and fathers."

"And you don't think that's sad?"

"Of course not. Our parents have done their job. They created us. What do we need them for after that?"

"Love?" she offered with sad smile.

"I don't mean to be disrespectful, Miss Austin, but we have all the love in the world here. We have friends. And friends are more important than parents. Everyone knows that."

"I suppose sometimes friends can be more important than family." She lowered her head so I wouldn't see her eyes clouding over. Her sadness left me disturbed. Knowing that I had almost made her cry made me want to cry myself. I quickly changed the subject.

"Maybe we should talk about something else."

"Okay. Why don't you tell me about yourself."

I shrugged my shoulders. "There really isn't much to tell. My life isn't very exciting. Nobody's ever been interested in me before."

"I am."

"Okay. But I have to warn you, life in Resurrection is pretty boring."

"Why don't you let me be the judge of that? I'm sure that there are many, many interesting things that happened to you."

"Nope."

"Tell my anyhow."

"Okay, if you insist. I live right upstairs from you in Greenkill House in room 311." I stopped and frowned. "But you already know all that."

"That's all right. I'd like to hear it from you."

I humored her and continued. "I've lived there ever since my parents created me more than thirty years ago. Ever since then I lived with Justin Frederikson. He's my roomie. We grew up together, went to school together, and became best friends. I'm lucky because we get along so well."

"That's a long time to live with someone," Private Austin commented while she scribbled in her notepad. "During all those years did you ever fight with him?"

"Of course not. Why should we?"

"Oh, I don't know, people fight all the time. Mostly about silly things."

"Maybe they do where you lived because you're all crammed together like rats in a cage. But Resurrection is different."

I knew she didn't believe me, and it dawned on me that Private Austin really didn't know much about us.

"Not even arguments?" she pressed. "C'mon, admit it. We all have arguments once in a while."

"Oh sure. Justin and I argue. But when we do, we talk it out intelligently until we agree."

"Who is right most of the time? Justin or you?"

"I am of course." I hadn't meant to sound so superior and wanted to explain myself when she interrupted.

"Why is that, David? Are you smarter? Or a better person?"

"No, not at all. Justin is probably the smartest man I know. He's just not as far along as I am."

"You mean in school?"

"No. Justin finished school a year before I did. I'm talking about Retooling."

"I see. Why don't we talk about that for a minute. Maybe it'll help me understand why Retooling works better with some than it does with others."

"Sure. Retooling is something we all go to once a month. I don't really know how to describe it. It's all very sophisticated, with computers and scanners and other equipment. Brauner tried to explain it to me once. He showed me one of the machines and explained how he can look inside someone's brain with it. I didn't understand it all, but he explained how a brain is like a computer, processing sensory impulses and transmitting information to the rest of the body. And how he can rewire the pathways, opening and closing gates, and so on. And how the brain is where we store our ideas and emotions and memory. Does all of this make any sense to you?"

"Oh yes. I do, and I'm quite impressed with you, David. But please go on. What happens when you go to Retooling?"

"Well, according to Dr. Brauner a brain can get sick, just like any other part of the human body. It could be a whole bunch of things. Like bad memory, for instance. When that happens your brain can store incorrect information. And that can cause a chain reaction. It can affect your other brain functions, like thought and decision making. If that happens, it has to be treated before it gets out of control."

"And that's where Justin has a problem?" she asked with interest.

"Oh no. Not a problem. He just acts a little different at times."

"How? Can you tell me?"

I felt trapped. I had promised Justin never to talk about him. And now, less than an hour into my session with Austin I was on the verge of breaking my promise.

Austin kept digging as if nothing were wrong. "What's the matter, David? Can't you tell me?"

"I promised not to say anything."

"Hmm. I know we have a deal not to embarrass each other but this could be important. What I'm trying to say is that your promise to Justin could be contrary to everything you believe in. I mean, if Justin is sick and he needs help, shouldn't you tell someone before he is out of control?"

"He's not out of control. He just asks too many questions," I blurted out. Trying to explain my relationship with Justin I had talked myself into a corner. For the first time I resented Private Austin. Despite all her talk about trust and confidentiality I felt that she had tricked me.

"What kind of questions?" she insisted. "Questions about the *Outside*? About *Them*?"

I shook my head. "Sorry, Private. I promised."

"All right. I understand. But don't you think that it's unfair of him to put you on the spot like this. Sounds to me like he's using you. And that is very un-Resurrection-like, don't you think?"

Annoyed by her simple logic, I didn't have a good answer.

"Talk to me, David." Her voice suddenly had a sting to it. "Don't you think if Justin has a problem he should have told Dr. Brauner rather than drag you into it? Isn't that what you would have done?"

Trapped again.

"What's the matter? Is it against the rules to ask questions or it just against the rules to ask the wrong kind of questions?" Not only was she like a ferret, she had also turned downright nasty.

"Can we talk about something else?"

"Sure. You already answered my question anyhow. Why don't we get back to your life? That's how this whole thing started, you telling me about how you've lived in the same room with Justin for the last thirty or so years."

"That's right," I said quickly, relieved to get off the delicate subject of Justin. "My normal day starts at seven in the morning. I have breakfast in the mess hall and I'm on my job by eight thirty."

"What is it that you do?" she asked with genuine interest as if the past five minutes had never happened.

"I actually have three jobs. In the mornings I work with Doc Brauner. I help him in the office with all sorts of things. Mainly I enter medical information in the computer for him. He's got terrible handwriting, you know, and I'm one of a few people who can decipher it. Then I schedule appointments for him, do some filing, that sort of thing. Every once in a while he lets me sit in on examinations, usually with the younger Disciples."

"Wow, you must know an awful lot about everybody in Resurrection. That's a big responsibility."

"Now you sound exactly like Doc Brauner. He said the very same thing. But he said I was the only one he could trust."

"So I suppose that whatever you learn on the job is privileged information?"

I agreed. "Right. As a matter of fact, he used the same term you used before, you know, doctor-patient confidentiality."

"And he isn't worried that you… Let's see if I can phrase this correctly, that you won't accidentally misuse this information. Or become inquisitive, like Justin?"

"Oh no. Dr. Brauner trusts me. Besides, I never get to see all the information. It's more like bits and pieces, like a jigsaw puzzle. And there are a lot of things I'm not allowed to do on the computer." I thought about it and added, "I guess his trust in me has a limit."

"Maybe. Or maybe he's just bringing you along slowly. Maybe you still have a little way to go before he's willing to let you put all the pieces together."

*****

We broke for lunch. Private Austin was off to the *Apostle's Lounge*, while I was on my way to the cafeteria after declining her offer to join her at the lounge. J knew Justin would be waiting for me.

I got myself a ham and cheese on rye. Instead of the usual chocolate malt I opted for black coffee. After this morning's session with Private Austin I needed all the help I could get to stay alert. Carefully balancing my tray, I made my way to the far corner where Justin had saved a seat for me at our usual table.

He looked preoccupied and hardly ate even though today was meatloaf and mashed potato day, his favorite. He picked at his food, slurped a mouthful of soda, then took another bite before pushing his plate aside and staring at his tray.

"You're late," he said.

"Sorry. I've been at Brauner's all morning."

"Talking about me, I suppose? Does the old bastard still want you to fire me?"

"Of course not. I told you, Brauner's okay with it as long as you keep your nose clean. And for your information I haven't seen Brauner all day. I've been with my new counselor."

"Oh yeah?" He perked up. "Who's that? The new broad who just moved in downstairs?"

I had no reason to get annoyed with Justin. After all, Private Austin meant nothing to me, but I found his language demeaning. "Yes. And the broad has a name, Private Austin. Dawn Austin."

Justin rolled his eyes. "Dawn, huh. She's the tall skinny one, right?"

"Yeah."

"How is she? Is she nice?"

"She's okay I guess. I didn't know why talking about Austin should make me feel uncomfortable, but it did.

"Is she good looking?"

"I guess. Let's drop the subject, okay?

"My my, aren't we touchy." He gave me a curious look. "I guess you like her. What did you talk about all morning?"

"Oh, this and that. You know, typical counselor stuff. She wants to know everything under the sun." I knew I sounded evasive and Justin picked up on it.

"You didn't talk about me, did you?"

I hesitated for a moment. "Not really."

"Not really? What does *not really* mean? Did you or didn't you?"

"Just in passing. Nothing…"

His hand clamped on mine. "You didn't tell her about Josh, did you? And what I said about Brauner?"

"Of course not. I promised, didn't I?"

"Yeah, I know. But sometimes, you know, especially with a woman…"

"It's not like that."

He released my hand. "I'm sorry, Davey. I didn't think you'd snitch on me. I just want to make sure you don't slip accidentally. Especially not now."

"What makes now so special?"

He leaned across the table and whispered into my ear. "Because I'm going in there tonight. I told you I'd find out. Well, tonight's the night."

"Are you crazy? You can't do that. At least sleep on it. You'll feel differently in the morning."

"No I won't. Besides, I don't have a choice. It's got to be tonight. You see, tomorrow I get Retooled. It may be too late by then."

Damn. I was right in the middle again. Austin's words were still fresh in my mind…*it's unfair of him to put you on the spot like this. Sounds to me like he's using you. And that is very un-Resurrection-like…* Neither had I forgotten what Brauner had said, about Resurrection working in mysterious ways and how I must be willing to endure pain if I truly wanted to serve.

Everything was happening so fast I couldn't think straight. I knew all about my duty as a Disciple and I knew all about keeping my word. But what if Justin went out of control, as Austin had hinted? Or if I said something and Justin wound up in trouble. With Austin's arrival life had suddenly become very complicated.

I was tempted to skip my afternoon session with Austin but couldn't think of a good excuse. Skipping out on her would only make her suspicious. And if anything went wrong with Justin tonight she'd put two and two together. I didn't have a choice but to go back to Terwilliger House.

*****

Austin picked up right where we left off the moment I got back to Doc Brauner's office. "You told me about your job with Dr. Brauner right before we broke for lunch." Austin sounded businesslike and no-nonsense. As a matter of fact, her demeanor had undergone a subtle transformation. She was still friendly but in a professional manner. Her charming modesty had vanished. Now, as she faced me across Brauner's desk, she looked and acted every inch a counselor. "What about your other jobs? You said you had three."

"My real job is in the afternoon writing for the Sentinel. Actually, it's more than just writing. I really run the paper."

"That sounds interesting. What do you write about?"

"Mostly human interest stories. Sometimes about current events. Like the annual Apostle Day celebration. Things like that."

"Does anyone ever tell you what not to write about?"

"Sometimes."

"I suppose you don't want to talk about that?"

"Right."

"I understand. Maybe we'll talk about it some other day when we know each other better. What about your third job?"

"It's not much of a job. I'm a room monitor. I have to make the rounds of a couple of homes and do a bed check. The whole thing only takes an hour or so."

"Compared to your other jobs it sounds kind of boring. But I suppose it strikes the right balance. Research in the morning, creativity in the afternoon, and then, to wind down the day, something routine that doesn't require much thinking. Actually it sound like an ideal combination to me."

She looked up from her notes. "In a way you're a lucky man, David. You do a lot of interesting things. Do you enjoy them?"

"Sure."

"Is that why you're happy."

Whatever relief I had felt evaporated. I sensed that she was about to probe again, try to catch me off guard. What did she have against being happy? Why couldn't she just believe me?

"I guess so. I have a lot to be happy about."

"I can tell." She looked unconvinced. "I envy you."

Her sarcasm was so heavy-handed that even I noticed it. "Don't worry. Now that you're in Resurrection you'll be happy too," I said.

"I suppose that's why Ezekiel wondered why anyone would ever want to leave Resurrection," Austin said.

"You knew Ezekiel?"

"Knew?" She looked puzzled.

"Yeah. Ezekiel died a few days ago. I'm the one who found him dead in his bunk."

Austin's face turned ashen. She was visibly shaken.

"Are you all right, Private? You don't look so good."

She tried to pull herself together but a quiver in her voice betrayed her. "Yeah, I'm okay, David. Just a little surprised. You see, I just talked to Ezekiel a few weeks ago and he looked fine to me. As a matter of fact…oh, never mind. You wouldn't know anyhow."

"Know what?"

Disregarding my question, Austin shrugged her shoulders. She suddenly seemed a million miles removed from Brauner's office. Her eyes were closed, her lips pinched. Twice she looked up as though she was about to speak but each time she thought better of it.

I grew restless. Facing Austin across the desk, watching second after second tick off the wall clock, and not being asked any questions, I had the distinct impression that today's session was over. Two minutes later I made up my mind. I cleared my throat. "Private Austin, is that it? Can I leave?"

She didn't reply. She didn't even acknowledge me.

"Private, if you're through with me I have a couple of things to take care of." With that I rose and turned to the door. I hoped to escape the office without getting into any more trouble but she stopped me.

"David?" She walked to my side and led me back to my chair. "David, what happened to Ezekiel?"

I shrugged my shoulders. "I, I…don't really know."

"But you just said you found him. You must have some idea what happened."

"I'm sorry but I really don't. All I know is that when I did bed checks he was dead. Other than that there's nothing to tell."

My answer frustrated her. It also made her more determined. She rolled Brauner's chair to my side of the desk and took a seat next to me. I didn't dare look up. She was so close that I could smell fresh soap clinging to her skin and hear a quick intakes of breath.

"You know, David, the one thing I want more than anything else in the world is to help you. I'm giving up two years of my life to live in this place. I gave up my mother and my friends, my comfortable room, my books, my whole social life. And I'd gladly do it all over again if I thought I could help you. But you got to meet me halfway. I can't do it all by myself. All I'm asking for are a couple of minutes of your time and some honest answers. Is that so much to ask for?"

I shook my head. I really wanted to cooperate and help her but there wasn't anything I could do. Why couldn't she understand that?

"David?"

I avoided her eyes.

"David?" she repeated, this time with more urgency.

"What?"

"Please tell me what happened."

"I told you. I can't tell you anymore than I already did."

"Can't or won't?"

Austin turned and faced the window. Mullioned glass panes revealed Albany Avenue and late-afternoon traffic. An endless stream of official Resurrection vehicles, clearly marked with the Camp's crossed sword and shield emblems, wound its way towards Uptown. Bus after bus carried Disciples home after a day's work. Interspersed among the green caravan were a handful of armored vehicles bringing night-shift Guardians to their posts.

It was the typical rush-hour hustle and bustle before Resurrection City settled in for the evening. In another hour the flow of traffic would ebb to a trickle. Sidewalks, now crowded with pedestrians would be deserted. By then everyone in Resurrection City will be enjoying their leisure time, eating dinner in cafeterias, attending prayer services, or simply hanging out in their rooms. Which was exactly what I wanted to do if Austin would only let me.

She however seemed to have lost all concept of time. Mesmerized by Albany Avenue, she stared at the street. Each passing minute increased my anxiety. I hadn't done anything wrong. As a matter of fact, I'd bent over backward to be nice to her. Had I lied to her? No. Had I refused to answer even a single question? Again no, although Austin seemed to think so. Had I been polite? Absolutely. So what did this woman who flip-flopped between nervousness and tenaciousness want from me? Why did she behave like this?

Maybe she was a set-up, I thought. It wasn't Brauner's style to pull something as underhanded as this, but who knew? Perhaps pawning me off on a new counselor, especially someone who looked insecure and came on like gangbusters about friendship and trust really was a test I had to pass. Damn. I didn't know what to make of her. Except that I didn't particularly like Austin anymore. Or I trust her. She had a habit of smooth-talking me and then trying to catch me off-guard. Come to think of it, I disliked her more and more by the minute.

The object of my dislike finally turned from the window. Picking up where she had left off earlier, she said, "I don't believe you ever answered me, David. You can't tell me what happened or you won't tell me. Which is it?"

"Can't," I said without conviction.

"Let me ask you something." Her voice hardened. "A few minutes ago you told me that you were happy. All the time. That's pretty much what Ezekiel told me too. Do you think he's happy now?"

"I hope so, ma'am."

"And what about you? Were you happy when you discovered his body?"

"I was happy to see that whatever had happened to him was over."

"Was he your friend?"

"In Resurrection we're all friends."

"And you were happy when you found that your friend had died? I can't believe that."

"Why are you trying to put words in my mouth, ma'am? That's not what I said. What I said was that I was happy that whatever was wrong with him was over. That's all."

She seemed pleased that I had raised my voice. "Go on, David."

"There's nothing else to say. That's it. Besides, what's so wrong with being happy? It sounds to me like the only time you're happy is when you're trying to make someone unhappy."

"That's not true and you know it. I have nothing against being happy. It's just not the way normal people are. The only people I know who are always happy happen to wear straightjackets and live in a rubber room at Bellevue. For God's sake, I'm only trying to show you that real people have highs and lows. They laugh and sometimes they cry. Sometimes they get scared and other times they think that there isn't a thing in the world that can harm them. And sometimes even the nicest people get angry for no good reason. Anything other smacks of indoctrination. Or moronic intransigence."

"Private, with all due respect, you're dead wrong, and please don't call me a moron. And I'm not intransigent. You of all people, with your degrees and all, should know that intransigence is the refusal to modify one's position, usually an extreme position. That's certainly not the case with me. My happiness is not an extreme position. I think it's an enviable emotion, one which Resurrection has taught me. If anyone is intransigent I think it's you, because you refuse to see the goodness and love all around you."

She scoffed at my outburst. "My, my. What a scholarly explanation from a Disciple."

Her sarcasm stung. Already on edge, I lost my temper. "Why do you assume that I'm stupid? Just because I'm a Disciple and not yet an Apostle doesn't mean I'm stupid. And if you think that it's unnatural to be happy you don't have the first idea what Resurrection is all about."

"And you don't have the first idea what life is all about. You're confusing blind faith with happiness," she accused me and stalked back to her desk.

For the next few moments she ignored me, randomly shuffling stacks of paper, pretending to be absorbed by the contents of various folders and charts that were scattered on Brauner's desk. The more she shuffled, the more irritated she looked. She wrinkled her nose at one page, frowned at another one, and shook her head when she read a third one. One page in particular seemed to catch her attention. She held it up with both hands, squinted over the top of her glasses, read it a second time, then marked it up with a blue pencil and at last put it back on a stack of papers. All the while her face was a dead giveaway. She was annoyed.

"All right, David," She started again. "If you don't want… Oh, I'm sorry, if you don't know what happened to Ezekiel I'll ask Dr. Brauner. I'm sure he'll be happy to tell me."

Once again a subtle change had taken place. I saw yet another side of Dawn Austin. Call it willpower, maybe anger, perhaps disappointment that I hadn't told her about Ezekiel, she had transformed herself into a different person. Her eyes were steely, her voice had an unpleasant edge. If a counselor was supposed to be comforting, she sure as hell didn't look like a counselor.

"Let's talk for a moment about that last job of yours. Room monitor is what you called it, right?"

"Yes ma'am."

"Maybe I was wrong when I called it a routine assignment. Finding Ezekiel dead in his bunk wasn't routine, was it?"

"No it wasn't."

"Did any other unusual thing ever happen?"

"No ma'am. The worst that usually happens is that I find someone breaking curfew."

"And what do you do then?"

"I report them to the authorities. That's the whole purpose of the job."

"So you're a snitch?"

"Ma'am, why are you trying to belittle me all of a sudden? What did I do to get you so angry?"

She ignored me and went on. "And that makes you happy? Reporting your friends to whomever you report these things to?"

"Yes, Private Austin. It means I'm doing my job, and I'm really helping others stay out of trouble."

"But you're not quite as conscientious and dedicated as you'd like me to think, are you David? Every once in a while you look the other way, don't you?"

I had no idea what Austin was driving at, but whatever it was it couldn't be good. As usual, when faced with accusations, I got flustered. "Ma'am, I don't know what you're talking about."

"You're a liar, David." She got up, stormed across the office, and slammed the hallway door shut. It rattled the frame and echoed like a gunshot. Brauner's medical diploma tilted on the wall. Outside, in the reception area, Rachel Firestein ceased typing, shocked by Austin's outburst.

Austin stalked past me, bumped against my arm me with a brusque *Sorry*, and pounced back into Brauner's chair. She swiveled one-hundred-eighty degrees and, with her back to me, tapped a rapid drumbeat with her pencil.

"You know damn well what I'm talking about. Your roommate, Justin Frederikson. Tell me you never covered for him."

I bristled with anger. How dare this woman, this stranger, one of *Them*, question my integrity and honesty? She knew nothing about me. She scoffed at me and thought she was better than me just because she went to this Barnard place and was a psychiatrist. Damn her, calling me a liar After all her talk about trust. Bitch.

At that moment, sitting like a lab specimen under her icy glare and having to defend myself against her half-truths and innuendos, my anger turned to hatred. I wanted to lash out and hurt her. I wanted to make her cry, make her feel miserable and lonely. I wanted to taunt her and laugh at her. I wanted to hold a mirror to her face and let her see what a pathetic misfit she was. But I summoned all my strength and swallowed my anger until it was nothing more than a faint rumble in my guts. I'd show her that I was better than her, that Resurrection was full of love and kindness and a hell lot better than this city of hers where millions of people were crowded into tiny apartments.

"Yes ma'am. You're right. I've looked the other way a few times. Maybe that was wrong. Maybe I even hurt Justin by not reporting him when I should have. But I thought I was doing the right thing. I'm sorry if I disappointed you, but I'm only human."

She crossed the room and stopped directly in front of me. "You could have fooled me, David. For a moment I thought you were perfect."

"I think it's best if I leave now, Private Austin. I still have some work to do on the paper and it's getting late."

"David."

"Yes?"

"Are you happy now, David? Are you still happy? Or are you upset? Angry? Do you hate me?"

Without realizing it, I had jumped out of my seat and found myself standing face to face with her. *Christ. I hate this bitch.*

"God damn it, David. Tell me. Are you still happy?"

"No, ma'am."

She did something completely unexpected then. She reached out and touched my shoulder. And smiled. "It's okay, David. It's okay to hate once in a while, as long as you have more love than hatred inside you. It's okay to be human."

Chapter 9

CECILIA AUSTIN DROPPED two grocery bags on the kitchen counter and sorted through her mail. Still out of breath from her near-sprint to make the two block trip from Gristede's to her apartment without getting drenched in a sudden downpour, and too anxious to put the perishables in the refrigerator before opening the letter she had waited for, she swept aside half an inch of junk mail and bills. Dawn's neat script was unmistakable. She fumbled with the envelope and ripped it open impatiently.

Dear Mother. Sorry it took so long to write, but I've been incredibly busy. You can't imagine how much there is to do and learn. I thought I was busy at Barnard, but this place has it beat by a mile. But I don't mind. It's what I wanted, and there really isn't much else to do in Resurrection anyhow. Social life here is as extinct as the dinosaur, and most of the Guardians, that's inside lingo for prison guards, are local yokels with negative IQs. Forgive my sarcasm, but after one month in this place I'll never make fun of the nerdy grad students at Columbia again.

My living quarters are small but comfortable (for a prison, that is). I have a suite (Up here that means a room with a private bath). Not bad for a lowly Private, huh? I'm not nuts about the interior decorator though. I think he has a green fetish. When I'm in my room with my uniform, actually a skirt, military style blouse, and jacket called Habiliments, (you guessed it, green), I blend into the walls. But enough about my life in the lap of poverty.

Resurrection is everything I expected, and then some. The best way I can describe the place is that it falls somewhere between a minimum security prison and a religious retreat. Quite a mix, huh? Guns and crosses. Still, the inmates (oops, Disciples) are a peaceful enough lot, although a very strange one. They're all happy. As a matter of fact, there's so much happiness here that I want to puke.

All of the above notwithstanding, I've already had some gratifying experiences. I've started working with my very own Disciple, a thirty-eight-year-old man who's as intelligent as Einstein and as simplistic as a village idiot. It's my job to remake him into a responsible member of society. He's going to be a tough nut to crack, but I have the feeling that if and when I do, he'll turn out to be the wunderkind of Resurrection. At first it was a bit scary playing God, but now I'm hooked (only kidding).

I've got to go now. It's almost time for my next session with my protegee and I still have to make my bed and clean my suite (remember my messy room?). I wish I had a phone but rules are rules, so I'll just have to write.

I miss you. I even miss your bitching, so feel free to write and bitch a little bit. And I miss my books. Please send…

Cecilia Austin squinted, put on her glasses, but still couldn't make out what Dawn wanted her to send. Water stains and bleeding ink had obliterated the words. She shrugged her shoulders and read on…*it'll be my mental dessert (chocolate cake for the gray matter). I think it's on the top shelf in the bookcase next to my bed.*

Please write and I'll write again next week. Love 'ya. D.

PS. I'm really surprised you didn't bitch about my sexual encounter in front of the whole class. You must be slipping.

Chapter 10

AT TWO MINUTES to midnight Justin Frederickson cut across Albany Ave on his way to Resurrection City's uptown library annex. So far, things couldn't have gone smoother. Sneaking out of Greenkill had been a piece of cake. The ensuing five minute walk had been equally uneventful. The only Guardians he'd seen came staggering out of the Apostle's Lounge. He ducked behind a rhododendron hedge and avoided them easily. In another five minutes he'd be at the library, well past the time when Perlmutter, the night watchman, will have dozed off.

Resurrection City had been lulled to sleep by late summer's nocturnal music of tree frogs and crickets. Albany Avenue was a deserted, moonlit ribbon slicing through an area of the city that at one time was home to some of the city's grandest mansions. Gingerbread Victorians, its turreted rooflines and intricate fretwork reminders of an era when architectural whimsy mirrored the excesses of their high-living, fun loving owners, stood side by side with somber Dutch colonial stone houses whose massive walls had withstood the burning of Kingston by the British. Expansive lawns and century old maples fronted each house, providing a buffer between the mansions and the bustling day-time traffic that lumbered along Albany Avenue on its way to the stockade district, home of Resurrection's administrative headquarters.

At the stroke of midnight a Guardian patrol carrier turned onto Albany Avenue and headed north towards Ascension Square, one of three vehicular checkpoints for the Stockade district. The carrier, a hybrid Humvee outfitted with bullet proof passenger cage, gun ports, and thermal imaging devices proceeded through a double-gated security zone then headed straight for Terwilliger House, the first of several administrative buildings that were patrolled every night.

At first sign of the approaching headlights Justin Frederickson hit the ground, flattening his one-hundred-ninety pound body against a carpet of overgrown grass adjacent to Terwilliger house. Already perspiring in his makeshift camouflage outfit of olive green hooded sweatshirt and black jeans, the trickle of sweat turned into a torrent. His heart raced out of control. Afraid to move, he remained on his stomach, face pressed into the lawn, a cloud of mosquitoes diving at him like kamikaze pilots.

He tried to calm down, taking deep breaths, convincing himself that there was nothing special about dodging Guardian patrols in the middle of the night. Hell, he'd done it for years now, outwitting these ersatz soldiers time and again. But never in the heavily guarded Stockade district. And the urgency of tonight's mission was obvious. Retooling was just around the corner. Getting caught by Brauner was still fresh in his mind. Justin's window of opportunity was closing fast. It was now or never. And that was enough to make him sweat no matter what he told himself.

Judging from the sound of the Humvee's engine, the vehicle was no more than thirty yards away. Close enough for him to hear the patrol's two-way radio. Close enough to pick up snatches of conversation. Close enough to hear a car door slam shut. Frighteningly close enough to make out steel-tipped boots hitting the pavement as two Guardians jumped off the running board.

Justin lifted his head in time to see them approach. Halfway up the front walk they stopped. And then the unexpected happened. Instead of proceeding to the front door they split up. The taller of the two, assault rifle slung over his shoulder, continued along the flagstone walk. The other Guardian, short and stocky, a flashlight in his right hand, a semiautomatic in his left, veered to the left and crossed the lawn to check the side entrance. His course would take him within ten yards of Justin.

Justin froze. Too late to make a move, he resigned himself that he'd be caught. Frantically thinking of excuses, he discarded each the minute he thought of it. *I lost my wallet when I was here yester-*

day to pick up my prescription. Even these two morons wouldn't buy that one. Or how about *To tell you the truth, I have no idea what I'm doing here. I must have sleepwalked right out of my room.* They'd laugh him all the way to headquarters, or even straight to *The House.* Shit! Maybe he should just come clean, well, sort of, and admit breaking curfew. *Hey guys, I know I shouldn't have and it's against the rules, but you know how it is, I just had to get away from my room, you see I was… blah, blah, blah.*

A flashlight clicked on and zig-zagged across the lawn in lock-step with the Guardian who was making his way to the side entrance. In a flash Justin jumped to his feet and threw up his arms. "Hey guys, I know I shouldn't…"

He stopped before he finished the sentence. The flashlight clicked off. The Guardian made an abrupt about face and rushed in the direction of the Humvee, trailing his partner by five steps. Amid the cacophony of crickets and tree frogs the two-way radio barked urgent orders, "Code 914. Code 914. All units to 164 Lindermann. Officer down. Repeat. Urgent. All units to…" Before the radio finished crackling both Guardians had clambered into the vehicle, gunned the engine, and raced north on Albany Avenue.

His arms still in the air, Justin broke into a wide grin. He was on an adrenaline rush. So what if he'd almost wet his pants? Who cared that his shirt stuck like glue to his sweat-soaked skin? What did it matter that he'd almost blown it? If ever there was a lucky omen, this was it.

After waiting two minutes to make sure no additional patrols were on their way Justin slowly got to his feet and headed towards Pearl Street. Along the way he stayed in shadows whenever possible, edging along trees and hedges, darting across intersections with quick bursts, sprinting crouched at the waist, until he was in the relative safety deep in the Stockade district. The area was a warren of crooked, narrow streets where houses stood cheek by jowl and extended to the sidewalk. Gone were the wide lawns that could have exposed him. Here, recessed vestibules and iron-gated stoops created a patchwork of nooks and crannies that would provide emergency shelter.

At the corner of Fair Street he paused and checked the intersection for signs of life. The street, which was brightly illuminated by one of the few remaining streetlights in the Stockade district, was the last danger spot. No one to his left. Nothing but a deserted stretch of Fair Street to his right. He darted across the street and huddled inside a doorway, surprised by the tremors that rattled his body. He was dying for a smoke, a habit he'd acquired recently after making friends with Paulette, a forty-two tear old Guardian who was more interested in his looks than his conduct, but the glow of a lit cigarette would be suicidal this close to the end of his mission. He reached into his pants pocket and felt for five keys looped around a wire ring. Reassured by the feel of metal, he whispered through clenched teeth. *Thanks Paulette. I'll make it worth your while.* There was no stopping Justin Frederikson now.

*****

Sixty three John Street was a building Justin knew well. It was where he worked as a janitor. It was also a building he could break into easily thanks to Paulette's generous and unbeknownst donation. By the time she missed her keys he'd be long out of here. With any kind of luck he'd be back in her place and she'd never know.

During daytime hours, the brick two story townhouse was a quietly sedate extension of Resurrection's public library. Every shelf, every nook and cranny of every room was crammed with books, periodicals, videos, and compact disks of special interest. It wasn't the place to find romance novels, children's classics, or back issues of the Sentinel. For those publications, Disciples went to the main Library on Clinton Avenue, just several blocks past John Street. In contrast, the John Street annex contained books that were of little interest to the average Resurrection resident. The only readers making their way through the extension's doors were academics and scientists who held special passes, men and women who had a demonstrated need to access scholarly works in conjunction with their daily activities.

Despite the wealth of information in its archives, the John Street annex was a low security admin building. Its contents had never attracted a thief or vandal. If someone wanted a specific book, one filled out a library pass, had it approved by Colonel Axton, and presented it to Mrs. Biedermaier, the kindly gray-haired, blush-cheeked librarian who presided at a desk near the front door and was known around town as the *book keeper.* Either Lucy Bramble, the dim-witted librarian's assistant, or Gerald, a retired history professor, would then disappear with the authorized withdrawal slip into a labyrinth of bookcases and reappear shortly thereafter with the requested volume. Although no books were allowed to be removed from the building, a small but comfortable reading room, outfitted with a wing chair, writing table, and Tiffany reading lamp was available. Photocopies could only be obtained by filling out another authorized form. The reading room was a haven of quiet serenity and academia in an area otherwise crawling with administrators and Guardians.

At night, with the doors locked and the Tiffany lamps extinguished, Quinton Perlmutter reigned over the library. Perlmutter, a retired literature teacher, was myopic and spoke with a lisp, two afflictions which forced him into retirement at the relatively young age of sixty. Perlmutter's tendency to doze off at any time, even during the middle of a conversation, was well known. He would certainly be no obstacle for Justin Frederikson.

Justin scaled a waist-high picket fence that surrounded an empty lot next to the library and dodged from tree to tree until he reaches a narrow side entrance. At one time the lot had been the beer garden of a German restaurant, and the door led straight into the restaurant's kitchen and bar. Now it led into the library's reading room, separated from the front entrance and Perlmutter's guard station by a narrow corridor, the public toilets, the copier room, and a supply closet.

The side entrance was no match for Justin's collection of keys. The third one did the trick and the door creaked open. He wedged himself through the narrow opening and closed the door behind him. As he had expected, the reading room was in darkness. To Justin's right, sounds of Perlmutter's uneven snore were muffled by thirty feet of hallway. An archway to Justin's left revealed the outline of bookshelves, arranged in twelve rows separated by narrow aisles. Beyond the shelves a locked door separated the main section of the library from the mixed media vault, which had once been the restaurant's walk-in freezer. Now it held a collection of video tapes and computer discs. The key to the vault was buried inside Perlmutter's pants pocket and was impossible to get at without waking him. That however was of no concern to Justin. He owned neither a video cassette player nor a computer.

He used a penlight to guide him through the narrow aisles and moved cautiously, avoiding floorboards he knew would creak under his step, playing the fist-sized circle of light along the spines of hundreds of books. He lingered several times to read a title, hurried past an entire section he knew to be of no interest to him, and stopped intermittently to listen for unusual sounds. But there were none, merely Perlmutter's sporadic snorts growing dimmer as Justin worked his way deeper into the library.

His watch told him that it was almost one o'clock. He was beginning to run out of time but resisted an urge to hurry. One wrong move, the sudden noise of a single book dropping to the floor and shattering the silence, could send Perlmutter scurrying into the room. If there ever was a time for self-discipline, this was it. But another problem nudged him to move more quickly. His penlight battery was weakening at an alarming rate. Already the circle of light was so dim that Justin had to pull book after book from the shelves to decipher its title. And he still faced the prospect of having to return them to their correct place when he was finished.

He estimated his battery had ten minutes or so left before it would die. And he needed to be back in Paulette's apartment before sunrise. He also knew he had finally arrived in the Geography section. It was time to take a chance before time ran out. Without hesitating another moment Justin snapped off the penlight and buried it in his pocket. Then, working with methodical care, he pulled a stack of large books from the top shelf. He ran his fingers across their spines and counted. Six books. That should be more than enough for a start.

He made his way back to the reading room, guided as much by his sense of direction as by the faint moonlight that filtered through the room's single window. Step by agonizingly slow step he felt his way through the labyrinth of books, through the biology aisle, past the political science section, and finally along the world history shelves, until he found himself back in the reading room.

He selected a chair furthest from the corridor that led to the front hall and Perlmutter, whose intermittent snorts had given way to a steady snore, and stacked the books on the writing table. Hidden by darkness, he wriggled out of his sweatshirt, still damp from his earlier encounter with the Guardian patrol, and draped it across the Tiffany shade. Shirtless, his naked torso streaked with beads of perspiration, he felt chilled, and cursed himself for forgetting his T-shirt in the rush to get out of Paulette's apartment.

He tugged at the lamp's metal chain. A muted circle of multi-colored light dappled the table. It was barely enough to read, but he'd manage. He opened the first book and almost let out a triumphant whoop. Bingo! He'd struck gold with his first book, a World Atlas. His fingers trembling with excitement, he flipped through the pages until he got to the North American section.

Gradually, a few pages later, Justin was completely absorbed by the maps. It was nearly two in the morning but he had lost all track of time. He hadn't moved, other than to flip from page to page. At last he knew he had the right page. The names on the map were all familiar. Kingston, Boiceville, Shandaken, the Hudson River. His fingers traced the outline if the river until he got to a mass of blue, the Atlantic Ocean.

His skin tingled. He could feel his blood rushing through his veins. He hadn't heard a single sound. Neither had he noticed the absence of Perlmutter's monotonous snore. A quick chill ran across his back. A faint motion, a gentle stirring of wind, caressed his naked skin. He spun clockwise, right hand balled into a fist. A sickening sense of pending danger set his heart racing.

A young woman, tall and thin, with shoulder length black hair and wire-rimmed glasses gasped as his fist came up and his eyes hardened with fear and determination.

Chapter 11

132 FAIR STREET was an unlikely building to house Resurrection's Violence Control Center. Graceful columns and marble steps, flanked by wrought iron railings, greeted guests. Six-panel palladian windows lent an air of dignified elegance. The house had at one time been the home of Jacob VanDyken, a wealthy local wine merchant, and the interior retained much of the grandeur and opulence its original owner craved. A winding staircase led from the center hall to the second and third floors. The oval hall held a collection of oil paintings depicting life in Kingston prior to the burning of the city by the British, although bronze plaques beneath each painting identified the scenes as historic Resurrection City. A custom woven oval carpet, hand knotted in Tabriz, muffled footsteps. Crystal chandeliers and matching wall sconces provided unobtrusive light. Six double doors fanned from the center hall and led to the former living quarters: a grand salon, front and side parlors, a music room, a smoking parlor, and the wine merchant's office. It was in this last room, measuring eighteen by twenty feet and fronting Fair Street on the eastern side of the building, that sensitive meetings were held nowadays. VanDyken had insisted on conducting his business transactions in complete privacy and security. Accordingly, his office was lined with an inner wall which deadened all sounds and made it impossible for servants to listen in on his conversations. The doors had always been kept locked and heavy brocade curtains drawn even at daytime. A pocket door, hidden within intricately carved mahogany paneling, led to a root cellar and provided an escape route for VanDyken, who suffered from severe paranoia during his later years. The office soon gained a reputation as a place of sinister and immoral events. Local residents

talked about it in hushed terms and never in front of VanDyken. The ghosts of the past were long gone, but locals still talked about the room with hushed voices accompanied by furtive glances. To be called into the *Office*, as the room was simply referred to nowadays, spelled trouble.

This afternoon, as in days past, the doors to the *Office* were locked. The brocade curtains, an exact replica of the originals, were drawn. A haze of cigar smoke hung like an atmospheric inversion beneath the ten foot ceiling. On a cherry wood credenza stood an uncapped decanter, half filled with Dom Perignon, and three snifters. Were it not for the occupants of the Office, the ghost of VanDyken could easily be seated behind the enormous wooden desk, trademark cigar in hand, alternately sending puffs of smoke into the air and swirling Dom Perignon in a crystal snifter, while conducting an important business negotiation.

But instead of VanDyken's powerful six foot three inch frame and unruly shock of gray hair, today's occupant of the leather chair was a thin, bespectacled gnome of a man with a fringe of grey hair whose only distinguishing features were pallid complexion, a prominent nose, and piercing blue-grey eyes. Colonel Xavier Axton, Resurrection's chief intelligence officer and, at the age of forty two, the Camp's most feared senior administrator, normally did not conduct initial interrogations himself, letting lieutenant Sanchez, his smooth-talking assistant who had an uncanny ability to convince suspects that he was on their side draw first blood. Then, after they had been lulled into a false sense of security, Axton took over. His short temper and abrasive attitude were legendary. Consequently, he was avoided like the plague. At this morning's meeting however Sanchez was conspicuously absent. The assault on Private Austin was by all indications a highly unusual and potentially dangerous development, one which demanded Axton's immediate personal attention. As soon as all parties were present Axton strode to the Cognac decanter. He lifted it and pointed at the office's other occupants. "Gentlemen? May I offer you some cognac?"

Two heads declined politely.

Axton's eyes swiveled ten degrees further. "Private? Something more delicate? Perhaps a glass of Sherry?"

Dawn Austin nodded in the colonel's direction. "Cognac please."

Axton's eyes lit up with surprise. He nodded stiffly and forced a smile. "Wise choice, young lady."

He poured an ounce and handed the glass to Dawn. "Here you go, Private. Enjoy. And if I were you I'd swirl the cognac in your snifter first. It will let the bouquet…"

"I've had Cognac before, colonel," Dawn interrupted him.

Brauner and Perlmutter smiled quickly and lowered their eyes, hoping that Axton hadn't noticed. The colonel replied with a smile of his own and a quick "But of course you have. I forgot that you come from a privileged background." With that he returned to his desk. Although his face was still frozen into a smile, Brauner knew that Axton was seething from the humiliating repartee. 'Axton' he thought, you've met your match.

The quick exchange between Axton and Dawn Austin signaled the end of introductory pleasantries. Back in his seat, the colonel turned all business and dropped any pretense of cordiality, glaring at Austin.

"Would you please tell us what the hell you were doing in the library between one and two in the morning?"

Dawn was momentarily taken aback by Axton's sudden coldness. *Your reputation is well deserved* she thought, still fuming at his sexist remark moments earlier. *Something more delicate indeed.* It seemed to her that, as he glared at her, a cruel curl of his thin lips, his prominent nose protruding from a cadaverous head, the colonel resembled a vulture.

Determined not to be intimidated by Axton, she answered with forced cheerfulness, "Looking for a book, Colonel. What else?"

"At that hour?"

"I couldn't sleep."

"I see." His eyes told Dawn that he didn't believe her.

She was quick to elaborate. "I needed a psychiatric reference book for my work. I had written to my mother and asked her to send it to me. But that will obviously take some time.

"Obviously."

The colonel's expression was a clear warning to tread lightly. It wasn't lost on Austin. He was obviously not a person to antagonize. But instead of badgering the Private for more answers, Axton suddenly turned his attention to Quinton Perlmutter.

"And you let Private Austin into the library after hours?" It was as much a question as an accusation.

"Yes, sir," Perlmutter lisped.

"And she was the only person you admitted that night?"

"Yes, sir."

The colonel frowned, then sneered at the ashen-faced night watchman. "I suppose we can therefore deduce that Private Austin's attacker entered the library illegally, perhaps through a window left open?"

"Oh no, sir. All the windows were closed and locked. I checked them myself before…"

"Before you dozed off?"

"Yes, sir." Perlmutter lowered his head, resigned to the fact that Axton would hold him responsible for this whole mess.

Dawn felt sorry for the old man. If not for her curiosity, Perlmutter would not face this inquisition now.

"Sir," she piped in, earning a reproachful glance from Axton and a silent *Thank you* from Perlmutter. "Mister Perlmutter was not asleep when I got there. I can vouch for that. He answered the door on the first knock and looked very alert." A lie, but a lie she'd swear to in court.

"Very well, if you say so. We'll find out soon enough how the perpetrator got in. And since you felt it necessary to interrupt, you might as well continue." He dripped arrogance and contempt. "Go on, Private, you have the floor. Please tell us everything that happened. Every detail please, up until the very moment you were bashed on the head and passed out." He pointed at a lump that had blossomed above Dawn's right eye.

She took a deep breath and replayed last night's incident. Convinced that Axton would pounce on her if she omitted even one detail, she was determined to be as truthful as possible. "As I said, I couldn't fall asleep. I was preoccupied with my assignment for the next day and wanted to look up a few references. Rather than fight my insomnia I decided to make better use of my time. I got dressed, walked to the Library, and asked Mr. Perlmutter to let me in."

"Were you not told of the 10:00 PM curfew?"

"I'm sorry, sir, but I forgot all about it. There have been so many things to remember. Everything has been like a whirlwind the last few weeks. I'm sure you understand. It won't happen again."

"Let me make one thing clear to you, Private. There is a reason for curfews. As you have witnessed firsthand life in Resurrection can have its pitfalls. We therefore go to great length to ensure peaceful coexistence between employees and inmates. In return, we expect our staff to act in a professional and responsible manner, and that includes obeying curfews. If you don't demonstrate these qualities in the future, perhaps you don't belong here."

"I thought with all the love and harmony in camp…"

She stopped in mid-sentence, but it was too late. Axton seethed with anger. "Love feeds harmony, Austin. And callous disregard for rules feeds anarchy. If you think for one moment that I'm concerned about the bump on your head, you overestimate my concern for your well-being. And if you think for one moment that I'll allow anarchy to reign, you're dead wrong. Do I make myself clear?"

"Yes, sir. Crystal clear."

"All right. Please go on, you were telling me about a reference book you needed for your work."

"Yes, that's right. Like I said, I was so wired that I couldn't fall asleep. Rather than fighting my insomnia I got out of bed, dressed, and went straight to the library. I think you'll understand that I forgot all about the curfew. Mr. Perlmutter opened the door and told me that the library was closed for the night. I'm afraid I talked him into letting me come inside. I told him I'd only be a few minutes, that I knew exactly what I was looking for, and he was kind enough…"

Axton interrupted her sharply. "Private Austin, please spare us your attempts at making Mr. Perlmutter an innocent martyr. It may be well intentioned on your part, but it's ill advised. I don't care what you told him. He is not supposed to let anyone in after hours. Anyone. And that includes me. But he's had a good record so far and I won't crucify him because of one incident caused by a careless recruit. Now, if you don't mind, let's get back to the events. What exactly was it that you were looking for?"

Smarting from his stinging rebuke, Dawn lowered her eyes and said "I told you before, sir. A psychiatry book."

"I know that." He sounded irritated. "What's the title?"

"Oh, I'm sorry. I see what you meant. It's called *Love and Hate. The Thin Human Line*."

"Thank you. Perlmutter, please see if we have that book. Private, please go on."

"Before Mr. Perlmutter let me in he checked my credentials and asked to sign the register. Then he told me what aisle psychiatric reference works were in and went back to his duties. I proceeded through a hall and into the reading room, beyond which Mister Perlmutter told me the actual library was situated.

"I was surprised to see a light at the end of the corridor but thought nothing of it at the time. I guess I assumed that someone else couldn't sleep and used the time to study, so I just walked in. I remember that I was very quiet. I tip-toed. It's a habit I developed living with my mother. She's an early riser and goes to bed early. I never wanted to wake her up at night when I got home late and always tip-toed around the house."

Dawn took a deep breath and fell silent, puzzled by Axton's changed appearance. He seemed to have dozed off in the middle of her statement. His eyes were closed. His head bobbed up and down as if he were fighting off sleep. In fact he was deep in thought, blocking out everything around him other than the private's voice. He listened carefully for telltale signs of lying. Her voice sure sounded like she was, but maybe she was just scared. And every so often she stopped in mid-sentence. But was she afraid of contradicting herself or merely nervous? And what about that annoying habit of hers, blinking and twitching? Axton was almost convinced that she was lying through her teeth. Almost, but not quite. With anyone else he would have made up his mind by now. But with Austin it was hard to tell. She looked and acted as if she was afraid of her own shadow. So, he asked himself, was she really that insecure or was it all an act?

He hated to admit it, but he really didn't know. All right, he told himself, there's more than one way to skin a cat. And he knew he had found it. Just act like a male chauvinist, belittle her, be obnoxious and condescending. That would get her pissed off. It obviously had before, during the Dom Perignon episode, when his unintentionally sexist remarks had gotten a rise out of her. Good. Very good, Axton congratulated himself. Get under her skin, get her so pissed that she'll react with emotion rather than intellect. And there'd be plenty of opportunities to remind Austin that, compared to him, she was "just a woman."

Something else puzzled him. Why was she making such a big deal about tip-toeing into the reading room? It sure sounded fishy how she'd gone out of her way to tell him about tip-toeing around her mother and all that. Who cared if she tip-toed or not? Obviously she did, which told Axton that she wanted him to be absolutely aware of the fact. Interesting. Why? Was she covering for someone? If so, whom? A lot of unanswered questions.

Axton roused himself from his self-imposed trance. It was time to get some answers. "Let me see if I got that right, Austin. You said you walked into the reading room. I think the term you used was tip-toeing, isn't that right. "Then what? Are you going to keep us in suspense or tell us what happened next?"

"Sorry, sir. When I walked into the reading room, I saw that one of the table lamps to the left of the door was lit. The light was dim because someone had draped something over the shade. I think it was a sweater or shirt, because the man sitting at the table was naked from the waist up. At that moment I realized that something was wrong. But before it sank in and I could run away or scream for help, the man turned. When he saw me he hit me right here." She pointed to her bruise and winced. "And that's it. That's all I remember until I came to and saw Mister Perlmutter bent over me."

"Would you please describe this man?"

"There really isn't much I can tell you about him. I told you it was dim in the room. But I do know that it was a man. He looked to be in his thirties. And he had blonde hair. Other than that…" Dawn shrugged her shoulders and gave the colonel an apologetic look.

"That's quite all right, Private. All we have to do now is find a man in his thirties with blonde hair who was not in his bunk between one and two in the morning and who had access to the Library." Axton allowed himself a rare smile. "That shouldn't be too difficult. The more interesting question however, is why. Why would he be in the library? What was he trying to find out? Do you have any idea, Private Austin?"

"No, of course not. How would I know?"

"I thought that perhaps you saw what he was reading when you surprised him."

"Sorry, but it all happened so fast. All I can tell you is that there was a stack of books on the table. And I think they were leather bound."

The colonel shook his head with admonition. "Details, Private. Details. Didn't I ask you to mention every detail? Now, is there anything else you didn't mention?"

"I'm sorry, sir. I forgot about the books. I was frightened and everything happened so quickly."

Axton nodded and turned his attention back to Perlmutter. "Did you see any books in the reading room?"

"No, sir. I rushed in as soon as I heard a noise. I saw Miss Austin on the floor and naturally I assumed she had tripped and fallen. I rushed to her side. When I saw she was unconscious I ran back to the copier room at once. The room has a sink in it, you know, and I got a washcloth and ran cold water over it. But by the time I got back to the reading room Miss Austin had already come to again. She was still a bit dazed. But she told me she had been attacked. That's when I called the guards."

"And you didn't see any books?"

"No, sir. But I'm afraid I was too concerned about Miss Austin to pay much attention to anything else."

Axton's expression was one of disgust. "You didn't search the library for her attacker? You merely stood at her side until the guards arrived?"

"Yes, sir."

"Didn't you think that Private Austin's assailant might still be in the building?"

"No, sir."

"Or perhaps you were afraid to look for him?"

"No, sir, that wasn't it at all. I just didn't think of it."

"Or maybe you didn't have to look for him because you knew all along who he was?"

Perlmutter turned as pale as a ghost. "Absolutely not, sir," he protested. "Are you implying that I had something to do with…"

Axton cut him off. "Nothing of the kind, Perlmutter. I'm only offering a number of logical explanations for your failure to do what anyone else would have done. Perhaps you can enlighten me further. The way I see it, you were either stupid, scared, or an accomplice. Which was it?"

"Stupid I guess."

Axton took a sip of Cognac and mulled over what he just heard. He was convinced that Perlmutter was telling the truth. The old fool was too scared and dumb to cover up for anyone. Austin, on the other hand, was quite another story. She was intelligent and, despite her little-girl looks, spunky and determined. Axton was also convinced that he wasn't going to learn any more from Austin at this time. It was probably best to get rid of her now, let her wonder for a while. She might even trip herself up. He waived his hand towards the door in a clear sign of dismissal.

"You may leave, Private. If there is anything else you remember, please let us know immediately. In the meantime, take the rest of the day off. Relax and take care of that bump of yours."

Feeling more like perpetrator than victim, Dawn was relieved to get out of Axton's office. She gave him a brief nod and a frosty "Thank you, Colonel" and waited for him to buzz her out.

As the door closed behind Austin, Axton turned his attention back to Perlmutter, seething at the night watchman's careless behavior. "As far as you're concerned, if you fall asleep on the job one more time you'll be assigned to clean toilets in Shandaken. Do you understand?"

"Yes, sir."

"And if you ever admit anyone after hours again, you'll wish you could clean toilets in Shandaken."

"Yes, sir." Perlmutter fumbled for his glasses. Without them, Axton was merely a blurred outline against the paneled wall. "May I leave, sir?"

"You may. And as soon as you get back I want you to check if any books are missing or misfiled. Let me know by tomorrow morning. I don't care if it takes you all night. Go through every shelf, every title. Do you understand?"

Perlmutter bowed his head and mumbled, "Yes, sir" for the third time. Despite the prospect of a sleepless night spent rummaging through more than ten thousand volumes, he was thankful to have escaped the Colonel's wrath with nothing more than a warning. The threat of being reassigned to the maximum security facility in Shandaken was all the motivation he needed to work around the clock.

*****

With Perlmutter's departure Brauner squirmed uncomfortably. He knew he was next, and with no one else in the Office things could turn ugly. But Axton seemed in a jovial mood now that everyone else has left. He even repeated his offer of a Cognac, which the doctor again refused reluctantly.

Axton drained the rest of his Dom Perignon and sloshed the liquid in his mouth. Eyes closed, he inhaled the cognac's bouquet and joined Brauner on the settee, taking the seat just vacated by the hapless Perlmutter.

"You know, Bruno, we go back a long way. We've been through a lot together, haven't we?"

Brauner nodded, wondering where the colonel was headed.

"As a matter of fact, you're like the older brother I never had. When you think about it, the similarities in our backgrounds are amazing. Neither of us ever married. We grew up in the same neighborhood. You used to live up in Yorkville, didn't you? Eighty-fourth and Lex, am I right?"

"Yes, and you were on ninety-first."

Axton agreed. "Yes, Ninety-First and Third. I remember there was a deli on the corner that had the best potato salad in the world. I used to go there to pick up a bite to eat every Tuesday night after school, always on Tuesdays and always a Liverwurst on Rye with a slice of raw onion. And I'd get a side of their potato salad and a six-pack of Becks and take it up to the apartment. Talk about ambrosia. But you know, that was the only good thing about living on the Upper East Side. The apartment was a dump. I don't think there was anything in the place that worked right. I know the air-conditioner never did and that lazy super they had, Lazar I think his name was, he never fixed a damn thing. As matter of fact, the only time you ever saw that Jew was at Christmas time sticking his hand out for a present. Imagine that, a Jew of all people, looking for a Christmas present."

Brauner nodded his head in complete agreement. It was a reflexive action. He seldom heard the colonel reminisce about his early years in Manhattan, but when dealing with Axton it was always better to agree. Still, he was pressed for time and checked his watch. Axton noticed the furtive glance.

"Relax, Bruno. I won't keep you much longer. But I'm telling you all this for a reason, so bear with me, will you. I think it's important to remember one's roots, one's heritage, don't you? So there we were, two young men growing up within a mile of each other and going to the same school. We probably even passed each other in the street a couple times, went to the same movies houses, shopped in the same stores. But it took this prison to bring us together. And look at us now. From a tenement to a prison. That sounds ironic, doesn't it, except that we're on the right side of justice. You know, sometimes I ask myself why I keep doing this. I mean, there are so many other things I could be doing. You too, Bruno. You're an educated man, a brilliant doctor. You could write your own ticket on the outside, have a thriving practice, rake in the money, live in an expensive condo and spend your free time playing golf. Tell me, did you ever think of leaving?"

Brauner nodded slowly. Tendrils of apprehension worked their way down his spine. Whatever it was Axton had in mind, it smelled like trouble. "Sure I thought of it," he said. "But that's as far as it went. I never seriously considered packing it in."

"Me neither," Axton smiled. "See, that's what I mean. We really are like brothers. We think alike. We're of the old school. Honor and values mean more to us than material possessions. I guess it goes back to the way we were raised. You don't realize it when you're young, but the older you get the more you see of your father in yourself. Not that I look like my father. I'm talking about something much more important. I'm talking about what we're made of, of character and personality, of the values instilled in us that are passed from generation to generation. You know, at the time I didn't appreciate my father, but I realize now what an influence he was on me. Him and some of my teachers at the academy. Remember Sticklemayer, the ethics professor? I think you had him too. God, I was so young then, so idealistic."

Axton poured a refill. "Tell me something Bruno. You were just as full of ideals too, weren't you? Do you still feel the fire? Do you still believe in the cause?"

"Of course I do. Like you, I also remember the old days. That's probably why both of us are still here."

Axton raised his snifter. "To the cause."

"To the cause," Brauner agreed.

"Unfortunately we're in the minority nowadays," Axton continued gravely. "Do you think Amadeus is still as committed as we are? I don't think so. Looks to me like he's slipping fast, the way he keeps confusing the past with the present. If you ask me, I think he's got Alzheimer's. I hate to say it, but a man in his condition can be a real hindrance to our mission. And that Stokowski. Arrogant sonofabitch, isn't he? Always strutting around like a peacock, acting like he's in charge. If he represents the future then I'll keep the old days anytime. The good old days, Bruno, when we were young and had fire in our bellies and dreams in our hearts."

It was the longest Axton had ever talked with Brauner. Completely out of character, Brauner thought, who was used to the colonel's terse orders and sarcastic one-liners. The longer Axton reminisced, the more apprehensive Brauner grew. Axton didn't indulge in sentimental remembrances unless he had a specific reason. Brauner expected the other shoe to drop any time now. But Axton seemed lost in the journey back to his youth, looking teary-eyed, speaking so softly that Brauner had to lean closer to hear him. As he did, Axton put his arm around Brauner's shoulder and softly slapped his back several times, the way people do at funerals to show their sympathy. The moment Brauner thought of the scary analogy, the other shoe dropped.

"I hate to say this, Bruno, but I'm worried about you too. You seem to have lost your focus. I'm not so sure your commitment is as unwavering as it should be. What's wrong, Bruno? Is there anything you want to tell me?"

"Of course not. There's absolutely nothing wrong. Why do you ask?"

"Well, don't get me wrong, but this whole mess, with Austin I mean, it's not like you."

So that was it, Brauner thought. It was all about Austin. He had the uncomfortable feeling that Axton was about to blame him for everything that had happened. "What do you mean it's not like me? What isn't like me?"

Axton squeezed Brauner's shoulder in response. "To be honest, I don't know what to think. I just think she's wrong for the job. I tried to tell you but you wouldn't listen."

"That's a lie," Brauner interrupted sharply.

"Bruno, please. You know, we talked about the good old days, we just toasted the cause, and now this. You're the one who hired her. You're the one who selected her for Koertner. And now you're denying any involvement."

"There's nothing to deny."

"Answer one question, Bruno. David Koertner is your choice, isn't he?"

"You know that, so why ask?"

"And you'd do anything to guarantee his promotion, wouldn't you."

"That's not true," Brauner objected again, knowing full well that Axton was closer to the truth than he was willing to admit.

"I think it is." The colonel's voice had suddenly turned to ice. He's like a chameleon, Brauner thought. Best friend one second, back-stabber the next. Axton continued despite Brauner's sputtering attempt to interrupt him. "I think you'd do anything in the world to protect your precious Disciple, including compromising your life-long ideals."

Brauner jumped to his feet, trembling with anger. "I don't have to stand here and listen to this. As a matter of fact, if your security guards had done their job none of this would have happened."

"Sit, Bruno. Sit and listen to what I have to say, and you'd better listen good because I'm only going to say it once. I think you hand-picked this Austin woman because you thought she was the easiest to manipulate. I'll bet as soon as you saw her you fingered her for a soft touch. A young, inexperienced, bleeding-heart psychiatrist who'd work her ass off to help poor David. How am I doing so far, Bruno? But you miscalculated, didn't you? David turned out to be a lot more receptive than you ever thought. I suppose that's good for him, but it sure as hell is bad news for you."

"If you're suggesting…"

"Tell me, Bruno. What do you know about Austin?"

"Not very much, Xavier. She is a new recruit. I just met her about a month ago. From what I've seen so far she's doing a good job. I know she is intelligent and compassionate."

"Too compassionate?"

"What do you mean?"

"The bitch lied. This washed-up excuse for a night-watchman was fast asleep. We have the whole thing on surveillance tapes. The question is, do you think she lied about anything else?"

Brauner shook his head. "I don't think so. Why should she?"

"That's up to you to find out, Doctor. She works for you. Watch her. And get me her folder. I want to know everything about her. Her background, her school transcript, her resume, her medical records. Her psychiatric profile. I want to know why she joined. I want to know whom she voted for, what she did in her free time, her love life, everything. If she's got an itch I want to know about it before she scratches."

"It'll be on your desk in the morning." Brauner, despite fears of opening a can of worms, was compelled to ask for a favor. "And when you do find her assailant, might I interrogate him?"

"Absolutely not."

"But Xavier. With all due respect, I think we can learn where we went wrong. Why he committed an act of violence."

Axton scoffed. "When we find him we'll let him go on as though nothing had happened. Do you really think I care who hit Private Austin on the head? She'll survive. But her attacker is more important to us than you can imagine. We need to find him, and when we do we'll keep him under surveillance around the clock. You see, Brauner, our assailant's inquisitive mind is far more dangerous than his random act of violence. The one thing we cannot and will not tolerate is a Disciple asking too many questions or reading the wrong books. I don't think I need to remind you of the consequences, do I?"

Chapter 12

PAULETTE KOWALSKI'S DAY was off to a bad start. The forty-two-year-old prison guard's bedside alarm clock went off at seven sharp, turning her migraine into a sledgehammer. For a moment she didn't know where she was, staring through bloodshot eyes at crumpled sheets and waiting for her room to come into focus. Her mouth was dry, her throat the consistency of sandpaper. Faint rumbling in her bowels warned her of an oncoming diarrhea attack.

She climbed out of bed slowly, lifting her right leg over the side, pushed herself up on one elbow, then slid her left leg over the edge until both feet were planted on the linoleum floor. By now she started to recall disjointed fragments of last night. She remembered an empty Scotch bottle. Puffing a Havana she had pilfered from Axton's personal supply. Vivid recollections of an arm draped across her breasts. That part of the memory was good, so good in fact that she relived it through closed eyes until she was able to associate a face with the arm. Mmmm, Justin Frederikson.

The rest of the night hadn't been as good though. She thought she'd woken up in the middle of the night, running into the bathroom and throwing up every ounce of Scotch. Everything else was a blank. The biggest blank was not remembering if she'd taken her birth control pill. Determined to fill in the blanks, she padded into the bathroom on bare feet and splashed handfuls of ice-cold water on her face. Coming to grips with last night wasn't that easy though. Wide awake now, her hair and face dripping, she was pretty sure that Frederikson's yummy memories weren't just wishful thinking. Apparently also real were getting drunk, getting laid, getting sick, and everything else she couldn't remember yet.

The most distasteful proof was her toilet, where vomit had dried along the porcelain rim. She scrubbed the bowl and washed her hands. Getting rid of the sewer taste in her mouth was more difficult. She ran cold water into a Dixie cup and splashed in a capful of mouthwash but spat the diluted mixture into the sink a moment later. This morning called for more drastic measures. Three mouthfuls taken straight from the bottle, followed by vigorous brushing that left her gingivitis-inflamed gums bleeding, she was antiseptically clean. It also seemed to improve her memory. She thought she confessed her infidelities to her late husband Hymie, whose photograph hung above her dresser. But she usually didn't talk to Hymie's picture unless she was tipsy, and last night by the time she had anything to confess about she'd been well beyond tipsy. All of which reinforced Paulette's suspicion that some form of damage control was called for.

She hurried back to the bedroom to check her pill supply. She turned her pocketbook upside down and dumped the contents on the dresser top. A small plastic case landed on top of the assorted junk she carried with her religiously. She unsnapped the lid and counted the pills that lay encased in the monthly-dosage supply wheel. Sixteen. "Whom the fuck am I kidding?" she told Hymie, who was watching reproachfully from inside his eight by twelve walnut frame. "I don't have a clue how many of these I'm supposed to have. I haven't had to use a pill in months."

Hymie didn't say a word and Paulette felt compelled to confess. "That's not really true, Hymie. I've had a couple of flings. Of course it hasn't been the same like it was with you but, well, you know what it's like living in this fucking place. It can get pretty lonely for a woman and you said yourself that if anything ever happened to you I should get married again. Well, I never did, but you know me. I have needs, so every once in a while I, you know…"

To her surprise, Paulette blushed. Her cheeks turned red talking to a photograph of her long-gone husband, the man she'd coaxed with street-walker talk whenever he'd been too tired to make love. "Anyway, last night was one of those nights. I had a tough day so I went to the Apostle's lounge after work for a couple of drinks. Well,

I never liked drinking by myself and I got real lonely and started feeling sorry for myself.

Then on the way home I stopped by the library and ran into an inmate who works there. Well, we got to talking and we kinda hit it off. So I invited him to stop by my place for a while that night and the rest is history. Actually I think you would have liked him. He's the kind of person who's easy to talk to, always ready to listen without interrupting. And that's what I needed, a shoulder to cry on. So I asked him to come up to my place. To make a long story short, we had a couple of drinks and one thing led to another and before you know it I was in the sack with him. I guess I was completely drunk by then because I gave this kid a pretty good lesson but I'm afraid I'm the one who's going to flunk out. You see, I don't know if I took my pill. All I know is I got sixteen of 'em left and I have no idea if I should have fifteen instead. I guess when you sleep with a guy only once or twice a year you get kinda sloppy with these things."

Thoroughly disgusted with herself, but feeling better for having confessed, she gathered her belongings and dropped them back in her pocketbook. And discovered that her key ring was missing.

"Shit."

A bit more frantic now, she turned her attention to a trail of clothes that were strewn on the floor. Among the fluff of fabric she found her Resurrection-issue skirt and blouse, black silk panties, her black lace bra which she hasn't worn since Hymie passed away, socks and sneakers, and a man's T-shirt. She poked through the clothes with her toes, then picked up each garment and shook it before dumping it into the hamper. No keys.

But Paulette was a pragmatist. The keys would turn up sooner or later. And if not she'd just confess to losing them, get reprimanded, at worst lose an accrued vacation day. The pill however was far more serious. Getting pregnant was probably the worst thing that could happen to a middle-aged woman who had never liked babies, especially if the father turned out to be an inmate. She'd be out on her ass before she could pack her personal belongings. And she could fit all of those in one suitcase. A dishonorable discharge with no benefits was the best she could hope for. Worst case she could be indicted and spend five years in jail.

What she needed was a black coffee to kick-start her brain. She usually picked up a cup at the commissary on the way to work but that wouldn't do this morning. She'd be late but *So what?* she thought, it wouldn't be the first time. Weighing her alternatives was far more important than punching in on time.

Sill wearing only her robe and slippers, Paulette added an extra spoonful of Columbian into her brew master and watched the black liquid drip into the carafe as if it were her own life trickling away. "Shit, I'm acting like a teenager who got laid in the backseat of a car. I don't even know if I'm pregnant, so why worry about something that may never happen."

She carried her cup to the dinette table, getting more worked up with each scalding sip. Not knowing if she was pregnant was bad. Now she'd have to wait for her period to come and she had no idea when that was supposed to happen. Just like she hadn't counted her pills, she hadn't found it necessary to pay attention to her time of the month. Sloppy, but not having sex had that effect.

"Shit," she said for the third time this morning. Hymie would have an answer, but how could she ask him about her dilemma? Telling him about sleeping with Frederikson was one thing, but this? "You're on your own," she told herself. So you better get your brain in gear and figure out what to do, just in case."

Figuring out her 'just in case' options wasn't that difficult. There weren't that many to think about. The most obvious was an abortion. It was also illegal, which made them expensive and risky. There were no doctors in Camp who would perform them. Jutta Firestein, her friend and patrol partner, had nearly died after drinking a labor inducing milky liquid she had bought from a quack in Shandaken for a thousand dollars. The sight of Jutta thrashing in agony on a sweat-soaked bed, vomiting, and finally forced to check into a clinic was still fresh in her mind.

Of course she could always find someone who'd admit that the kid was his. But the standard payoff was five-grand and all she had to her name were five-hundred in the bank and the clothes on her back. Scratch that.

Paulette stared at her empty cup and resigned herself to the fact that she had only one choice. Find some dumb schmuck inmate, seduce him, and then scream rape. They'd put the guy away but what the hell, these guys were in Camp for life anyhow so what's the difference? Then she could have her abortion, maybe even get some cash from the Victim's Aid Fund, and get herself reassigned to a cushy desk job. Of course there'd be one important detail to take care of. From past experience she knew that a good number of prisoners were so drugged-up and brainwashed that they couldn't get a hard-on no matter what. Frederikson of course didn't have that problem but she'd rather hold on to him for herself. "That's okay," she smiled, happy that she'd solved her potential problem, "I'll just have to test drive some other guys 'til I come up with a winner."

With only half an hour left before work she unwrapped her robe and took stock of herself in a full-length bedroom mirror. Viewed in the harsh reality of the morning after her image wasn't pleasant. At the age of forty-two, a hard life had left her looking old beyond her years. Her prematurely gray hair needed another touch-up. Onetime crows-feet had grown deep-etched. Forty pounds had played havoc with her once pleasing shape, leaving her breasts sagging, her stomach flabby, and her thighs looking like tree stumps.

She turned from the mirror in disgust. The woman who had won Hymie Kowalski's heart was long gone. Today's Paulette was a pathetic has-been who was content to have an occasional roll in the sack with the likes of Justin Frederikson, who, despite his youthful good looks and energy, was on the bottom rung of the social ladder. Paulette, who'd resigned herself to the fact that she'd always be poor white trash, certainly wasn't a snob, but still, a prisoner was a prisoner was a prisoner. And possibly a father to be.

Seeing her flabby self in the mirror had a twofold effect on Kowalski. On the one hand she was disgusted with herself. On the other hand she was more convinced than ever that last night had been a good thing after all. The way she was going, she'd only have a couple of years before she wouldn't be able to seduce anyone, even a horny prisoner. With that thought she threw on her uniform, put on her bravest face, took the stairs from her second floor apartment two steps at a time, and was about to climb aboard her Jeep when she realized that her car keys were missing as well.

*****

"Can I catch a ride?" Lounging in the passenger seat, his arms folded across his chest and wearing a sheepish grin, was the one person she'd like to forget all about this dismal morning, Justin Frederikson. Viewed through the sobering lens of a hangover he was the antithesis of the young man she had taken to bed last night. At ten to nine, despite bright sunshine playing off his blonde hair, creating sensuous shadows and highlights on his square-jawed rugged face, and despite his blue eyes which always reminded her of Frank Sinatra, she preferred the Justin of last night. Cloaked in darkness and softened by a haze of Scotch, her probing fingers weaving through his hair and tracing the outline of his face, fluttering across his lips and chin, teasing blond tufts of hair on his chest, cradling his penis in her hand, Frederikson had been her very own selfish creation. In the soft confines of her bed he had become her fantasy lover. This morning there was nothing magical about him. He was no better than countless other inmates.

She shook her head. *You poor bastard*, she was tempted to say. *You think you're some kind of Adonis because you fucked an overweight forty-two-year-old.* Refusing his help she climbed aboard. She held out her right hand, palm up, and said as matter-of-fact as she could, "Got the keys?"

*****

They rumbled along potholed streets, each preoccupied with their own troubles. She caught him staring at her every time she turned her head, and each time she did he avoided her eyes and shrank into himself. At the corner of Fair Street, less than a block from work, he got up enough courage to talk.

"Paulette? I need a favor."

"Oh?" A favor was the last thing she had expected. "What is it?"

"I need you to lie for me. If someone asks you, tell them I spent the whole night with you. You don't have to say anything about us, you know… Tell them we talked, or that I got drunk and fell asleep on the couch. But I never left your place."

"No."

He looked hurt. "Why not?"

"No." The light changed and she accelerated the jeep sharply.

"But why not? What's the big deal?"

She pulled up in front of 132 Fair Street and backed into a spot.

"Look, I have to go now and you better do the same before somebody sees us and puts two and two together. And don't bother coming to my place anymore."

"But why? What's going on, Paulette?" He looked confused. "Didn't you like it?"

"Yes Justin, I liked it. But there's more to my life than one night-stands with you."

"I guess there's no use in asking you for another favor then?"

She couldn't believe her ears. He was really pushing it. "What now?"

"I need the keys to Brauner's office."

"Forget it. You're out of your fucking mind." She slammed the car door behind her and hurried into Violence Control Headquarters. She was already ten minutes late.

Chapter 13

TROUBLE WAS SOMETHING I'd learned to smell from a mile away ever since I'd met Private Austin. So it came as no surprise that I smelled it the moment I got back from dinner at the Stockade Deli and found Justin sitting on his bunk, legs folded beneath him, arms dangling at his side, wearing nothing but sweatpants and a far-away look in his eyes. Wednesdays was bowling night, something he never missed.

Something else I'd learned was that whenever I had a sinking feeling in my stomach I was probably justified in expecting the worst. Seeing Justin sitting on his bunk like a statue, my nerves didn't merely sink, they plummeted.

Thanks to Private Austin my day hadn't been anything to write home about either. After rushing to Terwilliger House for my 8:00 AM appointment with her she'd been a no-show. No message. No explanation. Nothing. Rachel Firestein had been more tightlipped than usual, shrugging her shoulders and giving me a curt *How I should I know? Who do you think I am, your private secretary?* when I'd asked her about Austin. Then, about two hours later, Brauner had rushed in and made a beeline for his inner office. His response had been equally curt. *Not now, David, I'm busy.*

So when I walked into room 310 tonight I was in no mood to have any more problems dumped on me. I didn't say hello. As a matter of fact, I didn't say anything until I heard Justin stir. When he did, I glanced up and, seeing that he was about to start talking, I cut him off before he could open his mouth. "I don't want to hear about it."

"But all I…"

CAMP RESURRECTION

"Whatever it is, I don't want to hear about it."

*****

Tension in room 310 was rare. Sure, we had our share of arguments. On rare occasions they were of the knock-down, drag-out variety. Other times we bickered over stupid things, but afterwards we always shook hands and all was forgiven. The tension that hung in the air tonight was unusual. I didn't know how to handle it. Following my angry outburst a few moments earlier Justin had mumbled something under his breath. I occupied myself doing paperwork for Brauner that didn't need doing. By nine-thirty the mandatory power shutdown took care of my paperwork. The lights flickered off and on twice for the five-minute warning. I threw my papers on the desk and shuffled off to the bathroom.

When I returned a few minutes later Justin still hadn't moved. Pale moonlight cast a silver hue through the window. I couldn't help but think that I had walked into a surreal stage setting populated by inanimate objects and framed by elongated shadows. It also struck me that I wasn't a participant in the setting but a spectator. I waited for something to happen, for someone to enter the stage and breathe life into the play, for a plot to develop. The play, I was convinced, had to be a tragedy. Both the setting and the cast, an inert outline of a man backlit by the moon, had a chilling effect. The only character who could have come onstage and transformed the play into something other than a tragedy was I. And I couldn't. Hypnotized by the mysticism of the moment, I remained a spectator, seeing but not understanding Justin's role. I was also saddened. I had a premonition that I had become an outsider.

It must have been about an hour later when all hell broke loose. I was halfway between drowsiness and sleep, aware of intrusive sounds but not quite hearing them, sensing danger but not knowing if I had been dreaming. I sat up with a start. A thickening cloud cover had made it impossible to see beyond a few feet. From the hallway I heard footsteps but that wasn't unusual since Disciples regularly passed room 310 on their way to the bathroom. Something about the footsteps was all wrong though and it took me a second to figure out what it was. When I did, they had stopped outside the door. A blinding light exploded. The footsteps were inside room 310, the sound of steel-tips unmistakable.

I bolted upright, blinking and shielding my eyes against the beam of a high-intensity flashlight. A second light clicked on, this one brighter, bathing the interior in stark whiteness. Simultaneously a cacophony of sounds broke the quiet: several voices talking at once, a two-way radio spitting a succession of code words, intermittent beeps, rough idling of a patrol car at the curb. Someone shouted a string of obscenities in the hall. Doors opened and slammed shut.

"Get your ass outta bed. C'mon kid, move it, move it."

What happened next was incomprehensible. The entire incident took less than a few minutes but within that time span individual events stood out with freeze-frame clarity.

Sitting on the edge of my bed and trying to lace up my sneakers I was pulled to my feet. "Don't bother with them. You ain't goin' very far."

Not very far turned out to be the first-floor activity room, where I and Greenkill's nineteen other Disciples were ordered to line up single-file in room number order. One by one our names were called and we shuffled towards a card table behind which a Guardian was seated. It took less then ten minutes before it was my turn.

"Koertner, David."

I approached him, dazed and vulnerable. "What's this all about?"

"No questions please."

The Guardian sounded neither threatening nor pleasant. His pen hovered above my name on a residency list before him. He placed a checkmark next to my name, dated his entry, and gave me a cursory once-over, comparing me to a one-by-two inch black and white photograph.

"Is that it? Can I go?"

"Not so fast, Koertner. I just want to ask you a couple of questions."

A moment of silence followed. I didn't know if it was intentional, but it had the effect of making me nervous. I fidgeted, swallowed, and sweated, feeling like a criminal even though I had nothing to worry about.

"No need to be nervous, Koertner."

"Yes, sir, I'm not."

"Tell me, you're a room monitor, aren't you?"

"Yes, sir."

"You're the one who found Ezekiel, isn't that right?"

Again that sinking feeling bottomed out in my stomach. I nodded.

"Have you told anyone about that incident?"

"No, sir, I haven't"

"No one?" he asked. A doubtful expression crept over his face.

"Only Private Austin. That was okay, wasn't it? I mean, she's my counselor and…"

"Oh sure," he said. "That's okay. Oh, by the way, off the record, what's she like?"

"What do you mean."

"You know what I mean," accompanied by a conspiratorial wink and a lewd smile. "Pretty good looking, I hear. Is that right?"

"I guess."

"C'mon Koertner, you can do better than that. I told you, this is off the record."

"Yeah, I guess she's nice looking. Why do you ask, sir?"

"No special reason. It's just that from what I hear Ezekiel kind of liked her too and now the poor bastard's dead. That's all. But you're okay with her, huh?"

"Yes, sir. I think she's a good counselor."

"Better than Doc Brauner?"

"No, sir, I didn't say that. Just different."

"Yeah, I'd say she is. She's got tits. Okay, Koertner, thanks. You can go now."

I turned and was halfway to my place in line when he called me back. "Just one more thing, Koertner."

"Yes?"

"When was the last time you saw Austin?"

"Yesterday. I met her in Doc Brauner's office."

"You sure of that?"

Even though I was positive I hesitated long enough for the Guardian to notice. "Yes, sir. I am positive," I said louder than I intended.

The Guardian gave me a brief curious look, then said, "Okay. Thanks, Koertner."

*****

One thing was obvious; room 310 had been searched and they hadn't bothered to hide it. Every drawer stood open. The closet was a mess, wire hangers pushed to one side, jackets and shirts piled on the floor, shoes turned upside down. The hamper lay on its side. Of most concern however was the desk. My paperwork had been carelessly scattered. My notebook, in which I'd recorded all psychiatric sessions since the beginning of the year, had been flung to the floor. I opened it and found several pages missing. The last entry was dated August 23. The only remainders of my session with Private Austin were a few shreds of torn paper that remained wedged in the spiral wire.

Knowing that strangers had been in my room and gone through my private possessions left me feeling violated. It didn't matter that I had nothing to hide. It didn't matter that I firmly believed in Resurrection's spirit of sharing. I never considered my things to be my personal belongings. Everything I owned belonged to all of us. All they had to do was ask and I would have shared. Until this moment. Searching my room had changed everything. Now I thought of things as *Mine,* not *Ours.* And I was angry. Why did they do this? Why did they have to burst into *my* room in the middle of the night and go through *my* possessions and steal *my* things? Why?

"I'll tell you why," Justin said after picking up his meager belongings and stacking them next to his bunk. "It's because of Austin."

"What the hell are you talking about?"

"Austin, that's what I'm talking about. She's been nothing but trouble ever since she got here. Sticking her nose into things, asking too many questions, acting like she's our best friend. The last thing this place needs is another goody two-shoes fucking with our heads.

What we need are some answers, like what happened to Brannigan and Ezekiel, but nobody is talking about them. They don't give a shit about them because they're only Disciples. But I bet there's going to a lot of talk about Austin because she's one of them."

Justin's outburst didn't help matters. In fact, it made me angrier and nervous. Knowing him as well as I did, I suspected that he was right. He usually was. All you had to do was dig beneath his words and you'd come up with a kernel of truth. The kernel of truth this time had to be Austin. That would explain a lot of things, like all the questions about her and the fact that the only pages they'd torn from my notebook were about her.

"I get the feeling there's a lot more to your story," I said, trying not to sound sarcastic. "What's going on?"

"It's a long story."

"I've got nothing better to do," I said. "I doubt if I can fall asleep again anyhow."

"But you have to swear not to say a word to anyone, you hear. No one, especially not Austin."

Thud. Once again my insides hit rock bottom. "All right. I promise."

"I slugged your Guardian angel two nights ago."

"What?"

"Yeah, I know it was a stupid thing to do but it happened. I was in the library. You see, I broke into the place because I had to find out a couple of things and all of a sudden she was there and there was nothing I could do. I don't know who was more scared, her or me, but when I saw her standing there I just jumped up and hit her as hard as I could. Knocked her out cold. Christ, I thought I'd killed her, but I didn't bother to hang around. But then Paulette told me Austin was at Axton's this morning with Brauner and Perlmutter and now they're looking for me. Shit, when they find out what I was doing there in the first place they'll put me away for good. And the whole damn thing started with Paulette and those damn pills and…"

"Whoa, slow down," I interrupted him. "Maybe you better start from the beginning. Who the hell is Paulette. And what pills are you talking about?"

"Paulette Kowalski. It's her fault just as much as Austin."

I didn't understand. "You mean Kowalski the Guardian?"

"Yeah, her."

"What the hell are you doing with her?"

"That's what I was trying to tell you. You see, she's really a very nice woman. Her old man died a couple of years ago and I guess it finally got to her, being all alone I mean. About a month ago, I ran into her at work. She was looking for a book and Mrs. Biedermaier was busy with something, so she asked me to help Paulette. We started talking and one thing led to another. I guess she liked me because she asked me to come over to her place after work that night. We listened to the radio and talked for hours. And we must have polished off a bottle of Scotch. Around one in the morning she suddenly started kissing me. Then she took off her dress and asked me to kiss her breasts. I really don't want to go into every detail but let's just say that the night didn't turn out the way she wanted. After a while Paulette got this disgusted look in her eyes and told me *They made a fucking eunuch out of you, didn't they? Bastards. I'll fix them. I got something for you.* Next thing I know she went for a bottle in her medicine cabinet and gave it to me. *Stop taking whatever pills they're giving you*, she said, *and take one of these a day instead. But you have to swear you won't tell anyone about it. No one, you hear? Then come back in a month and we'll try again. I promise you won't regret it. You're in for the biggest thrill of your life.* Let me tell you Davey. She was righter than right. About that and a lot of other things."

Justin eyes glazed over when he recalled nights with Paulette. "It was almost good enough to make all of this worthwhile. Almost."

I interrupted him before he could get another word out. "I may be dense but if you're saying what I think you're saying…"

"That's exactly what I'm saying," he nodded. "You know me, right? You know I'm always game to try something new. I stopped taking Brauner's pills the next morning. Haven't taken one of them since."

"Are you out of your mind? Do you realize what you're doing?"

"Yeah," he said.

"That's why you've been acting so strange the last couple of weeks, isn't it?" Now it all makes sense."

"What makes sense?"

"All these crazy things you've been talking about. About Josh and Brauner and…"

Justin put his hand over my mouth. "Listen to me, David. There's nothing crazy except for what's going on in this place. Let me tell you, a couple of funny things happened when I stopped taking Brauner's pills. Little by little I noticed things I never noticed before. And the more I saw the more questions I had. I started asking Paulette but she played dumb. All she wanted was to get me in bed with her. Not that I minded but she didn't want to talk to me about anything anymore. Not like that first night when she told me about her husband. Now every time I ask her a question she says *Shhh. Just sit back and enjoy*, and she gives me a kiss and puts her hand here." Justin's hand found its way to my crotch. "Just like this."

I brushed his hand away and Justin blushed. "Sorry, David. I didn't mean to make you feel uncomfortable. I was just trying to show you what happened. Anyhow, being with Paulette was great." He looked sheepish. "Still is. But she won't talk to me about anything anymore. It's driving me nuts. And that's why I wound up slugging that counselor of yours."

"Because Kowalski didn't want to talk to you anymore?"

"Yeah. You see, the longer I was off the pills the more I wanted to know. Paulette wasn't any help, so I figured the only way I could get some answers was to break into the library. And that's when your Private Austin showed up in the middle of the night and saw me sitting there. I didn't hear her or see her until it was too late. I felt someone behind me at the last moment. I jumped up and turned around, and there she was, scared as hell. She started to scream. At least I think she was gonna scream. That's when I let her have it. I hit her as hard as I could. Knocked the shit out of her. She went down hard, banged her head on the floor and passed out."

"Did she recognize you?"

"I don't think so. Everything happened so fast. And she's never seen me before. The only reason I knew it was her was because after what happened with Ezekiel she was kind of a celebrity. You know, everyone started talking about her, about what happened and what kind of strange person she is, like she doesn't fit in here. But I doubt if she got a good look at me. And Perlmutter sure as hell didn't. The old bastard was sleeping as usual."

I panicked. This was my worst nightmare come true. Dammit! I should have talked to Brauner about Justin. Now it was too late, just like Austin had said.

As if he had read my mind, Justin's voice took on new urgency. "Remember, you promised not to tell anyone. If they ever find out they'll kill me."

"Oh come on, Justin," I objected. "People don't get killed here, not for sneaking into a library and not even for attacking a counselor. The only thing they'll do is make you go to Retooling to make you better again."

"No!" he shouted. "You don't understand. Breaking into the library was bad enough. Hitting Austin was worse. That alone can get me time in *The House.* But when they start asking questions, like *What were you doing there in the first place, Justin?* and *What kind of books did you want to see that you couldn't ask Mrs. Biedermaier for?* and *Just what did you read that was so interesting?* Then I'm done for. They'll put me away for good."

"Just exactly what were you looking for?"

"Does Auschwitz mean anything to you?"

I shook my head.

"What about Gulag?"

"No. Never heard of them before. Who are they?"

"It's not who they are but what they are. They're places. Places where society dumped people they thought were different and dangerous."

I was beginning to make the connection. Private Austin's revelations that I had successfully managed to block from my mind suddenly flooded my brain. I panicked again. Private Austin's story was scary enough. But now that Justin was headed into that forbidden territory it turned into ice-cold terror. My mind swirled. I had been sworn to secrecy by Austin. And now this. Christ. I wasn't used to lying. I was a bad liar. How could I keep it from Justin? I had to. But what if I couldn't?

Justin stared at me. "David, what's wrong? Are you all right?"

I swallowed with no spit in my mouth.

"David, you look like you're gonna throw up. What the hell is wrong?"

"Nothing," I managed to stammer and dry-swallowed again. I clenched my fists. "Just a sudden blast of heart burn, I guess. I'll be right back." I rushed out of the room, ran for the bathroom and splashed cold water on my face. I gritted my teeth. *You can do this. You have to do this. For your sake and Justin's.* I took a deep breath. Another. At last I regained some composure. The trembling ceased. My legs steadied enough to walk back and face Justin.

He was still sitting were I had left him. I took another deep breath and forced myself to say, "Sorry. Where were we?"

"You sure you're all right?"

"Yeah," I nodded.

"Okay. If you say so." Justin didn't seem convinced but picked up the conversation nevertheless. "Like I said, these places, Gulag and Auschwitz, they were just like Resurrection. They were places were society dumped people they thought were different and therefore dangerous. You see, there've been places like this for hundreds of years."

In my desperation I tried to make light of the situation. "Okay. So what does that make us? The sons of Resurrection?"

"Don't be a smart ass. You have no idea what you're talking about."

"And you do, I suppose?"

"Not yet but I'm getting there. Justin's eyes burned with frightening intensity. "I just scratched the surface, but what I found out is scarier than hell. For starters,…"

I didn't want to listen to him. Part of my denial was self-preservation. If what Private Austin had told me was all a lie I could hold on to my deep-rooted conviction that everything I'd been taught, everything I cherished, indeed that my entire life was still intact, that there really as no *Outside. No Thems.* And then there was the terror.

Terror of the unknown, terror of the truth, terror of the pain that came with the truth. And fear for Justin and what would happen to him.

His words drifted through fog. I didn't hear what he said, but I knew it was the truth. He finished an hour later with "Look Davey, I don't expect you to believe me. I don't even expect you to help me. All I want you to do is to keep your mouth shut and have an open mind. If you do, you'll see what the hell is going on."

Chapter 14

Dearest D. I just got your letter yesterday. I think the US Postal service is finally living up to the term "snail mail." It took more than a week for your letter to travel a lousy hundred thirty miles from Upstate New York to Manhattan.

I'm happy to hear that everything is okay with you. Sorry about your simple living quarters, but maybe now you'll appreciate your room at home. I hate to say I told you so, but I told you so. As far as my lack of bitching about your sexual encounter, sorry again, but I have no idea what you're talking about. It must have been a figment of your imagination. If it wasn't, I hope is was as good for you as I'm sure it was for the lucky guy. Just be careful though, dear. You know I'm not a snob, but a Barnard girl can do better than one of those "prison persons."

By the way, I looked for the book you asked me to send but couldn't find it. I tore your room apart last night and it's definitely not there. I went to three bookstores this morning but none of them carried it. I ordered a copy but it'll take two weeks before they get it in so I asked them to ship it straight to you. I did run across another book at Barnes & Noble that might interest you and had it shipped to you. You should get in a couple of days. It's called 'Sex in Prison—Our Deviant Secret.' Your mysterious reference to your sexual encounter prompted me to pick it up and read the dust jacket. I'm not sure how good a textbook it is, but it makes for salacious reading. I can vouch for it myself.

Everything is fine at home. We all miss you. You know how empty my life is without you. There's nobody to argue with about politics and religion, nobody to watch an old movie with, and nobody to bitch at. Of course there's always Max, but he's been kind of mopey lately. I'm sure he misses you as much as I do. Yesterday he didn't touch his food at all. I *bought him a new bone, one of those giant-sized ones, but he only chewed on it for a couple of minutes and then sat by the front door for the rest of the day.*

Aunt Bea and Uncle Art were by last week and send their love. They're renting a place in Florida for the winter and asked me to stay with them awhile. I told them no, but might take them up on their offer. You know how dreary New York can be in the winter.

I ran into Chaz in Gristede's this morning. You remember him, don't you? I think he still has a crush on you. I know he's not the best looking young man, but he's sincere and very smart. He told me to send you his love. I gave him your address, so expect to hear from him.

I'm dying to speak to you or see you. Not having a phone is a real bummer. I thought even prisoners are allowed supervised calls every so often. I asked about coming up to visit you but was told that due to the "delicate psychological balance of the camp's societal structure" (their exact words), visits are not permitted. This place is locked up tighter than Alcatraz ever was. I suppose letters will have to do until I can think of a better way. I promise to write often, at least once a week. You do the same, okay? In the meantime, take care of yourself, try to be happy, learn as much as you can, and never forget that you have a room waiting for you here. Love, Mom and Max. Kisses and barks.

Dawn suppressed a sudden urge to cry. She folded the letter in half and tucked it inside her notebook. She wouldn't have thought so two months ago, but she missed her mother more than she ever missed anyone. And Max. And she missed her room. And her freedom. And the city. Even Chaz.

Chapter 15

Austin's folder lay unopened on Axton's desk. He eyed it with disdain. The very notion that he, Xavier Axton, chief of Violence Control, had to be distracted by something as trivial as a common Private stumbling head-first into a botched break-in, was annoying to say the least. Under normal circumstances he would hand the case to Lieutenant Berger and be done with it. Unfortunately, the assault on Private Austin appeared to be anything but normal. Axton had a nose for such things, and this case stunk worse than the Resurrection City garbage dump on a hot August day.

He clipped a Garcia y Vega and lit up. As usual, Axton's office was sealed off from the rest of Violence Control Center. The foyer doors were bolted from the inside. The curtains were drawn, with only a hint of sunlight weaving its way through the brocade. In the near darkness his cigar glimmered like an angry eye.

Axton hunched into his oversized leather chair. If not for raspy breathing and an occasional puff of smoke directed at Dawn Austin's folder, the office looked unoccupied. But precisely at the stroke of noon, announced by the Westminster chimes of a hundred-year-old grandfather clock, Axton roused himself into action and called Rachel Firestein.

"Get me Brauner. Page him if you have to." He paused momentarily, then added "Tell him it's about...never mind, just tell him it's important."

He hung up and waited for Brauner's arrival, using the time to plot strategy, likening himself to a chess master moving pieces across the board. In his imaginary game Austin was the black king, her assailant the white queen. Axton's private cadre of security guards made up the rest of the black pieces. The strategy was simple. Attack relentlessly and flush out the white queen. When she surfaced, Axton would pounce.

A timid knock interrupted his game. Brauner, looking disheveled and out-of-breath, was ushered into the room. Axton's summons had obviously caught him at a bad moment. The doctor tugged at his vest, straightened his tie, and wiped his head with a monogrammed handkerchief. He didn't look nervous however, just rushed yet confidant. After talking a seat on the settee he swung one leg over the other, forced a cordial smile, and pointed at the Cognac decanter. "Mind if I help myself, Xavier?"

Axton nodded. The game had begun.

"Hmmm, good stuff," Brauner remarked and raised the glass in Axton's direction.

The colonel didn't answer. He drew in another mouthful of his Havana, held the smoke in his mouth, then curled his lips into an 'O' and sent a smoky ring into Brauner's face. "Dawn Austin," he said at last, pointing at the folder. "Tell me about her."

"It's all in there. Isn't that her folder?"

Axton rolled his eyes with exasperation. "I know it's in there, Bruno, but I want to hear it in your own words. You hired her. She's your protegee, so I think it's appropriate to hear your side of the story."

"I don't think it's my side versus anyone else's side," Brauner objected. "Yes, I hired her and if that makes me her advocate, well that's fine with me. So far she hasn't done anything wrong except get assaulted."

"So you don't think wandering off by herself after curfew is wrong?"

"Sure it's wrong, Xavier, but nothing we all haven't done in the past. Why throw the book at her because of one minor infraction?"

"And lying, that isn't wrong either?"

"If you mean Perlmutter, she's only trying to help him because she feels responsible."

Axton smirked. "She's a regular Mother Theresa, isn't she, always looking out for the downtrodden. Tell me, is David one of the downtrodden too? Or whoever attacked her, do you think she feels responsible for him too?"

"I think you're making something out of nothing, Xavier. You're forgetting she's new here. She's probably scared out of her mind. You intimidating her sure as hell doesn't help. Cut the woman some slack, will you."

Axton's smirk grew into a scowl. "I'm afraid your irresponsible defense of her only proves that that are two sides and which side you're on."

"Look Xavier, I got a message saying this was important and now you're rehashing the same old accusations. I really don't have the time right now, so unless you have something new to add I'll finish my cognac and get back to my patients."

Touché, Axton thought, and a good opening move. Brauner obviously wasn't intimidated, so a different tactic was called for. "Sorry, Bruno. I didn't mean to get on your case but I wish you wouldn't be that touchy. It's just that this whole affair has come at the worst possible time and I'm getting a little antsy. You know as well as I do what'll happen if we miss our target. Anyhow, that's not why I called you. I wanted to…, oh by the way, did you hear what happened last night at Greenkill?"

The surprise in Brauner's eyes was obvious. "No," he said warily. "What happened?"

"I had my men search the place."

"Why?"

"Isn't it obvious?" Axton asked. "I thought it would be as a good a place as any to start looking for Austin's assailant. If she's hiding something, perhaps she stashed it away in her place. And you never know what you find if you go through someone's personal possessions, a letter or note of some kind, perhaps even a library book. And let's not forget that her patient also lives in Greenkill. Besides, someone might have seen her leave. I mean, we have only her word that she went straight to the library. We know from the surveillance tape what time she got there, but wouldn't it be interesting if we found out that she left…oh, maybe an hour earlier. That would raise a number of questions, wouldn't it? Like did she go someplace else first or did she meet someone along the way?"

Axton could tell that he'd caught Brauner off guard. No longer as confidant, he shifted on the settee. "And did you find anything?"

"Well, sort of, although not what I had expected. Austin's room was clean as a whistle. All we found was a letter from her mother. But we did confiscate a few handwritten notes from her patient. Tell me Bruno, are you aware of everything that goes on during Austin's session with Koertner?"

"Of course I am," Brauner said with too much assurance.

"And you don't object to the rather stormy relationship that seems to have developed between them?"

By now Brauner's confidence was showing significant signs of cracking. "Sometimes a so-called stormy relationship is exactly what's needed to trigger a psychological breakthrough," he said.

"As long as it's a breakthrough and not a breakdown," Axton replied, allowing himself a sardonic smile. "But enough about last night's raid. Let's get back to Austin, tell me about her. You can skip everything that happened since she arrived here. I have Ritter's reports, I have her transcript, and I have your own evaluation. I want to know what she did before she came here. I want to know about Private Austin the woman. What she likes and dislikes. What turns her on. Why she is so, shall we say passionate, about her work here. And of course why she joined."

"I'm afraid you'll be disappointed. There's nothing special in her background."

"Why don't you tell me anyhow?"

"Well, let me see. She's twenty-eight years old, the only child of Cecilia and Thurston Austin. Her father is deceased and for the last twelve years she lived at home with her mother. From what I can tell she was always the perfect all-American girl. Straight as an arrow. Never got into trouble. Went to the right schools, got good grades. Graduated from Barnard College in Manhattan and just received her doctorate in psychiatry. She's well off financially from what I understand. Not wealthy, mind you, but rich enough not to have to worry about working."

"Don't you find that a little odd?" Axton wanted to know and stubbed out his Havana. 'She doesn't need this job and yet she's here, apparently willing to work her ass off."

When Brauner didn't answer, Axton went on, his voice low yet full of urgency. "It seems to me that Austin is diametrically opposed to our usual recruits. The vast majority of them come from disadvantaged backgrounds, blacks and others like them who need a job and the only place that'll take them is Resurrection. Austin on the other hand doesn't need a job, especially a low paying stint in a prison. She could make a lot more money counseling rich, paranoid Fifth Avenue millionaires. So why is she here? She sure as hell doesn't fit the profile of disadvantaged recruits taking care of disadvantaged prisoners."

"I don't know if I would put it quite in those terms," Brauner objected. "She's obviously passionate about her job. You said so yourself. She wants to help people."

"I don't care what terms you'd put it in, it's the truth. But let me finish. The other types of recruits we attract are the do-gooders, the bleeding heart liberals, the social masochists who want to flog themselves daily in front of the whole world to atone for the sins of their forefathers. From what you've told me, Austin doesn't fit into this category either. I did some checking of my own and found nothing. She never volunteered for anything. No causes seemed to interest her. The only organization she ever joined were the Girl Scouts. She never got involved with any radical groups and she's not on the FBI's watch list. I struck out with her medical history as well. No abortion, no substance abuse, nothing. The only thing I found was that she was in therapy for a couple of months after her father died. So you see Bruno, it seems that Austin is the typical average citizen who doesn't give a shit about anything."

Again Brauner remained silent.

"That leaves a tiny minority. Young men and women who have very specific personal reasons for being in this hell-hole."

"Xavier, I wouldn't call Resurrection…"

"Please don't interrupt me, Bruno. Let me do my job and you do yours. Find out why this woman is here. What's her personal reason for joining? You're a shrink, so by God look into her head and tell me what you see."

"If I may, why are you so interested in her? She hardly seems a big enough fish to concern you."

"Ahh, you're still not thinking, Bruno. I told you before, I don't give a damn about Austin. I'm even inclined to believe her story that she went to the library to look for a book. She may just be dedicated enough to spend the few precious hours she has to herself trying to get ready for an assignment. It's what happened from that moment on, from the precise moment she walked into the reading room, that I have a problem with. Like I said, it's not Austin I'm worried about, it's her misguided dedication. Which, I think, is a direct result of whatever it was that made her enlist."

"Well, to answer your question, I have no idea."

"Have you asked her?"

"No," Brauner admitted sheepishly.

"Then I suggest you do. Maybe she'll tell you the truth although it would be a first."

"That's all I keep hearing from you. You make her out to be a pathological liar. If that's how you feel, why don't you send me a request to have her discharged? I'm sure you can come up with a trumped-up charge and make it stick."

"The thought has crossed my mind, but I'm afraid it's too late for that. I think she's on to something. Besides, I don't think she's a pathological liar, I think she's a selective liar. Just look at the facts. She walks in on an unsuspecting intruder who has his back turned to her. Now, try to follow what I'm saying. She enters the room from a dark hallway. She sees a man sitting at one of the tables, next to a light, reading a book. She takes a few steps into the room. He notices her. He turns around and hits her. I know she wants us to believe that the whole thing happened quickly, but she made one big mistake. She told us how quiet she was, how she tip-toed into the room. I think she had more time that she led us to believe, certainly enough time to know that he was reading a leather-bound book. But not enough to describe him other than that he had blond hair and was in his thirties. All of which leads me to believe that she knows who her assailant is."

"Why don't you confront her with your allegations and ask her point blank," Brauner said, borrowing a page from Axton's book. "Maybe she'll surprise you."

"I might just do that," Axton said. "But I want to ask you a few questions first. Perhaps you'll confirm my hunch."

Brauner checked his watch. "My morning's shot anyhow so go ahead and ask anything you want. You're obviously leading up to something or you wouldn't have told me about your midnight raid on Greenkill."

"That's right, so let me run this by you. Austin's had quite a stormy first session with her *Disciple*." His emphasis made the word sound obscene. "She obviously got him so upset that he exhibited a rare emotional outburst. And this from a young man you yourself recommended for promotion to Apostle. I believe you praised him for his keen intelligence and inquisitive mind. Tell me, Bruno, who but an inquisitive person would break into a library? Who had a reason to believe she could identify him and therefore tried to silence her? Who had a reason to dislike Private Austin? And whom would Private Austin protect if not her own patient?"

Brauner looked stunned. "That's preposterous, Xavier. I refuse to believe that David is involved in this whatsoever."

"I said it was a hunch. I can't prove it yet, but I will. There'll be plenty of evidence. For one, our intruder was kind enough to leave his sweatshirt behind. We're running some tests on it now. We also found a number of fingerprints, but that's going to take some time to analyze. Obviously a lot of people were in and out of the place, including employees. But who knows, maybe we'll get lucky. If all else fails we can help jog Austin's memory. It's amazing how much a person's memory improves when they're interrogated properly. Sooner or later I'll find him. And when I do, your recommendation to promote Koertner may be a bit tarnished, shall we say. As could your own reputation, Bruno."

Brauner jumped to his feet. "Are you implying…?"

"I'm not implying anything, Bruno. I'm merely pointing out suppositions which may become facts. I think David Koertner fits the psychiatric profile of our intruder. And Private Austin has a damn good reason to protect him. And so do you."

Chapter 16

"Sill mad at me?"

The way she asked, looking apprehensive and very fragile, I didn't think anyone could be mad at Private Austin right now. A large contusion above her right eye was beginning to turn angry purple. Broken blood vessels extruded from its center and formed a spiderweb beneath her pale skin. If possible, she had lost more weight. Her uniform hung loosely off her body, hiding her muscular long-distance runner legs which were anchored by white tube socks and scuffed sneakers. She tried to hide behind a brave smile, but anyone could see right through it. Austin was a sorry sight and a nervous mess. So when she greeted me at Brauner's office with that little girl voice I immediately felt sorry for her.

"What happened?" I asked with genuine pity, but scared of what she would say.

"I ran into someone who didn't share your love for all things big and small."

"Do you know who did it?" I held my breath, praying she wouldn't give Justin away.

She lowered her head and bit her lip. "No. He didn't introduce himself."

"I'm sorry. Things like this usually don't happen here, especially not in the library."

"David?" She touched my cheek. Her fingers trembled, tears clouded her eyes. "David. Will you do me a really big favor?"

I brushed her hand away instinctively. The touch of her fingers was unnerving, making me feel guilty, making me hate Justin. All I wanted was to run away from Brauner's office and this pathetic waif of a woman who seemed determined to win my trust. I managed a brusque "What?"

She reached out to me like a drowning woman grasping for help. Her fingers clutched my shirt. "David, please tell me who did this to me."

I yanked at her wrists and pushed her away. "I don't know what you're talking about, Private Austin. I have no idea who hit you."

"How did you know it happened in the library?"

Caught. My mind raced a mile a minute but I couldn't think of anything to say other than a lame, "Yeah, so what? Everybody knows about it."

"Who's everybody?"

"You know, everybody. Look, I'm sorry you got hurt, but I don't know who did it."

"You're a bad liar, David."

"I'm not a liar at all."

"Okay, David, have it your way." She lowered her head and started to cry. I watched helplessly, trying not to hear her soft whimpers, trying not to see her tremble. "Please don't cry."

"I just thought you were different," she said between sobs. "I'm sorry that I put you on the spot. I know that whoever did this to me was really frightened and that's why he hit me. I don't think I've ever seen him before, and I probably couldn't pick him out of a lineup if I saw him again. Everything happened so fast. But I'll never forget the look in his eyes."

She turned her back to me. Small tremors wracked her body as she fought off tears. "You see, David, anyone who breaks into a library does so for only one reason, and that is to learn something. No one should be afraid of knowledge, but that's exactly the case here. The man who attacked me obviously thought that he'd get into terrible trouble if he got caught. Why, David? Why wouldn't he just go there and ask for whatever books he wanted to read?"

I shrugged my shoulders but didn't answer her, "Aren't you allowed to take out any book you want to?"

"Well, sure," I said and sounded unconvincing even to myself.

"Then I don't understand. Why would this man… You are telling me truth, aren't you David?"

Try as I might, I couldn't bring myself to lie to her. "Sort of, Private Austin. We're allowed any book as long as it's on an approved list."

A small hiss escaped her lips. "I see. And what kind of books aren't on the approved list?"

"I really don't know," I squirmed in my chair. "Every time I wanted a book I got it with no problem. Except once."

"And what book was that? Do you remember it?"

"Yeah. I was doing some research for an article I was writing for the Sentinel and wanted to know more about the history of Resurrection. That's when I found out it was called Catskill State Park at one time."

"That's right," she agreed and leaned forward as though trying to pull the words out of my mouth. "And then what happened?"

"I found a couple of books in the register. One was about the Catskill Mountains. The other one was about the origins of Resurrection. But Mrs. Biedermaier wouldn't let me have them. She said they weren't on the approved list."

"Did she tell you why?"

"No." I closed my eyes, remembering the incident as though it had happened yesterday. "She just said that if I wanted the books I'd have to get approval from Dr. Brauner."

Private Austin leaned even closer, sitting on the edge of her seat, trembling with excitement, as though she was on the verge of a major breakthrough.

"And? Did you?"

"Yes."

"Well, come on David. Tell me what happened."

I knew what I was about to say would only add fuel to the fire. "David? Go on," she urged.

"Dr. Brauner said that he couldn't release the books to me."

"Why?" She sounded as though she had expected the answer all along. "Did he tell you why?"

"He said that the books would only provide one tiny piece of information and when taken out of context, they would present a distorted picture of Resurrection."

"I see. And you didn't question him on this?"

"At the time... Well, no. Not really."

"Weren't you upset?"

I knew that she was hounding me again, just waiting for me to say something she could use to her own advantage. "I don't see what all of this has to do with you and me. I mean, you're supposed to be here to help me. Dredging up the past doesn't do anyone any good." It was the closest I'd come to refusing her.

"Please bear with me, David. Just a little while longer. It's important."

"You're acting like this is an inquisition," I objected. "Like you're blaming me for what happened to you."

She shook her head. "Of course I don't. I think you know that. I just want to know if you were upset when they wouldn't let you have those books."

"All right, I was. Are you happy now?"

"Upset enough to sneak into the library yourself and..."

"Now wait a minute. You're twisting this whole thing around."

She smiled quickly. "No I'm not. I'm just trying to show you that it's perfectly normal for you to want to know more about Resurrection. Not being allowed to know doesn't make any sense. And I think that's why the young man who attacked me did what he did. I think he may have found out things he wasn't supposed to know. And that's why he was frightened."

Private Austin didn't know how close to the truth she had come. She leaned back in her chair. "I just thought I could help him. God knows he needs help."

Rather than reassure me her compassion upset me. It validated Justin's theory that life in Resurrection was a lie and that we needed help, and not the kind of help Brauner's Retooling provided. She'd made me look at myself like Justin would have and it was scary vision. I quickly assumed the safety of denial, which in turn made me angry.

"Why would you want to help someone who attacked you? As a matter of fact, why do you want to help any one of us? What makes you so different from all the others?"

"I have my reasons."

"And that's all you can say?" I mimicked her, suddenly enraged by her kindness. "I have my reasons. I have my reasons. I have…"

Her hand came up with blazing speed. She slapped me, stinging my pride harder than my face. I was dumbfounded. This was another situation I didn't know how to handle. Damn her and her promise of friendship. Damn her for making me want to believe in her. Damn her. Damn her. Damn her. She was turning my world upside down.

"I'm sorry, I shouldn't have done that," she apologized at once.

"It's okay."

"No, it's not. Sit down David. I have to tell you something. And then maybe you'll believe me."

Whatever hopes I had of getting out of my session with Private Austin soon went up in smoke. She rolled Brauner's chair to my side, burying herself in it like a wounded animal. Her fingers wound around the armrests until her knuckles turned white. She took a deep breath and was about to start but hesitated, trying to find the right words. With her eyes closed she took another deep breath. Finally she did speak, and the words come haltingly, as though each caused her great pain.

"When I was sixteen years old my father took me camping in the Adirondack Mountains. That's about a hundred miles north of here. He had a cabin there. It was just the two of us. My mother stayed home because she had to teach a summer class at Barnard College. I remember those two weeks as being the happiest time of my life. I finally had my father all to myself. You see, he was always busy with work and I hardly ever saw him. This was my chance to be with him and bond with him. Without anyone else cutting in on our time. Without anyone, including my mother.

"The cabin was tiny, just one room and a bathroom, but it was the coziest place in the world. It had a large stone fireplace that we used for heat. You see, even though it was September, we were high up in the mountains and it got cold at night. We built a fire in the evenings and talked and talked until the fire died down and the last embers stopped spitting flames up the chimney. In the mornings I got up early and cooked breakfast for him. I never cooked anything at home. I hated cooking. But up there in the mountains, when the sun rose above the treetops and a raw early-morning chill made me shiver, cooking was fun. I loved it. I think that subconsciously I loved father's dependence on me. For the first time in my life I felt like I was needed. Instead of just being a pampered teenager who had no responsibilities I was doing something important. I took care of someone and it was the greatest feeling in the world. You know, all my life my father had been the breadwinner, working hard and making the decisions in our house. In that cabin I suddenly became his equal. I was his daughter and his wife and his partner. Making breakfast was the natural thing to do. So I made bacon and eggs and toast and the strongest coffee in the world.

"Our two weeks flew by and we drove home on September 17. I'll never forget the day as long as I live. We were both singing silly songs and talking father and daughter stuff. You know, everyone thinks that fathers and sons have a special relationship that daughters can't share. That's bull, David. We talked father and daughter stuff and I really got to know him. I think I knew him better than mother did.

"We stopped in Albany for dinner. By the time we left the restaurant it was already after eight and I remember begging him to stay overnight. That way I could have him to myself for one more night, but he had to get back to work the next morning. About half an hour later we ran into a heavy thunderstorm. It was really scary. The wipers couldn't keep up with the rain. The AC was blasting to keep the windshield defogged. But nothing bothered us. We were still talking and singing those silly songs.

"We had just passed exit 21 on the Thruway when something went terribly wrong. My father suddenly slammed on the brakes. Something, or someone, was in the road. I caught a blurred outline running across the highway. Our car went into a skid and turned over. I remember that the whole world was suddenly upside down. My head banged against the roof of the car and the windshield shattered into a million pieces. I screamed and screamed until my throat was raw with pain. My face was cut and I was bleeding badly, but I didn't know it at the time. The car just kept rolling and rolling and each time it did I was thrown against something else. Against the door. Against the roof. Against my father. The last thing I remember is staring at my father's face. I knew that he was dead.

"I don't know for how long I passed out but it couldn't have been more than a few minutes. The next thing I knew was that someone dragged me from the car. A man pulled me by my arms and got me out just before the car blew up. The next few minutes I drifted in and out of consciousness. All the time this man stayed with me. He had no idea how to help me. He just sat next to me in a ditch and waited for a miracle. And a miracle did happen that night. Someone must have seen the explosion and called an ambulance. All that time the man kept talking to me. Somehow he knew that if he kept talking I wouldn't die. So he just kept on talking and every time I started to close my eyes he shook me and talked a bit louder. I don't remember a lot of what he'd said, but I do remember a few things. I remember it because what he said scared me and I wanted him to go away. He said that he was an escapee from Camp Resurrection and that they'd kill him if they caught him. Then, when flashing lights lit up the black sky, he squeezed my hand and ran off. I never saw him again. I never got a chance to say thank you."

She opened her eyes and looked at me. "Now you know one of the reasons why I'm here."

"One? There is more?"

She nodded.

A gradual reversal had taken place. Suddenly I was the counselor in whom she confided. Me, David Koertner, thirty-five-year-old Disciple trying to help Austin, an intelligent, educated woman. I slipped into my role easily, actually believing that I could help her. "Do you want to talk about it? I can be a good listener."

"I'm sorry, I can't." She avoided my eyes and shook her head.

"Okay." I really hadn't expected her to say anything else.

"It's not that I don't want to. It's just…" She leaned across the armrest. Her lips touched my ear. "Come to my room at ten tonight. And don't breathe a word of this to anyone. Ten o'clock. My room."

Chapter 17

BRAUNER KNEW THERE was no time to waste. After leaving Axton's office he was in a rush to get back to Terwilliger House, cutting through alleyways, crossing Albany Avenue in mid-block despite a steady line of supply trucks, barely acknowledging hellos of passers-by. By the time he reached his office he was out of breath and perspiring freely. He ignored Rachel Firestein and a small cluster of Disciples lounging along the far wall, crossed the room and double-bolted the door to his inner office. Next he flicked off all lights except his desk lamp, then turned on the radio. To his chagrin, WREN was broadcasting an Oldie recital, the kind of mind-numbing hard-rock music that hurt his ears and deadened his brain. He gritted his teeth and lowered the volume, then hurried to the bookcase behind his desk. Impatient now that he was finally alone, he swept aside volume after volume of medical journals, oversized psychiatry books, and the collected works of Friedrich Nietzsche. Behind the empty shelf space was a two-foot square wooden panel, slightly lighter in color than the surrounding wood, and secured by a combination lock. He turned the dial, a hair to the right, three degrees left, two full revolutions right again, until he heard a faint click above WREN's horrid music. The secret panel swung open, revealing a television monitor and a disc player, one of only two in Terwilliger House.

Mounting excitement swept over Brauner. Chills rippled along his spine. Gray tufts of his tonsure stood up and quivered with anticipation. He was about to begin his journey into Austin's mind.

The disc slid into the player. Th nineteen inch monitor flickered to life. Paranoid as he was, Brauner stopped the disc to check the office one more time. Door locked. Window locked. Shade drawn. Radio volume turned high enough to drown out the video's audio. Lights out. He was ready.

He indulged in a rare mid-afternoon treat and splashed three fingers of Wild Turkey into a water glass. Then he pressed *Play* and settled into his chair.

The picture was sharp, the colors crisp. If he didn't know any better he could swear that Dawn Austin was standing before his eyes. Brauner leaned forward, hypnotized by the image. He paused the recording and zoomed in on her face. Magnified ten times, her scar was prominently displayed against pale skin, running in a concave line from the inside corner of her right eye to her mouth. Without quite understanding his feelings, Brauner was mesmerized by the scar, studying the tiny craters along its edge, unable to take his eyes off the path of puckered skin, saddened to see it blend into her upper lip.

He shook off the scar's sensuous hold and panned out until the entire room came into focus. Against the background cacophony of WREN, the video's sound was merely a whisper and Brauner turned up the volume one notch.

Dawn Austin and David Koertner. Two unsuspecting actors in Brauner's real-life drama performing against the familiar backdrop of his examination room. He watched their performance in a voyeur-like trance, hypnotized by their psychological interactions.

She was good, very good. The subtle changes in her body language were apparently not lost on David, who exhibited rare signs of emotion. The expression in his eyes was one of confusion, and Brauner felt a sudden chill. God only knows what she was about to unleash in her ingenuous patient. Maybe Axton was right, maybe a sudden transformation from innocent child into full-grown man was more than David could handle. One thing was obvious. Although David was making every effort to control his feelings, Brauner could see emotions bubbling beneath the surface.

Simultaneously Brauner tried to analyze his own reactions to Dawn Austin. To his surprise he found himself affected in much the same manner as David. Brauner snorted. Impossible. Yet he kept his eyes glued on the image of his twenty-eight-year-old assistant, trying to find what it was that fed his fascination. On the surface, she was one of the most ordinary looking women he had ever met. But Brauner knew that men often respond in a variety of ways to woman regardless of their physical appearance. Austin's appeal was much more enigmatic. Brauner searched for an answer among a variety of subtle clues. Her eyes, which conveyed a curious blend of childlike innocence and infinite sadness, the kind of sadness that comes from having experienced tragedy. Her voice, which was both fragile and determined. Her body language, which revealed an intense inner struggle. Struggle for what though? Brauner wondered. Affection for her patient while trying to maintain clinical detachment? Mother versus child? Brauner was willing to stake his professional reputation on one thing though: Austin had awakened a deep-seated instinct in David to protect Austin. Except that in this case David might very well be the one who needed protection.

Brauner's revelation wasn't much of a revelation though. He'd known all along that Axton's innuendoes had been way off base. Sex had nothing to do with it, at least not on David's part. Not yet. But preparing him for the future meant tinkering with a lot of emotions, and the transition would have to be carefully monitored. Brauner knew that he couldn't do it without Austin. What he didn't know was how large a dose of Austin he could feed David before he could potentially self-destruct.

He turned his attention back to the video. So far nothing of importance had happened. There hadn't been a single clue why Austin had enlisted in Camp Resurrection, or why she felt such sympathy for David Koertner. In the long run, did it really matter why she was here? Brauner didn't think so. Who cared if she was a bleeding-heart liberal or a guilt-ridden do-gooder? So what if she was a shy, sex-starved woman out to test her femininity or merely an ambitious professional who wanted to leave her mark on clinical psychiatry? He also dismissed the theory that Austin was nurturing a maternal instinct, transferring a mother's love to her patient. Austin didn't seem the motherly type.

Far more serious however was Axton's innuendo that David had been Austin's assailant. Of course Brauner didn't buy that for one minute but he considered the possibility, if only to defuse the charge. Could David prove that he wasn't at the library at the time of the attack? Perhaps, but most likely not. If he was innocent he would have been asleep along with all other Disciples, therefore no one would be able to vouch for his whereabouts. Was he the kind of person to break into a library? Yes and no. Although he was a model Disciple, the very quality that made him Brauner's choice was also his biggest detriment: intelligence. But could a gentle and peace-loving man turn suddenly violent? Until recently Brauner would have denied it categorically, but after the stormy session with Austin the other day Brauner wasn't so sure anymore. And what about Austin? Would she try to protect him? Absolutely, Brauner conceded. Whether misguided loyalty or professional ambition or, Brauner cringed at the thought, sex appeal, Austin had all the reasons in the world to protect her patient. And then Brauner asked himself the most difficult of all questions. If he were in Axton's shoes, would he suspect David? Brauner cringed again.

"This is getting me nowhere," Brauner said to himself and turned back to the video. He hit replay and started from the beginning. This time he ignored the psychological clues and concentrated on their conversation. It made for boring viewing for the first half hour and Brauner was tempted to stop the video. Then came her childhood story, her softly spoken account of a private tragedy. It at last explains her reasons for being here, Brauner thought. But he got only a small measure of satisfaction from his discovery. All he had to do is ask her. He's sure she would have told him.

But as he listened, Brauner gradually recognized that a far more important event was playing before his eyes than he could have imagined. More than anyone else in the past, indeed more than he himself had been able to, Private Austin was reaching David. He was responding to her. The tables had been turned. Private Austin became the one who needed help. David was the one to offer it.

His familiar voice was tinged with an unfamiliar compassion. "Do you want to talk about it? I can be a good listener."

"I'm sorry, I can't." She looked around the room and shook her head.

"Okay."

"It's not that I don't want to. It's just…"

She leaned across the armrest. Her lips touched David's ear. Brauner strained to hear what she was whispering but it was useless. He jumped out of his chair and zoomed in on her face. He replayed the scene in slow motion over and over and over. He zoomed in until her lips extended across the screen. Her teeth were frighteningly large. Glistening strands of saliva clung to her tongue. And as her lips moved, slowed to an infinite crawl, he read her whispered message.

"Ten…o'clock… My…room."

*****

The screen image faded. Brauner stared at *Classified Information–Property of New York State Department of Corrections* frozen in white letters against an olive green background. He clicked the TV off. Then he did what he should have done in the first place, asked Rachel Firestein to summon Austin to his office.

She was in his office five minutes later, looking apprehensive, even nervous, and avoided Brauner's eyes as she stood before his desk. He compared the real-life person to the video image he'd just seen but stopped himself moments later. Stop trying to read more into this than there really is, he thought and invited Austin to take a seat. She did. She appeared more relaxed now, folding her hands in her lap and waiting for Brauner to speak.

"I'll be brief," he began. "I just wanted to hear your side of the story now that we're alone. I can well imagine how unnerving this whole incident must have been, and then to be questioned by Axton must have made it even worse. To be honest, I don't understand him. I think his manners leave something to be desired." Brauner shook his head.

"I guess he's only trying to do his job," Austin said without conviction. "But I really don't know what else to say. I told him everything I know."

"I'm sure you did, but I'm less interested in the details than in your opinion. But before we go on I need your promise that what I'm going to tell you in this room stays between us."

Austin looked up with surprise. Her intuition told her to be careful. "Well, okay, as long as…"

"My dear, I wouldn't put you in a compromising position. It's just that if it got back to Axton he might get the wrong impression. You see, he's been unusually touchy about this whole affair. I think he's embarrassed that something like this happened right under his nose. Anyway, after you left his office he made some innuendoes. He feels that you haven't been completely truthful. He's convinced that you know who attacked you and that you're protecting him."

"That's ludicrous. Why would I do that?" Austin said.

"That's what I told him too but once the colonel gets an idea in his head, well, let's just say he can be very stubborn. Anyway, he thinks you're covering up for David."

"David? David Koertner?" Dawn was stunned.

Brauner nodded gravely. "That's exactly how I feel too. I even got into an argument with Axton. The man just won't listen to reason. The more I argued the more obstinate he became, telling me that you were directly to blame for what happened. You see, Axton's mind works in black and white. With him there's no gray area and he's convinced that what happened between you and David during your first session caused him to snoop around in the library. And he's also convinced that you recognized him but don't want to betray him."

Austin shook her head in frustration, feeling trapped. "I don't understand. Why would I do that?"

"Well, Axton thinks that there's professional pride involved. The way he put it, the better David looks the better you look. But I'm afraid there's something else."

"What?" Dawn asked with a sinking feeling.

"I'm sorry but there's no delicate way to put this," Brauner said, sounding embarrassed. "Axton thinks that you're sexually attracted to David."

"That's a damn lie," Austin shouted, trying to fight back anger.

"Now, now, don't get excited. Of course I don't believe it but you know as well as I do how hard it is to defend yourself against allegations. That's why we're having this talk. We have to figure out a way to prove to him that he's wrong." Brauner reached for a carafe, poured a cup of water, and handed it to Austin. "Here, have something to drink. It'll calm you down."

Austin waved Brauner's hand away. "The only thing that'll calm me down is an apology."

Ignoring her last remark, Brauner continued. "Tell me, do you have any idea why Axton would say something like that?"

Austin shook her head.

"Think back. Sometimes these things happen without anyone realizing it."

"There's nothing to realize." Austin was vehement. Following her initial shock she became angrier with every word. "Nothing happened. If you don't believe me why don't you check for yourself? I'm sure you've recorded every session I've had with David."

"Actually I already did," Brauner admitted. Now it was he who seemed annoyed. Avoiding her eyes he stared at his desk. His fingers knotted tightly, he furrowed his brow, then shook his head as though he had thought of something but rejected the idea. "No offense, Austin, but as soon as I got the chance I viewed the recording. I normally don't like doing that but in this case, well, I felt I didn't have any choice."

"Then you know there's absolutely nothing to the colonel's innuendoes," Austin said.

"Of course I know that. And I'd like to compliment you on your professional behavior. I've never seen a counselor get such quick results from her patient. I think the way you interacted with him, I mean the way you got the inner David to respond proves just how good you are. Considering that he was flooded with information overload he reacted better than most men would have."

"What's the problem then?" Dawn asked. "There's something in your voice that's, oh, I don't know, it's almost as if you're not so sure…"

"Well, to be honest, there were a few moments when I held my breath, particularly when you slapped him. And then when you told him your tragic childhood story… By the way, I'd like to offer my condolences. I had no idea what motivated you to enlist, but I think it's a noble reason. I wish there were more young men and women who shared your compassion, but anyway, my condolences once again."

"Thank you," Dawn said, trying to remember if she'd said anything to David that could come back to haunt her.

"Anyway, as I said, I was worried a few times that you'd pushed him too far. What really got me worried was the way David looked at you when you told him about your father's death. It was almost as if he felt your pain as acutely as you must have. The anguish in his eyes, the way he looked at you, the tremor in his voice, they all showed that he cares very deeply. And that's what I'm worried about. I'm not sure he's ready for that kind of relationship. So you see, even though I'm sure Axton is wrong with his allegations he may have stumbled upon something. But I'm afraid it's the other way around. I think David may be attracted to you. Mind you, I'm not saying it's sexual, but there's something there. Something that only exists between a man and a woman."

Dawn sat silently, trying to make sense out of Brauner's words. Intuition told her to be wary. His concern for her seemed out of character for a man who represented the higher echelons of Resurrection. These guys are all alike, she told herself, old cronies who ran a state prison as if it was their personal fiefdom. But she couldn't be one-hundred percent sure. What if there was a kernel of truth in what he'd said. What if…?

She took a deep breath and said in her calmest voice, "I think you're reading too much into it, Doctor. And I'm positive you overestimate my allure." She stopped and blushed, thinking how ironic it was that she'd downplay her effect on a man. "I think David just reacted the way any ingenuous person would have reacted under these circumstances. Let me assure you, a woman knows when a man is attracted to her, and there's nothing here. Nothing at all."

"I believe you," Brauner said, still with a twinge of doubt in his voice. "But I'm not the one who needs to be convinced, so I think it's better if you don't see David for a while."

"But…"

"Hear me out, please. I'll arrange the whole thing without dragging Axton's innuendos into it. I'm going to reassign you temporarily to our facility in Shandaken. I'll just tell him…"

"No!" Austin shouted, surprising herself with her vehemence. "The very fact that you're removing me from David lends credence to his allegations. It's an admission of guilt."

"Nonsense, Private. Besides, you've had a rough couple of days and I want you to rest up a bit." Brauner gave Dawn Austin a congenial smile, put his arm around her shoulder and led her to the door.

"But I can't just walk away from David now. I just…"

"Of course you can. David isn't going anywhere. He'll still be here when you get back. In the meantime, a week away will work wonders for you. Trust me. The fresh country air in Shandaken will invigorate your body as well as your mind. And you'll be doing me a great favor. One of our counselors there had to leave on a family emergency. As soon as she gets back you can return to Resurrection City. In the meantime, I'll take care of David personally."

He opened the door and steered her into the hall. She tried to stall him, hoping to come up with an excuse and buy herself at least an extra day. Dammit. She can't leave now, not when she's asked Koertner to meet her in her room tonight. Not when she's this close. She gave it another try.

"Of course I would be happy to help you, especially since you've been so kind to me, taking me into your confidence. But can't it wait until tomorrow morning? I'm really not feeling one-hundred percent today. I'm sure you understand."

Brauner's eyes flashed a quick warning. She ignored it. "My head…" She touched her bruise and pleaded apologetically. "You know, I probably do a have a mild concussion. I'm sure if I get a good night's sleep I'll feel much better. I can get an early start and still be there by ten or so."

"Now, now, I won't hear of it. I'll have a jeep at your place in an hour. You won't have to drive, I'll have someone take you there. Now I want you to go to your quarters, pack some things, and I'll see you in a week. You'll thank me, you'll see. A week in Shandaken will cure anything, even a concussion."

Defeated, Austin made her way through the outer office when Brauner called her back. "By the way," he said, "I meant to ask you, at the end of your session, right before the recording stopped, you kind of leaned against David and it almost looked as though you whispered something in his ear. Unfortunately I couldn't quite make it out because of the camera angle. Did you say something to him? Something I should know about now that I'll be subbing for you for a couple of days?"

Dawn's heart skipped a beat. Ice ran through her veins. "I just wanted to let him know that everything would turn out okay. I don't remember the exact words I used, but it wasn't anything important."

"I see. Well, okay then, off you go young lady. Pack your things. My driver will pick you up at, let's see, two o'clock."

*****

He closed the door and walked across the office with leaden legs. He suddenly felt tired, very tired. Despite months of careful planning and meticulous preparations his plan was in danger of collapsing like a house of cards. Ironically, he knew that he himself was partially at fault. If he hadn't selected Austin from a pool of recruits he probably wouldn't be in this pickle now. But she had seemed the perfect choice, exhibiting the blend of smarts and commitment that was needed to prepare David for his new position. How was he to know that she'd turn out just a little too smart and too committed? And how was he to know that David would react to Austin so… so? Brauner searched for the right words and was shocked when he found them. So much like a normal man. Yes, normal. Too normal.

He didn't want to admit it, but one other thing that galled him was that Axton had warned him about the very same possibility. *You better be careful of what you wish for,* Axton had started the argument which had suddenly become prophetic. Dismissing the colonel's warning (Axton would have said the same thing about any other candidate just to be contrary), Brauner had plowed ahead and defended Austin even though he knew next to nothing about her. And how did she repay him? She disobeyed curfew, got herself conked on the head, caused a full-scale investigation by Axton, and in the process dragged David into the whole mess. Damn the bitch.

Brauner walked to the window and lifted the shade. Standing in a muted puddle of light he peered at the street, straining his eyes to make sure Private Austin was on her way to Greenkill House.

Just when he wondered what was taking her so long he saw her. Half hidden by the Corinthian columns that flanked the front entrance to Terwilliger House, Dawn Austin buttoned her jacket and hurried down three steps to the flagstone walkway. Halfway to the street she stopped. She glanced over her shoulder and started to turn. For an instance he thought she was about to return and knock on his office door, trying one last time to change his mind. But then she resumed her pace and disappeared from view.

Brauner let out a deep breath. "Bitch," he said under his breath. "Bitch." If only he'd… He stopped his thought in mid-sentence, surprised by his lack of self-control. He usually managed to keep his anger bottled up, but Austin was sorely testing his equanimity. His brief outburst was therapeutic though, energizing him to concentrate on the task at hand, making the best out of a bad situation. Temporarily reassigning Austin to Shandaken was a brilliant move but only the first step. Dealing with Axton wouldn't be as easy. As a matter of fact, dealing with Axton meant turning the botched-up break-in to his own advantage, and for that he needed help from Austin. Brauner grimaced at the irony of it all. Austin had become both ally and obstacle.

Chapter 18

BED CHECK HAD passed more than an hour ago. Since then Justin Frederickson went over his plan step by step, weighing risks, thinking of and throwing out alternatives, and getting more worried by the minute. He knew that he was taking the biggest chance of his life. He also knew he was running out of time. He was going over the wall.

On the surface, life in Resurrection City had taken on a carnival-like atmosphere. Resurrection Day celebrations had started early. Curfews had been lifted until midnight and parties were in full swing in every group home. WREN extended its broadcast hours until ten at night. Crowds were abuzz with speculation about this year's Apostlehood nominee. Bookies were doing a brisk business—the odds-on favorite now that Ezekiel had been eliminated was Patricia Torrington at two to one, but David Koertner was closing the gap fast. The latest odds put him at six to two.

In keeping with the hoopla, tents had been set up in Ascension Square, offering everything from cotton candy to two-percent beer with a limit of three bottles per Disciple. Bands played, pennants flapped, happiness flourished. Even colonel Axton made an appearance, pinning citizenship medals on a group of visiting junior Disciples from High Falls, kissing their cheeks, and inviting them back for next year's celebration.

Most notable was the absence of Guardian patrols. Whatever Guardians could be seen were clustered in small groups, exchanging jokes, laughing, and passing the time with small-talk. All of them were unarmed. Not a single patrol Humvee rumbled through the streets. Rowdy Disciples were routinely ignored. And that worried Justin.

He knew damn well that quite the opposite should be happening after his unfortunate run-in with Austin. Instead of extending curfew, it should have been curtailed. Instead of selling near beer to underage Disciples, every drink except milk should have been pulled off the shelves. And instead of joking with Disciples, Guardians should be running them in for jaywalking. As a matter of fact, the place should be crawling with so many patrols that a simple stroll in the park would be a pain in the ass. So, Justin figured, security in Resurrection had moved underground. And that was bad news.

There were subtle signs that not everything was as it seemed. For starters, Perlmutter had unexpectedly taken ill. The official explanation was influenza, which had settled in his lungs. Then there was a hastily arranged meeting at 132 Fair Street. Violence Control Center received very few visitors and most of them never returned after being summoned. So when Justin saw Perlmutter, Brauner and Austin enter Axton's private domain, Justin had taken notice. When they came out the front door a while later, first Perlmutter who looked shaken, followed ten minutes later by Austin who looked pissed, and finally Brauner who looked like he was in a mad rush, Justin put two and two together. And that wasn't the end of it. The next few days a procession of men and women made their way into the building, most of whom Justin had never seen before. Since they weren't door to door salesmen, Justin assumed they were security agents. But the clincher undoubtedly was the party atmosphere that suddenly flourished, which Justin recognized as an attempt to lull Resurrection City into a false sense of security. Which put his mission in peril.

*****

It was one o'clock in the morning. Steady breathing rose from David's bunk. The twelve-thirty Humvee patrol was well on its way back to barracks by now. The moon was blanketed by clouds. It was dead-time when no one was likely to see him.

He kicked off his sheets and got out of bed. He quickly climbed into his jeans and buckled up. A black sweater would be uncomfortably warm but provide him with cover. He reached under the bed and found his survival kit, one of Paulette's nylon stockings filled with the essentials of making it to the wall: a pack of Marlboros, two books of matches, two photocopies, the first a map of Resurrection courtesy of the library annex and the second Paulette's assignment sheet which gave him the times and routes of all patrol schedules within ten miles of Resurrection City, the key to Paulette's apartment, and three candy bars. He stuffed the rolled-up stocking into his back pocket and said a quick prayer, thanking Paulette for her unwitting generosity and praying for her soul should anyone ever discover her role in his escape. He would have liked to thank her in person but a prayer would have to do. For a split second he considered waking David and telling him but shook off the impulse. Instead he tip-toed barefoot around David's bunk, sneakers in hand, and was out of room 310.

The hallway was dark except for an emergency exit sign next to the communal bathroom. It was also Justin's first danger zone. Seeing a Disciple in the hall at this hour of the night, fully dressed and carrying what looked like a lumpy satchel, would raise every alarm in Resurrection. He couldn't take the chance of running into someone. He scanned the length of the corridor. Not a soul in sight. A quick intake of breath and Justin darted to the bathroom, zigzagging around ten outward opened dorm room, and ducked into the bathroom.

He found the nearest stall and latched the metal door behind him. Sitting on the bowl he put on his sneakers when a sudden noise to his right made him jump. Damn it. One of the stalls nearby was occupied. Justin cursed his bad luck and held his breath. He silently counted the seconds away and hoped his stall neighbor wouldn't start a conversation. He didn't, but neither did he seem in a rush to get back to his room. Finally, after what seemed like an eternity, Justin heard the toilet flush and footsteps recede in the distance.

A quick sigh of relief. The first hurdle had been cleared. In a hurry now to make up for lost time, and pumped up by an adrenaline rush, Justin nevertheless forced himself to proceed methodically. He made sure his sneakers were double-tied (he couldn't risk tripping, not tonight) and pulled a black nylon stocking, courtesy of Paulette, over his head. With it, darkness suddenly got a lot darker and Justin literally couldn't see more than three feet in front of him. It also got a lot hotter. Perspiration was trapped between skin and stocking with no place to run except into his eyes, which made it even more difficult to see. Justin, who prided himself on being calm under pressure, discovered that he was human after all. His level of calmness was directly related to the amount of pressure he felt. By the time he left the toilet he was a nervous wreck.

Breathing hard, he stared at the staircase leading to the ground floor. Once again, running into someone would be deadly, but he had no choice. Justin descended quickly but carefully, making sure not to trip. Never had the seconds ticked off the clock more slowly. Never had it taken this long to get to the ground floor. The front door swung open easily. No creaking noise to attract attention. He shut the door behind him.

He took a deep breath and let the cool night air fill his lungs. *Relax*, he told himself. *You've broken curfew a thousand times. Nobody ever saw you leave this place at night. Why's it different tonight?* He knew the answer. All the other times were for fun, for Paulette. Or for trivial reasons. Minor infraction. Tonight was for keeps. Tonight he wasn't coming back. Ever!

He drew a succession of deep breaths until he felt a familiar calmness spread through his body. His knotted muscles relaxed. The old Justin was back. In the night sky, pale moonlight filtered through tattered clouds. It was bright enough for what he needed to do, but not bright enough to give him away. Perfect conditions. His frayed nerves calm, his heart rate at near normal, he felt good. He'd made it. He was as ready as he'd ever be. Nothing could stop him now.

He wasn't afraid but he was worried about time. He checked his watch and was surprised that only fifteen minutes had elapsed since he'd left room 310. Right on schedule. Moving quickly now, staying close to buildings whenever possible, darting across occasional wide patches of front lawns, crossing streets in mid-block to avoid risky intersections, he made good time. At the corner of Clinton and Fair a roadblock surprised him. Apparently not all security had moved underground. A Humvee was parked at the curb. Sawhorses narrowed the pavement to one lane. But the two Guardians manning the post were seated inside the passenger compartment and apparently not interested in keeping an eye on the street. More confident, Justin grinned and gave them the finger. If that's the way they would guard intersections, the rest would be a piece of cake. He was outside Paulette's three-story frame building five minutes later.

He took a moment to check his surroundings. All windows were closed and dark. Two cars were parked at the curb, a black Toyota, which belonged to apartment 1A and a gray Plymouth that was owned by 1B. In the driveway, Paulette's olive-green, canvas topped Jeep was hidden by shadows. The chain-link gate to the driveway was unlocked. At the rear of the driveway was a wood-frame garage, its door open, revealing the typical assortment of garage junk.

Justin swung the gate open and climbed into the Jeep. He struck a match and checked the gas gauge. It read less than a quarter full, not enough. He blew out the match and dismounted, walked the length of the driveway and went into the garage. As he had expected, two gasoline canisters stood on a shelf along the back wall. Justin picked up both. The first was empty, but the second weighed at least twenty pounds. He unscrewed the cap and held the opening to his nose. The fumes made his eyes tear and his heart jump with joy. He re-screwed the cap and carried the canister to the Jeep, placed it on the passenger side floor, and crammed his stockinged survival kit into the glove compartment.

One last visit to Paulette's apartment. Not for pleasure this time but for her car keys. He was tempted to skip her place and hot-wire the car. He'd done it once before, two years ago, but wasn't sure if he could pull it off it the dark. Reason won over impulse and he made his way to the building's back door. It would only take a minute or two. He had the key to her apartment, he knew exactly where she kept her car keys, and he needed to take another look at the map to trace his route. And he was dying for a smoke and Paulette's apartment was the safest place. He knew she was a heavy sleeper. Nothing short of an explosion would wake her. And a quick glance at his watch told him he had plenty of time for a short cigarette break.

Justin had been in Paulette's building often enough to know its layout well. There were four apartments on each floor, each opening into a center hall. Doors A and B led to large two-bedroom units that were reserved for senior Guardians. 1A was out of town, vacationing in a tent camp by the Ashokan reservoir. 1B was on long-distance patrol along route 209 and according to Paulette's work schedule probably somewhere around Tannersville at this hour. The other two ground-floor apartments stood empty. Judging by the paint smell and tarps in the hall, both would soon have new occupants. Paulette's place was on the second floor. The other apartments on her floor belonged to nightshift Guardians. Justin knew all of them. In his opinion they were typical of most Guardians he'd met: men with surly attitudes and IQs of village idiots. The top floor had just received new tenants and Justin had no idea who they were or when they worked but was little concerned about them. He had no plans to knock on their doors and introduce himself. And at two in the morning, they should be asleep or at work.

He let himself into 2C and locked the door behind him. The same adrenalin rush he had felt in the street outside Greenkill's front door less than half an hour ago set his mind racing. He went straight into Paulette's bedroom, headed for the ashtray on the dresser where she kept her car keys and held them triumphantly.

He didn't glance at her bed, didn't listen for her familiar snorts and uneven breathing. This was not the time to take unnecessary chances. He turned quickly and softly closed the bedroom door behind him. Not a single hitch. Right on schedule. Not a worry in the world. Success. Deliriously intoxicating.

Back in the living room he sank into the couch and lit up, drawing deep, holding the smoke in his lungs. The intoxicating tingle spread through him, as did something else. He didn't notice it at first and when he did, he blamed it on a nicotine rush. Wow, he thought, what a high, he'd never had one like this before, not from one butt. He closed his eyes, savoring the feeling, hoping it would last another four hours and two-hundred miles. Wow!

Another drag. And one more. Slow down, he told himself, your cigarette is burning too hot. Take it easy, make it last longer. The tingle spread, making him hyper-sensitive until he thought he could see though closed eyelids and hear his hairs grow. Even his insides were on a high, gnawing and growling and gurgling and making the kind of noises he'd only heard whenever something was about to happen.

He bolted upright and studied the room. The front door was still locked. The window shades drawn. Except for his own heavy breathing it was silent. So why did he feel so creepy? He scanned the room and found it comfortingly familiar yet uncomfortably different. He drank in every detail, examined every item.

Slowly, one image at a time, reality sank in. Several gardening magazines were stacked neatly on the coffee table. Fresh flowers provided a splash of color against white walls. Lace doilies graced both arms of a recliner. In the kitchenette, the drain was empty. Coffee mugs hung from a carved wooden stand. The counter was set for two. Blue and white place mats and white china and gleaming silverware. The linoleum floor sparkled. The garbage pail had been emptied. As a matter of fact, the faint odor of cleaning fluids and disinfectants hung in the air.

The hairs on the back of his neck stood at attention. Paulette was a slob. She hated gardening almost as much as fresh flowers, which she claimed gave her a headache. She never used disinfectants because the smell made her feel worse than that of flowers. She always left dishes in the sink. And she never had place settings on the counter because she was usually too hung-over or running too late in the morning.

The overhead lights clicked on.

"Mister Frederikson. I've been expecting you."

Where had he heard that voice before?

"I'm afraid Mrs. Kowalski isn't here right now, but don't let that stop you. Won't you have a seat?"

The sarcasm in the voice triggered Justin's memory. He turned in the direction of the speaker. Utter helplessness swept over him. Stepping into the white glare of the overhead fluorescent light was Colonel Xavier Axton.

Chapter 19

AT FIRST I blamed it on the flu. The symptoms were identical. It had started this morning with a headache. Nothing too bad, just a nagging pain in my temples. By mid-afternoon it had grown into a full-fledged migraine and the rest of my body joined in. Aching muscles, stiff joints, and lightheadedness that made me miserable. I was in front of my keyboard trying to finish tomorrow's edition of the Sentinel and decided to take a quick break.

I took a couple of Aspirins which only made my stomach queasy. Coffee didn't help either. After two refills my insides churned, I felt hot, had chills, and became dizzy. I didn't want to bother Brauner, who seemed to be busier than usual, and fought my way through an article about the upcoming Resurrection Day celebration. By the time the column was finished and I turned off my PC I felt so bad that I did interrupt Doc Brauner.

He agreed that it probably wasn't anything to worry about and told me to go straight to bed, take another aspirin, and drink plenty of fluids. So by four in the afternoon I closed shop for the day, took twenty minutes for a ten minute walk to Greenkill House, and fell on top of my bunk without bothering to get undressed.

I must have fallen asleep immediately, but it wasn't a restful sleep. I had weird dreams. Not really dreams but more like hallucinations brought on by high fevers. Anyhow, whatever they were they left me with a bad taste in my mouth when I woke an hour later.

It wasn't dark yet. Twilight painted the room with gloomy shades of gray. I got out of bed and trudged to the toilet, toothbrush in one hand, a bottle of aspirin in the other, and splashed cold water on my face. I looked a mess. Flushed skin and shiny eyes stared at me from the pitted mirror above the sink. I really didn't want another aspirin but figured Brauner knew best. It turned out he didn't. Less than a minute after washing it down with a handful of water I threw it back up. I brushed my teeth again and walked back to my room, shuffling like an old man and holding on to the wall to steady myself. Resigned that there was no quick cure I sat on the bed and untied my sneakers. The room started spinning like a merry-go-round gone amok. I let my head drop against the pillows and waited for a wave of nausea to subside. Five minutes later I was asleep.

When I woke again to total darkness I felt worse than ever. Muscle-twitching, bone-chilling, teeth-clattering, sweat-pouring worse. By now I was really getting worried regardless of Brauner's off-the-cuff dismissal of my symptoms. I've had the flu before. This wasn't it.

My mind was playing tricks on me. My brain was a labyrinth with hundreds of mice scurrying back and forth, trying to find a way out, running into each other, bumping into dead ends, nibbling and clawing and screeching. But instead of finding an exit they merely succeeded in getting hopelessly lost and jamming themselves into tiny crevices.

I buried my head in the pillow and noticed something extraordinary. The mice were still scurrying back and forth, but at the same time I heard a muffled conversation. It took me only a few second to realize that I overheard two Guardians talking outside my window. Of course that by itself wasn't extraordinary. Guardians always talked. What was extraordinary was that the window was closed and they were in the street. Three floors below me. Against the Guardian's background chatter, I heard other sounds as well: the raspy noise of thousands of cicadas, leaves rustling in a soft breeze, my bedside alarm clock ticking seconds away.

I immediately knew that I was going insane. Working with Doc Brauner, who knew more about the human brain than anyone I had ever met, I was familiar with some of the symptoms. Mice scurrying in my head and hearing a muffled conversation through a closed window was all the proof I needed. I was going crazy, plain and simple.

*****

The following morning I turned to Doc Brauner for help. I caught him just as he was getting into the office. His desk was still locked, his briefcase was at his side, and he was about to hang his coat on his clothes tree when I burst into his office over Rachel Firestein's objections. He looked up, but instead of being annoyed he went out of his way to make me feel at ease.

Sitting in the familiar surroundings of his inner office where I had spent countless hours working side by side with him, I suddenly felt foolish.

He prodded me. "What's wrong, David? I know I sent you home with the flu but the way you look, I don't know, I'm getting a little worried myself. Is anything else wrong?"

I nodded sheepishly. "I'm sorry to bother you, but…"

"No bother, why don't you tell me what's wrong."

I hesitated and blushed. Telling someone that you're losing your mind isn't the easiest thing in the world. Ironically, I worried that I'd sound like a lunatic telling him that I was a lunatic. At last I blurted it out. "I think I'm going crazy. Actually, I *know* I am."

Doc Brauner's response was a gale of laughter, the kind of eye-tearing, gasping-for-air laughter that turned my blush into deep crimson "You're serious, aren't you?" he asked and wiped his eyes with a monogrammed handkerchief. "Now I've heard everything, but this… tell me, David, what makes you think that you've lost your mind?"

Squirming in my seat, I told him everything. The scurrying mice, hearing things that shouldn't have been audible, the entire series of events from the moment I'd left work until I burst into his office a few moments ago. He regarded me sympathetically but I couldn't help thinking that that's exactly how you act with any raving lunatic. I wanted reassurance, answers, anything but sympathy.

"Doc," I started, a little miffed by his cavalier behavior. "I'm worried out of my mind and all you can do is laugh at me. You know as well as I do that it's not normal to hear voices."

"I'm sorry, David. I shouldn't have laughed. It's just that I've had a rough day already and, quite frankly, the sight of my brightest Disciple bursting into the office to tell me that he's hearing voices is, well, you have to admit it's funny. Look, I'm sure there's a logical explanation for this and I'm just as sure we're going to find it. And I'm absolutely positive that you're as sane as I am. Now, has anything happened recently that might have stressed you out? Let's say in the last week or so?"

"Other than Private Austin?" I asked.

Brauner reflected on this with a moment of silence. "Hmm, I suppose she could have triggered some repressed feelings to surface. Tell me, David, how do you feel about her? I mean, *really* feel about her."

"Well, she's different. Don't get me wrong, I don't mean that in a bad way. It's just that she has some different ideas about… I can't really explain it."

"Different ideas about what?"

"I told you, I don't know. Just different, I guess."

Brauner frowned and walked to my side. He placed his hand on my shoulder and gave it a reassuring squeeze. When he did, I stiffened involuntarily. I knew he only wanted to set my mind at ease but I resented his gesture. I didn't want him to touch me. And I sure as hell didn't want him to blame Austin for my problems.

Brauner went on. "I didn't mean to imply that she is a bad influence on you, but I think it's important that you're honest with me. Sometimes good intentions can have a bad effect. I think that perhaps she might have said something or done something to upset you. She told you about herself, didn't she? About her life, where she lived, about her family and so on. Perhaps it was too much for you to take in all at once."

"That's not it," I objected. "I've heard about *Them* before. I guess I knew all along, I just never really believed it."

"And now you do?"

I nodded. "She wouldn't lie to me. But who cares if there's a different world out there? From what she told me I wouldn't want to live there anyhow. It doesn't sound like such a great place to be."

"What makes you say that?"

"Just look at what her wonderful world made of her," I said. "Some of her ideas of good and bad are all twisted. If that's what happens outside of Resurrection, well, then I don't want any part of it."

"Now I think we're getting somewhere," Brauner said. "Those ideas of hers, is that what you were referring to when you said she was different?"

"I guess so," I said unenthusiastically, unwilling to pursue it further. But Doc Brauner wouldn't let go.

"Give me an example," he demanded.

"Okay. She thinks it's all right to get angry. She actually made it sound as if it's okay to hate people. She thinks hatred can be healthy emotional outlet. Don't you see, Doc, it's against everything we're trying to live by. Instead of love and harmony she's saying go ahead and get angry. When I told her how I felt, well, she wouldn't listen. Instead she kept pushing and pushing until I did get angry. And that made her happy. She said it made me human."

Brauner fell silent, turning inward. When I was about to speak again he held up his hand to stop me. We sat like this for a minute, each pursuing private thoughts. I was conflicted, wrestling with a stubborn desire to defend Private Austin even though I knew she was wrong.

Doc Brauner wrestled with his own issues. His eyes closed, his hands folded on the desktop, he began to speak in an animated voice. As he spoke his voice became louder and more fervent. "I'm afraid that her talk of being *human* may be what triggered your emotional reaction. You see, of all the differences that exist between our world and hers, the most critical is their wide-held belief that all humans are imperfect. They call it original sin and cling to it with religious fanaticism. In a world ruled by crime and hate it's not unusual that people look for excuses, hence original sin. After all, they argue, it's normal to be imperfect if that's how our maker made us. It also creates a value system that is corrupt, rewards greed, tolerates the antichrist, and idolizes those who use their shortcomings to rise from the cesspool.

"We on the other hand reject the concept of original sin. Our father made us in his image and we are kind and loving and compassionate. That's what makes us human, and that's what Private Austin refuses to understand. She feels threatened by us. So you see, David, it's not that she has turned your world upside down. It's you who turned her world upside down. You have nothing to worry about. What you're feeling at this moment is a normal reaction. Oh sure, you've been bombarded with a lot of information and it's going to take some time before it sinks in and settles down. The things you feel and hear are nothing more than conflicting ideas fighting for supremacy. But it's not insanity, it's coming to grips with knowledge, it's part of growing up. And a part of growing up is recognizing that we're not all the same. Just like you and I are not the same, you and Austin are not the same. I anticipate that you'll become increasingly aware of other differences as time goes by. You are one of us, you aren't saddled with their pitiful original sin. You'll recognize the differences between our world and hers. And believe me David, in the end good will triumph over evil. Purity will win defeat impurity. Resurrection shall prevail."

Doc Brauner paused for a moment. His eyes shone with religious fervor. His voice cracked with emotion. He walked to my side and placed both hands on my shoulder, "So you see, David, Private Austin isn't a bad person at all. It's just that she's been conditioned all her life to look at humans differently than we do. I'm willing to bet that someday very soon she'll come around to our way of thinking. She too will see the light. Until she does it might be better if you had no contact with her. That's why I'm taking over your therapy for the next week or so." Hearing Doc Brauner say that I couldn't see Private Austin for the foreseeable future angered me to the point of objecting, something I would never have done in the past. I forced myself to be diplomatic however and said, "I'm sure you're right, but I'd like to have Private Austin stay with me a while longer. You see, I'd like to have a hand in changing her way of thinking, of making her see the light, as you put it. I think I owe her that much."

"Why this sudden loyalty for Austin?" Doc Brauner asked. "I thought you'd be thrilled to be rid of her for a while."

"It's not loyalty," I said defensively. I was about to tell him about my ten o'clock appointment with her but bit my tongue. Why complicate things, I thought, and suddenly knew that I had already changed. I was withholding information, harboring dislikes, choosing sides. And for now at least Austin had won over Brauner, a shocking development considering that Doc Brauner had been my mentor for as long as I could remember. *Maybe there was something to this original sin after all.*

"I just thought that, given my relationship with her, I'd be the perfect candidate to help," I tried one last time."

Doc Brauner gave me an odd look and escorted me to the door. My impromptu meeting with him was over. He shook my hand and said, "Perhaps you've grown up faster than you realize. I too would have growing pains if I'd been force fed the amount of information you had to digest. Now I want you to take the day off, go home and rest. Believe me, you'll be as good as new in the morning."

I found myself on the steps of Terwilliger House, wondering exactly what Doc Brauner's diagnosis for my insanity problems had been and why I wasn't allowed to see Private Austin any more. Puzzled by these developments I returned to room 311 and fell onto by bed.

Today Doc Brauner hadn't helped me at all. Sure, the voices in my head had subsided along with the mice, But the confusion Doc Brauner had sown and the self-doubt he had awakened were far worse. And I knew only Private Austin could help me regain my sanity.

*****

I spent most of the day in my room, resting to shake off whatever bug I'd had and recovering from my unsatisfying session with Doc Brauner. By eight at night I went to the cafeteria for a light meal. I sat by myself and ate quickly. By eight-thirty I was back in my room, impatiently waiting for my rendezvous with Austin.

The door to her suite was closed but not locked. After two unanswered knocks and a half-whispered *Private Austin, are you there?* I turned the knob and found myself inside her room. Normally I wouldn't have been brazen enough to walk into a counselor's suite but these weren't normal times. I had a feeling that tonight could turn out to be a watershed for me.

Private Austin wasn't in her room. Everything pointed to a hasty departure. The place was in disarray. The bed was unmade. The dresser drawers stood half-opened. A few of her personal belongings were strewn on the bed. Next to her bedside lamp I found a sealed envelope addressed to me.

David. Sorry to run out on you like this but I was called on an emergency assignment. Dr. Brauner insisted. I'll stop by your room as soon as I get back. In the meantime, please see Dr. Brauner for your psych sessions. He really cares for you and is very concerned about your wellbeing. He knows you much better than I do and can probably help you more than I ever could. Please give him your complete trust. Without it, no one can help you achieve your important next step. And remember what I told you. "It's okay to be human." Private D. Austin.

Her note left me sad and flattered at the same time. Although it wouldn't have taken much time to stop by my room and tell me she wasn't going to be home tonight she had gone to the trouble of leaving me a note, and that meant a lot. A few hastily scrawled words which proved that she thought about me. Funny how a short letter can make you feel better. What the note said wasn't nearly as important as its existence. The piece of paper in my hand was something very private and personal, even precious, something I'd never throw away or show to anyone. Especially not Doc Brauner.

*****

What a difference a day makes. When I woke the next morning, my life was back to normal. I felt good considering I'd probably had a massive anxiety attack. Yesterday's events were a million hours removed. Austin's note was tucked in my nightstand drawer, something to hold on to whenever I needed a boost. Everything was good with the world again. Everything except for that damn hyper-sensitivity that I still felt.

Justin, whom I hadn't seen since yesterday afternoon, was sprawled on his bunk and snoring up a storm. Some things never changed.

Thinking about the past twenty-four hours, I realized how lucky I was. What could have turned out to be a disaster was a blessing in disguise. Something had changed, but the changes were all good, sort of like being able to say good morning to a brand new David Koertner. I liked the new me. The new David was confident even if he didn't have all the answers. The important thing was that the new David wasn't unsure about his role. Doubts about his identity as a Disciple were gone. So what if there was another place besides Resurrection? The old David had suspected it all along and suppressed it. The new David wasn't afraid to confront it. He knew where he belonged. The new David had a brand new friend and a note from her to prove it.

Unconcerned about Justin I made enough noise to wake the dead. I hummed a tune, off-key, whistled, and got dressed. Justin stirred, rolled on his side, and buried his head under the pillow. What a shame, I thought, you're missing a glorious morning. I pried open the window to let in fresh air. Autumn was here, accompanied by cool breezes and low humidity. The morning sun hung low on the horizon, throwing slanted fingers of gold across the street.

Resurrection City stirred to life, as did Justin. He blinked and rubbed his eyes.

"Good morning, buddy," I said loud enough for every Disciple in Greenkill to hear.

Justin didn't share my good mood. "You're a real sadist, waking people this early." He glared at me with daggers in his eyes.

"And I ought to report you for being AWOL last night," I countered.

"You don't have to," he said. "They already caught me."

"What?"

"You heard me. Axton himself caught me. I almost shit in my pants when I saw him."

"How did he…?"

"Yeah, that's what I'd like to know too. You wouldn't know anything about that, would you?"

"I don't even know where the hell you were, so how could I snitch on you? By the way, where were you?"

"At Paulette's."

"Christ, you'll never learn, will you? I thought that was all over."

"It is."

"Then why'd you go to her place?"

"It's a long story." He corrected himself, "Actually it's a pretty short story. All I wanted was to borrow her car for a while."

I should have known Justin would be involved in another humdinger. But I guess the new David wasn't quite as savvy as the old one. I was shocked. "In the middle of the night?" I asked. "Where the hell were you going?"

"Guess."

I made up my mind right then and there to talk to Brauner. Just as Private Austin had suggested, Justin was spinning out of control. "I'm telling Brauner," I said. "I should have said something long ago, like when you first started seeing Paulette. I just hope it's not too late."

Justin smirked. "Don't bother. I'm sure that old faggot knows by now. Axton probably called him the minute he caught me. Maybe he knew before. Maybe the whole fucking world knew before I did. Axton sure as hell did, and I bet Paulette did too. You know, that really hurts, after the good times we had, selling me down the river. Just goes to show you, you can't trust a broad. Paulette, your precious bitch counselor, they're all the same. Making believe they want to help, giving you a little tease, and then, wham! You get screwed."

His vehement outburst was so uncharacteristic that it caught me off-guard. I'd known all along that he had a knack for getting into trouble but he was also good-natured. This didn't sound like him. "What the hell's come over you? I never heard you talk like this before."

"Yeah, well maybe that's because I haven't been in this kind of trouble before. This time I'm really fucked. And so are you, buddy. You and that bitch Austin."

"Don't you dare drag Private Austin into this." I was furious. "This is your mess. Nobody got you into it but you."

"Oh yeah? Well, let me tell you something, pal. If it hadn't been for her, nothing would have happened. Perlmutter would have slept through the whole thing, Austin wouldn't have surprised me in the Library, and me and my ass would be long gone. Out of Resurrection. Instead I gotta see Axton this morning and face the grand inquisition. I'm sure Brauner's gonna be there and probably Paulette. Wouldn't surprise me if Austin was there too."

"She won't be. She's been reassigned."

"Well, well," Justin sneered. "You're getting pretty chummy with the lady, aren't you? Did she tell you where she's going or is that privileged information?"

"You're really getting me pissed off, you know that?"

Justin disregarded my outburst, instead finding solace in goading me. "I'll tell you what, Davey, maybe someday we can compare notes. My money's on Paulette."

"Fuck you."

*****

Doc Brauner unlocked his desk and extracted David's file. Without hesitating, he started writing. *Fifty milligram reduction in Libidex-M produced expected results. Although withdrawal symptoms are evident they are of a non-violent nature. Hypersensitivity is more pronounced than expected but still well within acceptable tolerance. Current dosage of placebos will be continued until hormonal balance levels are achieved. Physical and Spiritual Maintenance session will be modified and accelerated until all gender related conflicts are eliminated. Patient will be transferred to my care and will undergo psychological evaluations once a week. Bruno B. Brauner, MD.*

Chapter 20

COUNSELOR MICHELLE ABRAMS' family emergency was apparently more serious than Brauner had told Dawn Austin. Following a bumpy one-hour ride west along state route 28, Dawn Austin was processed through Quadrant 2's checkpoint in Shandaken, shown to her new quarters, and told that Abrams was not expected back until next month.

The contrast between Resurrection City and Quadrant 2 was shocking. Although a prison mentality was always apparent in Resurrection City, it was run like a minimum security facility. Inmates were allowed to move about freely. Male and female prisoners saw each other socially. Education was mandatory, as was work. At the end of the workday, inmates were on their own until curfew. Crime was virtually non-existent. Guards generally treated inmates fairly and, although frowned upon, socialized with them occasionally. Indeed, it appeared that the great social experiment was working.

By comparison, Quadrant 2 was a living example of a living hell. A sense of doom was reflected in the eyes of inmates. For the first time in her life Dawn felt as if she had arrived in purgatory. It wasn't that the prisoners looked particularly hopeless; most prisoners did. Dawn was haunted by the fact that they shuffled from place to place without ever arriving anywhere. They displayed no emotions whatsoever, be it despair or hatred or even the will to live. They truly were the living dead.

The seven thousand-acre complex was secured by high-tech laser scanners along its perimeter and a twelve-foot high concrete wall topped with concertina rolls of barbed wire. Nothing, after all, reminded inmates more of a prison than razor sharp teeth glittering in the blinding glare of floodlights.

Within the Shandaken complex, two-story concrete-block barracks stretched in endless rows like headstones in a cemetery. They were connected by pot-holed asphalt ribbons that dissected Shandaken into six rectangular camps, each housing one-thousand prisoners. And at the core of it stood a three-story windowless building known simply as *The House*.

The House was similar in shape to a wagon wheel, with eight spokes extending outward from a central elevator shaft to the wheel's perimeter. The sole entrance to the facility was located at the eastern spoke of *The House*. It was a prison checkpoint within a prison, a large fire-proof, bomb-proof tunnel-like structure through which all traffic passed. The checkpoint's nickname *Eerie Canal* was more than a play on words. The tunnel was separated into three chambers, each secured by hydraulic steel partitions that resembled a canal's locks. Only one of the steel partitions could be opened at any given time. Each of the three chambers could be injected with a deadly nerve gas. No prisoner had ever escaped from Shandaken.

It was where Private Austin was about to live and work for the next two weeks. *So much for the fresh country air of Shandaken* she thought bitterly and shrugged her shoulders as she was escorted to her third-floor room.

*****

"Private Austin? Is that you?"

She craned her neck and stared around the crowded mess hall. A sea of faces stared back at her.

"Over here, Private." An arm rose above the crowd and she squinted to make out the face it belonged to. It was Quinton Perlmutter.

A rush of joy at seeing a familiar face lifted her spirits. Hard as it was to believe, two days in Shandaken had demoralized her so completely that Perlmutter, whom she had seen only twice before, seemed like a long-lost friend. Anything associated with Resurrection

City was a pleasant surprise in the abject despair that permeated Quadrant II. She squeezed through the crowd, balancing her lunch tray above her head, and took a seat at Quinton's table.

He beamed a broad smile at her. "What are you doing here, Private Austin?"

"I'm not sure," she said. "Officially I'm here to substitute for counselor Abrams. That and to get some fresh country air to help heal the bump on my head. But the whole thing happened so fast that I'm really not sure. Dr. Brauner hustled me out of his office the other day and before I knew it I was on my way. What about you?"

The question apparently confused Perlmutter. He rubbed his forehead and seemed lost in thought. "They sent me here to help me," he finally said. "Yeah, that's it. They wanted to help me."

Something in the way he replied made Dawn take notice. An unusual inflection in his voice, perhaps the way he emphasized the phrase, made him sound like… Dawn tried to think of the proper analogy and was surprised by the answer that came to mind. Religious fervor.

"Help you with what?" she asked cautiously, hoping to sound casual, and avoided his eyes, concentrating on a forkful of Chicken Chow Mein.

"Inward reflection," he answered and looked at her as though he had just revealed a secret.

"I don't follow you, Mr. Perlmutter." Dawn was puzzled and a bit taken aback by Perlmutter's strange answer.

He leaned into her and whispered. "It's really quite simple. I've let down my brethren when I fell asleep on the job. If I hadn't, you probably wouldn't have been attacked. No, no, let me finish." He put his forefinger over her mouth and she pulled back instinctively. "It's true, you know. But it's hard to see one's errors unless one is removed from the scene of the failing, if I may call it that. Distance provides perspective. Distance in miles as well as time. I now know where I went wrong, and I thank my superiors for having the vision and faith to help me see my faults. With their guidance I can become worthy of their trust once more."

Perlmutter was beginning to scare her. The man sounded like a certifiable lunatic. *Careful,* she told herself. *Watch what you say.* "I see, Mr. Perlmutter. And how much longer do you think you'll be here?"

"Not much longer. I'm in therapy right now, and phase I is almost completed."

"Phase I?"

"Yes, that's the first step to recovery. I'm finally able to admit my shortcomings to myself. It's like being a recovering alcoholic, you know. No one can help you until you admit that you're an addict. I've passed that step and I can go on to phase II. But what about you? What brings you here? Or did I ask that already? I can't remember."

"Gaining perspective."

*****

A common thread was woven through the fabric of Quadrant II. Unlike Resurrection City, which reminded Dawn of comfortable denim jeans and warm flannel shirts, Shandaken's cloth were soiled bandages unraveling from festering wounds. The stench of necrotic tissue assailed the senses along with a whiff of embalming fluid.

There were of course the obvious differences she had noticed upon arrival: Quad II's ever present barbed wire fences and the vast communal dormitories that housed up to one hundred inmates each and resembled concrete silos. Another difference she had noticed on her first day was the aimless existence of Shandaken's inmates. They worked at menial jobs and received no training. There was no effort to rehabilitate the inmates. Dawn wondered why the Camp's administrators bothered with counselors in Quad II. It was obvious that the prisoners here were throwaways. But there was another intangible difference between Resurrection City and Quad II that escaped her.

She found the answer in the eyes of the inmates, and when she did she was astonished it had taken her this long to recognize the obvious. Everyone she looked at and spoke to projected the same sheep-like acquiescence that Quinton Perlmutter had. It was as though someone had sliced away individual personalities and infused them with unquestioning subservience to a higher entity. For Dawn it was an awakening. Quadrant II was doing its job more effectively than she had ever realized.

Her revelation made her want to return to Resurrection City as soon as possible. There was real work to be done there. She was convinced that David Koertner could be helped without becoming one of the homogenous and mindless. She started counting the days much as prisoner would, each morning crossing out another entry in her diary. Three…five…eight…nine. Her fourteen day assignment seemed to stretch into eternity.

*****

One bad morning followed another. Restless night piled upon restless night. Her frustrations mounted. She rose each morning not knowing if the sun was shining or if clouds blanketed Quad II. Her room, like every other room in *The House*, was windowless, a hermetically sealed, temperature controlled, artificially illuminated, antiseptic chamber inside the sterile nether-world of *The House*.

Wakeup call was at six, when a central computer system activated an alarm and blared her into wakefulness with a shrill wail. She was allowed half an hour to wash and dress before her assignment for the day was displayed on a TV monitor that was mounted hospital-style on a wall opposite her bed.

Her only social interaction occurred during meal breaks, twenty minutes for breakfast, forty five minutes for lunch, and sixty minutes for dinner. Thirty minutes after dinner, the same computer system that woke her each morning shut the lights and dispensed 20 milligrams of Somnific-200 through the cooling vents. Fifteen minutes later she fell into a coma-like sleep.

By the end of her tenth day Dawn Austin had lost track of the traditional concept of day and night. Sun and moon and stars became meaningless. So did rain and wind and the early morning cawing of crows so prevalent in Resurrection City. Sequestered from the outside world, she relied on Shandaken's computer to regulate her life. She discovered that the thirty minutes she was allowed each morning to prepare for the day was more time than she needed, a notion that had been unthinkable when she first arrived here. At night she welcomed the near silent hiss that preceded the sleep-inducing Somnific-200. The pine-scented gas made it easy to slip into forgetfulness. Realizing that she, like everyone else around her, was in danger of becoming a mindless and obedient subject became a horrifying possibility. As an antidote, she threw herself into her work with abandon.

Her patient was a twenty-two-year-old woman named Anne who was unresponsive to every effort Dawn had made so far. Anne didn't have a last name. Like the other inmates in Shandaken, she simply had a first name and a number. The number identified Anne as a violent offender who had been committed to Quadrant II for treatment of antisocial tendencies. The specific nature of her crime had not been disclosed. Dawn argued to no avail that she should have access to Anne's medical records.

"How can I treat her if I haven't the slightest idea what she did?"

Dr. Callahan, Dawn's immediate supervisor at Shandaken, regarded her with cold contempt. "Your job is to treat the underlying reasons that caused her to commit a crime and to evaluate why she was able to resist twenty years of behavior modification. You don't need to know anything other than the woman's medical and psychiatric profile, as well as the treatment she received. Anything more than that is unnecessary and an invasion of her privacy."

In a rare outburst of temper Dawn stalked out of Callahan's office and slammed the door behind her. That had been the high point of her day. After that it had been all downhill.

Shortly after nine in the morning, and five minutes into the day's session with Anne, Dawn received a phone call. It was Callahan.

"Can't it wait, Doctor? I'm in the middle of…" She listened with growing irritation as Callahan explained why he needed her in his office immediately.

"But, sir, you don't understand. This woman is in a very agitated state right now. If I…"

She shifted the phone to her right ear. This stupid imbecile didn't understand. Or maybe he just didn't give a damn. She took a deep breath and tried one more time. "Just give me five more minutes. I'll be right over, I swear."

Callahan's rebuke made Dawn blush and she replied a tight-lipped "Yes, sir," hung up, and hurried to Callahan's office.

Ten minutes later, still fuming at the interruption and out of breath from running the length of *The House's* hallway to get back to examination chamber sixteen and her overwrought patient, Dawn burst into the room.

It took a second to sink in. When it did, Dawn felt uncontrollable tremors pulsing from the base of her spine to the center of her brain. Tendrils of panic gnawed at her guts. She screamed. And screamed. An inhuman, high-pitched shriek wrested from her throat and echoed off the walls and reverberated in her ears until her screeching threatened to suffocate her.

Five feet in front of her, swaying grotesquely as though the sound of Dawn's scream had set her body in motion, her eyes frozen in a fixed stare, her mouth twisted with the shocking realization that she had succeeded in taking her life, a trail of foamy spittle still glistening on her chin, her head twisted sideways, Anne hung like a rag doll. One end of Anne's bathrobe belt was knotted around her broken neck, the other end was tied securely to a ceiling mounted steel bracket which supported a closed-circuit television monitor. A chrome, leather covered stool lay on the floor three feet behind Anne.

The door flew open and two orderlies burst into the room. One rushed to Dawn's side and tried to calm her, holding her by the shoulders, shaking her, saying words she didn't hear. The other stared dumbfounded at Anne's dangling corpse, afraid to touch her, and shouted at the top of his lungs for a nurse.

Dawn had stopped screaming. She had the absurd notion of being on stage, playing the role of straight man in a comedy, that any moment now the curtain would fall to thunderous applause. This can't be real, she told herself, it's only a play, but I can't remember my lines. As she stood mute, the play unfolded. A male nurse had arrived to help the orderly. Together they lowered Anne to the floor and covered her body with a blanket. A stretcher arrived and Anne was wheeled from the room. From the doorway, several other nurses could be seen staring into the room, talking in hushed voices, then stepped aside as Callahan walked through the door.

"I think you can let go of Private Austin," he said to the orderly. "I'm sure she doesn't appreciate being shaken like a sack of potatoes."

The orderly did as told and Callahan turned to Dawn. "Austin, what the hell happened here?"

With Callahan's harsh question the curtain dropped, the play ended. She was back in the reality of examination room sixteen. "What happened?" she shouted, hating him with a fury. "You have the nerve to ask what happened? If it weren't for your arrogant stupidity nothing would have happened and this woman would still be alive. I told you she was agitated. I asked you to wait five lousy minutes but you insisted on seeing me right away. And for what? Just to tell me that you're changing my fucking shift? Fuck you, Callahan."

"Are you through?"

"You bet I am. I'm through with you and this place and everybody in here. And while you're at it, you can change my shift right out of here. I'm going back to Resurrection City."

"I'm afraid that won't be possible." Callahan said, seething with anger, his face crimson, veins protruding prominently from his neck. "Your orders are to serve at Quad II until Counsellor Abrams returns to duty. If we granted every capricious request by overwrought psychiatrists, this institution would be in shambles. Permission for transfer denied." He added, "And consider yourself lucky if I don't bring you up on charges."

Dawn couldn't believe what she had just heard. "Charges for what?" she asked, stunned by Callahan.

"Take your pick, Austin. Malfeasance, not following established procedures, insubordination, I'm sure I can think of lots more. Remember, you left a patient unattended when, by your own admission that patient was in an agitated state. You know damn well that it's standard procedure to call for an attendant whenever you're called away. Why do you think we have attendants stationed in every ward? To be your private gofers? They're here to care for patients when attending doctors are called away on emergencies."

Callahan stormed out of the room only to return seconds later. "One more thing, Austin. If you hadn't been personally recommended by Dr. Brauner I'd have you court-martialed. I think you're inept in your job performance and a trouble maker. As a matter of fact, trouble seems to follow you wherever you go. Let me remind you that this isn't a private institution for troubled society psychiatrists. This happens to be a maximum-security facility housing dangerous prisoners and we expect our employees to follow orders. Fortunately your incompetence only resulted in the death of an inmate who had nothing to live for anyhow. The next time you might not be so lucky."

Against her better judgement Dawn allowed her anger to get the best of her. "Meaning what? That it's okay if a prisoner dies?"

"You forget that these people gave up their lives the moment they got here. They're useless, going through useless motions."

"Then why don't you just kill them instead of prolonging their useless lives?"

"That would be cruel and unusual punishment," Callahan said and spun towards the door."

"Bastard!"

"That'll earn you another letter of reprimand. Keep it up and you'll have quite an interesting personnel file. It may even earn you some additional time in Quadrant II."

The time before she was allowed to return to Resurrection City seemed light years away. The next forty-eight hours blurred into a nightmarish fog. Every so often the blanket of fog lifted. During brief moments of lucidity Dawn tried to come to grips with her patient's senseless death. Although she had met the woman only a week ago and knew nothing about her, she knew that the sight of Anne's lifeless body would be etched into her mind forever. Simultaneously she experienced a personal metamorphosis, transferring her guilt to Callahan and the entire Camp. He might be nothing but a hard-ass, but he was to blame for Anne's death, not she. And he was dangerous. Dawn hadn't paid attention to it in the heat of passion but was now convinced that he had threatened her with confinement. His parting words stuck in her craw…additional time in Quadrant II. Paranoia wasn't an affliction she normally suffered from but now she wasn't so sure anymore. Somehow she managed to shrug it off and concentrated on a much more important matter, a fanatical resolve to return to Resurrection City and finish her work. She had failed Anne. She could not afford to fail David Koertner.

*****

At lunch she ran into Perlmutter again, whom she had successfully avoided since her first day in Shandaken.

"Over here, Private. I saved a seat for you."

There was no graceful way to get out of sitting with him. Dawn pushed through the crowd and slid her tray next to his. Perlmutter looked pleased to have spotted her and brushed a trail of bread crumbs off her seat.

"Sit down. Where've you been, hiding from me?" He chuckled. As he did, his tongue clacked, reminding her of a duck.

"Of course not," she smiled weakly. "Just been busy."

He looked offended by her answer. "That was a rhetorical question, Private. I didn't really think you were avoiding me." He clacked again, and Dawn noticed that his Adam's apple jumped in his throat with each cluck. "Unless I make you feel uncomfortable."

"Of course not, Mr. Perlmutter, don't be silly."

He didn't look mollified and seemed to have ignored her remark completely. Without looking at her he dug his fork into a heaping plate of spaghetti and tried to maneuver it into his mouth without losing a single strand of tomato sauce soaked pasta. His lips turned into a perfect circle, and, with a quick motion belying his pudgy appearance, he plunged the fork into his mouth. Inch-long tendrils of pasta dangled from his lower lip. Unconcerned with table manners, he sucked and the spaghetti slipped into his mouth with tiny pops, showering his shirt with red sauce. Dawn didn't know whether to laugh or cry and looked away at the last moment.

"Silly?" he picked up on her answer, his fork poised midway between plate and mouth. "You just said not to be silly. Why did you say that?"

By now Dawn was convinced that Perlmutter, like everyone else in Shandaken, had gone over the edge. The best thing she could do was to eat as quickly as possible and get away from him. The less said the better. But Perlmutter wouldn't let go. He looked at her with piercing eyes and repeated his question. "Why silly?"

"Because I don't have a reason to feel uncomfortable around you. Not a reason in the world."

Her answer seemed to please him and he resumed eating, but three forkfuls later his fork stopped in midair and he said, "Well, you should."

"I should what?" Dawn got a prickly feeling that things would get worse before lunch was over.

"Feel uncomfortable. I sure would if I were in your shoes. It's the Christian thing to do."

"Mr. Perlmutter, I have no idea what you mean by that."

"Oh you don't, do you?" He clacked again and his Adam's apple jumped up and down like a yoyo. He stared at her bug-eyed and shook his head admonishingly. "If it hadn't been for you I wouldn't be here right now."

Ever so slowly his meaning sank in. The crazy old coot blamed her for the incident in the library. She decided to disregard him. Another few bites and she'd be done with lunch.

"Yes," he went on. "Don't you see, it's all your fault. I would still have my job. I would still have my respect. And you don't even have the decency to acknowledge your guilt."

"Mr. Perlmutter. I had absolutely nothing to do with you falling asleep on the job. As a matter of fact, I tried to save your ass. And now, if you'll excuse me…"

She slid her chair backward and started to get up.

"Sit down, Private. I'm not finished talking to you."

"But I'm finished with you."

Dawn reached for her tray when the sound of his ice cube filled soda sloshing to the floor alerted her. She watched with disbelief as his hand came up, clutching his fork tightly, and descended in a quick motion. She opened her mouth and wanted to scream. She tried to pull back her hand. It was too late. Perlmutter's fork caught her between thumb and forefinger and pinned her hand to the table. For a split second Dawn had an uncontrollable urge to laugh. Her hand was covered with spaghetti and tomato sauce. Then a searing flame shot from her hand through her wrist and up her forearm. And she knew it wasn't tomato sauce.

Chapter 21

AT SEVEN THIRTY on Friday morning Brauner was woken by sharp raps on his apartment door. Frustrated by the events of the last few days, Brauner had overindulged the night before, consuming a third of a bottle of Wild Turkey. He was therefore in no mood for an early visitor. Fumbling for his slippers, he drew a robe around striped pajamas and slipped his eyeglasses on his nose. Annoyed by another round of impatient raps and unwilling to face whoever it was without first running a comb through his hair he barked, "Hold your horses, will you. Don't you know what time it is?"

He retreated into the bathroom and emerged moments later, looking at least somewhat presentable. He made his way to the front door. Outside, a jeep was parked curbside bearing the familiar crossed-saber emblem of Colonel Axton's private security cadre. A tightlipped corporal waited at the door to deliver an ominous wakeup-call.

"A message from Colonel Axton, sir." With that the corporal handed Brauner a sealed envelope, saluted, and drove off, his jeep leaving wispy puffs of white exhaust in the brisk air.

The message was terse and offered no explanation. *Urgent that I see you in my office at nine. Axton.* Since the note had been delivered personally, Brauner assumed that his day wasn't off to a good start. He washed his hangover away with a hot shower, forced scalding coffee and burnt toast into his queasy stomach, and hurried off to 132 Fair Street at a quarter to nine.

An armed guard led Brauner into Axton's office and locked the door behind him. Inside, a grim-faced Axton paced the floor with quick strides, too preoccupied to acknowledge Brauner's arrival. The colonel's trademark Havana lay smoldering in a cut crystal ashtray. Judging by the bluish haze in the room it wasn't the colonel's first cigar of the morning.

A halogen lamp spread a cold glare on the colonel's cherry-wood desk. The desktop, usually cluttered with reams of papers and messages, was bare with the exception of one thin manila folder. Next to the folder lay two passport-sized photographs of Private Dawn Austin.

Brauner cleared his throat tactfully. "Good morning, Xavier."

Axton glanced in Brauner's direction and nodded in recognition. He waved his arm in the direction of a loveseat. "Have a seat Bruno. Sit." Then he took a seat next to Brauner and said calmly "We have a problem."

"Again? What is it this time?"

Axton shook his head. "I'm not sure. But every time he wants to talk to both of us, it's a problem.'

The telephone rang five minutes later. Axton jumped to his feet and picked up on the second ring. "Yes, sir. He's here. Wait, let me put you on the speakerphone."

Brauner waited with a growing sense of dread as Axton adjusted the volume control. Brauner, who prided himself on being prepared at all times, felt like he was caught with his pants down. Having to participate in a conference call without knowing all the facts made him tentative. And a migraine courtesy of Wild Turkey didn't help.

Axton finished fiddling with the speakerphone. "Is that better? Can you hear me now?"

The voice on the phone was brisk and businesslike. "Yes, that's fine Xavier. Good morning Bruno."

"Good morning, sir."

"Gentlemen, let me get right to the point. I've heard some disturbing news. Rather than overreact, I thought it best to get the two of you on the phone and find out first hand if I should worry. Are my sources correct?"

Axton's usual equanimity was shaken. Brauner knew the colonel well enough to interpret the telltale signs. Instead of his normal relaxed posture, leaning comfortably into his deep-cushioned chair, legs crossed, hands folded casually in his lap, Axton was fidgety. He shifted, then leaned forward in his seat and planted both forearms on the desk. His Havana remained untouched, its white ash growing to an inch. Even the disdain that normally characterized Axton's expression was missing. Axton was clearly worried.

The Colonel sent a questioning look in Brauner's direction. But Brauner shrugged his shoulders in a gesture of ignorance and returned a blank look, and Axton started cautiously. "Well, since I don't know what it is you heard I don't know how to answer that, sir."

Instead of providing an explanation, the voice on the intercom came back with a question of its own. "Let me rephrase my question then, Xavier. Is something worrisome going on in Resurrection that you would like to share with me? And Bruno, please feel free to jump in any time. My question is directed at you as much as Xavier."

Axton looked at Brauner and placed his forefinger across his lips. Brauner was happy to comply with the colonel's silent gag order.

"I don't know if I would call it worrisome, sir, but there have been two incidents that bear watching. I assume you're referring to…"

He was interrupted at once. "I'm referring to Private Dawn Austin."

Axton nodded. "Yes, I thought so, sir."

Axton and Brauner exchanged quick glances before the colonel picked up the conversation. "And I assume…"

A hint of annoyance came loud and clear from the speakerphone. "Instead of telling me what you assume, why don't you tell me the facts? Who is she? What happened? And most importantly, what is she after?"

Damage control was in order. Brauner leaned forward and motioned to Axton *let me take this one*. "Sir, this is Bruno. Private Austin works for me as a counselor in Quad I. I've done some background checks on her. Nothing in depth yet, of course. There simply hasn't been enough time but from what we know so far she looks solid. She comes from a good background. Upper middle class white, has an excellent education, no run-ins with the authorities, nothing. No skeletons in the closet. However…"

"Why did she join then? She doesn't sound like your typical recruit."

"I was just coming to that, sir. Private Austin was in a car accident when she was sixteen-year-old. Her testimony to the State Police at the time shows that an escapee from Camp Resurrection pulled her out of the wreckage moments before the car exploded and saved her life. According to Private Austin, the man stayed with her until an ambulance arrived at the scene. He was never found and the story was not substantiated, but we know that an inmate did in fact escape on the night in question.

"I examined her psychiatric profile and her school records, and one fact stands out. That accident, in which her father died, changed Austin's life. Up until then she had been a normal, well-adjusted teenager. After the accident she became an introvert. She had no social life to speak of. Instead she buried herself in her studies. Eventually she lost touch with the few friends she had. It looks like a classic case of withdrawal. The only person she confided in was her mother and even she wasn't privy to everything in her daughter's life. Over the years Austin's lack of social interaction left a void which she had to fill with something. Some people turn to drugs and alcohol. Others seek out promiscuous relationships which give them a sense of power over their sexual partners. Austin filled her void with an obsession to come to Resurrection and help the inmates. She saw it as chance to repay her debt."

"Sounds very touching. Is there more?"

"Well, yes, sir. What I've told you so far is fact. It can all be substantiated. The rest is conjecture on my part." Brauner hesitated for a moment. He knew he was taking a chance but also knew it was worth the risk. He simply couldn't let Axton get the upper hand. "I think Private Austin is potentially dangerous."

A sharp intake of breath by Axton and a glaring *Why haven't you told me this?* look. A momentary pause on the intercom. "What makes you say that, Bruno?"

"She is determined to succeed. Not so much because of a particularly strong work ethic but because of something that escapee told her. I don't know what he told her, not yet, anyhow. But whatever it was, it fueled her obsessive need to come here. Now that she's here she keeps pushing and digging. Sooner or later, well, you know what I mean."

"I see. Does she know anything?"

"Not yet."

"Put her under surveillance."

"It's already done, sir."

"Good. By the way, who's her patient?"

The question made Brauner feel uneasy again. "David Koertner."

"The same David Koertner you recommended for elevation to Apostle?"

"Yes, sir."

"Was that a wise move, pairing her with Koertner?"

"We didn't have a choice at the time, sir. You know yourself how shorthanded we are. But it may turn out to be a blessing in disguise."

"Why's that?"

"Well, I think there's a certain chemistry between her and Koertner. He's responding well to her but more importantly, I think she's responding to him. If there's anyone she'll open up to, it's him. Right now Koertner is our best shot at finding out what's at the root of Austin's compulsion."

"I think I know what you're leading up to, Bruno, but aren't you taking a chance? I understand we already lost our primary candidate for apostle this year. Losing another could be catastrophic. I don't think I have to remind you how bad it would be for morale if no one makes it this year. Not to speak of the…" Sounds of a throat being cleared burst from the speaker. "The other thing. You know how closely our quotas are being watched."

Brauner considered the comment for less than a second. "You're right, of course. But if I may explain, I think you'll agree. Losing Ezekiel was a blow. Ironically, Private Austin was involved in that as well. But Koertner is quite another matter. He is probably our finest subject so far. Unshakable in his conviction."

"So far," the intercom cautioned Brauner.

"Yes, so far, sir. And I'm convinced he'll hold up well. No matter what she does."

"No matter what?"

"Yes, sir."

"My dear doctor, I think you've been in Resurrection for too long. I'm afraid you have lost touch with reality."

"Sir?" Brauner was puzzled. And a bit wary. He waited for the other shoe to drop.

The voice on the speakerphone taunted Brauner. "Has she fucked him yet?"

Brauner jumped to his feet. His face was flushed with shock. His tonsure stood at attention. "Of course not, sir."

"I know, I know. That would be against all the rules, wouldn't it? You might encourage it though, Bruno. I mean, it's inevitable, isn't it? Sooner or later Koertner is going to find out what he's been missing. So it's probably best if he had his first fling in a controlled environment. Clinically speaking, of course. And Austin might be more than willing to go along, just so she can help him, of course. You said yourself that there was chemistry between them, so why don't you sit back and wait for a chemical reaction. If anything is going to make her spill the beans about her past, this should do it. In the meantime it'll add some spice to your surveillance, wouldn't it?"

The ensuing silence was deafening. Brauner fought to regain his composure. The idea was preposterous. Unthinkable. He balled his hands into tight fists. For a fleeting moment a vision played in his mind. The image of a faint scar blending into the corner of Private Austin's mouth.

Chapter 22

DEAR MOTHER. DON'T get alarmed. I'm okay now.

Cecilia Austin's heart started to race. Her hands trembled. What did she mean by 'I'm okay now'? Why was it that children, even after they were grown and should have more sense, still had an uncanny ability to scare the hell out of their mothers?

I had a little mishap, actually more than a little. I was stabbed in the hand. And it happened at the worst possible time, right after I found one of my patients had committed suicide and I was really depressed. But I'm getting ahead of myself. You see, I was temporarily reassigned to a maximum security facility in Shandaken after what happened in the library...ooops, I guess you don't know about that either, do you?

Despite Dawn's claim that everything was okay she couldn't calm herself. What on earth was going on? She'd had a bad taste in her mouth ever since Dawn had sprung Resurrection on her. Now her worst fears had apparently come true. A prison was no place for someone like her daughter. Self-recrimination mixed with anger, except she wasn't sure if she was angry at Dawn or at herself. Both, she thought, because Dawn was so damn thick-headed and she hadn't been thick-headed enough. Damn, damn, damn.

It's a long story and I don't want to alarm you unnecessarily so I'll just give you the bare facts. This whole thing started a couple of days after boot camp. It was all very innocent, and I guess I was a little naïve. You see, I needed a book from the library and didn't want to wait until the morning, so I decided to get it right then and there. Except it was after curfew and I wasn't supposed to be out by myself. Anyhow, I talked the night watchman at the library into letting me in. And that's when I got slugged. I mean, it wasn't much of a mugging by Manhattan standards but in Resurrection things like that just don't happen. Apparently someone had broken into the place and punched me when I surprised him. The end result was that I was knocked out, the night watchman who let me in got into trouble and I was reprimanded for breaking curfew. I thought that was the end of it but obviously it wasn't.

A couple of days later they reassigned me to Shandaken (I'll tell you more about that place in a minute). They said they needed someone to cover for another counselor but I don't believe it. The way they hustled me out of Resurrection City, like I had the plague, well, let's just say they didn't throw me a bon voyage party. And guess whom I ran into over there? Yep, none other than the night watchman I just told you about. So I guess being sent to Shandaken is the standard punishment in this place.

Anyway, things weren't going all that great. I was just coming out of a bad case of depression after one of my patients had hanged herself. So when I ran into this guy in the cafeteria I was happy to see a familiar face. I guess that's why I let my guard down, or maybe I wasn't thinking too clearly. Whatever, even though I noticed he was talking kind of strange, like a lunatic actually, it didn't really register. That's pretty funny, huh, considering I was trained to recognize strange behavior. Well, in this case I blew it. I must have said something to set him off and by the time I realized he was actually blaming me for getting sent to the Siberia of Resurrection it was too late. Before I could get up and find another seat he attacked me. It was really weird. You see, he was eating spaghetti and meatballs and all of a sudden he stabbed me with his fork, spaghetti and all. At first I thought I had tomato sauce all over on my hand. When I found out it was blood I almost fainted.

Let me tell you mom, this place can give you the creeps. As soon as I get a chance I'm going to do some good old fashioned snooping and find out what's going on. I have a hunch but that's all it is right now and I don't really want to say anymore. Anyway, I got this creepy feeling as soon as I got to this place. At first I thought it was because it was a prison. I mean, you can call it Camp or, as the people here like to call it, a "social experiment," but it's still a prison. There are guards and walls and barbed wire. And everybody here knows it. Despite all the subliminal propaganda they feed you, a prison is a prison is a prison. I don't want to sound disenchanted, because I'm not. But I'm not a Pollyanna any more *either. I guess the best way to describe Resurrection is that it reminds me of a body farm, like they're raising people but none of them have a mind of their own. It's creepy.*

There are some exceptions though. My patient is a real nice guy. If I can get through to him I think I can really help him. He must have been hiding the day they gave everyone around here a lobotomy. He still thinks for himself. Once I even got him angry. Around here that's real progress. And then there's my boss, Bruno B. Brauner. What a piece of work this guy is. If anyone ever fit the description of a wolf in sheep's clothing, Brauner does. He keeps watching me with a funny look and when I catch him staring at me he smiles and acts like he's my father confessor. Maybe he's got the hots for me. Ugh. Either that or he doesn't trust me.

Well, enough of that. Now for the good news. My hand is healing fine (I didn't even catch rabies or mad cow disease from the food), the tetanus shot didn't hurt at all and David (that's my patient) was just approved for elevation to apostle this morning. That's inside lingo for being paroled. It takes effect tomorrow, on Resurrection Day. That, just in case you didn't already know it, is the biggest holiday of the year around here. I know it's all hype and hoopla, but even I got caught up in it. I was so proud when I found out that he made it. I'm just sorry I'm going to miss it. It's kind of hard to explain, but in a way I feel like I'm his mother. Imagine that. The guy's seven years older than me and I think of him as a little kid.

Sorry to be babbling on and on about myself. How are you? I bet you're miserable not having me to boss around, huh? How's work? I hope you're not spending twenty hours a day in the office. Go out and have some fun, mom. Now's your chance. Imagine, you can bring a date home without having to worry about me busting in on you and embarrassing you. And how's Max? I really miss that dopey mutt. I'll never complain again about him jumping into bed with me. By the way, thanks for giving Chaz my address. I'll be nice' to hear from him again. I bet you never expected to hear that from me but after a couple of weeks in Resurrection even a Columbia nerd looks good. Please write soon and I'll do the same. Love, D.

Chapter 23

"SO HOW DID it go with Axton?"

For someone who'd just faced the grand inquisition Justin seemed in a pretty good mood. From the looks of it he was more relaxed than I was, sauntering into our room and dropping a handful of papers on the desk.

"Not bad," he said. "Actually I think Axton did me a favor when he caught me last night."

I couldn't believe my ears. This wasn't the Justin I knew. I said, "Wow. They really must have done a number on you. You're the last person in the world I expected to say something like that."

Justin grinned sheepishly. "Yeah well, you never know how you react until it happens to you. All I can say is that I must have been a real pain in the ass all these years."

I agreed. "You're right, about being a pain in the ass, I mean. But I can't believe that you're admitting it. I've been trying to talk some sense into that thick head of yours for years and now you see Axton one time and all of a sudden you're a changed man. What the hell did he tell you?"

Justin was evasive. "Oh, just stuff."

"I can't believe it. Tell me, who was there, what'd they say? C'mon man, don't keep me in suspense."

"It's really not a big deal," Justin said. "Nothing special happened. It was just Axton and me and Brauner. No Paulette, no Austin, nobody else. Instead of shipping me off to *The House* Brauner gave me a special Retooling session. Imagine that, one hour with that little weasel was all the punishment I got. And you know, when I was done with Retooling Axton made me feel right at home. I mean, he didn't try to intimidate me or threaten me or anything like that. He even offered me some of his private stuff, some real smooth cognac. And one of his cigars. Let me tell you, David, those things are wicked. I never had one before but I didn't want to look like a wimp, so I said okay, I'll have one. Well, let me tell you, I inhaled it like it was a cigarette and I started coughing so hard I almost busted a gut."

"Okay, okay," I interrupted him, getting impatient. I wanted to hear the meat of the story. "I don't care about his cigars. Tell me what happened, like what you talked about and what happened at Retooling.? Didn't he ask you what you were doing at Paulette's?"

"Oh sure. At first I tried to give him some cock and bull story. I told him that I, well, you know, that I wanted Paulette, which of course meant that I had to confess that she I and I got it on before. I didn't really want to say that to him but I figured it was better than admitting what I really wanted to do. But he didn't buy a word of it. He just smiled and said *C'mon Justin, we both know you didn't come here for that. You didn't even look for her in the bedroom, so what's the real reason?* When I didn't answer he poured me a refill. Then we clinked glasses and he made a toast. *To the truth*, he said. *Go ahead, Justin, why don't you come clean and tell me. You were trying to bust out of here, weren't you?* Well, I thought that's it, straight to the House and adios Resurrection City."

"And?"

"And nothing. Instead of arresting me he said 'Why don't you talk to David. He knows about all that stuff. He'll tell you all about it.' So I guess that's what I'm gonna do, talk to you about it I mean. So go ahead, David."

Talk about having the tables turned on you. I wasn't so sure I really understood what I'd learned, so how could I explain it to Justin? Neither did I know how much I should tell him. Some of this stuff had to be confidential, I thought, certainly what Private Austin had told me about herself, and the rest, well, what would Brauner say if I repeated all this stuff to Justin? It's one thing to talk about the outside, but how do you explain things like original sin?

Now it was Justin's turn to prod me for answers. "Well, come on, I'm all ears."

I squirmed. "I really don't know all that much either. I heard a couple of things, you know, the same kind of stuff you've been bugging me about for years."

"Like?"

"Like about the outside," I admitted, cursing Axton under my breath. "Private Austin told me about where she used to live, some place called Manhattan, and a school she went to. I don't know if she was telling me the truth though. I mean, the whole story could have been some sort of subliminal suggestion therapy."

Justin was impressed. "Them's pretty big words for a Disciple. How about telling me in plain English what it means."

"Well, this is all way above my head, but what it boils down to is this. If you plant some ideas in someone's head you can create inner conflict. According to Brauner that conflict can then be used to let patients differentiate between fact and fiction, or good versus evil, and if the good wins out you'll be able to suppress evil feelings."

I wasn't so sure that that's exactly how Brauner had put it but it sounded good. Justin apparently thought so too. "Makes sense," he said. "Like in my case, I now understand that it was wrong to see Paulette. You see, when I put it in perspective I can see what she really is, a selfish woman who used me for her own personal gratification." He smiled sheepishly. "Those are Axton's words, not mine. I guess he and Brauner went to the same psych classes."

"That's what he said about Paulette?" I asked. "Didn't he ask you how you felt about her?"

"No, why should he?"

"Because Brauner wanted to know how I felt about Private Austin. And that's what bothers me about this whole thing. Like I said, I don't know if this wasn't just some psych test, in which case I have no idea if what she told me is true or not. The only thing I'm sure of right now is that I'm not sure of anything anymore except that I know how I feel about Private Austin."

If I had expected Justin to give me a smart-ass answer I was disappointed. Instead of making a suggestive remark, which is what he would have done in the past, he seemed genuinely interested in my explanation. He said to me, "And how do you feel about her? Believe me, I'm not trying to embarrass you or anything like that. I'm really interested.

I shook my head. "I wish I knew. All I know is that I kind of like her. Don't ask me why but there's something about her. I can't really explain it, but it's different than how I ever felt about anyone else before."

Justin whistled softly and gave me an odd look, a sort of faraway gaze as though he'd just heard something of profound importance and was letting it percolate inside his brain. Finally he spoke, and what he said scared the hell out of me. "You know, David, that sounds a lot like I used to feel about Paulette. Maybe you ought to tell Axton. I mean, if the guy can help someone like me I'm sure he can cure you of Austin."

*****

Brauner had two surprises waiting for me.

"Congratulations, David. I just got word from the Justice Ministry. You will become our newest Apostle. In just one week you…"

One word ran into the next. Here was something I'd wanted all my life and now that it was coming true I had a tough time dealing with it. I recalled what I'd told Justin just half an hour ago, about inner conflict, and I suddenly had more inner conflict than I knew what to do with.

Brauner was surprised by my reaction. I'm not sure what he had expected, but this obviously wasn't it. "David, what's wrong? I thought you'd be thrilled and instead you look like your best friend just died."

Come to think of it, that's pretty much how I felt, too. If I'd thought that my life had become complicated ever since meeting Private Austin, this news turned it upside down and inside out. All I could think of were the negatives, like what it would do to my friendship with Justin, my relationship with other Disciples, and if I could handle the responsibilities, even though I had no idea what my new responsibilities would be.

Brauner must have guessed what was going through my mind. He patted me on the back, a kind of complimentary and reassuring gesture rolled into one, and said, "I know how you feel, David. I know it's a shock but I thought it be best if I told you personally, before you heard it from someone else. No use beating around the bush, right? I mean, if you're going to be an Apostle you must act like one, and dealing with surprises is probably one of the responsibilities you'll have."

He'd said the magic word, responsibility. Here was something concrete, something I could ask about without giving away the way I really felt. "I guess that's what I'm worried about, Doctor. Of course I'm thrilled, but this is all kind of overwhelming. I mean, what'll I do? What kind of responsibilities will I have?"

"Oh, that's easy, I'll tell you all about your duties." He smiled and winked and for some strange reason his gesture offended me, like I was about to be turned into someone like him. He went on, "Of course I'll ease you into it, there's just too much to learn all at once, but before you know it you'll feel comfortable with your new role in life. Believe me, you'll take to it like a duck to water. I think we'll start with your new working quarters, your office, the lab, things like that. What do you say, David. Ready to roll?"

I guess I was. Obviously there was no use in delaying it, and it seemed as good a place as any to start. I nodded.

"Good. Then let's get going." He winked again. "We'll start with Brauner's Kitchen."

Brauner's Kitchen. That was the name given to the labyrinthine warren of offices and labs and vaults and hi-tech computer rooms that occupied the basement of Terwilliger House. Of course it had an official name, *Psychiatric Evaluation and Behavior Control Center,* but everybody called it Brauner's Kitchen. It was where Brauner and his assistants kept their recipes for Retooling and cooked up whatever treatment they prescribed if you needed help. The place was shrouded in secrecy. It was also off-limits.

But no longer off-limits for a newly appointed Apostle. Brauner led the way, down a flight of stairs, through a turnstile that was activated by a card-key, through an inner door that wouldn't open until he placed his hand on a glass panel, and then along a narrow corridor lined with numerous doors and security cameras.

First impressions stay with me. In addition to being intimidated by all the security, a couple of sensations were etched into my brain immediately. Brauner's Kitchen smelled. It wasn't a single odor but several: a strong chemical or medicinal smell, a distinct stench of something so unpleasant I nearly gagged, and an undertone of cleaning fluids. It felt as if I had entered into a hospital ward that had just been scrubbed clean of blood and vomit.

It was also cold, but not the kind of raw winter-cold you experience outdoors. It embraced me with a clammy chill that made me shiver. And above all, Brauner's kitchen hummed. It hummed with a constant drone of generators and unseen machinery, a monotonous thrumming that grew louder the deeper we descended into Brauner's Kitchen. All in all, I thought, a spooky place, but I didn't know if I was spooked by the sudden assault on my senses or because of the mystique associated with Brauner's kitchen.

Brauner hustled me along the corridor, explaining where each door led as we passed it. "This is the video vault. And this door leads to the computer room. Everything in there is connected to the Resurrection network, so we can share information with our other system in Shandaken." He added with obvious pride, "Our computer however is the master system and controls all data throughout Resurrection. And this," he stopped in front of a double-door, "this is our lab area. It's not your typical kind of lab though, not with slides and tubes and all that old-fashioned alchemy stuff you've learned about. In here we do virtual reality research, so it's more like a mixed media room that's connected to the network."

"So this is where you do a lot of Retooling research?" I asked.

Brauner seemed pleased with my question. "That's very astute of you, David. Yes, a lot of what you call retooling was developed in this very room."

I was impressed. And curious. "Can we go in?"

Brauner shook his head. "I'm sorry, David. Not yet. Some areas are going to be off limits, even to you. At least for now," he added. "Someday I'm sure you'll have access to every room down here, but for now I'll have to ease you into it. Call it a need-to-know basis. I'm sure you understand."

I didn't but nodded anyhow. There didn't seem to be much hope of inducing Brauner to show me the entire place, so why bother? But another door caught my attention. This one, unlike all others, was made of metal and didn't have wire-mesh windows of opaque glass. Instead a square sign with a yellow background and three black triangles was mounted eye-level. "What's this? I asked. "It looks ominous."

"It's supposed to," Brauner explained. "It's our nuclear medicine lab. And this one by the way is strictly off limits. As a matter of fact, it's probably best if we don't even discuss it."

"Okay." I followed Brauner, who had accelerated his pace and tried to remember his every word. We passed numerous other doors, most of which led to less ominous rooms. There was an equipment room, a maintenance room, a library, a supply room, the janitor's closet, and on and on and on.

By the time we mounted the steps to the main level I was thoroughly confused as well as amazed by the sheer size of Brauner's Kitchen. I could be wrong, but it seemed to stretch beyond the foundation of Terwilliger House. I didn't mention this to Brauner. For whatever reason, I didn't want him to know how interested I was in the footprint of Brauner's Kitchen. I'd find out sooner or later, I told myself, and was convinced that right now was not the time to be overly inquisitive. Instead I filed it in the back of my brain for future investigation.

Next on Brauner's tour was my new office. It wasn't much of an office, a small, windowless room where Rachel Firestein used to keep her office supplies and ate lunch. Judging from the dagger-look she gave me she resented my invasion. A desk. chair, and book case left little space for anything else. The walls looked the color of pea soup, and the place smelled musty, but it was mine. It had a door. And a nameplate, which made it officially mine. And just like that any misgivings about being Apostle were gone. I had never thought of myself as vain but seeing my name made me tingle with pride. I could learn to love this job.

Back in Brauner's office and eager to get started, I got my second surprise of the day. Unfortunately, this one wasn't pleasant. Brauner sprung it on me toward the end of our conversation. After explaining what my initial duties would be and running through an elaborate and confusing security scheme, which left no doubt that most of Brauner's Kitchen would still be off limits, he escorted me to the door, shook my hand, and dismissed me with a jovial, "Take the rest of the day off, David and enjoy yourself. You're going to be one busy young man from now on. And by the way, you'll be seeing an awful lot of me. I'll be counseling you myself."

His words deflated me immediately. His Wild Turkey rose in my throat like a lick of fire. My coveted private office suddenly loomed as a lonely place. "Oh? What happened to Private Austin?"

I said this as casually as I could but I'm sure Brauner noticed my disappointment. He said "I thought it best if I stepped in at this point. I discussed it with her and she agreed."

I lingered at the door and he shot a probing look at me. "Anything else, David?"

"No, not really, You wouldn't mind if I stopped by her room on my way home, would you, sir? I'd just like to thank her."

A steely hardness glazed Brauner's eyes. "I'm afraid that won't be possible. Private Austin is gone. It seems she didn't quite fit in here. She felt that the progress she made with you was poor. Although she didn't come right out and say so, I think she didn't want to see you any longer. I think you turned out to be a bigger challenge than she'd bargained for. I'm not sure what her real motives were, but there was a fair amount of animosity. Maybe she blamed you for her own shortcomings. In any event, she asked me to get her an emergency discharge. I agreed, and so did Colonel Axton."

Chapter 24

CECILIA AUSTIN SLIPPED into her nightgown, poured a glass of Sherry for a nightcap and allowed Max to curl up next to her on the couch. Her day had been stressful, a common experience lately, and she looked forward to a few moments of relaxation. She turned to channel 27 and was watching *NY In The News* when the doorbell rang.

Startled, she checked her watch. It was fifteen minutes to midnight. The presence of someone at her front door at this hour was frightening. When she realized the concierge hadn't rung her apartment to let her know she had a visitor she became doubly frightened. Her heart thumping in her chest Cecilia drew a robe around her shoulders and walked to the front door. Afraid of making any noise and letting the intruder know that she was home, she pressed her eye against the peephole and stared at the dimly lit corridor. Staring back at her was the face of a stranger.

He stood too closely to the door to let Cecilia see anything other than his head and shoulders. From the looks of it he was in his thirties, athletically trim, with closely cropped brown hair and pink complexioned. He seemed to be the stereotypical all-American, quietly confident, intelligent, and devoid of any ethnic facial characteristics. Certainly not a door to door salesman, she thought, and definitely not a religious fanatic trying to convert her to the sect of the moment.

The man stepped back from the door, affording Cecilia a look from his waist up. He was well-dressed, wearing a dark blue suit, white button down shirt, and red tie with diagonal white stripes.

A leather attaché case completed the look of a corporate executive who'd gotten lost on his way to the boardroom.

The doorbell rang a second time.

"Who is it?" Cecilia asked, her eye still glued to the peephole.

The man leaned forward until his mouth filled her field of vision. "Ma'am. This is Officer Warner. US Department of Justice, Internal Affairs. I need to speak with you. It is a matter of some urgency."

Cecilia hesitated. Every night the news was full of yet another scam designed to trick people into opening their doors to strangers. But the US Department of Justice? She kept her hand on the safety chain, asking her sixth sense if the stranger could be believed.

"Ma'am. If you'll permit, I'll slide my identification under the door. We recommend that you also call Internal Affairs to verify the ID. You can find their number in the on our website. Their address is DOJ.gov/intaff. They'll confirm my identification. Warner. Emmanuel Warner, shield number 7749553."

*****

Emmanuel Warner was thoroughly practiced in these after-hour calls. His facial expression was one of complete stoicism. He looked devoid of emotion. Once inside Cecilia Austin's apartment he opened his attaché case and extracted a thin envelope. His hands were as steady as the rock of Gibraltar.

"Mrs. Austin. It is with the United States Government's deepest regrets that I have to inform you that your daughter was killed on November 2 in an automobile accident on her way to…"

The words refused to sink in. Cecilia Austin looked at Officer Warner with disbelief. Her fingertips started to tingle. The tingle spread up her arms and into her chest. The cheerful colors and fabrics of her living room dissolved into slushy gray. Somewhere, a million miles away, Max began to bark and nudged her with his wet nose.

"…will be returned to you as soon as it is released by the Medical Examiner. Since your daughter died while serving her country, she qualifies for interment in a National cemetery. You may, of course, decline to avail yourself of this option and bury her in a plot of your choosing. Furthermore, since Private Austin…"

How could she feel so dead inside when it was Dawn he is talking about? How could a total void of feeling, a complete absence of physical and emotional sensations, be so painful? If she were to cut off her arm she wouldn't feel anything other than numbness. A knife could slice through her flesh and bones, blood could spurt from the wound, and it wouldn't hurt as much as this numbness. Nothingness caused ultimate agony. With nothingness came hopelessness. Without hope there was no foundation upon which to rebuild her life. Without hope there was only eternal pain.

"…in the amount of three thousand six hundred forty eight dollars and twenty two cents. In addition, your daughter's personal belongings will be released by the Internal Affairs Department within one week.

"The United States government is deeply saddened by your daughter's untimely death. You may take some solace in the fact that your daughter was a dedicated soldier on the side of truth and justice. Her immediate supervisor, Dr. Bruno Brauner, has recommended that the *Sword and Cross*, Resurrection's highest medal, be posthumously awarded to your daughter for her dedication and valor in the fight against crime."

Max was barking louder by the minute. What on earth was wrong with him? He usually ignored strangers in the house. Tonight he was downright surly, baring his teeth and snarling. Officer Warner slid his chair several inches backwards to distance himself discreetly from Max. He snapped his attaché case shut and rose.

"Again my deepest sympathy, Mrs. Austin. You can be sure that the government…"

Warner's lack of emotion made the pain worse. Running through his speech as if it were a sales pitch he might as well be selling vacuum cleaners. He probably hadn't even known Dawn's name until he rode up the elevator, casually checking his folder between floors. He probably did this sort of thing all the time. The government's town crier delivering obituaries as if they were singing telegrams. Cecilia wondered how Warner slept at night. Probably very well, she told herself bitterly. After all, nobody came knocking on his door in the middle of the night.

"Do you have any children, Mr. Warner?" she asked.

"No ma'am."

"I didn't think so."

Chapter 25

"You know, you have an attitude problem."

Justin's observation summed up my state of mind perfectly. It was the day before Resurrection day, a glum and dreary afternoon that matched my mood to a tee. He went on, "I don't know what's bugging you, but if it's your coronation to exalted Apostle, I sure as hell hope they never kick me up a rung on the resurrection ladder."

Sarcastic bastard, I thought but bit my tongue. Justin really had become insufferable since Axton caught him at Paulette's apartment and turned him into a model Disciple. Now he wasn't just a plain, ordinary pain in the ass, he was a sarcastic, holier-than-thou pain in the ass. Nobody likes a smart ass, especially if that smart ass happens to be right. I did have an attitude problem and it was getting worse the closer I got to my coronation.

I guess it had started the day I thought I was going crazy. As a matter of fact, I was still miffed at Brauner laughing at me. But that wasn't the only reason I was miffed at him, nor was he the only one I was pissed off at. As a matter of fact, my hate-list grew longer as my temper grew shorter. For some strange reason, Brauner occupied the top spot. He was condescending and pretentious. I hated it when he put his arm around my shoulder. I hated the smell of Wild Turkey on his breath. I hated his fringe of gray hair, always neatly trimmed, surrounding his glowing pink scalp, making him look like an ersatz angel with an ersatz halo. I hated the liver spots on his hands. I hated his arrogant control of what I could and couldn't do. And I hated it when he looked at me like a benevolent father. Most of all though I hated him for taking Private Austin away from me. That's how I viewed it. She belonged to me, she was my guide on my journey into a new life I knew nothing about. I desperately needed her and now she was gone. Gone. God I hated Brauner.

Brauner may have been at the top of my list but he wasn't the only one. I hated Rachel Firestein and her supercilious and meddlesome ways. She ruled Brauner's office like a queen bee and treated me as if I were her personal minion. And to be perfectly honest, there weren't too many Disciples I liked nowadays. They were all jealous and it showed. Even Justin wasn't immune. Last on my list, but certainly not least, was yours truly. I didn't want to admit it, but I didn't like what I had become. Oddly enough, even though Private Austin was primarily responsible for the change in my personality, she hadn't made it on my hate-list. As a matter of fact, I missed my stormy sessions with her more than ever.

So when Justin lectured me on this gray afternoon my first reaction was to lash out at him. But we were brothers and deep down I knew there was more than a kernel of truth in what he said.

"I'm sorry," I said to him. I really meant it too. A rush of emotions swept through me. Love and hate and sorrow and disappointment collided. Shit! Life had sure become hard. "I'm sorry," I said again. "I know I've been a bit edgy lately. Just bear with me for a little while longer. I'm sure that as soon as it's official…" I didn't finish the sentence.

"Well, I sure hope so. Except it won't matter then. I mean, you'll be an Apostle and I'll just be the same imperfect Disciple I've always been."

"That's not fair," I said. "Why are you doing this?"

"It's the truth, isn't it?" he said. "You'll move into your own place, right? And you'll hobnob with the upper echelon. I bet you'll have a bunch of new friends too, like Private Austin."

"I doubt it," I said. "Private Austin is gone for good. Quit. Ran out on me."

"No shit." Justin was surprised. "Did she say why?"

"I didn't talk to her but Doc Brauner said she gave up on me, didn't want anything to do with me anymore."

Justin looked puzzled. "Well he's lying," he said. "Brauner shipped her off to Shandaken."

"What makes you say that?"
"That's what Axton told me and why the hell would he lie?"
Yeah, I thought. Why would he?

*****

Justin and I made peace. Sort of, anyhow. We both retreated into our own worlds and left each other alone. For him that meant lounging on his bunk and reading comic books, a habit he'd gotten into lately. For me it meant packing a few last minute things and moving to Schryden Hall.

By five in the evening I was finished. Two cardboard boxes stood next to the door. One contained what I called 'work stuff': a couple of notebooks in which I recorded interviews and reports, back issues of the Sentinel, including the prized first issue with my name on the masthead, a PC manual, more number two pencils that I'd ever need, paper clips, erasers, markers and so on.

The second box held my meager personal belongings, primarily knickknacks of dubious value, like a debating team trophy, a battery operated radio with two dead batteries, and a photo album. The plastic-sleeve album was a trip back in time, picturing me during high school graduation, hiking Mount Tremper with troop 17 of the Resurrection City boy scouts, and me blowing out thirty-five candles at a surprise birthday party Justin had thrown me a few years back. Nostalgia isn't my thing but for some inexplicable reason I treasured this album and its fading memorabilia.

My Resurrection Rags were still in the closet. I wouldn't need them any longer. As an apostle, I'll be issued new clothing. Real clothes for real people. Suits and shirts and ties and leather shoes. No more jeans and sneakers for David Koertner. Now it was Apostle Koertner, and his new status demanded appropriate attire. So why couldn't I bring myself to dump my rags in the trash?

At the last moment I remembered my most prized possession. I retrieved Private Austin's letter from my nightstand. I turned it over in my hands, then gave in to an impulse to read what I now knew was her goodbye. *David. Sorry to run out on you like this but I was called on an emergency assignment. Dr. Brauner insisted. I'll stop by your room as soon as I get back. Please see Dr. Brauner for your psych sessions. He really cares for you and is very concerned about your wellbeing. He knows you much better than I do and can probably help you more than I ever could. But you have to give him your complete trust. Without it, no one can help you achieve your important next step. And remember what I told you. It's okay to be human. Private D. Austin.*

It had all the elements of saying goodbye. It sounded very much as if she wanted to explain why Doc Brauner was good for me. It also sounded as if she had anticipated my new-found irritability and wanted to reassure me that it was normal behavior. But it sure as hell didn't sound like she had abandoned me. If she had run out on me as Doc Brauner claimed she would have said so.

I replaced the letter in the envelope and put it inside my photo album. That's where it belonged, with other memorabilia, other events frozen in time. Events that belonged to Disciple Koertner. And Disciple Koertner was a thing of the past.

Farewells with Justin were unemotional. We shook hands.

"See you around, Davey. And good luck."

"Yeah, see you."

And that was it. No teary-eyed embraces. No phony protestations of staying buddies. We both knew that a lot more than three blocks would separate us and neither tried to deny it.

I walked the three blocks to Schryden Hall with a cardboard box under each arm. A uniformed guard was stationed outside the front door to check credentials. His job wasn't to limit my own movements or even to monitor them. Rather it was his responsibility to make sure that only a limited number of Disciples, those authorized by Colonel Axton, were allowed to visit. Justin's name was not on the list.

My new quarters were impressive by anyone's standards. Fifteen square meters of luxury, outfitted with comfortable furniture. Color coordinated sheets and pillowcases and towels and curtains. A TV of my own and a radio. A private bathroom. And above all, a front door with a lock.

I dropped my boxes on the bed and waited for the guard to bring me a set of keys. He knocked on the door five minutes later and handed them to me. One key was attached to a metal ring. I signed for it, he saluted, and left. As far as I was concerned, the damn key was as much to lock me out of Resurrection City as it was to guarantee my privacy. I shrugged my shoulders.

I really had to do something about my attitude.

*****

My most vivid recollection of Resurrection Day was a confrontation with Colonel Axton. Among the class of over two-thousand Disciples, including ten candidates for Apostlehood next year, I stood out like a sore thumb against a sea of green Disciple robes, white shirts, and ties. At the last minute, with my belongings already unpacked in Schryden Hall, I had made an impulsive return trip to Greenkill House and room 311.

It led to an uncomfortable encounter with Justin. His new roommate was there, a young Disciple whom I'd never seen before. I disliked him the moment I saw him, probably because I resented him taking my place in room 311. I ignored him and headed straight for Justin, throwing my arms around him and giving him an old-fashioned bear hug. Justin stiffened and drew away, obviously embarrassed. My replacement seemed equally as embarrassed, going to great lengths to avoid looking at me and stealing from the room as soon as he could.

"I just came back to get some clothes," I said.

"Help yourself," Justin said. He pointed to an overflowing bag in the closet. "I was just going to bring them to the laundry." He looked at me, letting his eyes linger on brand new chinos, a flannel shirt, and docksiders. "What you want them for anyhow? Didn't they give you new rags?"

"Just a whim," I said. "I guess I wanted them for nostalgia."

"Whatever turns you on," Justin said and looked at me as if I had two heads. "But if I were you I'd bring them to the laundry anyhow. They're kind of wrinkled now."

"That's okay," I said and left without another word.

*****

And now, standing in a light drizzle on the parade grounds, feeling uncomfortable and out of place with my wrinkled Resurrection Rags, Axton regarded me with disdain as I made my way up three steps to the reviewing stand.

"Apostle Koertner, isn't it?" A smirk curled his lips. "Isn't this a rather peculiar choice of attire for today?" He sized me up and wrinkled his nose. "Didn't they issue you some decent clothes?"

"Yes, sir, Colonel. But I thought it appropriate to wear my familiar Rags."

"And why is that, Koertner?"

The coldness in his eyes should have warned me, but my newfound rebelliousness and stubborn refusal to obey the rules made me glad that I had left my new clothes hanging in the closet. "These have served me well all these years, sir, and I wanted to reinforce my belief that although I am now an Apostle, I come from the same humble beginnings as all of them." I raised my arm and swept it in a wide arc across the more than two thousand Disciples who had been ordered to attend today's ceremonies.

"I suppose you succeeded," Axton added with another smirk. "But I think it would have been more appropriate to point out to your ex-brothers and sisters that you have attained a new station in life."

"With all due respect, sir, that is exactly what I'm trying to avoid. If I'm going to keep their trust they must think of me as one of their own and not as an ex anything."

"Admirable, Koertner, admirable, but misguided. You will soon enough learn that you are a different person now. You're supposed to be better than them and that means dressing better than them. Perception is reality, Koertner, and reality is that you're an Apostle."

"Reality is that I'm still the same person."

Axton smiled. "But you're not, Koertner. Judging by your looks I'm not so sure what you are, but for your own sake I hope you're not the same."

"With all due respect,…"

"This discussion is closed, Koertner. I want you to get rid of those disgusting rags and start acting like an Apostle. So you may as well stop trying to be everybody's friend. Remember, friendship and respect don't mix. Your first loyalty has to lie with the Camp."

"I thought that's what I was trying to express, sir. According to everything I've learned, loyalty to Resurrection isn't possible without respect for its citizens."

Axton shot a questioning look at me and followed up with something totally unexpected. "Perhaps Private Austin taught you more than we all realized."

Perhaps she had.

Chapter 26

"How's she doing?"

A stocky middle-aged man in scrubs leaned forward and watched for dangerous variations in a horizontal line flickering on a computer monitor. During the last ten minutes the spikes had become less pronounced. Now they were mere flickers. Disappointed by the flatness of the line, the man shook his head and switched the computer to display historical activity. The decrease in reactionary activity had become pronounced at the seven minute mark, which coincided with a five percent increase in the impulse module.

"Not so good, she's not reacting at all. I think we better bring it back down to fifteen thousand pulses per minute. I'm afraid she'll be useless if we keep it at this rate any longer. We can always adjust the time-distortion factor to attain maximum impact."

A second man in scrubs agreed reluctantly with the diagnosis. "I'm afraid he's right."

The intercom crackled back to life. "Okay, guys. You know what to do with her. Let me know when you're done."

*****

Paulette Kowalski was fastened to a hospital bed in room 17C. Plastic straps around her ankles and wrists secured her to the bed's safety bars. A thin cotton sheet covered her nude body. A leather harness held her head in place. Several color-coded metal wires ran from the harness to a router, then disappeared into what looked like a wall-mounted power strip.

For the last three minutes she lay in a near catatonic state, wide-eyed, motionless, her chest rising and falling a precise sixty-four times per minute. Despite giving the appearance of sleeping, Kowalski was wide awake. She had never been more terrified in her life. When the unimaginable horror had gradually ceased three minutes ago she prayed that she were dead, but constant electrical impulses wracking her body reminded her that the end had not yet come.

She tried to blot the last day from her mind but the memories were etched into her brain. She knew that she was tied to a hospital bed. She had witnessed with her own eyes as two men in hospital greens fastened plastic straps to her ankles and wrists. But she couldn't feel the straps any longer. All sensations had left her limbs. Neither could she move them. She tried to wriggle her toes and twitch her fingers but her extremities were dead weight, numb and inert.

She also recalled that her head had been shaven. That had occurred at the very beginning, before the pain had started. They had blindfolded her, but the snipping sounds of scissors, followed by an angry buzz, were unmistakable. When they had removed the blindfold she'd kept her eyes closed, afraid of what she might see, but they had forced her eyelids open, held a small mirror before her, and made her stare at her bare skull. Then they had fastened her head inside a harness, a horrible contraption that resembled a gas mask and made her look like an alien monster. The harness dug into her temples and constricted her nose, while keeping her head elevated at an uncomfortable angle. Even more terrifying though were the yellowish goggles that covered her eyes and transformed the room around her into a sulfuric hell. And then the nightmare had started.

Kowalski was shocked that she could remember every minute detail of her ordeal with such amazing clarity. She still felt agonizing pain sear her body. She still saw the assortment of surgical instruments. She could still smell the stench of vomit and feces. She still remembered the lulls, when she had apparently blacked out, only to be jolted into wide-eyed terror by renewed agonizing horrors. Those interludes of relief were the worst. They never lasted long and they foretold the next wave of agony.

She had screamed for hours until her throat was raw and the slightest vibration of her vocal chords sent flickers of pain through her body. Eventually her screams had turned to whimpers. Now she waited in silence, counting seconds, trying to brace herself for what she knew would come next.

She didn't have to wait long. Viewed through her yellow goggles, the door to room 17C opened and two opaque figures walked to her bed. She saw them speak but couldn't hear the words because the harness's earflaps dulled all sounds. As they approached, Paulette willed herself to speak. But her lack of muscular control left her tongue motionless. She managed a hoarse croak and both men turned their heads in her direction. Desperate, she tried again, ignoring the pain, and whispered, "Please let me die."

"Did you hear that?" A yellowish outline of a man's face filled her goggles.

"Hear what?"

"It sounded like she said something. Listen."

"You're nuts. She's out cold."

The face disappeared from her field of vision, replaced by shadowy outlines of the hospital room. Paulette made one more desperate effort to let them know that she was wide awake, that she could see and hear and feel the pain that slashed her insides with increasing regularity. She inhaled, filling her lungs with air, waiting until she was about to burst, then hurled a scream as she exhaled, hoping against hope that her voice would be audible above the hiss of escaping air. Nothing, not even a whimper this time.

"All right, let's get going."

At that moment Paulette knew. She didn't understand how she knew. She couldn't see the two men any longer. She couldn't make out their garbled voices. She didn't see rubber-gloved hands or gleaming instruments. But she knew. She knew someone was cutting and scraping and slashing inside her uterus. And for the first time, raw terror was worse than physical pain.

She fainted. The room turned from yellow to gray to black. Voices slowed to an infinite crawl until they were a constant drone. She sobbed and prayed again for death.

When she came to, she screamed silently. No one heard her. As the haze lifted, patch by patch like fog dissipating beneath a brightening sun until the yellowish glow spread over her goggles, she saw the room and the men and a metal cart being wheeled out the door by a nurse. "Hurry up, will you. They want the embryo in the lab right away. And tell Callahan we're just about done with her. We just have to cauterize her, stitch her up and put her on ice."

*****

How do you commit suicide when you are strapped to a bed, without the use of arms, unable to turn your head and smother yourself with a pillow? Paulette stopped breathing. She pressed her lips together and clenched her jaws and held her breath only to have her body rebel fifty seconds later. With her heart racing, her blood slowing to a trickle in her veins, her lungs threatened to implode, she sucked the sterile cold of her refrigerated room and cursed herself for her weakness.

Her tongue had swollen into a grotesque lump and she had trouble swallowing. Saliva built up in her mouth until she choked and began to cough. Each convulsion intensified the pain. At last she managed to spit out the mucous fluid, feeling the slime slither across her lips and chin and collect in her harness' mouthpiece.

A voice drifted through her curtain of agony. "Hello, Paulette. I know you find it uncomfortable to talk, but maybe you can nod your head?"

She didn't move.

"No? That's a shame. Quite frankly I am disappointed in you. I thought your threshold for pain was greater than this."

Why couldn't they let her die? She had told them everything hours ago. The thought of slipping into death became an obsession. She dreamed of oblivion, of sweet darkness.

"Pain is only a state of mind, Paulette. If we numb your mind, we'll numb your pain as well. But that would be counterproductive. And all of this will have been for nothing. No, I'm afraid we can't do that. Not just yet. You see, we need you just a little while longer. Pleasant dreams, Paulette."

Chapter 27

I took Axton's Resurrection Day warning to heart and got rid of my "disgusting rags." I wasn't worried about what he'd do if I didn't, but why make waves? I had enough problems, not the least of which was trying to act like an Apostle. So when I arrived at Terwilliger the Monday after Resurrection Day I looked like I belonged there. I was decked out in a brand-new camp-issued pinstriped suit, white cotton shirt and conservative blue silk tie. On the outside at least I was ready.

Brauner made sure that the inner Koertner was prepared as well. Minutes after I took a seat behind my desk he knocked on the door and waited for me to ask him in. I was duly impressed. The mere fact that he didn't barge in spoke volumes about my new stature.

"Good morning, David," he said and surveyed the tiny office. "Very nice, yes very nice. I'll have to dig around for some tchachkas to dress it up. In the meantime, I have something for you that'll look perfect right there." He pointed to the wall behind my desk and handed me a framed certificate, proclaiming me Apostle, graduating class of 2089. "I had it framed yesterday."

"Thank you, sir."

"What's with this *sir* stuff?" Doc Brauner said and gave me a conspiratorial wink. "I've been Doc all these years, so let's keep it that way."

"Okay, Doc."

"That's better. Now then, I'd love to chat for a while and welcome you properly but I'm afraid there isn't any time for that. I know you're raring to go and so am I. And I want to make sure that you're ready before I leave."

"Leave?" I looked at him with surprise and panic. I had visions of sitting alone at my desk. No Doc Brauner, no Private Austin, no help whatsoever, trying to answer phones, answer questions, and cope with everyday problems by myself. The vision didn't have a happy ending. "Where are you going?"

"Did you forget? I'll be off to attend the annual Correction Facility Psychiatrist's convention on Friday morning."

"Oh yeah," I said, my voice trembling with fear. I had forgotten. Once a year Doc Brauner and Axton went on a two-day sabbatical, an event that obviously had never mattered to me. Business went on as usual during their absence. Lieutenant Sanchez took over for Axton and the newest Apostle took over for Brauner. Except that this year I was that newest Apostle and I had no idea what I was supposed to do.

"Don't worry, David. I'll only be gone for two days and we'll have the rest of the week to get you up to snuff. Besides, you already know most of the things you'll have to take care of. So all we have to do is fill in the blanks for you."

Easier said than done, I thought. Before you can fill in the blanks you have to know what and where the blanks are. I started saying this to Doc Brauner but he waved aside my doubts with uncharacteristic ebullience. Apparently he felt better than I did about my promotion. "Don't you worry. It'll be a piece of cake. I bet by the time I return you'll wish I'd stay away for the rest of your life." With that he took me by the arm and dragged me into his office. Once there, he closed the door and whispered, "Dreadful snoop, that Firestein. That's the first thing you'll need to learn. Watch what you say in front of her and never trust her. She'll twist everything around and broadcast it all over Resurrection. But enough about her. Let's start with the most important and complex issue you'll have to deal with for the rest of your career, the human mind."

Again I was shocked. I had expected a cram course in paperwork and computers and things of that nature. Judging from the reams of paper that covered every square inch of Brauner's desk and the amount of time he spent in front of his computer, that's where he clearly needed help. But psychiatry? This was going to be harder than I'd thought, but also a lot more interesting. If I played my cards right I could even find out some of the things I wasn't supposed to find out. Unless of course being an Apostle meant that there wasn't anything left I wasn't supposed to know.

Nevertheless the practical aspects of my job worried me as much as the intangibles. I asked Doc Brauner, "But what about the day to day things, you know, like scheduling appointments and filling out reports and things like that?"

"What do you think we have Rachel the ferret for?" Brauner said. "She's good at stuff like that. Menial paperwork for a menial mind. The real work, the glue that binds Resurrection, concerns the mysteries of the brain. And that's where you and I come in."

"And people like Private Austin," I ventured. As soon as I'd blurted it out I knew I had made a foolish mistake. Brauner reacted angrily. His face turned crimson, his lips tightened, and for a split-second I saw hatred in his eyes.

"That's the second lesson you ought to learn, David, not relying so heavily on your feelings for that woman. There are many things that make people tick, and believe me, not all people tick alike. Again, it goes right back to the crux of things, their minds. Try to look past the obvious, past physical appearances and mannerisms, and try to find out what motivates them. You see, lots of people pursue their own goals at the expense of others. I'm afraid she was one of those. Oh, I admit she was good at it, manipulating your emotions, twisting words, planting suggestive ideas in your mind, getting you to act out of character."

Brauner's attack on Private Austin angered me more than he realized. For whatever reason, probably because I considered her a friend, I blurted out my second foolish remark of the morning. "Sounds to me like Retooling in reverse."

To Brauner's credit he didn't lose his temper. Instead he avoided looking at me, thinking of a diplomatic answer to give to an upstart Apostle like me. "That's an interesting analogy, David, although a dangerous one. We'll get back to Austin a little later but for now I think we had better get going with the business at hand. Now then, what were we talking about?"

"The glue that binds Resurrection," I said sarcastically, giving myself a mental kick in the butt. Obviously I was still having an attitude problem and what made it worse was that I enjoyed goading Doc Brauner. Politically incorrect, I knew, but a lot of fun. Chicken soup for the soul.

He went on as though he hadn't heard me. "Yes, the glue. And now that you mentioned it, Retooling as well. Which by the way will bring us full circle to Private Austin and her... Well, let me keep quiet about her since you obviously still harbor feelings for her. You'll see the truth when the time comes."

I made my first politically correct statement of the day and didn't like myself for it. "I'm sorry I was sarcastic before, Doc. It's just that my nerves are a little frayed right now. I think you can understand that, with all my new responsibilities and all and you leaving in a few days."

"Apology accepted. Tell me, David, since you're in such a, let's see how I can put this delicately, in such a combative mood this morning, what do you think I meant when I said that you still harbored feelings for her?"

I shrugged my shoulders. "I'm not sure. Maybe that I trusted her too much?"

"Well, that's part of it, but there's more to it than that. Obviously you know that there's more to Resurrection than meets the eye. I mean, Private Austin told you about growing up in a place called Manhattan so you know that there's a place besides Resurrection. You've learned some pretty shocking truths in a pretty short time. Obviously it affected you. The once trusting and ingenuous David seems to have become a doubting Thomas. And I think it changed your personality in other ways too. It's pretty clear that you've become sarcastic and angry at times. I'm afraid that's not the lot of it though. How about deceitful? How am I doing so far, David? Would you care to comment?"

Talk about being combative. This was a side of Brauner I hadn't seen before and although I didn't know exactly what Brauner was referring to. I had the feeling that he was maneuvering me into a corner. *Be careful*, I told myself. Regardless of how I felt about him lately, one thing hadn't changed. He was still Brauner, smart and shrewd and perceptive.

"What's the matter? Cat's got your tongue?"

"I have no idea what you meant," I said. "Yeah, I'm changed all right but I thought that was the purpose of my sessions with Austin. And yes, I get angry at times and I know I was sarcastic before. But deceitful?"

Brauner smiled unpleasantly. Satisfied that he apparently had me right where he wanted me, he rose from his chair and turned his attention to the wall behind his desk. He touched a concealed button and I watched as two wall panels slid open noiselessly, revealing a disc player and television. Agitated now, Brauner unlocked his filing cabinet, reached into the bottom drawer, and came away with a disk which he slipped into the player.

"I'm going to leave you alone for a while. I want you to watch this video and give me your analysis when it's over. I should warn you though, some of the things you'll see will surprise you, others will shock you. Be that as it may, I want you to watch with scientific detachment. Don't form any hasty opinions until it's over. Then throw out your initial reaction because it will be biased. Instead take a few minutes to think. Have a cup of coffee or help yourself to some Wild Turkey. Put yourself in my shoes. After you've done some serious soul-searching you can buzz me and we'll continue our discussion. One word of warning, David. Everything we've talked about so far and everything you'll see must remain confidential. Not a word to anyone, you understand? No one. Including your best friend. Including any security personnel, especially Axton."

With that Brauner slipped out of the office, leaving the remote control in my hand. As if his lecture hadn't been ominous enough, mentioning Axton had been downright chilling. Axton and I had never talked before, except for that short conversation on Resurrection Day, and I had absolutely no reason to think that I'd ever talk to him again. But the mere mention of his name raised the specter of a sinister cabal that made me queasy. Add to that Brauner's inference about deceitfulness and I wished I could turn the clock back a couple of years. Life was getting more complicated by the hour.

I hunched forward in my seat, clicked *Play*, and watched.

On the screen, white letters against a black background marched left to right. *Property of the United States Department of Justice, Internal Affairs. This video contains information classified as confidential by the National Security Act of 2037. Case # 0411-56378. Access by unauthorized personnel is prohibited and punishable under provisions of Article 17 of the criminal code of the United States.* The warning was followed by a white bar code. Then the interior of a room all too familiar came into focus.

I was stunned as I followed the crystal clear images of David Koertner and Dawn Austin move about in Doc Brauner's examination room. I felt increasingly like a voyeur spying on two strangers. I was furious that my privacy had been violated. And I felt empathy for this frail young woman with a sad smile and compassionate eyes.

I didn't listen to the words, I didn't have to. I could recite them from memory. Like a second-rate melodrama, the scene built to a dramatic climax. She turned on me, taunting me, pushing me to the limit, until I reacted angrily.

I stopped the video and sorted out my feelings. I guess I had known all along but needed to confirm it in my own mind. Yeah, I was angry, but I wasn't angry at her. Whatever she'd done and said was an honest attempt to help me. Or maybe I had it all wrong. Maybe she was the one who needed help and I cut her off. Coming to grips with that possibility convinced me of a couple of things. First, Brauner was right. I had become angry and sarcastic and a whole lot more. Second, Brauner was dead wrong. Austin wasn't to blame. The real target of my anger was me. No, I corrected myself, not just me but everything I stood for, which meant everything I'd been taught, which in turn meant I was really angry at Resurrection itself.

That made me feel a whole lot better because it meant that I wasn't the one having an attitude problem. Hell no, it was the other way around. Brauner was the one with the problem, Brauner and Axton and everyone else in Resurrection. As a matter of fact, Resurrection was the problem, and it wasn't just that there was another world outside its borders. The real problem was why all of us, me and Justin and everyone else, were in Resurrection in the first place. And who put us here?

So Justin had been right all along. That was a bitter pill to swallow. Here I sat, Mister Perfect, Brauner's pet, Resurrection's newest Apostle, and now the laughing stock of Resurrection's powers to be. Well, my halo might be tarnished but that wasn't going to stop me from finding out what the hell Brauner and his equals were doing to us.

And that's when it hit me. The one person who could help me, who'd already told me half the reason she had for coming to Resurrection, had been conveniently removed from my life. *Damn you, Brauner.*

I restarted the video which had less than a minute of drama remaining, but the final seconds were the most powerful. Austin moved to my side and leaned over my chair. I saw and felt her pain as though an electric spark had jumped from her body straight into my soul. Her lips touched my ear, so close, so agonizingly close. Her hair mingled with mine. Her breath touched my skin. I read her silent words, "Come to my room at ten tonight. And don't breathe a word of this to anyone. Ten o'clock. My room."

The drama was over. The screen went blank. I reached for the remote when another set of bar codes appeared and another segment of film started playing. It was only one minute long. There was no sound and the picture was grainy. A date and time stamp played in the lower right hand corner.

At first I didn't recognize where the video was recorded. It was a small room, similar in size to my new quarters, with sparse furnishings and no personal belongings to brighten up drab green walls. A metal frame twin bed was placed alongside the far wall. A night table holding a digital clock radio and an ash tray stood next to the bed. Below the window was a petite wooden desk equipped with a high-intensity desk lamp and a blotter. An office chair on casters, a metal filing cabinet, a three drawer dresser, and an incongruous wing chair completed the furnishings. Judging by the messy appearance, the room's occupant must have left moments ago with all intentions of returning momentarily. The bed was unmade. The dresser drawers stood half-opened. A few personal belongings were strewn on the bed. Next to the bedside lamp I could see a sealed envelope.

It was then, at the precise moment that I noticed the envelope and a split-second before I saw myself entering the room, Chills ran down my spine. I watched as David Koertner looked around the room, whispered a near silent *Private Austin, are you there*, picked up the envelope, placed it in his pants pocket, and left the room a few seconds later.

I clicked *Off* quickly, afraid of seeing any more footage of myself. I must have been too stunned to notice anything. I didn't feel the sweat which had soaked through my button-down shirt. I didn't feel the heart-pounding staccato in my temples. I certainly didn't hear the door opening and Brauner walking into the office.

"Shall we talk about deceit, David?"

Brauner's self-righteous attitude almost made me snap. How dare he, this relic of a Resurrection I no longer belonged to, lecture me about deceit when he was the one who had snooped on me? How dare he show up in my office, looking confident and smug, telling me about deceit?

I took a deep breath, then another. Slowly I regained control of my nerves, forcing my anger into the pit of my stomach. I knew I couldn't afford to make any enemies, least of all Doc Brauner. I had bigger fish to fry and Brauner would provide the fuel.

I lowered my eyes and tried to look remorseful. I guess I was a pretty good actor because Doc Brauner bought it hook, like, and sinker. He took off his jacket, unbuttoned his vest, and made himself comfortable. Mollified by my apparent repentant attitude he was magnanimous. "Ah, David, David, David. I knew you'd come to your senses. You're too good a man to pursue misguided goals. All you needed was some soul-searching, some inner reflection. So, are you ready to discuss the matter of honesty and trust?"

I nodded.

"Good. Would you like to show me Private Austin's letter?"

I didn't hesitate a second. "Sorry, but I lost it when I moved my stuff to Schryden Hall. I had it in my night table and must have thrown it away by accident when I cleaned out my drawers."

Brauner looked doubtful. "That's too bad, but maybe you can tell me what she had to say."

Again I didn't hesitate. "Nothing important. I guess she just wanted to let me know that she wasn't going to work with me anymore. And she made a point of asking me to give you the same cooperation I had given her."

Brauner thought about this for a moment, then pursed his lips and said, "Why did she ask you to come to her room? Didn't that strike you as odd?"

"I never really thought about it," I lied, surprising myself with my glibness. "But after she told me that story about her and her father, she mentioned that…"

"Yes, yes?" Brauner asked a little too quickly. "I meant to ask you about that. I knew she said something else but unfortunately the video didn't pick it up."

I hemmed and hawed, calling on every acting skill I never knew I had. "She…well, I'd rather not talk about it."

"Don't you trust me," Brauner sounded hurt.

"It's not that. Oh, I guess there's no harm in telling you, now that she's gone. She said she wanted to get to know me better. That I was an interesting patient and that by improving our relationship…"

"I think you've said enough, David. I thought that's what it was." Brauner smiled as though he'd know the answer all along.

God, I hated him, this pathetic old man reveling in his phony benevolence. But he had taught me well and I continued playing the part. "I'm sorry, Doc. It's just that I'm a little upset right now, so you'll have to bear with me. I'm sure you understand. I mean, it's kind of embarrassing to be caught red-handed, especially by someone who's taught me so much."

I shook my head and wished I could force tears to my eyes. Unfortunately I wasn't that good an actor but I knew I looked contrite enough. Brauner nodded, agreeing with me, looking pleased and flattered that his hand picked Apostle had apparently returned to the fold. "It's okay, David. I understand and there really is no need to blame yourself. The important thing is to learn from mistakes. God only knows I've made my share, not the least of which was to entrust you to Austin."

If that last remark was intended to get a reaction I disappointed him. I merely agreed. I stuck out my hand. "Friends?" I offered.

Now it was his turn to struggle with tears. He wiped his eyes with his monogrammed handkerchief and shook. "Friends," he said.

It was only a skirmish and there were plenty of battles to be waged, but for today at least I'd won.

Chapter 28

FRIDAY MORNING BROKE with bleak sunshine and gathering storm clouds. An ominous beginning to the biggest day of my life. Friday, *B Day*. The day of Brauner's pilgrimage to his psychiatric convention. The day I'd be alone at Terwilliger. My best shot of unlocking Resurrection's secret. My best shot and quite possibly my only shot.

I arrived at Terwilliger at eight-thirty in the morning. Brauner's overnight bag waited at the front door, as did his locked briefcase and umbrella. Rachel Firestein was on the phone, arranging for a car to pick up Brauner and Axton to take them to the Rhinecliff train station. She glanced up when I entered and smiled, apparently pleased that the boss would be out of her hair until Monday.

I breezed through the office and asked, "Is Dr. Brauner in yet?"

Before she could answer Brauner showed his face and pumped my hand, bristling with energy and anticipation.

"Good morning, Dr. Brauner," I said cheerfully.

"Call me Bruno," he said. Wow. Considering what a stickler for etiquette he was, his gesture was impressive. "I'm glad you showed up early. I want to go over a couple of last minute things with you. Come along." He cocked his head in the direction of Brauner's Kitchen and walked toward the door leading to the subterranean maze.

I followed two steps behind him. He was the picture of distinguished lecturer, attired in an impeccable navy-blue pinstriped three-piece suit, starched white shirt, and natty red tie with a perfect Windsor knot. The gleam of his wingtips rivaled that of his scalp, both reflecting the glare of overhead lights.

We made our way downstairs into a long, narrow corridor. This was only the second time I'd been allowed here and again I was intimidated by the aura of secrecy that surrounded *Brauner's Kitchen*. Except that this morning I tingled with anticipation of what lay ahead.

My first visit had been a blur of impressions, a sensory overload that left me totally awed and confused. I remembered the elaborate security, the stench and faint medicinal smell that hung in the air, the clammy, bone-chilling cold, and the constant drone of far-off machinery. But there hadn't been enough time to digest any of it. This morning was no different. Brauner was in a hurry and I didn't have time to familiarize myself with anything.

I did come away with another prickly feeling though, *Brauner's Kitchen* was an anachronism. Located in the basement of a Dutch stone house that dated back more than three hundred years, state-of-the-art security was everywhere. No attempt had been made to hide it. In fact, it was displayed so prominently that its visibility was a deterrent in itself. Ceiling mounted cameras, palm-print and retina scanners, key-card access locks, turnstiles, lasers, alarms, you name it, this place had it. And that was just the security equipment you could see. Who knew what else there was down here? Yes, Brauner's Kitchen was an anachronism all right, but that shouldn't have surprised me. Resurrection City itself was an anachronism, an old city adapted to twenty-first century objectives. Whatever those objectives were, I knew I'd find them here.

The enormity of my undertaking became clear as Brauner passed from door to door, explaining what I could and couldn't do. The longer he talked, the more apparent it became that I was allowed to do very little. Being an Apostle, especially a rookie Apostle, apparently carried less weight than I'd thought.

Brauner explained. "I've updated security to allow you access to these two rooms." He pointed at two doors side by side at the far end of the corridor. "Library C and video vault 1A. You'll need materials from both of them to complete your assignment. The rest of the place is off-limits. Here, let's try it. I hope I didn't screw up."

I placed my hand against the video vault's palm scanner and the door swung inward obediently.

"Okay, good. Now let's try the library."

Again the door obeyed immediately. We made a U-turn and headed back to the staircase when Brauner suddenly stopped. "Let's make sure I didn't screw up and give you more access than you're supposed to have. Try a different door. Go ahead, any one will do."

I placed my hand against the nearest scanner. The door ignored me and Brauner sighed with relief. "Good. There probably wouldn't have been time to reset security." He checked his watch. "We're running late as it is and I still have to tell you what your assignment is."

I got a sudden idea. "What if I run late? This'll be my first assignment without you being here. Will I be able to get into the library and the vault after hours?"

It could have been my imagination, but I thought Brauner gave me a curious look. He said, "Normally access is limited to regular business hours, but I've anticipated that it might take you a bit longer, so I've set you up for twenty-four-hour access."

I was going to ask him what would happen if I accidentally violated security but didn't. Better not arouse his suspicion, I thought and followed him upstairs.

He hustled me into my office, pulled two folders from a shelf, and dropped them on the desk. He said, "I'm going to start you off with these two cases."

I reached for the folders but Brauner pushed them out of my reach. "Don't bother looking at them now. There'll be plenty of time for that later. The important thing is that you understand your assignment.

"It's really quite simple. Once a year we evaluate every Disciple's progress. Most of the time we're satisfied with what we see and that's the end of it. But every once in a while we run across a case that requires some action. It could be any number of things, like recommending treatment to correct behavioral problems, adjusting medical treatments for someone who is ill, rewarding personal achievements, and so forth. Whenever we make one of these recommendations,

Resurrection's laws require that the recommendation is reviewed by a third party, and that's where you come in.

"You're that third party, someone who hasn't been involved in making the initial recommendation. It's kind of a safety net to make sure that we give everyone fair treatment. So what you'll have to do is familiarize yourself with your cases, really get to know them inside out. You'll have to evaluate all kinds of test results, interviews, progress reports, and so forth. When you're done with that the computer will prompt you to answer a series of questions and supply your answers to a central data base. The official name for this process is ADE. I think it's an acronym for Analytical Data Evaluation, but what it really does is to make sure that a third party perspective is included in the evaluation of a Disciple's progress. Or lack of it. Most of the materials you need are right here but if you need additional information you'll find it in the library or the video vault."

"Then what?"

"Then nothing," Brauner said. "That's all there is to it. I told you it was simple."

"How will I know if me answers are correct?" I asked.

"I think you're missing the point," Brauner explained, exasperated that I should be so dense as to ask a stupid question. "There isn't a right answer or a wrong one. That's not the point here. The point is to gather opinions from a variety of sources. The computer already has my evaluation along with a slew of others. What it boils down to is that the computer will use psychiatric evaluations as well as educational records, police investigations, reports by clergy and so forth. The only thing missing from your two cases are peer evaluations, which you'll supply. Believe it or not, the opinions of a Disciple carry as much weight as my own. So, as soon as you're done the computer does what it does best. It'll crunch numbers, run through a number of algorithms, and spit out it's blessing."

Just then a horn blared. Axton's car was curbside, engine idling, billowing exhaust fumes into the cold morning air. The horn sounded again. Brauner threw up his hands in disgust and headed for the door.

"Sorry, David, but I have to run. Axton doesn't like to wait. Do your best and I'll see you in two days."

*****

I settled into the office and, borrowing a page from Brauner, closed the door behind me. It earned me a reproachful glance from Rachel Firestein and the peace and quiet I needed to put my plan into action. Thanking my lucky stars for my private office, I took a deep breath and reached for both folders. There was no stopping me now.

Until I got a nasty surprise. The name on folder one read *David Koertner.*

What I didn't need at this point were complications, and seeing my name complicated things exponentially. Evaluating myself was probably the ultimate test of honesty and integrity. I prayed that I'd strike the right balance between humility and confidence without appearing arrogant or self-serving, And what would happen if my answers were incorrect. I know Brauner had told me that there weren't any right or wrong answers, but was that designed to trick me? Could I flunk? And if I did, could Apostle Koertner soon be ex-Apostle Koertner? Shit. This was a complication with a capital *C*.

The beginning of my file made for boring reading. I saw a lot of things I'd known all along and learned some things that I couldn't care less about. As expected, the first two years of my life were a blank. Actually not a blank but classified. I found out that I had measles when I was six, that I had the third highest average in grade school, that my high school football coach thought I was a lousy athlete, and that I cheated on a biology test in my senior year.

My folder read like a normal a case history of a normal young boy growing into a normal Disciple on his way to becoming an Apostle. For all intents and purposes I was way too normal and average to become Apostle. But who was I to argue?

More interesting were the omissions and classified sections. The first two years of my life were classified and absent from my file. Therefore I still didn't know who I was or why I was here in the first place. When I checked Retooling I found the entire section, all thirty-eight years of it, missing. More puzzling was my medical record. I had apparently been in and out of the hospital six times before I was four years old but the only reasons for admission were *Pediatric Recommendation* and in all six cases the final discharge comments were *Satisfactory Health*. Strange, considering I didn't have any scars, my tonsils were still intact, I still had my appendix, and didn't wear glasses.

I thought about this for a while but didn't come up with a logical explanation other than that I must have been sickly. Well, whatever ailed me, the doctors must have corrected it. My school records indicated near perfect attendance, and the only other hospital visit was due to a broken pinky finger playing football.

Appendix A was only one paragraph long but made me cringe. It referred me to the video vault for taped interviews with "psychiatric professionals." Private Austin was back to haunt me. Well, here was one video I didn't need. Every scene was still fresh in my mind.

Becoming increasingly nervous I took a break. I poured a cup of coffee, chatted for a minute with Rachel who seemed a lot more pleasant now that Brauner was gone, stuck my nose out the front door to get some fresh air, chatted some more with Rachel, and returned to my closet-sized office. It was already eleven-thirty. I had spent two and a half hours reading about David Koertner and learned absolutely nothing of importance. Not that I was ready to panic. I still had plenty of time, but two-and-a-half hours were two-and-a-half hours and who knew how much time I'd need to evaluate myself or how many questions I'd be confronted with.

Exasperated, I put aside my own case history and concentrated on the second case I had been assigned. Jasmine Devin, case number 33846-5276463. Poor Jasmine was a mess who'd made a mess of her life. Compared to me, she was at the opposite end of the spectrum. Not willing to spend more than thirty minutes on her, I ran through page after page, getting to know Jasmine Devin as a lonely teenager who'd gotten into trouble time and again, flunked out of high school, and stood accused of sexual misconduct with Disciple Jarred Fitzsimmons. According to Appendix A, details of her transgression, as well as comparative case histories of similar transgressions, could be found in the library and video vault. It was time to bite the bullet and snoop around in Brauner's Kitchen.

*****

At one time I had thought that Brauner's Kitchen was the end-all and be-all. All I had to do was get inside and rely on my instincts to sniff out the truth. But after getting Brauner's tour last Monday I had changed my mind. Sure, Brauner's Kitchen was the place that held all the answers, but I still needed a road map. And although the road map was buried somewhere inside Resurrection's system, I had no idea how to find it. I had spent the last two days cramming in front of my computer and immediately ran into dead end after dead end. Being an Apostle might have meant a lot of things, like respectful salutes by passing Guardians and privileged housing, but as far as Resurrection's computer system was concerned, Apostle Koertner was hardly more important than Disciple Koertner. I was only allowed access to a limited number of functions, certainly not enough to unlock the truth. To attempt additional access would probably be denied, documented, and result in review by Security, possibly Axton himself. Brauner might trust me, but Brauner wasn't the person who controlled security. Which left me with nothing but my gut instinct. But by the time I'd made my way across the outer reception area and past Rachel Firestein's raised eyebrows, my gut started to gurgle.

Everything was going wrong. It was too early in the day to spend a lot of time in the vault without tipping someone off. After all, Brauner had left me with the videos and documents I needed to get started. It was also too early in the day to put my crude plan of hacking computer security into action. In fact, as far as my gut was concerned, it was too early for me to do anything other than what I was supposed to. And then get the hell out of Terwilliger.

So when I reached the basement turnstile and inserted my brand-new cardkey I was a mess. The locking mechanism clicked, the turnstile turned, and I found myself inside a four-foot square room Brauner had called the mantrap, staring at the inner door and a wall mounted security camera. I looked dutifully at the lens and waited for it to snap my picture. Then the inner door released and I pushed into Brauner's Kitchen.

So far so good. I walked quickly, making the thirty-foot long trek past forbidden doors until I reached the video vault. I thought of each step along the way as a personal victory. No alarms had gone off, no security guards had mysteriously appeared, and my gut calmed down. With my hand against the scanner, I took a deep breath, waited for yet one more click, and entered the video vault.

Inside, the sheer volume of videos was overwhelming. Staring me in the face was shelf after shelf, each reaching from floor to ceiling, each crammed with plastic-encased discs, dissecting the vault into a bewildering array of numbered sections. A wall-mounted floor plan next to the door told me that Jasmine Devin's video, case number 33846-5276463, could be found in aisle 14, section C. My own video, case number 565783637-32843 was in aisle 24, section G.

I made my way along a five foot wide central aisle until I reached section C and turned left into aisle 14. Here the shelves were a mere two feet apart and blocked overhead lights, creating a murky shadowscape. Fortunately each shelf was marked clearly with fluorescent numbers and I found Devin's video at once. I snapped her disk from its slot, marked the place with a yellow withdrawal slip, and repeated the process when I located section G and my case video.

The whole process had taken less then five minutes, including navigating my way through turnstiles and doors, finding both videos, and beating a hasty retreat to my office. During that time I became more apprehensive. The wealth of information that was buried in the subterranean maze was frightening. In the wrong hands, that information yielded absolute power. In Doc Brauner's hands it could be deadly.

I watched Devin's video. She was an ordinary looking woman, a skinny brunette with bad complexion and unevenly spaced front teeth. As she stared into the camera, her eyes red from crying, she spoke with a slight lisp and in an accent peculiar to people raised in the mountains of western Resurrection. I didn't know the exact nature of her crime yet, but I felt sorry for her. Devin didn't look like a criminal and she didn't sound like a criminal. If anything, she sounded like a young woman at the end of her rope. The look of terror in her eyes was frightening. What could she have done that was so bad?

What she had done, it turned out, was talk to a friend about a book she'd read. Speaking tearfully, she read a prepared statement to the camera and when I heard her admission I became furious. Not with Devin but with Brauner. Brauner probably had nothing to do with the case but he was a convenient scapegoat.

The book in question was a historical novel I'd never heard of, called *Of Sons And Lovers.* Devin's crime lay in succeeding where I had failed. She had managed to get a book out of the library, where I, like the obedient Disciple I'd prided myself on being, had asked for permission and accepted a resolute *NO* from the local librarian. So much for moral superiority. I wasn't any better than Devin. I just hadn't had the balls to do what she had done. *How the hell do they put blinders on all of us? And why? And why am I allowed to see the truth now?*

*****

Five hours later it was time to put my amateurish plan to work. Rachel Firestein was gone after sticking her nose into my office to inform me that she was leaving for the day. All Guardians except one, who was lounging outside Terwilliger's front door, left five minutes after Rachel. I was fortified with a fresh pot of coffee and a ham and cheese from the Stockade Deli.

I made a quick round of the first floor, ignoring the security cameras I knew were hidden somewhere. The front door was locked. An emergency exit leading to the side yard was activated, a red bulb flashing above the steel door in ten second intervals. No one was downstairs in Brauner's Kitchen. All other doors, except the one leading to my office and a supply closet, were closed. Rachel's computer was turned off and her telephone routed to the security department's switchboard. I was on my own.

Back inside my office I powered up my PC and picked up Devin's file. I navigated through several layers of security to access her case history. As Brauner had promised, the computer guided me from one question to the next with beeping prompts. Nothing to it. Piece of cake. And I made my first intentional mistake.

The computer didn't like what I did and beeped. I put on a little show for the hidden security cameras and reacted with a start and a confused look. Then I fat-fingered my next answer and was promptly kicked out of Devin's file.

This time I didn't have to play-act. I was confused and more than a bit annoyed. I had expected another beep, but to be kicked back to the main menu was disturbing. I started from scratch and got an immediate message from the computer *Warning: Second attempt to access confidential data.* I held my breath, said a quick prayer, and selected the *Admin Function*. I wasn't sure where it would take me, but it sounded like the place I should be. The computer thought otherwise. It beeped again and flashed a message *Unauthorized Function Selected. User ID Reported To Violence Control Center.*

I knew I was on thin ice. With nowhere to go and zero knowledge of the system, I played it safe. I returned to Devin's file without a hitch. Hating myself for evaluating her the way I thought Brauner would like me to, I completed her file quickly. I took another coffee break, hoping that fifteen minutes between warnings would calm down the computer, or me. I checked my watch. It was time to stumble through some more menu options. This time I tried Network Maintenance. It sounded interesting and was also right above Personnel Maintenance on the menu. Close enough to explain an errant mouse click. I clicked, the computer gave me an angry beep, and flashed *Unauthorized Function Selected. User ID Koertner Suspended.*

The screen went dark. The keyboard locked. With nearly two days remaining before Brauner's return, I was dead in the water.

Chapter 29

GOTHAM TOWERS WAS a beehive of activity. Every room had been booked for weeks. An endless stream of taxis discharged guest after guest beneath the hotel's massive Park Avenue canopy. Mountains of luggage were piled on the sidewalk. Bellhops maneuvered their carts through milling guests with the agility of slalom skiers. A doorman's shrill whistle pierced the night in a futile effort to attract empty cabs for the hundreds of guests waiting for a ride to the theater or a restaurant.

Inside the marble-floored main lobby, the dinner line for Antoine's, the hotel's main dining room, snaked around potted palms, past the concierge's desk, and halfway to the check-in counter. The continuous hum of hundreds of simultaneous conversations competed with a Jazz quintet playing in the Gotham Lounge. The mood in the hotel reflected Manhattan's atmosphere: controlled and joyous chaos.

In contrast, the mood in suite 4511 was tense and somber. Room service had just delivered dinner. Roasted Long Island duckling for Brauner, broiled Maine lobster for Colonel Axton. An unopened bottle of Corvoisier and two snifters waited next to a silver coffee urn and a sumptuous Sacher torte for desert. A humidor held Axton's private supply of Havanas.

The two men ate in silence, Axton too busy cracking his lobster in a diligent attempt to get at every last morsels of meat, Brauner too preoccupied with what he left behind in Resurrection to enjoy his meal. Even the crispy duck skin, which he considered ambrosia, failed to whet his appetite this evening. He picked at the meat with his fork, pushing pieces of duck back and forth on the plate, and finally abandoned his meal.

"What's the matter, Bruno. Something wrong with the duck?"

Brauner shook his head. "No, it's fine. I'm just not very hungry."

"Look, relax, will you. I thought you told me everything was under control."

"It is," Brauner answered without conviction. He was obviously worried. There were too many loose ends. For the first time Brauner considered the possibility that he may have been too hasty with Koertner. Leaving him free to roam Terwilliger had been a calculated risk, but one he felt he had to take. Still, David's state-of-mind was extremely fragile, and Brauner's Kitchen could prove to be the candy shop every kid dreamt of.

And that whole Austin mess. The woman was a real thorn in his side. Perlmutter hadn't helped either. Just when she had been safely tucked away in The House that stupid old fool had to go off the deep end and screw things up royally. Brauner still couldn't believe it. A fork of all things, how dumb how dumb could you be?

Brauner's logical side told him that everything was okay. His intuition told him it wasn't. His logical side also told him not to listen to his intuition, but his intuition had seldom failed him in the past. *What if* after *what if,* too many *what ifs* to shake off. But what really galled him was seeing Axton eating like there was no tomorrow, cracking lobster shells, dipping forkfuls of meat into drawn butter, acting like he didn't have a care in the world. Which he obviously didn't, because Axton always managed to pin the blame on others. Oh, he was good at that, so good that Brauner often wondered why Axton had chosen Resurrection over a political career. Funny how life turns out, Brauner thought. How his own life and Axton's were inextricably intertwined, bound by private ambitions and undermined by mutual dislikes. Like a bad marriage, with each partner staying with the other for the sake of the children. The *children.* If not for the children there wouldn't be a need for Resurrection.

Brauner wiped glistening goose grease from his lips and folded his napkin. Having to sit in these luxurious but unfamiliar surroundings, sharing a meal with a man he disliked intensely, his mind kicked into overdrive conjuring up visions of everything that could go wrong. He knew there was nothing he could do but remain at Gotham Towers for one more night. This is the last time though, he promised himself. The lure of mingling with other psychiatrists in this annual safari to civilization was wearing thinner each year. His fifteen minutes in the limelight, receiving a standing ovation from the gathering of prison authorities after delivering this year's opening speech had hardly been worth the nagging doubts that haunted him.

Brauner's thoughts were interrupted by Axton. The colonel sucked noisily on his remaining lobster claw, pushed his dinner plate aside, and concluded his meal with a belch. Comfortably sated, he lit a Havana and reached for the after-dinner Corvoisier.

"Ahhh, that was good. You know, Bruno, you don't know how to relax. Sometimes I think the finer things in life are wasted on you. Relax, will you. The Camp will still be there when we get back."

Brauner didn't answer.

Axton continued sarcastically. "I know what'll take your mind off things. You need a woman. What do you say we get two of New York's best up here." He whipped an address book from his pocket and thumbed through it. "Here you go, Big Apple Escort Service. I heard they have the best looking broads in the city. Real high class, not your average hooker. And they're very discreet."

Brauner rolled his eyes.

"Don't be such a tight-ass, Bruno. I can have them up here as soon as we're done with the annual report. So what's your pleasure? Big boobs and a tight pussy?"

"My only pleasure right now is to get this meeting over with and get my own tight ass out of here."

"All right, Bruno, have it your way. If that's how you feel, we might as well get everything ready. He'll be here in thirty minutes."

Brauner almost said it out loud. *Pig!* But he stopped himself at the last moment and rose with an abrupt motion. He couldn't resist an icy glare in Axton's direction, which the Colonel acknowledged with a sarcastic smile and a raised cognac snifter. "Prosit, Bruno. To the Camp."

*****

Three copies of Camp Resurrection's annual report were spread out on suite 4511's conference room table. Next to each report was a notepad bearing an imprint of Gotham Towers silhouette. A supply of sharpened number two pencils, three water glasses, and a filled ice bucket completed the place settings. At the head of the table, a disc player and large-screen television were ready. The curtains were drawn. Ten minutes prior to their dinner service, Colonel Axton's men had swept the room for bugs. It was a precaution Brauner considered unnecessary but which Axton had insisted on nevertheless.

*****

Their visitor arrived at nine o'clock sharp.
"Welcome to Gotham Towers, sir. I trust you had a pleasant trip?"
"Yes, thank you, although the timing was somewhat unfortunate. I'm swamped right now. I hoped that I could squeeze in a rare evening in Manhattan but it'll have to wait. I have to catch a flight out of La Guardia right after we're finished."
Axton bowed stiffly and pointed to the conference table. "I understand, sir. We're all ready for you. Why don't you take the middle seat?"
"Thank you, Xavier. Hello Bruno. It's good to see you again. Is the fresh Catskill air keeping you and your Disciples in good health?"
"Yes, sir, indeed it is."
"Good. I was a little worried for a minute. You look a little peaked."
"It's nothing, sir, really. Just a mild case of intestinal irritation."
Axton smiled. "Bruno gets it every time he ventures away from Resurrection. Must be the Long Island duckling, sir. Such delicacies are strictly verboten in Resurrection."

"As long as it doesn't affect his intestinal fortitude."

Both Axton and Brauner laughed politely.

Their visitor didn't join their laughter. Looking straight at Axton he asked, "Is your little problem taken care of? You know, the incident we discussed last I week?"

Axton didn't miss a beat. "Bruno handled it all, sir. He took personal charge because he felt it was a psychiatric issue more than a security problem. Of course I agreed. I'm sure it's well under control. Am I right, Bruno?"

Brauner was livid. With that one single statement Axton had dumped the entire Austin mess directly into his lap. If the shit hit the fan, the fallout would splatter all over him while Axton escaped unblemished. Visibly angry, his voice thick, his cheeks approaching the color of ripe tomatoes, Brauner forced a weak smile. "Yes, sir, it's taken care of, all with Xavier's expert guidance, of course."

A weak attempt at covering his ass, but he made his point. Their visitor didn't miss it and responded with a rare smile while Brauner and Axton exchanged daggers. "It's a pleasure to see how well the two of you work together, always willing to share the credit. Shall we get started?"

Glad to have the introductory sarcasm out of the way, Axton and Brauner concurred eagerly. Brauner put on his glasses. Axton opened the annual report and flipped to the financial statement. "If you'll direct your attention to page 17, I'll…"

One hour later, they had reviewed the entire report in minute detail. Considering how much Brauner had dreaded the meeting, it had been fairly painless. He felt a tremendous sense of relief. Now he could concentrate on more important matters. Being a methodical person, Brauner had found it difficult to take care of things on the home front while preparing for tonight's meeting. On paper everything looked good. No snags, no delays. Maybe his premonition had been nothing but jittery nerves after all. He closed the report and finished his water.

"Thank you, gentlemen. As always, it's been a pleasure. I must really make good on my promise and send the two of you on a well-deserved vacation. How does Hawaii sound? Maybe shortly after the twenty-fifth? Assuming of course that your shipment is received by my clients as promised."

Axton and Brauner responded in unison. "It will be, sir. Everything is ready."

"Good. I can't impress upon you enough just how important this is. I'm getting immense pressure. It's been nearly nine months."

"We know, sir. But you must understand how delicate our situation is. One cannot rush these things. Prudence is of the utmost importance."

"I understand." Another rare smile, followed by quick handshakes. "I'll talk to you on the twenty sixth. Good bye, Xavier. Good bye, Bruno. Have a safe trip back."

Chapter 30

EVERY DARK CLOUD has a silver lining. In my case that black cloud came when my computer shut down. The silver lining turned out to be yellow.

It was two in the morning. I was frustrated and tired and ready to call it quits. The only thing that kept me going was knowing that I'd never get a chance like this again. Not until Brauner went on another trip and that wouldn't happen until next year.

Sitting in front of my dead computer and fresh out of coffee, I remembered that something had caught my attention while making my way through the video vault's narrow aisles. And I recalled that I had promised myself to check it out, except that by the time I'd returned to my office I couldn't remember what it was I that had struck me. I knew I was grasping at straws, but whatever it was, I was determined to take one last shot at remembering it.

I grabbed a notebook and my two case folders and headed for Brauner's Kitchen. Down thirteen steps, through the mantrap with its palm and retina scanner, and along thirty feet of hall, I started getting excited. I knew that the answer was in the vault. I just hadn't looked in the right place or for the right thing. With my PC reduced to a useless pile of electronic chips I went straight to the horse's mouth.

The door clicked open on command. I retraced my earlier steps, passing by Jasmine Devin's DVD slot flagged with my withdrawal slip, then made a U-turn to section G where my own video had been.

I went to great pains to take the exact same route I had earlier in the day, passing through the same narrow aisles, but this time I walked slowly, determined to study the floor to ceiling shelves on both sides, convinced that it was here, among the thousands of videos, that something had struck me as odd. But I struck out.

My sense of déjà-vu was stronger than ever, but turning déjà vu into déjà reality was harder than I thought. Still, it was all I had to go on. I retraced my steps, step by step, back to the vault's entrance door, back to aisle C, back to aisle G, and when it still didn't come to me, I did it one more time.

This is silly, I told myself fifteen minutes later. I was tired. The vault's refrigeration system was beginning to make me shiver. I'd made my way along aisle after aisle three times now and still didn't have a clue. Frustrated, I slammed my right hand into the side of a shelf. It wobbled, twenty-five hundred discs rattled, and a yellow piece of paper fluttered to the floor.

Of course. Yellow. That's what it was. Yellow withdrawal slips plastered here and there like signal flags. I retrieved the errant slip from the floor, wrote the case number and date in my notebook, and pasted it back to the only empty slot on the shelf. Then I made my way along aisle after aisle, recording case numbers and withdrawal dates. By the time I finished forty-eight entries lined my notebook. Forty-eight cases which had all been withdrawn over the last three weeks. Forty-eight cases numbers, but no names.

No problem. I'd just take myself and my notebook back to my office and enter each case number into my computer and I'd have... Nothing, that's what I would have. I called myself a few choice names, most of which I'd never used before, and came to the conclusion that I had been better off before making my breakthrough withdrawal slip discovery. Fifteen minutes ago I had only been frustrated. Now I was frustrated and furious with myself.

Still, everything was not lost. It was time to get out of this icebox and make an attempt to crack case numbers in the warmth and comfort of my office. Besides, I didn't dare spend another minute in the vault. If Brauner's security system was half as good as I suspected it was, it would record the time I entered and left the vault. Having already spent more than twenty minutes in here I was sure to make someone suspicious.

*****

It was three-fifteen. My eight by ten foot office wasn't the comfortable haven I had assumed it to be. Reminders of my less than equal status were all over the place. Bare shelves to my right reminded me that what I needed were reference books which I wasn't allowed to have. Behind me, my certificate proclaiming me Apostle showed me that being an Apostle didn't matter as long as Brauner still pulled the strings. My computer was shut down by security. My office door, which I had closed behind me for no reason, gave me privacy from no one. Hidden security cameras probably recorded every move I made. Even my telephone was restricted to three lines. Brauner's office, Rachel Firestein's desk, and Security.

And ultimately that's whom I called, Security. It was time to admit defeat and get out of Terwilliger. I flipped open my leather-bound office diary and searched for Security, GUARDIAN. Never having owned a phone before, I fumbled with the letters and promptly entered a wrong number. A tinny recording at the other end gave me a nasty message about restricted lines and told me to dial GUARDIAN.

I started to translate the numbers to their corresponding phone pad letters when it hit me. There was no elaborate encryption here, no random assignment of case numbers. This wasn't a computer generated code, especially since every case number was of a different length. This wasn't some sort of sophisticated algorithm. This was pure Brauner, simple, logical, old-fashioned, and totally consistent with his disdain for computers.

I started with Jasmine Devin's folder. Using my phone as a guide, I matched each letter of her name to its corresponding phone pad number. Bingo! I nearly let out a triumphant cry. Translating case number after case number with feverish activity, I scribbled the resulting name in my notebook. It was tedious but not difficult, as each number was limited to three corresponding letters. Less than forty minutes later forty-eight names stared at me from my notebook. Forty-eight names revealed. Some of the names on my list were unfamiliar. Two, Jasmine Devin and my own, I had withdrawn myself. I recognized some of the other names. Four names I knew intimately. And when I saw their withdrawal dates, I saw the common thread than linked them.

My skin started to crawl. Josh Brannigan, withdrawn two days before he died. Ezekiel Vandeman, withdrawn two days before he died. Paulette Kowalski, withdrawn the day Justin was caught breaking into her house. Dawn Austin, withdrawn the day before she left for Shandaken.

Chapter 31

FUNERALS SHOULD BE held on rainy days. Mourners should be shrouded by swirling mist, hunched inward to fight off bone-chilling dampness, huddled against each other to share their grief.

Cecilia Austin remembered telling her daughter that the heavens had shared their anguish and cried the morning she laid her husband to rest. This morning's torrential rains had turned Saint Mary's cemetery into a quagmire. Lightning ripped through black clouds. Thunder reverberated among endless rows of gravestones. The skies were not merely crying, they were angry that Dawn Austin has died.

Long after the gravesite ceremony had ended and the few mourners who had braved the raging storm had returned to their cars and driven off, Cecilia Austin and Max remained at Dawn's open grave. Mud splattered the flag draped coffin. Floral arrangements were immersed in ankle deep water. But she welcomed the chill that a nor'easter had spread across New York. It was fitting retribution for the guilt she felt. If only she had tried harder to talk Dawn out of enlisting. Maybe things…

First a husband. Now a daughter. If it weren't for Chaz's phone call last week, Cecilia Austin would have given up. She had seriously considered suicide the morning after Emmanuel Warner's late night visit. She had gone so far as to look for an adoptive family for Max. But Max, who seemed to be more perceptive than most humans, had followed her around the house all day, plodding just inches behind her, and thumping his eighty pound body on top of her feet whenever she sat. That terrible first night, long after Warner had left a death certificate and a letter of commendation signed by faceless strangers, strangers who had been closer to her daughter in death than she herself had been, hours after Warner's announcement played in her ears over and over like a broken gramophone record, Max had nudged his way into bed with her and had miraculously warmed her body with his. Only then, with Max at her side, his chest rising and falling quickly with sleep, had she finally fallen asleep herself.

The next morning, after making the funeral arrangements, suicide still seemed her only way out. Until Chaz called her. Something he had told her hadn't make any sense. She hadn't caught it at first. But after reading Dawn's last letter again she had called Chaz. *I'll see you at the funeral*, he had said. *I can't begin to tell you how terrible I feel. Of course nothing compared to what you are going through, but Dawn was very special to me. I just wish my letter could have reached her. If there's anything I can do, anything at all, please let me know. And if it's okay with you, I'd like to have lunch with you after the service. If it's okay with you*, he had said again.

Max shook the rain off his body and thumped Cecilia with a muddy paw, signaling that it was time to leave. She knelt reluctantly and reached across the gaping chasm that separated her from the coffin, touching it for the last time. Calling on an inner strength she didn't know she had she got back on her feet, took Max's leash, and walked back to the limousine. Chaz stood next to the car, drenched and windblown despite his oversized golf umbrella. Seeing him like this, seeing the pain in his eyes, Cecilia managed a sad smile. Dawn could have done a lot worse than poor nerdy Chaz. If only…

They rode back to her west-side apartment without saying a word. Sitting next to Chaz in the spacious limousine, insulated from the stop-and-go traffic of the Long Island Expressway, magnified her feeling of isolation. While the rest of the world went about its business she felt as if she were shut inside a two-hundred-fifty horsepower coffin, being drawn towards her final resting place in Manhattan. That's what her apartment had become, a joyless fifteen-hundred square foot tomb in which mementos of a previous life were piled high to honor the dead. There were photos of Thurston and Dawn, an antique writing desk that evoked memories of a family antique-hunting trip to Vermont, her husband's three pipes, her daughter's collection of psychiatry books, a boxed set of Mozart's violin sonatas which they listened to religiously every Sunday morning over coffee and bagels, all reminders of a life gone forever.

An hour later, they pulled up in front of 721 Riverside Drive. The rain had stopped by the time they descended into the Midtown tunnel, but a trickle of water cascaded from scaffolding that had been erected along the building's second floor. Chaz insisted on settling with the chauffeur while Cecilia tried in vain to remove mud stains from the jump seat Max had occupied. Hector, 721's doorman, greeted them with an appropriately sorrowful expression, offered his condolences, and escorted them into the lobby.

"This came for you, Mrs. Austin." He pointed at a cardboard box filled with sandwiches and sodas. "Shall I bring it up for you?"

"I'll take it," Chaz offered and slipped Hector a five dollar bill.

*****

Cecilia had insisted on having lunch at the apartment. She couldn't stand to sit on public display in a restaurant. After a short argument Chaz had relented and ordered sandwiches from the Carnegie Deli. At his insistence Cecilia waited in the dining ell while he unloaded the food and brought it to the table. It was only the two of them but Chaz had ordered enough Pastramis on rye, kosher pickles, and coleslaw to feed a small army.

Cecilia couldn't help but smile. Poor Chaz, she thought, he's really coming through, doing his best to make her feel better. She wasn't very hungry but he hovered over her, making sure she ate her share, while discreetly dropping a few slices of pastrami for Max.

Still, it was a painful meal. Neither were willing to bring up the real reason why Chaz was here. If not for her suspicions, Cecilia would have preferred to be by herself. But surprisingly, seeing Chaz act like a mother hen and chatting aimlessly about this and that, helped her more than she had thought possible. In very different ways they both felt the same grief.

Chaz finally screwed up his courage. Having cleaned his plate and too full to eat one more bite, he unfolded a paper napkin, wiped his lips, and lowered his eyes. "Mrs. Austin, about what you said, you know, about our conversation the other day? I don't know what it was I said, but I'll try to help. Just let me know what it is you want to know."

His words signaled the end of lunch. Cecilia collected the paper plates and walked them into the kitchen. "I'm not so sure I know what I want any longer."

She returned with two coffees and took a seat on the couch. "I'm so confused. I can't even think straight. But something doesn't make any sense to me. You said that you wrote to Dawn, didn't you?"

"Yes." Chaz looked puzzled. "I did. But why shouldn't that make sense?"

"Because Dawn..." Cecilia halted in mid-sentence, trying to think clearly. "Didn't you tell me that you wished she could have received your letter?"

"That's right. My letter was returned. She never received it."

"Did you bring it with you?"

"Yes, of course. You asked me to. Here." Chaz picked an envelope from his jacket and gave it to Cecilia. "Here. This is it."

She looked at the envelope bearing the familiar post office symbol of a hand with its index finger pointing at the inscription *Forward to Quad 2 Facility*. Cecilia pointed at the imprint.

"Here. Look at it, Chaz."

Chaz shook his head, convinced that Cecilia Austin was still in shock. "Sorry, Mrs. Austin, but I still don't get it."

"I wouldn't have either, if you hadn't told me that your letter was forwarded. That's when I started to get confused and I read Dawn's letter again. After I did, everything suddenly started to make sense. Or," she shook her head, "maybe I should say nothing made sense anymore."

She closed her eyes and tried to sort through the chaotic ebb and flow of thoughts in her head. For a moment she considered forgetting the whole thing. What difference did it make? So what if there was a discrepancy? It wasn't going to bring Dawn back.

Chaz put his hand on hers. "Mrs. Austin, maybe I'm missing something. If you'll explain the whole thing…"

"Maybe I'm making something out of nothing. Forget I ever mentioned it. And thanks for being Dawn's friend."

*****

Senator Waldemar Kerr's office in the Nassau County Executive building in Mineola was bursting at the seams with petitioners. His influence with the Department of Internal Affairs had made him the last resort of hope for relatives and friends of Resurrection's inmates. On any given day he received more than a hundred requests for early pardons. On bad days, as this one had been, the line of visitors stretched into the marble-clad halls of the Executive building, where petitioners waited patiently for their five minutes with the senator.

At three thirty in the afternoon Cecilia Austin was led into the senator's office, passed through a metal detector, checked her handbag with a guard at the door, and surrendered visitor's pass number 179, which she had been assigned at eleven in the morning.

Austin liked the senator the moment she laid eyes on him. He was a kindly looking man in his sixties. A real gentleman, she thought, soft spoken and with a warm smile that set her at ease immediately. Compared to the stony-faced bureaucrats from the Department of Corrections she had encountered until now, Kerr's rosy complexion, light blue eyes, and thinning gray hair inspired trust and compassion.

He rose from behind his desk to shake her hand. "What can I do for you, Mrs. Austin?" He checked her appointment slip and smiled, "Cecilia, right?"

She shrugged her shoulders with pessimism. "I don't know if you can help me, Senator, but I'm at the end of my rope. Everyone I've spoken to so far has treated me as though I belong in Bellevue's Psycho ward."

"Well, why don't you tell me whom you're trying to get out and I'll see what I can do."

"I'm not trying to get anyone out, sir. That's not why I'm here. I'm trying to get some information about my daughter's death."

The senator's expression changed to deep compassion. "Mrs. Austin, I'm so sorry to hear about your loss. Please accept my deepest condolences." He walked around his desk and put his hand on Cecilia's shoulder. "It grieves me every time I hear a story like yours. We sometimes lose sight of the real purpose of Resurrection. Despite all the political sloganeering and government budget fights, we must remember that Resurrection is the only real hope these unfortunate youngsters have. And then the story of an unfortunate death comes along and…" He shook his head. "Do you know when your daughter was scheduled for parole?"

"You don't understand, Senator. My daughter wasn't an inmate. She worked there."

Kerr's eyebrows shot up in surprise. He turned to his desk and pushed the intercom. "Louise, no more petitioners, please. I'll be tied up for the rest of the day."

Turning back to Cecilia Austin he continued, "You said you were trying to get information. Haven't they told you what happened?"

Cecilia nodded, but Kerr went on without noticing. "The laws are very specific, Mrs. Austin. Besides the obvious, like death certificates and Medical Examiners reports and so on you should have received all of your daughter's belongings, transcripts of her employment history, evaluations and performance appraisals, and so forth."

"I received all of that," Cecilia said.

"Then I don't understand…"

"I got all of their official documentation all right. "Austin said bitterly. "All I wanted was to ask them some questions but they treated me like I was some kind of nut. They wouldn't give me any information."

Kerr seemed suddenly agitated. He paces the length of his office, breathing hard and trying to control himself. "I think I understand, Mrs. Austin." He interrupted himself. "May I call you Celia?"

Cecilia nodded and Kerr went on. "Please forgive me if I seem upset. I realize the last thing you need right now is for an old man like me to act like a self-righteous fool in the face of your sorrow. It's just that something like this occurred last year, and the brass up there stonewalled it. Wouldn't give the poor woman who came to see me the time of day. They seem to be more concerned with preserving their lily white image than with upholding the constitutional rights of our citizens. So they conveniently hide behind a wall of secrecy."

He took a notepad from his desk drawer and uncapped an old-fashioned fountain pen. "Now then, Cecilia, why don't you tell me your story. Try not to leave anything out. And please don't feel embarrassed or afraid of sounding crazy. I'm on your side."

Cecilia Austin started with an anguished plea. "Senator, all I ask is that you keep an open mind. Just listen to what I have to say before you dismiss me as some kind of crazy lunatic. You see, you're really my last chance. I don't know where else to turn if you don't believe me. I've tried everything I could think of. I even went to the camp myself, but they turned me back at the main checkpoint. They were all very polite, telling me how sorry they were. But regulations are regulations they said. I got nowhere with them. That's when I called your secretary."

Kerr nodded quietly and tapped his fountain pen against a notepad. After years in his position as Resurrection's watchdog he had come across many distraught women. But this one was different. She wasn't looking to free a prisoner. She was looking for the truth. He looked at her and wondered, was it truth or revenge?

Austin mistook his quiet for skepticism and went on. "At first I believed what this Colonel Warner said. I didn't have any reason not to. And it made sense. According to her records, Dawn was reassigned to a facility in Shandaken. On the way there she died in an automobile accident on route 28, halfway between Resurrection City and Shandaken. But when I read her letter…here, read it yourself."

She handed Dawn's last letter to Kerr, who read it carefully. At last he handed it back to Cecilia. "I'm sorry Cecilia, but I'm afraid this letter doesn't prove anything. I agree with you that she was in… Shan…what's the name of this place again…?"

"Shandaken," Cecilia volunteered quickly.

"Right. Shandaken. There's no question she was there. But I fail to see…"

Cecilia took a deep breath to control her trembling. "What about this? This is what I got from this officer Warner the night he told me Dawn was dead. Here." Cecilia pushed the letter in front of

Kerr's face. "Here… *regret to inform you that Private Dawn Austin was killed on November 2 in an automobile accident while driving to the Shandaken Facility.*"

"I don't want to seem unsympathetic to your plight, Mrs. Austin, but I think you're grasping at straws. The government's letter doesn't state that she died when she was first transferred there. She could have been there for quite some time. Most likely she was out on furlough and driving back to Shandaken when the accident occurred."

"That's what I assumed as well. Until Chaz mentioned something that…"

"Chaz?" Kerr looked puzzled.

"I'm sorry, Senator. Chaz is an old college friend of Dawn's. He called when he found out that she had died. And he said something that didn't make any sense. I just didn't pick up on it at first."

Kerr looked at his watch and fidgeted with his shirt sleeve, knowing that he was running late for a dinner appointment. Cecilia went on to explain. "He said *I just wish my letter could have reached her.*"

"But what's so odd about that? I'm sure he felt very badly."

Cecilia wasn't listening to Senator Kerr's rationalizations. Desperate to have someone, anyone, believe her, she handed Chaz's returned envelope to the Senator. He looked at it for a moment before handing it back to her.

"Mrs. Austin, I still don't understand. I'm sorry, but…"

Her voice turned shrill with frustration. "Don't you see the postmark? The letter was forwarded to her in Shandaken."

Kerr walked to her side and shook his had sadly. For a moment Cecilia thought he was about to embrace her as though she were a little girl who had been frightened by a bad dream and needed a father's comforting touch. Then his arms dropped to his sides and he shook his head slowly. Compassion lined his face, and infinite helplessness. When he spoke, his voice mirrored the pity he felt for her.

"Cecilia, I know how you feel. I would probably feel the same way. When a tragedy like this strikes, we cling to the smallest hope. We refuse to give up. But I'm afraid this only confirms what agent

Warner told you. And what your daughter herself wrote to you. She was reassigned. She was there for some time. Long enough for the post office to have her forwarding address. That is exactly why her friend's letter was forwarded and ultimately returned to him."

"Read her letter again, Senator. Read it and you'll see what I mean."

"All right," he said, resigned to the fact that this poor woman won't leave until he did as she asked. He read the letter. And read it for a second time. Suddenly he tensed. He let out a sharp hiss. And read the words again. *…By the way, thanks for giving Chaz my address. It was nice hearing from him again. Please…*

This time his words were deliberate and had a definite edge to them. "Mrs. Austin, how many times did this Chaz write to your daughter?"

"Just once. I asked him."

For the first time Cecilia had hope. Finally someone believed her. Yet she was afraid to ask him. He seemed to read the question in her eyes and said, "I'm sorry it took me this long. You're right, of course. Absolutely right."

"You believe me then?"

"I do."

She started to cry.

The senator's reaction was dramatic. His earlier kindness drained from his face and turned to stony hardness. He stalked to his desk and picked up the phone.

"Louise, will you get me the Attorney General on the phone? Thank you. Yes, I'll wait on the line."

He turned back to Cecilia Austin. He fought to control his temper, but his voice cracked with emotion. "Mrs. Austin. I think that someone is trying to cover up a terrible tragedy. I think they went through your daughter's personal belongings. When they found this letter and saw the forwarding instructions they checked with their outgoing mail facility. Someone there must have screwed up and missed her letter to you. You see, all mail in Resurrection is tracked and censored, not just the inmates but employees as well. When they didn't find any outbound mail from your daughter they just sealed

Chaz's letter and returned it to him. I guess they hoped that it would lend legitimacy to their cover-up. All they'd have to do is return it to the sender and the whole world would think it never reached her, that she was already dead. Obviously they never checked this."

He held up Dawn's letter and waved it in the air. "Unfortunately it won't bring your daughter back. But you may take some small solace from my promise. So help me God, I'll find out what is going on up there in Resurrection."

Chapter 32

At four o'clock in the morning life as he had known it unraveled for Justin Frederikson. Two soldiers of Axton's elite guard burst into room 311. One was a tall, red-haired man, the other a stocky black woman. They wore combat fatigues and hip boots. Assault rifles were slung over their shoulders.

They made their way to Justin's bunk, clicked on a flashlight, and shook him from a deep sleep. He blinked into blinding light and sat up with a start.

For a moment he thought he was having a bad dream but a pair of hands locked around his ankles and yanked hard. Frederikson slid halfway off the bed. Instinct told to run for his life. The grip on his ankles loosened. He drew his knees upward, then kicked with all the strength he could summon. About to lunge sideways and make a dash for the door, the flashlight slammed against his right temple. Dazed, he fell backward. The light clicked off. Someone laughed, a low, piggish kind of laugh. Desperately trying to remember what he'd done to get into trouble Frederikson drew a blank. Ever since the Paulette incident he'd been a model Disciple. So what…?

"Get your ass out of bed, Frederikson," a woman's voice ordered. "Hurry up, we don't have all night."

He weighed his options. There were at least two of them. They were armed. His pants legs were around his ankles, making escape all but impossible. Even if he managed to get away from them there was no place to run to. They probably had a backup at the front door. There was only one thing to do, obey and wait for the right moment.

He lifted himself off the bed and leaned forward to hitch up his pants. As he did it occurred to him that the slightest move on his part could be misinterpreted. He threw up his arms and said, "I just want to pull up my pants, okay? I'm not gonna make a run for it."

The woman snickered. She took one step in his direction and put her hands on his shoulders. She stood close enough for him to make out her face. Acne pocked skin, gleaming teeth, thick-lipped mouth stretched into a broad grin. He felt her hands slide along his shoulders. Her fingers clasped behind his neck. For one crazy moment he thought she was about to kiss him. He tensed. She continued smiling. And spat.

It hurt more than a punch. It was degrading and vile. It proved that she was in control. She had power. He was worthless. Frederikson snapped. He brought his hands up and caught her under her chin. There was a popping sound and her hands fell away from his neck. Her eyes widened with shock. The force of the blow drove her teeth into her lips and tongue. Blood streaked from her mouth and she let out a yelp. He knew what would happen next and tried to prepare himself for it. And he knew that whatever they'd do didn't matter. He'd shown that bitch who was in charge.

*****

When Frederikson came to he found himself on the floor of a jeep, wedged between the backseat and the driver's compartment partition. He was hogtied with rope, his arms stretched behind his back, wrists tied to ankles, lying face down on the car's metal floor. A cloth satchel covered his head. He found it difficult to breathe. Clumps of dried blood clogged his nose and he sucked air through his mouth. Nausea rose and he fought it back desperately, afraid of choking on his vomit.

He assessed his condition, running his tongue across his teeth to check for gaps or jagged stumps. To his relief there were none. He thought his ribs might be broken but couldn't be sure. His nose however was a different story. Judging by the blood and pulsing pain, it had been broken. His body was too numb to tell him if he had any other injuries but he suspected that he was okay. What he wasn't sure of however was if he'd stay okay much longer.

He didn't know where they were taking him but suspected the worst. Judging by the frequency with which his head bounced against the car's floor, they were still driving along potholed streets somewhere in Resurrection City, probably in the Stockade District where the streets were notoriously bad. The Jeep stopped a few times, probably for traffic lights, and another time to refuel. He heard muffled conversations and the whirring of a gas pump before the car's doors slammed shut and they resumed their ride.

Refueling had been a bad sign; they were preparing for a lengthy trip. Now, as potholed streets gave way to smooth pavement his suspicions were confirmed. They had left Resurrection City and were driving at steady highway speed. His worst fear was coming true. They were headed for the House.

Keeping track of time and distance was difficult. He kept drifting in and out of foggy consciousness. During moments of lucidity he was too preoccupied with his physical condition to notice much of anything. Survival became a chore; breathing, flexing his hands, ignoring pain, staying awake, staying alive, planning his next move. Once they stopped. The driver's side door opened. Moments later the engine started again and Justin speculated that the driver had relieved himself at the side of the road. While the door had been open, he felt cold air surge into the car, another sign that they were heading into the mountains, climbing at a steady pace and putting the Hudson valley behind them.

Justin knew he was slipping quickly. The longer he remained silent the worse it would get. He started talking to himself. It didn't help. What he needed was a conversation, hearing a voice other than his own.

"Hey guys, I gotta go," he shouted. "I'm gonna pee in my pants."

There was no reply.

Maybe they hadn't heard him? He shouted at the top of his lungs. "You hear me? I can't hold it in anymore."

"We're almost there," someone answered.

"Where?" Justin yelled back. "Where we goin'?"

"The Resurrection Hilton," a different voice replied. "Your private suite awaits."

This was followed by laughter. Justin was infuriated that they were laughing at his expense and had no idea what they meant by "Resurrection Hilton." But he felt better nevertheless. As long as he could speak and someone answered him there was hope. His sense of suffocating isolation was broken.

"What's a Hilton?" he asked.

There was no answer. They had tired of him. They were also busy talking to someone on their two-way radio. The words were unintelligible but it sounded like they were preparing for the end of their trip. Muted two-way chatter and static and beeps drifted into the back of the passenger compartment.

Minutes later the Jeep braked and came to a stop. Doors flung open. Steel-tipped boots pounded macadam. Cold air engulfed the car's interior and Justin shivered. He felt a pair of hands trying to yank him free but he was wedged in too tightly.

"Hey, gimme a hand. He's stuck in there."

"Christ. Try the other side."

Another door opened. This was followed by renewed pulling and cursing. "Shit, you got him trussed up like a fuckin' turkey. No wonder I can't get him out. Cut the friggin' rope and grab his ankles."

Moments later Frederikson's arms and legs were freed from the rope and he was pulled from the car by his feet. The satchel still covering his head, his upper body and head hit the ground first. He blacked out.

Although he regained consciousness quickly, his recollection of the next few hours was fuzzy at best. He knew that he was being dragged feet first along a smooth floor. The temperature kept dropping. Judging from echoing footsteps, they were proceeding through a tunnel. Chemical odors permeated the air. Straight ahead, an alien sound droned incessantly. Other impressions assaulted him. Doors opened and closed in rapid succession. He heard people talking. Throughout their conversations he heard occasional moans, babies crying, and never-ending beeping. The noises were disjointed yet vaguely familiar, but he was too disoriented to recall where he had heard them before. His brain was as dysfunctional as his body.

Little by little, inch by inch, Frederikson regained feeling in his arms and legs. As he did, numbness turned to pain and hopelessness to panic, fueled by a conviction that his worst nightmare had become reality. All the rumors in the world couldn't do justice to this place. The House was unimaginable, representing every fear and phobia. It was a descent into hell, a personal hell customized to fit personal fears.

Millions of fears inflamed his psychological terror. How long could he survive without food or water? How badly was he hurt? What would they do next? What if they did nothing? Would they just let him die? And all the time, over and over, he aske himself. Why?

He knew his journey was over when they dragged him across a threshold and shut a door. At once the frightening sounds ceased. But instead of relief the sudden silence was more ominous than the noisy cacophony that had invaded his body, it added to his isolation.

He also knew that he was locked inside a cell. His hands were cuffed behind his back. A cloth satchel still covered his head. But they hadn't bothered to shackle his legs. He flexed them gingerly, one at a time. His spirits soared when he found that each movement eased the cramps. Cautiously, he tried to get to his feet. He rolled on his back and attempted a sit-up, an exercise he'd done a million times in the past. But that was the old Justin. Today's Justin was handcuffed and exhausted and it took him three tries before he succeeded. He drew a deep breath and considered his next move. What he needed was leverage, something to push off against, something to steady him.

What he needed was a wall. He inched along the floor, using his feet to push himself backward until he reached a wall. Using every ounce of strength in his legs, he arched his back, dug his feet against the floor, and slipped. *Goddam!* Without shoes to give him traction it was an impossibility.

But Justin wasn't the type to give up easily. He began to talk himself through his next task. *Okay, You've made it this far. Now what? How the fuck do I get traction with woolen socks on a smooth floor. Simple. Take* my *socks off and use my sweaty feet.* Not so simple without using your hands. *Okay, smartass, now what?*

Frederikson struggled for nearly thirty minutes, peeling back his left sock with his right foot, then reversed the procedure. He didn't succeed completely, but far enough. He dug in with bare heels and pushed and raised himself a few inches. And pushed again. And again. Five minutes later he'd made it. He was drained beyond exhaustion, wobbly, and bathed in perspiration, but he had done it.

He set out to explore his world, working his way along the perimeter of the cell, using the wall to steady him and guide him. Eight steps from corner to corner, ten steps along the wall that held a doorway. Judging by the cold air seeping though the frame, it was much warmer inside his cell than outside.

Encouraged that he'd made it this far, Frederikson took stock of his situation. With the exception of a broken nose and more aches and pains than he could count he seemed to have escaped serious injuries. Most importantly, they hadn't killed him yet. Therefore, he reasoned, they needed him. And that, whatever it was, would be his ace in the hole. Sooner or later someone would come for him. Sooner or later they'd have to reveal their hand. It was up to him to make the most of that moment.

This revelation was a small triumph in an apparently hopeless situation. Sure, he was grasping at straws, but what the hell, there sure wasn't anything else to grasp. The bastards had brought him to the House. He was cuffed and blindfolded and wearing nothing other than a T-shirt, sweatpants and socks. And it wouldn't be long before he'd have to use a bathroom.

He wondered if they'd come to get him before he wet his pants. Which made him wonder if they'd come to get him at all. Maybe they didn't want anything from him after all. Maybe this was the way they did it all the time. Let people rot in this place and dump their bodies in a ditch and wait for vultures to pick them clean.

Once again he was on the verge of going over the edge. *I can't let that happen*, he told himself, and suddenly froze in mid-thought. He strained his ears, convinced he'd heard someone. It was a familiar voice, right next to him, so close that his skin prickled.

"Who's there?" he croaked and recognized the voice he'd just heard. *Oh Christ, I'm losing it. Now I'm hearing voices and what I hear is myself.* But for good measure he shouted again, "Who's there?"

There was no answer.

*****

There wouldn't be an answer for the next twelve hours. During that time Frederikson paced the length of his cell, talked to himself, wet his pants twice, dozed off on his feet, fought cramps in his arms and shoulders, cried, screamed at the top of his lungs, and then did the unthinkable. Too tired to stay on his feet, he eased himself to the floor, and sat. Gone was his small victory. Gone was his determination. All he wanted was something to drink and a few hours of sleep.

*****

"Hello Justin. Nice to see you again."

Even in a state of semi-consciousness Frederikson recognized the nasal, clipped voice immediately.

"I bet you're surprised I'm here, right? I'm sorry they roughed you up a bit, but it's really not too bad, not compared to what they did to your friend. You remember her, don't you? Paulette? Although I don't think you'll find her quite as attractive as you once did."

"What do you want from me?" Frederikson croaked, the words getting stuck in his throat.

"You have it all wrong, Justin. I don't want anything from you. You're the one who wants something."

Frederikson didn't answer.

"I guess you're not in a talkative mood. That's too bad. I thought we could have a little chat and clear the air. But that's all right. I have all the time in the world." The man chuckled and nudged Frederikson with his shoe. "And you do too, don't you? Have all the time in the world, I mean."

"No, wait. Don't leave me like this."

"Like what, Justin? Handcuffed? That's nothing. We've had prisoners cuffed for weeks on end without doing any permanent damage to them. The worst thing that'll happen is that your arms are going to be a little stiff for a while. As long as the cuffs don't cut off your circulation you have nothing to worry about."

"I'm thirsty," Frederikson croaked, hating himself. At least let me have something to drink. And take this blindfold off."

"Sorry, but I can't do that. You're not in any danger of serious dehydration. Not yet, anyhow. And as far as the blindfold is concerned, it's for your own good."

"Please." Frederikson pleaded, ashamed that was reduced to groveling.

"Soon, Justin. But for now it's better if you stay just the way you are. You'll understand when the time is right. Until then a blindfold will help you look inside your soul."

Confined to his cell, minute bled into minute, hour into hour. He didn't know if five minutes or five days had passed since Axton's surprise visit. As time bled away he was increasingly convinced that he would die. Not of injuries, which he didn't think were life threatening, but of abandonment and thirst. Already he gave in to mindless illusions. Slipping into the past was so much easier than dealing with the present. The past was good. The present was hell. And with it came a horrible question. "Why did I fuck up my life?"

*****

"Hello, Justin."

This time the voice was unfamiliar, soft and mellow, with an undercurrent of compassion. The cord around his throat loosened. The cloth was pulled from his head. He blinked against blinding light. His pupils followed a flashlight's circular motion. As his eyes adjusted, shapes emerged.

For the first time Justin saw his eight by ten foot cell. It was unfurnished. The walls were grayish blue and constructed of plastic panels. The floor looked like flecked marble and was pitched inward towards a rectangular metal grating covering a sump hole. There were no windows. Above him, a rush of cold air fell from a ceiling vent. Directly in front of him was a steel door. Next to it, a calendar was taped to the wall. One date, November 15 was circled in red. A one-sentence message, also in red, gave him chills. *Today is the first day of the end of your life.*

"Where am I?"

"In a criminal hospital. I'm Dr. Callahan."

Justin squinted at a tall man wearing a green hospital gown and rubber gloves. A livid purple birthmark stained his right forehead and disappeared in sparse gray hair.

"Why did they arrest me? What the hell am I doing here?" It was so much easier to talk to a stranger than to Axton.

"Don't you know, Justin?" Callahan's voice was as gentle as a summer breeze. "You have sinned. Impure thoughts have poisoned your mind and you were brought to The House to be healed."

Justin didn't believe a word of it. "If that's all they wanted why did they beat me up? Why didn't they just tell me to come with them?"

"Because you wouldn't have come, you know that. You would have resisted. Believe me, this was the only way. Someday you will understand, just like you will understand the wondrous ways of Resurrection. Think of it, Justin. Think of the name, Resurrection. How could we resurrect you unless you had perished first?"

Frederikson was stunned. Everyone in this place was infused with so much religious fervor that it almost sounded believable. "Then how come…?"

Although Callahan's kindness was unflappable, he cut Justin short. "Enough of this talk. I'm not here to heal your mind. I'll leave that to those who understand the miracle of the human brain. It's your body I'm concerned about. You look a mess."

"How bad am I?" Justin asked with alarm.

"Probably not as bad as you look. I'm sure it looks worse than it actually is."

The man lowered himself to one knee and touched Justin's cheek. Even a gentle touch made him wince.

"Hold still, Justin, don't move. I think it's just a bruise, but let's make sure." He ran his finger along Justin's cheekbone. "This will hurt a little."

Justin clenched his jaws and watched as Callahan looked with concern at his cheekbone.

"My, my. It does look like your cheekbone may be cracked. It's not the end of the world though. You'll be as good as new in a few weeks if they let you."

The words sent tentacles of fear up Justin's spine. "What do you mean by *if they let me*?"

"Oh my, is that what I said? What I meant was that you'll be as good as new by the time they let you out."

The reply was accompanied by a reassuring smile, which didn't reassure Justin at all. He wanted to say *Bullshit* but changed his mind. Instead he asked, "What about my nose? I think it's broken."

Callahan agreed. "I'm sure it is, but that's nothing. No bones there to worry about, just cartilage. I'll set it and pack it in ice. I'm more worried about any neurological damage you might have sustained. It looks like you've got quite a nasty bump on the back of your head."

"That happened when they dragged me out of the car feet first," Justin said, recalling the moment vividly. "They grabbed me by the ankles and pulled and the next moment my head hit the ground. That's why I blacked out."

"I wish someone had told me earlier. You can't be too careful when it comes to neurological injuries. Nature does a pretty good job protecting the brain but all the fluid in the world isn't going to help if you get a real nasty blow."

Callahan raised his hand and moved it slowly from left to right. "Look at my hand, Justin. Can you see my hand?"

Justin nodded.

"How many fingers do you see?"

"Two." Justin stumbled over his words. "Three maybe. No, two. Definitely two."

"And now?"

Justin followed the hand's slow motion and started feeling dizzy.

"Do you feel like you're going to throw up?"

"No."

"Good. How about dizziness? Does it look like everything is spinning?"

Frederikson nodded. "A little bit."

"Well, it's a concussion all right. We'll run some scans to make sure there isn't any serious damage but it looks like you're going to be okay. Anything else bothering you? Any chest pains, shortness of breath, that sort of stuff?"

Frederikson shook his head. "No. Just the handcuffs."

Callahan looked troubled. "I'm sorry, Justin, but I'm not allowed to…" He put his lips to Justin's ear and whispered, "but if you tell me that there's something wrong with your shoulder… Well, then I wouldn't have a choice, would I? I mean, in order to examine you properly I'd have to remove your cuffs, wouldn't I?"

Frederikson nodded.

Callahan's face creased with a quick smile. "Okay then, let's have a look at that right shoulder of yours. If you'll just move over a bit…"

And just like that Frederikson's arms were free. The cuffs dropped to the floor. Callahan retrieved them and slipped them into his jacket pocket before turning back to Frederikson. "Go ahead, stretch your arms. Go easy though. You've been cuffed for a long time. Here, let me massage them."

Callahan's fingers worked Justin's arms. They moved along his forearms to his elbows and up to his shoulders. Throughout, he spoke with the gentlest voice Justin ever heard. "Slowly, that's the secret. Work out the kinks and get the old blood flowing again. Feels better already, doesn't it?"

Frederikson agreed.

"Go ahead, you do it."

Inch by inch numbness gave way.

Callahan gave Frederikson a conspiratorial wink. "Good. And I'm so glad your shoulder's okay. You feel better now?"

"Yeah."

"Good. I'll see to it that they get you something to drink. Juice okay?

"Sure."

"Consider it done. Just one more thing though and then I'll be out of your hair. I'm going to give you a shot to relax you."

"But…" Frederikson objected with a stricken look.

"Don't worry, it won't harm you. It's just a sedative."

Frederikson hesitated. "I feel okay now."

Callahan wouldn't take no for an answer. "Shhh, trust me. I won't hurt you. I'm here to help you. Now, give me your arm and make a fist. Okay, that's good. Believe me, you won't even feel it."

A quick sting.

"See. That wasn't so bad, was it? Now lean back and close your eyes. This stuff may make you dizzy for a while so it helps if you keep your eyes closed for a couple of minutes. I'll let you know when you can open them again. By then you'll feel much better, you'll see. All your anxiety will be gone. Good boy, keep them closed. Perfect. Feels better already, doesn't it? And you're not afraid anymore, right? Just a few more minutes. Feels so good. So good. Soooo good…"

*****

A tall man with gray hair and a birthmark above his right temple took his eyes off the monitor. He picked up a phone and waited patiently for the connection to be established.

"Phase I is completed." He glanced at the monitor again. Frederikson's eyes were closed in peaceful sleep. A content smile curled his lips. "He's ready for phase II. Do you want me to use the usual method?"

The man listened with growing concern, then frowned. "Are you sure, Bruno? That's pretty powerful stuff. Okay, if that's what you want. I'll start transference immediately."

*****

When Justin woke up he found himself in bed, his arms and legs strapped to sidebars. He was dressed in a green hospital gown. Subdued light filtered through overhead louvers whose slats were angled to deflect glare away from his eyes. He smelled fresh linens and antiseptic cleaning fluids.

He moved his head from side to side, feeling as if he were floating in an ethereal void. Indescribably delicious nothingness filled his body, matching a delicious void inside his head. For the first time in a very long time he was at peace with himself. He was free of troubling thoughts and pain and fear. He felt clean and uncluttered.

Frederikson smiled.

Chapter 33

LIKE IT OR not, I had to go back to Brauner's office one more time. I had a crisis on my hands, and I found out about it as soon as I woke up.

One of the perks of being Apostle was that I now owned my own drip coffee maker. And after the kind of night I'd just had, I could really use a cup to get me going. So I brewed a pot and decided to spend a couple of minutes going through my notes. That's when I discovered I didn't have any notes to read. In fact, I didn't have my notebook.

I searched high and low, but with living quarters as small as mine it didn't take long to figure out that the one place my notebook wasn't was in my apartment. And since I'd hightailed it from Brauner's Kitchen without making any detours, there was only one place where it could be.

Of course I had every right in the world to return to the office. As a matter of fact, I was probably expected to be there, doing my job, trying to act every inch the honorable Apostle. So what was the problem?

For one, I was scared. I felt like a criminal returning to the scene of the crime. For another, the very last thing I'd done last night was to call Security and tell them that I was finished, thank you very much, and that I didn't need to come back. At the time it sounded like the right thing to do. Now it turned out to be the dumbest thing I'd ever done. Today was Sunday, off-hours security was still in effect, and if Security didn't let me back inside my office, my notebook with all its scribbling and a list of forty-eight names was there for the taking. Doc Brauner's taking.

I threw on my clothes and ran to Terwilliger where I was greeted by security guard Oliver who took his job very seriously. He gave me a once-over, demanded to know why I needed to get inside a secured building, and was unimpressed when I told him that I was Apostle Koertner, here on official business. He checked his security log, found my name had been crossed out, and told me to go home.

I tried to convince him, explaining my call to security last night. He simply shook his head and folded his arms across his chest.

"Just check with headquarters," I pleaded. "They can verify everything. Dr. Brauner cleared it with them."

"So why don't you get Dr. Brauner to call them?" he asked.

"Because he's out of town."

"I see," guard Oliver said. His expression told me he thought I was full of it.

"Look, I know what you think, but all you have to do is call them. Please."

"I can't do that," he said.

"Why not?"

"Because my two-way is in the car and my car is parked over there," he pointed in the general direction of a municipal lot at the corner of Front Street. "And I'm not allowed to leave my post."

Guard Oliver was unmoved. He wasn't about to budge. I was getting desperate. Visions of Brauner's return from his sabbatical, making the rounds of the office, and stumbling upon my notebook loomed larger than life.

I decided to play on Oliver's sympathy. "Isn't there anything I can do, sir? You see, if I don't get my job done by the time Brauner gets back, well, I'm afraid he'll fire me."

Oliver was still unmoved.

"What if I go to security and get a note from them?" I offered. Counting on a half-hour walk there and another half-hour to plead my case with them, I could be back at Terwilliger before ten. Plenty of time to find my notebook, shred two pages of incriminating evidence, and be out of there before lunchtime.

"That'll work," Oliver said. "But you'll have to go the Rondout office."

"Huh? I thought they're at…"

"They are," Oliver said with a smile. "But today's Sunday and on Sundays their Stockade district office is closed. Happy walking, Koertner."

*****

Happy walking indeed. It was five-and-half miles to the Rondout office on Wurtz Street. I made it there by eleven, pleaded my case at the gatehouse, and was allowed inside ten minutes later. Being inside a police station, let alone Violence Control's dreaded headquarters, can make even the most innocent person nervous. I was a basket case.

I waited on a wooden bench in a shabby waiting room. Three rows of benches faced a counter, behind which a lone duty sergeant was busy answering a barrage of telephones. Half an hour later, he acknowledged me, informed me that he'd be back by twelve-thirty, and said that I could get a bite to eat in the employee's cafeteria. So much for having plenty of time.

I wasn't hungry but didn't have a choice. I was escorted from my bench and the waiting room was locked behind me. The duty sergeant hung a hand-lettered sign proclaiming *Closed For Lunch* from the door and led me downstairs to the lunchroom. I spent my last three dollars on a ham and cheese I didn't want and waited for twelve-thirty.

Finally, Violence Control was back open for business and to my surprise no one gave me a hassle. The duty sergeant made a phone call and issued me a pass. Then I got lucky. He called me back just as I was about to close the door behind me. "Hey Koertner, you want a ride?"

I made an about face and watched him walk around the counter. "Sure," I said, trying not to sound too excited.

"I'll meet you out front in five. I gotta run into town and pick up a package from Terwilliger anyhow."

"Sure," I said again. "Thanks."

"No problem. Some big shot just called from Shandaken for a priority pickup from Terwilliger. Besides, It'll be nice to have some company. By the way, I'm Tim."

Guard Oliver was still standing out front, still in the same position, still being a hardass. He waved Tim through without checking his credentials and then made a big deal out of checking my pass. By the time he was satisfied that everything was in order Tim reappeared at the front door, a book-sized package under his arm, and waved goodbye.

"See ya around, Koertner."

"Yeah, and thanks again, Tim."

*****

The office was a lot neater than I'd left it last night. Pails stood empty with new plastic liners. Desks were dusted, floors vacuumed. Rachel's droopy plant wasn't droopy any longer after receiving a much-needed watering. I didn't bother checking my own office. I remembered putting my notebook on a shelf when I reached up to slide Jasmine Devin's video into its slot, I headed straight for Brauner's Kitchen, hopefully for the last time. I descended into the basement, through the turnstile, and into the vault. And there, just I'd thought, was my notebook, wedged halfway under a shelf, undisturbed by cleaning crews, out of security camera reach, ready for the shredding. I let out a deep breath and saw something odd. Something green. Something I hadn't seen before.

It was a withdrawal slip. Color-coded, green for Sunday. Dated today. Signed out by Timothy Steckel, badge 8861. Case number 37333745766-587846.

I scribbled the case number in my notebook and left the vault with a bad taste in my mouth. So bad that I headed straight for the front door. Not so bad though that I didn't stop at Rachel's desk. Using her telephone pad, I translated case number 37333745766-587846.

Justin Frederikson.

Chapter 34

ON THE EVENING of their departure from Gotham Towers, Axton and Brauner were heading west on State Route 28 on their way to *The House*. They made the sixty-five mile trip from the Rhinecliff railroad station to the facility's outer checkpoint in a little over an hour and a half. Torrential rains pelted the Jeep, reducing visibility to a hundred yards. Axton drove, peering intently through a pie-shaped patch of windshield that the wipers barely managed to keep clear. Inside the passenger compartment, humid air was thick with cigar smoke, making Brauner's eyes tear and his stomach queasy. Neither spoke, each exhausted from a train ride that had been delayed by signal problems for over two hours.

Both were glad to be back, but for very different reasons. Axton had a nagging foreboding that things weren't quite as rosy as Brauner led him to believe. Why else would the doctor be so damn edgy? Brauner on the other hand was increasingly worried that Axton was on to something. Although the colonel always looked at everything with a suspicious eye, his circumspect behavior since the Austin incident had been unusual even for him. Brauner had worked too hard for too long to let someone interfere with his plans now.

By the time the checkpoint became visible in their headlights it was six-thirty. They pulled up at the gate, Axton lowered the driver's side window, and returned a guard's salute. He barely checked their credentials, recognizing both of them from numerous prior visits, and raised the gate. Axton gunned the engine and they drove off. The *House* loomed one mile ahead.

Brauner, his hands knotted and jaws clenched, couldn't wait to get the last leg of the trip out of the way. He detested the five minute ride through a virtual no-man's land that ringed *The House*. Speed bumps were placed at one-hundred yard intervals. Glaring spotlights illuminated the man-made devastation. On either side of the road was dirt the color of ashes. All trees had been felled. Defoliants had killed off vegetation, rendering the ground permanently barren. Even weeds couldn't survive in the poisoned earth. Spring rains turned the no-man's land into muddy quagmires. During summer's prolonged dry spells, haze and dust filtered out daylight. In the winter, when the countryside was ethereally peaceful, two giant incinerators transformed freshly fallen snow into a sooty blanket. Only for a brief spell in October, when the fall foliage painted nearby mountains with a riot of colors, did the complex seem remotely inhabitable.

In the middle of this desolation stood *The House,* a squat, windowless, concrete structure rising three stories into a permanently sulfur-laden sky. From a central core, eight spoke-like arms extruded like roots, seemingly anchoring the main building to the earth. In reality, they were the top-most floors of a vast underground structure that plunged six floors beneath the ground, supplying ventilation, solar energy, and security installations. Buried from view lay an efficient, self-contained city, the heart and soul of Resurrection.

Reaching that heart was unnerving, leaving it without permission was deadly. Even Brauner, who had made the trip many times, felt apprehensive as Axton pulled up on a concrete pad. Straight ahead was a reinforced steel door and a sign proclaiming *Pull Onto Conveyer. Shut Engines. Close All Windows.*

They were about to enter Spoke Six, the main vehicular artery leading to the central core. A security camera made a sweep of their car. Armed with a hand-held explosives detector, a white-robed technician scanned the Jeep, then punched an access code into a keypad. The steel door cranked open and the conveyer was activated.

They inched into Spoke Six, aptly nicknamed Eerie Canal because of three chambers located along the quarter-mile stretch of tunnel. Progress was a slow three miles an hour. Making the five minute ride seem even longer were the ominous sights gliding past their car windows: overhead floodlights, security cameras, gas jets protruding at fifty yard intervals from the tunnel's walls, and of course the massive steel gates that separated the tunnel into three chambers.

They approached the first gate and Brauner's claustrophobia ran amok. He turned to Axton. "The next time I come here I'm taken the pedestrian tunnel. This place gives me the creeps."

Axton continued chewing his Havana.

"I don't know why you insist on driving in the first place. You can't do anything with your car when you get there."

Axton was amused. "Because I like the tunnel, Bruno. As a matter of fact, I'm damn proud of it. I think it's ingenious, especially the gates. Look at them." He pointed at the bars of an approaching gate, suspended from the tunnel's ceiling like giant teeth. "They look like guillotines, don't you agree? One move and wham!" Axton's hand slammed the dashboard for emphasis. "They can crush a car like it was a cockroach."

Brauner winced. He didn't find the idea amusing at all.

Axton chuckled, his bald head bobbing, and exhaled a cloud of smoke. And he was more convinced than ever that something was up. This was unusual behavior, even for Brauner.

*****

They signed in at the guard's station and changed into mandatory white coveralls. Axton barked a curt goodbye and headed for a second-floor conference room meeting with the local chief of security, Lieutenant Blaufeld. *Good riddance* Brauner mumbled under his breath, glad to be rid of the colonel until midnight. He took the elevator down to the third floor and headed for Dr. Callahan's office. Wheezing and out of breath after rushing along Spoke A he opened the door to Callahan's office without bothering to knock.

Callahan jumped to his feet and beamed a broad smile when he recognized his visitor. "Bruno, you're late. What happened?"

"Don't ask. Everything. First there was a signal problem and my train got in two hours late. Then right outside Resurrection City the skies opened up and it took an extra half hour to drive here. I'm just glad I made it in one piece. Axton drives like a goddamn maniac."

Callahan put his arm on Brauner's shoulder and led him to a wing chair, next to which waited an ice filled tumbler and an unopened fifth of Wild Turkey. "Well, better late than never." He pointed at the bottle. "Help yourself. You must be exhausted."

"Well, maybe just one." Brauner poured two fingers and downed the bourbon in one gulp. "Ah, that's good. Thanks for making me feel at home."

"Glad to do it. I'm just sorry we missed dinner. I had reservations at the club but they stopped serving half an hour ago. I'm afraid the best I can do under the circumstances are… Let me call the commissary real quick and see if they can send something up."

Brauner waved him off. "Don't bother. To be honest, my stomach still hasn't recovered from last night's roasted duck. Besides, we need to talk. Are you sure everything is okay? Are we still on target?"

"Relax, Bruno, there's no need to worry. I told you yesterday everything is under control."

"I know, I know, but Axton has been very antsy lately. He's acting as if he smells trouble. You know him as well as I do. He's usually right."

Callahan smiled. "Don't worry. Whatever the Colonel is smelling, it's got nothing to do with us. I'll tell you what, let me order a couple of sandwiches. It'll take them half an hour before they get them up here anyhow. In the meantime we'll take a few minutes and make the rounds to set your mind at ease. Then we can have a bite, catch up on some gossip, have a drink…"

"What gossip?" Brauner interrupted with sudden alarm.

"For God's sake, Bruno, relax and don't be so jumpy. It was just a figure of speech. You know, we'll kick off our shoes and reminisce a bit, talk about the old days. That's all I meant."

He refilled Brauner's glass and pushed it into his hand. "Here, have another. I insist. You need it. I haven't seen you this uptight in a long time."

*****

A circular hallway wound its way around the building's core. In the sub-basement, the core housed a computer center, three laboratories, a decontamination room, a battery of examination and treatment rooms, and the morgue. Fifty single-occupancy patient rooms lined the outer perimeter of the hall. Each room was monitored by closed-circuit cameras which were hooked up to the Camp's computer network, supplying twenty-four-hour life support and surveillance. Steel doors with one-way windows were kept locked at all times. Tonight, only twelve of the fifty rooms were occupied. The other patients had completed their treatment two days ago.

Shortly after their makeshift dinner of cafeteria sandwiches Brauner and Callahan made their rounds for the night. Brauner, holding a computer printout, led the way. He was closely followed by Callahan as they made their way from door to door, pausing occasionally to look at a patient, checking off name after name on his list. Door seventeen held his interest longer than the others.

"How's seventeen doing?"

"Not as well as I had hoped," Callahan admitted. "We doubled her phase I therapy, even gave her a secondary stimulus, but she hasn't responded well. We managed to extract most of her short-term memory and neutralized ninety percent of her thought processes, but there's something in her long-term memory that resists everything we've tried so far. I don't really want to go on to phase II unless we clean her out completely."

"I agree. Leftover clutter can be very unpredictable, even dangerous."

"What do you suggest, Bruno? We don't have a lot of time to waste."

"What about radical desensitization?"

Callahan looked doubtful. "I don't know. There's always a risk that it'll leave her virtually brain dead. I'm not sure we should take that chance. Not yet, anyhow."

Brauner shrugged his shoulders and headed for the next door when he stopped abruptly.

"I have an idea, Callahan. A more direct approach might work better with her."

"Such as?"

Brauner rubbed his hands with glee. "Why don't we try a virtual reality overdose." He held up his hands to fend off Callahan's objections. "I know, I know, it's risky. But unless you have a better idea…"

Callahan shook his head.

"All right then, this is what you do. Program the module to play back some kind of horrible experience, a car accident for instance. Yes, this should be her scenario. She's in her teens, sixteen I think. She's next to her father in the front seat when he suddenly loses control of his car trying to avoid a man running across the road. The man is an escaped prisoner from the Camp. Make sure she knows that. And make sure she blames this man for the accident. That's critical. And for emphasis, make sure she sees her father die. Let him burn to death. Pull out all the stops. You know, the sizzling, the smell of burning flesh, whatever else you can think of to traumatize her."

Callahan whistled softly. "Christ, Bruno. What did she ever do to you?"

"Everything."

The two men resumed their rounds in silence, passing door after door, engrossed with their work, when Brauner stopped and put an arm around Callahan. "If the patient in seventeen doesn't respond to the virtual reality module she's probably useless. Just have her shipped to the warehouse. No use wasting any more time on her."

Chapter 35

DAYLIGHT SLITHERED THROUGH drawn blinds into Terwilliger House like a snake's tongue. A pale glow cast monochrome shadows against the floor and crept towards Brauner's couch. Half an hour after sunrise it reached Brauner, who was curled up lengthwise on this couch, right arm dangling to the floor. The light worked its way along his fingers, across his wrist, and towards his elbow. His pale skin and white shirt sleeve glowed in the advancing light, giving them the appearance of a bloodless limb that had been severed from a torso.

Brauner stirred and turned on his side, curling up into a ball. But his sleep was broken. Thoughts began to stir. Apprehension grew into full-fledged worry. As fitful as sleep had been, facing the day loomed even worse. He allowed himself another five minutes in the fetal position, hoping for his pounding headache to subside. It only worsened. His stomach was queasy, his nose stuffy. He blinked and the light hurt his eyes. He was suffering from yet another old-fashioned hangover, courtesy of way too many Wild Turkeys and not enough time to sleep it off.

Reluctantly, Brauner scrambled to his feet and ran a hand through his gray tonsure. He thought back to last night, trying to recall if anything had happened between leaving Callahan's office and the moment Axton had deposited him outside Terwilliger's front door with a sarcastic *Clean yourself up, Bruno. You smell like a distillery. And be at my office at ten sharp.*

As far as he could remember, it had been a routine evening followed by a routine meal he didn't want, half a pint he shouldn't have had, and a routine drive back to Resurrection City during which neither he nor Axton spoke very much. All very routine. Except for the fact that he'd stayed at Terwilliger for the night, which wasn't routine at all. And that worried Brauner. Sleeping on his office couch was completely out of character. So, if he'd been too drunk or too tired to go home and sleep in his own bed, what else had he been too drunk or too tired for?

Brauner stretched to work out the kinks in his bones and made his way to a small powder room. Inspecting himself in the mirror, he saw a pasty-faced old man with a fringe of disheveled gray hair, a soiled white cotton shirt, and trousers so wrinkled he normally wouldn't be caught dead in. He checked his wristwatch and winced. Already nine-thirty. There was no time to shave, let alone run home and change into a new suit. He splashed water on his face, ran a comb through his hair, and gargled with week-old orange juice. Then he popped two aspirins into an empty stomach and was out the front door.

*****

Axton greeted him with a sneer. "You look like shit, Bruno."

"It hasn't been a good night, Xavier. I'll be all right."

"No you won't. Not when I tell you the bad news." A cruel smile flickered on Axton's lips. Compared to Brauner, Axton looked well rested. His skin glowed from a recent shave and not a hair was out of place, reminding Brauner painfully of his own bedraggled appearance.

As quickly as it had appeared, Axton's smile evaporated and he fixed Brauner with a contemptuous glare. "It seems you have a problem, Bruno. Actually two problems."

Brauner squirmed and hated himself for his jittery nerves, knowing that any sign of weakness in front of Axton could be deadly. He managed an unconvincing smile and asked casually, "What's the matter, Xavier?"

"This is what's the matter." Axton punched the phone's message replay button. "Listen carefully. I think you'll get the drift."

Brauner listened to an all too familiar voice. His heart sank. Halfway through the recording his hands started to tremble…*represents not only a serious problem for the December 24 shipment, but for the entire operation. I cannot and will not tolerate these careless mistakes any longer. If unsuspecting civilians can discover such glaring discrepancies, think of what our enemies might come up with. I want this matter resolved immediately and hold you personally responsible…*

Brauner felt cold sweat break out on his back. But things got worse. Axton blasted another salvo at him.

"And that's not all. I have a video showing your wonderful apostle snooping all around Brauner's Kitchen. It seems your young man is quite the detective. He's come up with a list of thirty names."

"No. That can't be. I…"

"Shut up, Bruno, shut up and listen to me. This has gone too far. Don't you realize you're jeopardizing everything we've worked for? I can't let that happen. I want all loose ends tied up. Get rid of the woman now. You're good at things like that. I don't want a trace of Private Austin left anywhere in the Camp. Anywhere. Do you understand?"

Brauner nodded.

"And then I want you to take care of Koertner. Your experiment is over. Get rid of him."

"But…"

"Don't but me, Bruno. You have until midnight tonight to take care of him and Austin. I just hope it's not too late."

"She's no problem, Xavier. I'll take care of her today. But David, let me talk to him. I think I can…"

Axton cut him off in mid-sentence. "I don't think you heard me, Bruno. He's become a liability. I want him terminated by tonight."

Seething with anger, Brauner nevertheless kept himself under control. He knew that his confrontation with Axton had been inevitable, a moment he had both dreaded and looked forward to. Now that it had arrived he recognized it as a defining moment. A stony silence followed Axton's last remark. They glared at each, then Brauner rose and made an about face to head for the door. He was overcome by ethereal tranquility and wondered, is this is how it feels to lose the final appeal on death row? The similarity was fitting in more ways than one.

He turned to Axton and aid, "As you wish. I'll be on my way. No use wasting any more time. I'll let you know when I'm finished."

He was gone a second later. Axton drew aside the brocade curtains and watched Brauner descend three steps to Fair Street and head briskly around the corner. It was only a five minute walk and although the morning air was icy, Brauner didn't notice the chill. His jacket was unbuttoned and his tie, having worked its way free from his vest, fluttered in a gusty breeze. His sparse hair was in disarray but his mind wasn't. A crucial decision had just been made for him and now there was no turning back. Brauner smiled. It was the first ray of sunshine on a day that had risen with dismal gloom.

*****

An ingenious plan had germinated during what should have been Brauner's darkest moment. Back in his office, the doors closed and shades drawn, the noise and clatter of Rachel Firestein and this morning's Disciples in the outer office a muted reminder that life in Resurrection continued on a hectic pace, Brauner reflected and nurtured his idea into a full-fledged plan.

He called Callahan on his private line and waited patiently for the doctor to pick up. When there was no answer he depressed the *Page* button. Two minutes later an out-of-breath Callahan called back. Hearing the anxiety in Brauner's voice, he was immediately alarmed. "What's the matter, Bruno? Is there a problem?"

"Not at all, just a change of plans."

"That's a problem," Callahan responded warily. "What happened?"

"The time has come."

Silence from Callahan's end. Brauner started tapping the desk. "Callahan, are you there?"

"Yes, of course. It's just… Well, you know, it's so soon before the shipment is scheduled to leave. What is it you want?"

"I need a report on patient thirty-eight immediately."

"I don't have it yet, Bruno. They just brought him in yesterday, you know that. And he wasn't in the best shape. They really did a number on him. He's got a concussion, broken nose, contusions, bruises, you name it, he's got it."

"I know, I know. Did you start phase II yet?" Brauner asked impatiently.

"No, I thought it best to give him a day or two."

"Good, don't start it."

"I don't understand," Callahan said. "I thought…"

"Can he travel?"

"Yes, of course. None of his injuries are life threatening, but without going on to phase II he's going to be unpredictable at best."

"Don't worry. I'll fine-tune him myself."

"What?" This time Callahan's reaction was unmistakable.

"Look, Callahan," Brauner said, forcing a calm note. "I told you, it's time. We have to do it now. Immediately, before Axton finds out. I need thirty-eight in Resurrection City by this afternoon. Can you get him here?"

"I guess so," Calahand said. "There's a supply convoy leaving at noon. I guess I can have him on it."

"Good, that's settled then. Just get him on the truck and wait. Do you understand? It's absolutely crucial that you do nothing at all. Just go on with your everyday business and wait until you hear from me. I'll take care of things on this end."

Callahan frowned. "Are you sure? I don't like last minute changes. I mean, we've been over this again and again, and now all of a sudden you're changing things."

"I'm not changing anything," Brauner corrected him. "I'm just accelerating it."

"How can you say that? Patient thirty-eight never figured in our plans."

"I know," Brauner admitted, feeling twinges of apprehension himself. Of course Callahan was right, plans had changed, but for the better. He decided to come clean with Callahan. "But that's because we didn't know Axton was going to have him sent to *The House*. Let's not look a gift horse in the mouth. He'll be perfect and we won't have to risk one of our own. Besides, Axton forced my hand. He gave me an ultimatum. We've got until tonight. If we don't pull it off by then we can kiss our plan goodbye."

"I guess that's it then, huh?"

"Yeah, that's it. Oh, I almost forgot. There's one more change. Ship patient seventeen to the warehouse."

This time Callahan objected and Brauner listened with growing annoyance, beginning to have second thoughts himself. The man obviously didn't have the foresight or the guts. He wondered how long it would be before Callahan too would have to be dealt with. It was probably best to make contingency plans shortly. But for the moment at least he needed him, so it was best to appease him. "Trust me, it's the only way. I know what you're going to say, about the deadline and the shipment and all but it has to be done. As a matter of fact, those are Axton orders. If you don't believe me, call him yourself. He was quite emphatic about it. He wants her shipped to the warehouse by midnight tonight. Those were his exact words."

He smiled at Callahan's lack of response, knowing the man's aversion of dealing with the colonel. *Definitely no guts,* he told himself. *No guts.*

Brauner glanced at his watch. It was time to get moving, time to get off the phone. "Thanks, Callahan. I'll give you a call as soon as thirty-eight gets here. In the meantime do nothing. As a matter of fact you should keep out of sight. Plead a headache or the flu or whatever and stay in your room."

*****

Brauner hung up and walked to a filing cabinet. He unlocked it and slid out the top drawer. Hidden beneath a stack of pads and folders was a semi-automatic handgun. Brauner lifted it from the drawer and slipped it under a stack of papers on his desk.

It was still before noon and the day that had started so badly was turning into a pleasant surprise. Brauner sat back and folded his hands. All he needed to do now was be patient and wait. The problem would take of itself.

Chapter 36

TWO SOUNDS WOKE Cecilia Austin from her first deep sleep in over a month. One was Max, who had stationed himself at the side of her bed, tail thumping, front paws scratching at the sheets, barking furiously into her ear. The other was her phone.

Cecilia turned on her side and saw that it was nine-thirty. Having been roused from a realistic dream, in which she, Thurston, and baby Dawn had relived a vacation in Disney World, it took her a moment to return to reality. It was a reality she'd rather not have faced, accentuated by drab daylight and haunting memories. She was tempted to let the machine pick up but Max refused to quit barking, the phone refused to quit ringing and her conscience refused to keep ignoring the interruption.

She cradled the phone between shoulder and cheek. "Hello?"

"Mrs. Austin? This is Senator Kerr's office. Will you hold while I connect you with the senator?"

Cecilia was instantly awake. While she listened to a series of rapid clicks as a connection was made at the other end, her brain was bombarded by hundreds of impulses. But before she had a chance to sort them out the senator's voice filled her ear.

"Mrs. Austin, sorry I took so long to get back to you."

Max's tail whipped against the bed in a mad frenzy, rivaling her racing heart. Cecilia sat up with a jolt. After waiting to hear from Kerr for three weeks, she suddenly dreaded his call. "Please don't apologize," she said. "I know how busy you are."

"It's not a matter of being busy," he said. "It just took a while to find out what happened. Unfortunately I don't have any good news for you."

It was exactly what Cecilia had expected to hear. Now that Kerr was about to confirm her fears she refused to believe him.

"Mrs. Austin, are you all right?"

"Yes," she whispered, her voice cracking. She started to cry. "No, I'm not," she sobbed. "I'm not all right. How do you think…"

"I'm sorry. That was a very insensitive thing to say. Of course you're not, but at least I can tell you that you were right in your suspicions. Something went terribly wrong up there and they tried to cover it up. I know it won't bring your daughter back, but maybe you can get some sort of closure knowing that the people responsible will be fully prosecuted and punished."

She heard his words but didn't believe them fully. If they had lied before why wouldn't they be lying now, she wondered. Why should she believe anything coming out of that terrible place? Why wouldn't they be concocting another cover up? Why couldn't Dawn be alive and well?

Kerr went on with his incredibly soothing voice. "To be honest, at first I believed them myself. It sounded so logical. A young woman driving alone on an unfamiliar mountain road. Heavy rains, pitch black, all the conditions for a terrible accident. But I couldn't get your suspicions out of my mind, especially that discrepancy with the letter. So I dug a little deeper. Thank God I have some contacts in the place. Of course they're not always reliable. Most of them are inmates themselves, stoolies who'd sell their mother for a dollar. But your daughter's case was different. She was relatively new in Resurrection and didn't know too many people there, but the one's she knew all seemed to like her, including her immediate supervisor. So when I didn't get anywhere with my usual sources I became suspicious myself. Something was going on. They were afraid of talking to me and that is always a red flag. That's when I decided to talk directly to her boss, a Dr. Brauner. Is that name familiar to you?"

"I think so, Cecilia said, vaguely recalling a reference Dawn had made in one of her letters. "I think Dawn mentioned him to me."

"Well, I spoke to Brauner a few days ago and he mentioned how your daughter had been attacked in a public library and how she'd been sent to a maximum security facility in Shandaken and how there'd been another incident there in a lunch room…"

"Oh yeah" Cecilia interrupted. "The stabbing incident."

"That's right. Anyhow, this Brauner also mentioned some other disturbing facts, like how your daughter seemed depressed over a suicide, and how she missed working with a Disciple she'd been assigned to, and so forth."

"David," Cecilia said. "She wrote to me about him. She thought he had a real chance of making something out of himself."

"Anyhow, to make a long story short, this fellow Brauner seemed honest and sincere and he seemed to be very upset about your daughter's death. And then he said something that struck me as odd. He mentioned that he'd just been in Shandaken and wanted to see your daughter. But when he asked for her he was told that she was unavailable. He thought that was curious but didn't pursue the matter because at the time the place was on high alert. Apparently one of the inmates had managed to escape and since it was the second successful attempt in three months the whole place was in an uproar. It seems that the chief of security there was under intense scrutiny and that they'd clamped down hard. You know, things like curfews, restricted movement by everybody in the place, strip searches, double-checking absentee logs, and so forth. So Brauner didn't push it and he never got to see her."

Cecilia didn't understand how any of this had anything to do with Dawn's death, but continued to listen. "So after speaking with Brauner I talked to my source again and found out some interesting things. This escapee I just told you about had apparently stolen a Jeep and was heading east on route 28. Don't ask me how he managed to steal a car and get through security, but somehow he did. He was speeding. About two miles west of Arkville, well there's a sharp curve in the road, and…"

"And he collided with Dawn?"

"I'm sorry, yes. I'm not exactly sure how it happened. He could have skidded. Maybe he didn't have his lights on, who knows. What seems to be certain is that he sideswiped your daughter's car. She lost control and went over a guardrail. There's a fifty or sixty foot ravine there and when she went off the road her card exploded on impact. She died immediately."

"But I don't understand," Cecilia said. "What was Dawn doing on that road in the first place." Her voice turned increasingly hysterical. "For chrissakes, she didn't even have a driver's license."

"I know," Kerr answered. "I found that out when I went through her records. But the logs show that she signed out a Jeep that night at the Shandaken motor pool. Apparently nobody bothered to ask for her license. I guess they just assumed she had one. You see, up there everybody drives. It's not like Manhattan where a car can be an inconvenience. Anyway, she signed for the Jeep. She filled out the log, stating that she was going to Resurrection City to keep a meeting with this David she'd mentioned, and took off. About twenty-five miles later the weather turned really nasty and she was forced to turn back. As fate would have it, she ran right into this escapee."

Cecilia sat in silence, trying to make sense of what she'd just heard. If that's what had happened, and she had no reason to doubt Kerr, then why the cover-up. Why this elaborate scheme to keep the truth from her? "Senator," she asked. "If that's all there's to it, why did they lie? Why didn't they just tell me the truth?"

"I'm afraid there's a simple explanation, Mrs. Austin. You see, you have to understand the culture that prevails in Resurrection. It's a closed and secretive place. Everybody there assumes that the outside world wants to meddle in their affairs and is out to get them. When you add the fact that the chief of local security was under fire and on probation for the last escape attempt, it all makes perfect sense. What it boils down to is plain and simple, they're covering their asses. They didn't want another scandal. And they are arrogant to the point of taking the law into their own hands."

Long silence on Cecilia's part. Finally she spoke. "Now what?"

"Well, I've started a full investigation. I can promise you one thing, the people responsible will be brought to justice. The chief of security, a career officer named Sanchez, has been relieved of his duties and will face a tribunal. My guess is that he'll be sentenced to at least five years for obstruction of justice."

"And the other man?" Cecilia had trouble asking her question. "The man who killed Dawn."

"He was captured and returned to Shandaken. He's banged up a bit but not seriously hurt. He too will face a tribunal and will probably be sentenced to solitary confinement for life."

"I would like to see him," Cecilia said. "I just want to look him in the eye and ask him what it feels like kill a woman who dedicated her life to helping people like him."

Kerr hesitated. "I'm afraid that's not possible."

"Then at least tell me who he is," Cecilia asked with morbid fascination. "I need to know more about him."

"I suppose there's no harm in revealing his name. You'd find out sooner or later anyhow since it'll be part of your daughter's permanent record. They tell me his name is Justin Frederikson."

If Cecilia had thought that knowing who had killed her daughter would bring her closure she was mistaken. Justin Frederikson. A faceless unknown. Just another inmate. Just another man whom Dawn had given her life for.

She sat in stony silence, hearing Kerr breathe on the other end. There seemed to be nothing else to say. "So this is it?"

"I'm sorry, yes. Except for my formal report and some other paperwork. I have it all in front of me right now. There's an accident report, sworn statements by security, the coroner's report, the transcripts of my conversations with people in Resurrection, everything I've been able to document. The people in camp normally don't release this to the public but I pulled a few strings. If you're going to be home today I'd like to messenger it to you."

"Thank you."

"If it's okay with you I'll have one of my assistants bring it to you personally. There are some pretty graphic photographs in there along with the DNA report used to identify your daughter's remains. I'm afraid it's a bit gruesome and I'll feel better if one of my people brought it to you."

Cecilia still sat silently.

"Mrs. Austin, will that be okay with you?"

She nodded. "Yes." All she could manage was a whisper.

"Good. I'll ask Gertie Samuels to bring it. She is a lovely person. She's been with me for years. I know she's only a stranger to you, but sometimes even a stranger's shoulder can help. And Mrs. Austin, I'm…I'm so terribly sorry.

"It's okay."

"If there's anything else I can do for you…"

"No, thank you, Senator."

*****

Kerr hung up and walked to the window. He opened the curtains and stared into a light drizzle falling on Nassau County's Executive Complex. Beyond a wide expanse of lawn, the domed roof of the Nassau County Court was obscured by low hanging clouds. Beyond it, the usually heavy traffic on Old Country Road was at a near standstill. Kerr seemed transfixed by the scene. And he wondered how Cecilia Austin would cope.

After several minutes of silence he tore himself away from the window and returned to his desk. He took a deep breath, shook his head, and picked up the phone. By the time the connection was established he was as steady as a rock.

"It's Kerr. I've taken care of it. But let me warn you Xavier, this is the very last time I'll save your ass. No more slip-ups, do you hear me? And make sure Bruno doesn't screw up or you'll both be history. And make absolutely sure that all traces of Private Austin are gone. As far as I'm concerned, she never existed."

He set the phone down and shook his head again. Incompetent fools. God dam incompetent fools.

Chapter 37

AT TEN THIRTY in the morning Nurse Bruce McDaniels and Orderly Schlomo Minsk deactivated a heat scanner, unlocked door seventeen, and rolled a gurney into the room. A young woman lay comatose in bed, sheets covering her lower torso, leaving her abdomen and breasts exposed to fifty-five degree refrigerated air. She was deathly white, her translucent skin bearing a bluish tint that was eerily contrasted by shiny black hair and accentuated a jagged scar running the length of her right cheek. Her mouth was cracked open, revealing perfect teeth between bloodless lips. As the gurney was noisily maneuvered next to her bed and the sidebars lowered, her stare remained fixed on the ceiling, her dilated pupils eclipsing the white of her eyes. If not for a steady beep and recurrent spiking of a heart monitor she would appear to be dead.

Nurse McDaniels lifted her right wrist and removed a clear plastic tube. He let go of her arm and let it drop to the bed. A trickle of blood formed in the crook of her elbow and seeped along her forearm. McDaniels dabbed the puncture with a cotton wad and removed two suction cups from her chest. The monitor's jagged spike turned into a flat line.

Minsk tugged the top sheet off the woman and dropped it into a soiled-laundry bag. He studied her body with curiosity. "For a skinny broad she's got some legs," he said. "Get a load of them muscles. I bet 'ya she used to do a lot of running."

"Well, I guess she didn't run fast enough," McDaniels snickered. "A lotta good that's gonna do her now."

"You think…?

"I don't think nothin'," McDaniels interrupted him and turned his attention to a black leather bag on the gurney. "You're wasting time, so let's get her ready. We're running late." With that he unzipped the bag and handed it to his partner. "You get to do the honors this time."

Minsk shrugged his shoulders and without saying another word extracted a pair of scissors and an electric razor. While McDaniels lifted the woman's head to free her hair Minsk sheared to within an inch of her scalp before switching to an electric razor. A few moments later the woman's shorn head was dropped against the pillow and Minsk ran the razor across her pubis.

"Okay, all done," Minsk said. "Let's get her cleaned up."

They worked in silence, gathering up hair and dropping it into a medical waste bag. With the long strands removed, Minsk plugged in a handheld vacuum cleaner and ran it's soft-brush attachment across the woman's body. He worked meticulously, making sure to suck up all residual fuzz. Two minutes later he was done. He emptied the vacuum into the medical waste bag, sealed it with a sticker bearing the woman's ID number, and chuckled. "Okay, baby. Cleaner than a plucked chicken."

Ten minutes had passed. Six hundred seconds during which patient seventeen was stripped of her hair and dignity. Her depilated and nude body lay unmoving under the glare of overhead lights while McDaniels and Minsk left the room for a cigarette break. A few hurried drags later they returned and positioned themselves on either side of the bed.

"Okay, baby, time to get dressed. You're goin' on a trip," Minsk said. He lifted her ankles while McDaniels slipped her feet into a cryovac bag. They worked the plastic up her calves, past her knees and thighs.

"Okay, you lift her up."

McDaniels rolled the woman on her side and worked his right arm under her waist. "On three," he said and took a deep breath.

"One…two…three." He arched her waist upward and Minsk quickly slid the bag across her buttocks.

"Shit, for a skinny broad she sure is heavy," a red-faced McDaniels announced.

"Stop your bitching," Minsk said, "I'm going as fast as I can," glad that he'd won the coin toss and didn't have to do the lifting today. "Just sit her up."

McDaniels did as told, climbing into the bed and positioning himself behind the woman. He looped his arms under her shoulders and tilted her upper torso forward while Minsk folded the woman's arms across her chest and taped them into place with electrical tape. When she was securely trussed in the required position, he pulled the cryovac bag over her shoulders and head. Obscured by opaque plastic, the woman's body seemed to float inside the bag like an otherworldly alien suspended in space.

Both men took a moment to rest. McDaniels wiped his forehead. Minsk sat on the edge of the bed, looking at the body next to him with morbid fascination. "You know," he said, "no matter how many times I do this I still can't get used to it. I mean, just look at her lying in there. Sort of reminds me of a supermarket. You know, like at the meat counter where they have them bulk cuts all packaged airtight and then when you take it over to the butcher and he starts trimming away…"

"Oh fuck. Will you shut up already," McDaniels interrupted. "You're making me sick. I swear this is the last time I'm gonna work with you. The last fucking thing I need is your fucking commentary. Lets get her out of here before I puke up my breakfast."

They worked quickly now, running their hands from the bottom of the bag toward the top, smoothing out air until the plastic clung to the woman's body. Then they activated an electric pump to suck out the remaining air. With the last of the bubbles gone, Minsk peeled back a protective covering from the bag's adhesive strip and sealed the bag. Once more on the count of three they lifted her onto the gurney.

"I wonder what she did to wind up in the warehouse?" Minsk wanted to know. "I thought she had another day."

"Beats me. All I know is that Callahan gave the order himself. When he says jump I ask how high.'"

They maneuvered the gurney into the hall and headed for the elevator. "All right, sweetheart. Enjoy the ride. You're off to see the wizard of Oz." McDaniels chuckled. "Sorry, sweetheart. I meant the wizard of ice."

Dawn Austin was living inside her private nightmare. Her body had been paralyzed by drugs. Unable to move, not even capable of blinking her eyes let alone scream for help, She had watched with horror as two men entered her room, unhooked her from life support systems, stripped her, and shaved her. Her paralysis had not lessened the shame she felt at the touch of the men's hands. Her horror had set her heart racing with such fury that it felt as if a jackhammer was pounding her chest into her bones. For a while she thought her terror would kill her. When the plastic bag had imprisoned her body, clinging to her skin and ultimately fogging up until an opaque film blocked her vision, she had prayed for a quick death. But she couldn't close her eyes or stop her heart from racing, and endured her ordeal with wide-eyed horror.

Nothing was as terrifying as witnessing her own death with absolute certainty and clarity. Nothing equaled the horror of being buried alive in her plastic coffin. She had no choice but to endure the trip from her room along a deserted hallway, and her descent in a freight elevator, praying for death. By the time she was lifted off her gurney and placed on top of a sliding platform her mind short-circuited. As it did her terror receded and dark oblivion took control of her senses. She realized that she was losing her mind. During her final seconds of lucidity she recognized the signs of insanity that she had looked for so often in others. She became lightheaded. She wanted to giggle. She wanted to tell the two men that the plastic bag tickled her skin. She wanted to…

The platform slid backward. Inch by inch Dawn Austin's world grew blacker and colder. Then the platform stopped with a jolt and was locked into place. A trapdoor by her feet was latched shut. Iciness worked its way through her opaque casing. She slipped into unconsciousness. Frost bloomed on her skin like sparkling diamonds. Her eyes were wide open.

Chapter 38

AT TWO-FIFTEEN IN the afternoon a Jeep broke away from a convoy that had left Shandaken hours earlier. It rounded the corner of Albany Avenue and proceeded to Terwilliger House. After pulling up curbside the driver gunned the engine and shut the ignition. Sergeant Dietrich of the Shandaken Psychiatric Center security force clambered from the Jeep, threw the passenger side door open, and escorted a man in handcuffs to Terwilliger House's front door. Justin Frederikson had returned to Resurrection City.

Throughout the two-and-a-half hour ride he had been animated and talkative, hardly believing the sudden turn of events. From beaten-up prisoner to freedom in two days was more than anyone had a right to hope for, especially if prison consisted of a cell in The House. Of course he was still wary. Someone with Justin's street-smarts believed in kindness and fairness about as much as he believed in the Easter bunny, but stranger things had happened lately. And although Justin had a built-in distrust of anyone wearing a uniform, and Callahan's hospital whites were as much a uniform as the camouflage outfits worn by Axton's goons, he wanted to believe that maybe this guy wasn't so bad after all.

From the moment Callahan had told him that he'd be released into Brauner's custody Justin had tried to focus his dim recollections and wrestled with a lot of questions. Could he trust Callahan? More importantly, could he trust Brauner? He went from a tentative no to a tentative maybe. Or maybe the whole thing was a trick? He'd heard about tactics like that. But he'd heard a lot of things lately. So when Dietrich put him in the Jeep and started the trip back to Resurrection City Justin became a believer.

About ten miles east of The House Justin started feeling even more confident. They were really taking him home. It wasn't a trick after all, and although he was still cuffed at least he wasn't wedged in the back. No, sir, this time he was in the front seat without a blindfold, watching mountains speed by as the Jeep ate mile after mile until Resurrection City's familiar landmarks appeared in the windshield. And ever since the ten-mile point he'd been talking. Mostly to himself because Dietrich wasn't a talkative man. Neither was he happy about having to go out of his way to deliver a prisoner to Brauner. But when Dietrich offered him a smoke during a rare break in his silence, Justin kept talking to Dietrich, uniform or not. So he sat and took drags on a Resurrection Gold, holding the king-size cigarette carefully between cuffed hands, blowing smoke rings at the windshield, feeling better about himself than he'd done in a long time, and wondering less and less why Brauner had been kind enough to spring him.

Brauner. Thinking about Doc Brauner was confusing, but so was seeing Resurrection City's outskirts. Justin knew he'd been dragged from his bunk just three days ago. Or was it two? Regardless, it felt like a lifetime. His brain was fuzzy, his memories foggy at best. When he'd complained to Callahan about it, the doctor had nodded knowingly. *Quite normal,* he had informed him. *Don't forget, you have a nasty concussion. Temporary short term memory loss is one of the side effects. It'll be gone soon,* Callahan had promised.

Well, not soon enough, Justin told himself as they made their way into the Stockade District. Somehow he knew that he'd rebelled against Brauner and this city. So why was he feeling so good about coming home to a place he'd wanted to run away from? And why the hell was he feeling so kindly toward a man he'd probably never liked? But thinking hurt his brain and after a while he stopped asking questions and decided to go with the flow. Maybe Brauner wasn't his favorite person and maybe Resurrection City wasn't his favorite place, but compared to the last two days this was heaven, wasn't it? He was coming home. He had another butt, courtesy of Dietrich, and when the Jeep pulled up in front of Terwilliger Justin's heart raced with anticipation.

Brauner met them at the front door, more jovial than Justin remembered him, bouncing about with nervous energy, smiling broadly, slapping Justin on the shoulder, and welcoming him like a long lost friend. "Welcome back home, Justin. It's good to see you."

Justin was taken aback by the effusive greeting. "Thank you, sir."

Brauner gave him a hug, then inspected him from head to toe. His eyes stopped at a patch under Justin's right eye. "Just look at you. What have they done to you?" He touched the patch but withdrew his hand as soon as Justin flinched. "Oh my. Is it broken?"

Justin nodded. "Yeah, I think so."

"Well don't worry. We'll take care of it. As long as the rest of you is okay we'll…" He interrupted himself in mid-sentence and pointed at Justin's shackled hands. "Sergeant, would you please?"

Dietrich shook his head, disgusted by Brauner's show of affection for a prisoner. In his opinion, letting Frederikson bum a couple of smokes was the civil thing to do, but hugging him? These bleeding heart liberals in Resurrection City should spend a couple of weeks at *The House*, he thought. They sure as hell wouldn't treat scum like this Frederikson as though they were long-lost friends.

He tossed the keys at Brauner. "Here you go. You want the cuffs off, you take 'em off. My orders are to deliver him to you. It said nothing about releasing him."

With that Dietrich handed Brauner an official transfer order. "But before you do, I'll need you to sign for him. After that I don't care what you do. He'll be all yours."

Brauner did as told. Still shaking his head, Dietrich turned and headed back to his Jeep while Brauner led Justin by the arm and closed the door. "Come on in, Justin. We have a lot of things to talk about. Come on, hurry up."

Brauner hurried with quick steps to his inner office, Justin in tow. "In here, Justin. We'll have more privacy in here. Hurry up, will you. I can hardly wait. It'll be just like old times."

Sitting in the familiar surroundings of Brauner's private office, Justin's instinctive wariness returned. His subconscious gave out hundreds of signals, all of them unpleasant. Each signal by itself was insufficient to let him know exactly what bothered him. But there were enough of them to paint a disturbing picture. Together they said *Watch your ass!*

Brauner didn't take note of Justin's apprehension. Hovering over his new ward like a mother hen, he was the picture of concern. He kept bouncing about the office, rolling his chair around the desk so he could sit by Justin's side, and called Rachel to brew a fresh pot of coffee. Finally he sat still, planted his elbows on his knees, and leaned forward.

"Let me look at you," he beamed. "My God, you're a sight for sore eyes. When I heard about them taking you to *The House* I thought I'd never see you again but now you're back. It just goes to show you that you can never take anything for granted. Here today, gone tomorrow. The good Lord and Resurrection work in mysterious ways, don't they? Well, the most important thing is that you're safe and sound and… Oh, I'm sorry, Justin. Here I'm babbling and you've still got those darn cuffs on. Here, let me…"

He freed Justin's hands and let the cuffs jangle to the floor. "That's better, isn't it?"

Justin nodded silently, which earned him a quizzical look from Brauner.

"What's the matter? You look like something's bothering you. What's wrong?"

Justin shrugged his shoulders. "I'm not sure."

A light bulb seemed to go on in Brauner's head. "You know where you are, don't you?"

Again Justin nodded, with more conviction this time. Yes, he knew where he was but nothing else made sense.

"And you know who I am, don't you? I mean, you do remember me, right? Brauner? Dr. Brauner?"

"Yeah. I mean I remember you. That's just it though. I remember faces and names but somehow I don't remember much else about them. It's really weird."

"Not as weird as you might imagine," Brauner said. "It could be your mind blocking unpleasant events to protect you from trauma. I've seen that happen."

"What unpleasant things?" Justin asked. "Something happened, didn't it and that's why they took me to *The House?*"

Brauner nodded gravely. "Yes," he said without further explanation.

"Yes what?"

"Yes, something did happen and I feel terrible about it."

Frederikson didn't know what to make of Brauner. Something told him not to trust the doctor but in the same breath he wondered why he should feel this way about a man who was obviously trying to help him. "Oh man, I'm all screwed up," he said. "I can't remember what happened, I hardly know who you are and well, everything I do remember is kind of fuzzy. You know, like something in my life got screwed up and maybe it wasn't perfect but I want it back anyhow."

"Of course you do," Brauner reassured him. "And that's exactly why you're here. I can help you, but it'll only work if I have your trust."

Another flash of wariness. "Boy, I heard that one before," Justin blurted, knowing that it was the wrong thing to say.

Brauner shook his head, his jowls quivering sadly. "I know. That's exactly why I feel so terrible, almost as if I failed you and the whole thing is my fault. It was my job to make you see the goodness all around you and instead…"

"You're not gonna cry, are you?"

"Of course not," Brauner said gruffly and swiveled his chair to avoid Frederikson's scrutiny. He took a deep breath, then rose to his feet. Walking to a corner filing cabinet, the spring was gone from his step and he looked like a beaten man, stoop-shouldered and weary. He opened the top drawer, reached for his stash of Wild Turkey, and returned to his desk. "I think it's time you learned the truth," he continued, concentrating on pouring two fingers for himself and Frederikson. Avoiding Justin's eyes, he handed him one of the tumblers. "Here you go, drink up. It'll make you feel better."

Justin took a sip and grimaced. This stuff tasted worse than iodine.

Brauner noticed. "I'm sorry, but that's all I have. Scotch is your favorite poison, right? Isn't that what you and Paulette used to drink?"

"Paulette?" The name triggered another signal, this one both pleasant and sad.

"Yes, Paulette. Don't tell me you forgot about her too." Brauner looked surprised. "I would have thought that if anyone stayed in your mind it would have been her. But maybe that's a blessing in disguise. I'm sure you'll remember her sooner or later. Here, drink up. I know you're not supposed to, but…" Brauner smiled, "I won't tell if you don't."

"Why are you being so nice to me?"

Brauner looked hurt. "Justin, Justin. Please."

Justin tried to arrange his memory into chronological order. He smelled trouble.

Brauner went on. "Have I ever treated you unfairly? In all the years I know you, have I ever done anything to hurt you?"

"That's the problem." Justin blurted. "I don't remember. I don't know if you have or haven't."

Brauner's face changed into sympathetic sadness. "I was afraid this might happen. I warned him not to go through with it but what could I do? I'm only a doctor."

"Warned who?"

"Never mind who. But I'm sure it's not too late."

"Goddammit, Brauner, too late for what? You make it sound like I have some incurable disease. What the hell happened to me?"

Brauner came to Justin's side and placed his hands of his shoulders. He leaned forward and continued as though he hadn't heard Justin. "Tell me exactly what you remember. Every last detail. Try hard, Justin. It's important."

Brauner's order made Justin realize just how little he could remember. With the doctor hunched forward, hovering inches from his face, making eye contact, Justin tried one more time to nudge his memory. The harder he tried the more confusing the kaleidoscope of memories became. Not surprisingly, most were unpleasant but there were also brief flashes of exquisite pleasure and warm comfort.

"Well?" Brauner asked impatiently.

Frederikson shook his head. "I can't. I don't know where to start."

"Why don't you start with the last thing that you just thought of," Brauner urged. "It's not important if it's something from the past or not. Surely you remember what you thought of a second ago."

"Well," Justin blushed. "Believe it or not I was surprised that something as awful as this," he pointed at the Wild Turkey, "could make me feel so good."

Brauner smiled. "That's good. It shows memory association. And that's all we're after right now, associating things with past events. Bourbon evokes good memories. Now how about this office? Anything?"

Frederikson looked uncomfortable, yet Brauner urged him on. "C'mon, Justin, don't be afraid. Just tell me how you feel when you look at my office."

"Not as good as I did when I thought about your Bourbon."

"That's wonderful," Brauner interrupted him with obvious excitement. "Not that you don't feel comfortable in my office. That means that subconsciously you remember something unpleasant, or frightening that you experienced here. See what I'm saying?"

"If you say so," Frederikson said lamely, missing the significance. "And it's not that I feel uncomfortable in here. I mean, not really. It's that other office, that one over there." He pointed to Brauner's examination room.

"Excellent. That's where I do all the Retooling and that's where you spent a lot of time."

"Retooling?"

"Oh, that's just slang for psychiatric examinations."

"Like you're doing now?" Frederikson asked.

This brought a chuckle from Brauner. "Sort of. Except in Retooling we try to emphasize the positives. Today we're after everything, good and bad, because without remembering the bad we can't differentiate positives from negatives. You see, it all comes back to what I was just telling you, associating events with emotions or feelings."

"Like Scotch and feeling good." Justin said, pleased with himself.

"Exactly. Brauner could hardly contain his excitement. "Excellent, Justin. You're making phenomenal progress.'" Justin gave him a wide-eyed stare. "I am?"

"Absolutely," Brauner said. "You said Scotch. Not the Bourbon you just drank. You remembered Scotch. That'll lead to a very important association. The person you drank it with, and the pleasant experiences you shared."

Frederikson thought about this for a moment. He didn't see how this association stuff was going to help him remember but Brauner probably knew best. Worst case, he'd waste some time, which wasn't a big deal because now that he was out of the *House* he probably had all the time in the world. And without knowing the past, the future was a big question mark. So the thing to do was to listen and learn. And do whatever the doctor wanted him to do.

When he looked up Brauner had shifted in his seat. No longer leaning forward, he had settled back and crossed his legs, confident that he was on the right track. Brauner's confidence was contagious. Frederikson relaxed.

"Shall we go on?" Brauner asked, refilling Justin's glass.

"Sure."

"Okay, tell me about David."

"That's easy. He was my brother, right?"

"Still is," Brauner said. "Not only your brother but your best friend as well. You've lived with him all your life. Do you remember any of that?"

"A little. Not the everyday things but the important ones. I know that whenever I needed something he was there to help me."

"That's exactly how I feel about him too," Brauner agreed. "Like a good friend." Brauner stopped, looking embarrassed by what he was about to say. "In a way I think of him as my son," he confided. "Does that make sense to you?"

Actually it didn't, but Frederikson didn't know why it didn't, so he said nothing. Brauner didn't pursue it. Instead he announced a ten minute break and left the office in search of Rachel Firestein, leaving Frederikson alone with his thoughts.

Confused. Frustrated. Scared. Frederikson was all of that, but mostly he was scared. But he knew he was making progress. Where there had been a void in his life there was now some order. There were things like Retooling, people like Brauner and David, places where he'd lived. All he'd have to do now was to connect the dots and he'd be back to normal. And Brauner would help him do just that.

Brauner, Justin thought, where the hell was he? A lot more than ten minutes had passed. The afternoon sun slanted toward the horizon. Shadows lengthened. From the reception area came a steady background noise of activity, muffled by a closed door but audible nevertheless.

Frederikson was about to go in search of Brauner when the door opened. "Sorry, Justin. I got caught up in a couple of things. You know how it is, everything takes twice as long as you think."

With the apology out of the way Brauner took a seat. "What do you say, ready to go on?"

Frederikson nodded. "Sure."

"Okay then. I'm going to throw out some names and you tell me the first thing that pops into your head. Okay?"

Again Frederikson agreed without saying a word.

"Paulette."

Hearing the name hit Justin hard. His reaction was immediate and obvious. Brauner looked pleased and waited for an answer.

"Well, come on Justin. Talk to me."

"Was she a good friend?" he asked cautiously. "Like David?"

"I thought I was the one supposed to ask the questions," Brauner said. "But yes, she was a very good friend, although not at all like David."

When Justin looked confused, Brauner added with a sardonic smile, "Let's just say that Paulette was good to you but not necessarily good for you."

"I don't understand."

"You will soon enough." Brauner said. "But for now, just go along with me, okay? Remember, you're supposed to tell me the first thing that comes to mind when you hear a name, not ask questions.

Now go ahead, what do you think of when you hear her name? Paulette." For emphasis he repeated it. "Paulette."

A bitter-sweet memory emerged. A small bedroom. Tangled sheets. A pile of Resurrection Rags on green carpeting. Skin against skin. Delicious warmth turning into searing heat, lips touching. Clutching, flailing, sweating, pleasure becoming pain. Pleasure ebbing and turning evil. A hateful image of a thin, bespectacled gnome of a man with pallid complexion and a prominent nose emerged from the shadows. Axton. Xavier Axton.

Visibly shaken Frederikson changed the subject back to safe ground. "Can I see David?" he asked.

"Oh sure. I'll bet he'd love to see you himself. He's an Apostle now, you know, and I'm afraid he feels kind of isolated. So seeing you would probably help him cope."

"Now?" Justin asked, ready to get out of his chair.

"Not right now," Brauner said. "First we have to make sure you're all right."

"What about Paulette?"

Brauner squirmed in his seat. "I'm afraid that won't be possible," he finally said.

"Why not?"

"Do you remember what I said before, about her being good to you but not good for you? Well, it wasn't too good for her either. What I mean is that she broke some rules and isn't with us anymore."

Justin's heart plummeted. "Where'd she go?" he asked.

"To a far better place," Brauner said. "But the important thing is for you to remember the time you spent with her, the happy moments, the joys and pleasures you shared." He stared at Justin. "You do you remember, don't you?" His voice trailed off to a whisper. "The pleasures. The passion. Passion. Passion."

The same bitter-sweet memories returned. The same searing, all-consuming pleasures. The tender touch of skin against skin, The sweaty clutches. It all faded to slushy gray as the same evil vision of a man intruded. Justin swallowed hard. Spasms of hatred roiled his body. He knew. His vision of the man crystallized. He saw him clearly. He associated a name with the face. And a painful memory came to life.

Brauner glanced at him with obvious concern. "I think this is enough for now. We'll continue later on tonight. I'm going to meet Colonel Axton for dinner at the Apostle Lounge at seven thirty. Why don't you go and get some rest. Let's see, examination room three is available. There's a comfortable bed in there. And if you want some more Bourbon, go right ahead and help yourself. Just don't overdo it. Relax and remember the good moments you shared with Paulette. The pleasures. The passions" His voice became a whisper. His eyes shone like beams of light. His whisper died among gradual darkness.

Brauner rose abruptly and hurried from the office. In doing so, he brushed accidentally against a stack of papers on his desk and sent them scattering to the floor. Beneath the remaining papers Justin saw the outline of a dull black semi-automatic handgun.

*****

Colonel Axton's body was discovered at seven-thirty-two in the evening by patrolman Classen outside the Apostle Lounge's side entrance. Classen had been alerted by a single gunshot and raced around the corner to the wooded area abutting the lounge.

The Colonel was on his back with a single gunshot wound to the head. The bullet had entered through his right eye and exited in the back of his head. Blood and specks of his brain littered the ground. Flies had swarmed to feast on the Colonel's detritus.

A semi-automatic handgun was found approximately ten feet from the colonel's body. The gun was registered to Dr. Callahan of the Shandaken Facility for the Criminally Insane, who had reported it missing two days ago. A single shot had been fired from the gun.

Classen surveyed the crime scene, recognized immediately that it was too late to help the colonel, and raced after the outline of man who disappeared around the corner on Fair Street. He alerted Axton's security force on his two-way radio. Within minutes more than one hundred guards fanned out from headquarters on John

Street, forming a dragnet that combed through Resurrection City's Stockade District.

At seven forty five a man was spotted cowering in a doorway. He bolted in the direction of Albany Avenue. When he disobeyed orders to stop Axton's security forces opened fire. The fugitive was killed instantly by fifteen bullets to the head and chest. His head was shattered beyond recognition. He could not be identified until an autopsy had been performed. Dr. Bruno Brauner signed the death certificate himself. Justin Frederikson was buried in Resurrection's Potters' Field immediately following the autopsy.

*****

Bruno Brauner finished his third Wild Turkey of the night and loosened his tie. A belch escaped his moistened lips. He picked up the phone and punched in the familiar number. Two rings later and a low voice answered, "Hello."

Brauner allowed himself a second to bask in satisfaction. "It's done, Callahan. You can proceed with our plan." Brauner hung up the phone. "And now for David Koertner."

*****

Colonel Axton was buried the same morning with full military honors. His flag-draped coffin was interred in Resurrection's Federal Cemetery. Graveside eulogies continued for more than an hour. Dr. Brauner gave a moving speech and nearly collapsed at the conclusion, overcome by grief for his friend and associate of over twenty-five years. Senator Kerr, who had made the trip from Long Island to bid his trusted friend farewell, called the Colonel "A soldier on the side of truth and justice who will live forever in our hearts. A loyal fighter against mankind's evildoers. He may have left this earth, but he will always sit close to God."

Chapter 39

AN UNEASY CALM hung over Resurrection City. The usual bustling pace of the Stockade District had slowed to a trickle. Knots of Disciples gathered at street corners and spoke in hushed tones, stealing furtive glances over their shoulders. Guardians patrolled the streets in pairs, something they hadn't done since Rebecca Sachem's nude body was discovered in an overgrown lot on the banks of the Rondout creek more than three years ago.

Barricades had been set up on Fair Street and were manned by Axton's elite guard. Known for their arrogance and a policy of shooting first and asking questions later, there was no doubt about their mission today. They looked more menacing than ever. Dress-blacks and spit-shined shoes had given way to green combat fatigues and studded boots. No one was allowed within one block of Security Headquarters. 132 Fair Street was under lockdown.

Starting at eight in the morning, Resurrection's top administrators arrived, had their credentials checked, and were ushered into Headquarters. General Amadeus was the first, followed closely by Alderman Stokowski and Senator Kerr. Dr. Brauner was the last to make his way to the front door, present his ID card, and enter. As usual, he was impeccably dressed in a charcoal gray three piece suit, herringbone overcoat, and black wingtip shoes. Unlike most other times, he was calm and confident, dismissing the guard's salute with a condescending wave of his hand. As soon as Brauner disappeared inside the building the front door was locked and two guards took their positions on the stoop.

When the doors reopened four hours later, rumors spread like wildfire. In an effort to stop the wild speculation, WREN broadcast a special news report, confirming Colonel Axton's assassination. No motive was given and no mention was made of Justin Frederikson. Sunday was proclaimed a day of mourning. Attendance at prayer services throughout Resurrection was mandatory. General Amadeus would personally take over Axton's function until a new security chief was appointed. Dr. Bruno B. Brauner was named Resurrection's acting Chief Administrator, filling the position vacated by Amadeus, the broadcast went on to say. And then a bombshell poured from every radio and every loudspeaker and reverberated throughout Resurrection. Apostle David Koertner had been appointed Dr. Brauner's second in command.

Fallout from the assassination was immediate. In his first act as Chief Administrator Brauner announced an eight o'clock curfew. Violators were to be arrested and shipped to Quad II. All Disciple privileges, including the right to assemble, were suspended until further notice. Disciples were not permitted to enter administrative buildings, libraries, local shops or restaurants, including the *Apostle's Lounge*. Broadcasts of WREN were limited to two hours a day and would be dedicated to classical music. Publication of the *Resurrection Sentinel* would cease immediately. A total news blackout was in effect.

*****

"And what if I refuse the job?"

Ten minutes after hearing of my promotion I arrived at Terwilliger and was ushered in by a saluting Guardian at the door. The fact that he saluted me was incongruous. Just yesterday he would have asked for my ID card and arrested me if I refused to show it. This morning he snapped to attention, clicked his heels, and touched his cap.

Brauner was equally as respectful, though in an infinitely friendlier way. He didn't click his heels or salute. Instead he pumped my hand and smiled broadly. Being treated with all this respect should have made me feel proud but it left a sour taste in my mouth. As far as I was concerned, things had only changed for the worse. They were trying to turn me into one of them. Them, who were responsible for

Justin's death. Them, who were hiding something terrifying and evil from every Disciple in Resurrection. Them, whom I detested. Them, who'd get rid of me, just like they had murdered Justin and probably Private Austin, when they didn't need me anymore.

I've never been a two-faced schemer but forty-eight names convinced me I had better play their game. Standing face to face with Brauner I saw past his façade of old-world dignity. Behind his immaculate suit and starched shirt, beneath his glowing skin, hidden behind his pleasant smile and gleaming eyes was a manipulative, hideous, deceitful, old man. And an extremely dangerous one. I was convinced that he knew me better than I did and that he'd use his knowledge to control me.

I was also convinced that that was the only reason he had made me his assistant. It was so much easier for him to control me if I worked at his side, never out of sight. How else could he pull the strings and have Assistant Koertner jump like a marionette at his very command? As long as I moved in concert with each tug of his strings I was safe. I corrected myself almost immediately. I was only safe as long as he needed me. But I had my own trump card, and Brauner was it. I just had to find out how far I could push him. So in a very small way they'd already won. Lying and cheating never came easy to Disciple Koertner, but Apostle Koertner had no trouble deceiving Brauner and his cohorts. My reasons may have been noble, but my methods were as deceitful as theirs.

"And what if I refuse the job?" I repeated and glared at Brauner. His eyes showed genuine hurt.

"Why are you doing this to me, David?" Brauner shook his head in disbelief and wrung his hands. Turning his back on me he walked to the window and stared at Albany Avenue. Nowhere was the aftermath of Axton's assassination more apparent than in the transformation of this grand, tree-lined avenue. Its usual civilian traffic was all but gone, replaced by occasional troop carriers bearing Resurrection's cross-and-shield markings, and a steady stream of armored vehicles patrolling the Stockade District. Resurrection was hunkering down.

It was a dismal day. Light drizzle had spread over the city. Black clouds hung threateningly low in the sky. Over the past hour the temperature had been in a free-fall until it hovered near the freezing mark. The rain was sure to turn into the season's first snowfall, a painful reminder that winter was just around the corner.

I've never liked the holiday season very much. Knowing that I would be spending Christmas by myself this year made it more depressing. The prospect of four months of long nights and bleak days, living in the isolation of my new quarters, was like a death sentence. And as far as I was concerned it was all *his* fault, that hateful man with a holier-than-thou attitude. God, how I wished I could kill him. How I hated him. How much I needed him.

He turned from the window and poured two ounces of sour mash, downing it in a single gulp. After wiping his lips with the back of his hand he returned the bottle to its hiding place and turned his attention back to me. I could see right away that something had transformed him. He looked like a man possessed. Anger shone in his eyes.

"I asked you a question, David. Why are you doing this to me? Did I miscalculate when I placed my trust in you?"

I didn't know how to answer his question.

"Answer me, David." The fire in his eyes was intense.

"I never asked you to trust me," I said sullenly.

"Very true, and I probably shouldn't have. You proved that when you snooped around my office while I was away."

Damn. Caught. What now? My first reaction was to deny everything. "I wasn't snooping, I was only trying to do my job. And while we're on the subject of snooping, obviously you did some of your own so don't talk to me about misplaced trust. Look, either let me do my job or fire me but don't preach to me. You made a big deal about giving me free access to anything I need in Brauner's Kitchen and then you accuse me of spying on you. Looks to me as though you're trying to hide something.'

He was at my side with three quick steps. His right hand tightened around my forearm and shook me violently. "Don't play me for a fool, David. I may be many things, but I'm not a fool. You were snooping like a Goddamn little weasel. You sneaked back and forth all night long. You tried to do things you weren't supposed to, and if

I hadn't been careful enough to safeguard the computer's security you would have snooped even more. And you have the nerve to deny it. You're nothing more than a common liar."

I'd never seen Brauner this angry before. He flung the words at me amid a spray of spittle, still digging his fingers into my arms and shaking me as hard as he could. But as quickly as his outburst had come, it stopped. He measured me with contempt, let go of me, and turned his back. "I trusted you. I defended you. Dammit, David, what did you hope to find?"

"The truth."

"The truth?" he sneered. "The truth? I don't think you're man enough to face it."

"Try me. And you can start by explaining what happened to forty-eight people. If you're man enough to tell me."

His hand came out of nowhere. A sharp slap and stinging shame reddened my cheek. "That's none of your business."

"What's the matter, don't you trust me? I thought I was your assistant. That's what I heard all over the radio this morning."

I should have known that I'd pushed him beyond his limit. Trembling with rage, cold hatred in his eyes, he picked up his whiskey glass and flung it at the wall. Shattered glass sprayed to the linoleum tiles and crunched under his feet as he made his way back to the window. He'd lost control, but so had I.

"Damn you, Brauner," I shouted at his stoop-shouldered back. "You didn't do me any favors with this promotion. All you managed to do is to turn me into a pariah. Nobody trusts me anymore. Nobody wants to be with me. I don't want the job. I don't want to be an Apostle anymore either. I quit."

"You can't do that." His response was a whisper.

"And why the hell not?"

"Because you know too much."

*****

The office turned silent. Neither of us knew what to say next. We stood ten feet apart but it might as well have been a mile. An invisible line that had always existed between us, separating the teacher from the student, had been crossed. Brauner's word's hung in the air like a menacing cloud. *You know too much!* I saw the terrifying truth of his words. With that single sentence we had achieved parity. If I wanted to live I needed to become one of *Them*. Brauner had become my equal. Both of us knew that we could never return to the way it used to be. We also knew that we needed each other. For better or worse we were stuck with each other.

I cooled off. Hoping to do damage control I reasoned with him. "I want to believe in Resurrection, Doc, I want to help. But too many things have happened. Everyone in Resurrection knows that something is wrong and you can't stop the rumors. Not as long as people suddenly disappear or change their personalities overnight. Justin did. He was one of the smartest men I've ever known and fanatical in his belief that you were hiding some terrible secret. But as soon as Axton caught him he changed his tune. He actually told me that there was nothing to all the rumors, that he had been wrong. That's not like Justin. And he sure as hell wasn't violent. He may have been crazy, but he would never kill anybody. Something changed him. I think someone planned it and Justin just followed orders."

Brauner swiveled on his toes. "What makes you say that?"

"His records disappeared the day before he was shipped to the *House*. Not the day he killed Axton, not the day he died. The day before. They did something to him in the *House*. Something changed him."

"That's hogwash. You don't know what you're saying."

"What about the other people?"

Brauner tried to reason with me. "Wouldn't you expect their records to be removed after they resigned or passed away?" He suddenly had reverted to his scholarly personality, trying to give a simple answer to a simple question asked by a simple-minded student. "There's nothing sinister here except what's in your mind, David. These people are no longer with us. They resigned. They died. That's life, you know that. And when they're no longer with us their records are removed from active status and placed in the archives in Shandaken."

It all sounded so convincing and logical that I almost believe him. Almost, but not quite. "If that's the case, then explain to me why Justin's records disappeared the day before he was sent to Shandaken?"

Brauner shook his head with disappointment. "David, David. What an active imagination you have. His records didn't disappear the day before he died. They were removed from the vault the day before he was sent to Shandaken for treatment because that's the day his diagnosis was made and his transfer papers were signed. I personally signed off on his papers. There's no sinister plot here. The fact that he was returned the day Axton was shot was strictly coincidence."

I had to admit that he made sense. And I was beginning to waver. Admitting to myself that I might have been wrong was both troubling and soothing. Troubling because I still had nagging suspicions. Soothing because life would be so much simpler if Brauner was right.

"What about Private Austin?" I asked.

If I had thought to catch him off-guard or get a reaction from him I was disappointed. He remained unflappable.

"What about Private Austin?"

"Well, how come she quit? I don't believe that she didn't want to see me anymore. She left me a note and…"

"I know she did. We've been over this before, David. Don't you remember?"

"I know I told you about her note. But why did she say she looked forward to working with me again."

Brauner did a bad job concealing his surprise. "She did?"

"Yeah. Why would she say that? Why, if she was going to quit?"

Brauner recovered quickly. "Because she changed her mind? David, People change their minds all the time. You know that."

We had reached a stalemate. With it came a moment of silence.

Brauner was the first to speak. "Why can't you just accept the fact that she quit? Does it hurt your ego? Is that it?"

I shook my head, even though he was probably right.

Brauner's voice was soothing when he spoke again. "Look, David, she quit. That's all there's to it. Both Axton and I tried to talk her out of it, but she wouldn't listen to us. She was quite adamant. And whether you want to believe it or not, she really didn't want to see you anymore. She gave us some cockamamie story about not fitting in, about coming from an incompatible background, but I suspect the real reason for her resignation was you. She may have felt a certain…oh, how shall I put it?…a certain romantic interest in you. You are a fascinating young man, you know, and the right age for a woman like Private Austin. Unfortunately she wasn't blessed with exceptional beauty. She may have found it difficult to attract men on the outside. When she realized that you didn't share her feelings, well, you know."

"I don't believe it. She never once…"

"Oh come now, David," he interrupted me. "You saw the tape of your sessions with her. It seems quite obvious that there was more to it than a purely professional interest. Just look at her body language or listen to her voice. I'm not suggesting that she tried to seduce you on purpose. On the contrary, she was probably convinced that she was helping you. But subliminal expressions of her feelings for you got in the way and when you didn't reciprocate, well, I think she felt hurt and rejected. I suppose she finally recognized what had happened and knew that she had compromised herself. So the easiest thing was to walk away from it. This way you weren't hurt and she didn't have to admit that her advances went unanswered."

As flattering as the thought was I dismissed it at once. The idea that one of *Them*, an outsider, an attractive and intelligent young woman, might have been attracted to me was absurd. If anything, our situation was reversed. Maybe it was I who had liked her too much. Anyhow, I was convinced Brauner was up to his old tricks again, playing with my emotions, pulling strings. Brauner was a master at that. But he hadn't seen her note. I had. I didn't know how it had slipped past him. She had been very explicit. *Sorry to run out on you like this but I was called on an emergency assignment. Dr. Brauner insisted. I'll stop by your room as soon as I get back.*

Brauner continued, warming up to the role of analyzing Austin's relationship with me. "So you see, David, there is a perfectly logical explanation for everything. No skeletons in the closet. No ghosts lurching in the attic. If you try hard enough you can read something sinister into everything. Life is simply a matter of perception. Now I wish you would stop your foolishness. We have a lot of work to do."

"All right. But I'm going to write Private Austin a note. Just to let her know I appreciate what she did for me."

"I don't think that would be wise, David."

"If you say so." It was time to play a hunch. I turned so he couldn't read the lie in my eyes and said, "Well, it doesn't matter. I can always write to her later. I still have her home address."

"You what?" The words exploded from Brauner's mouth.

"What's the matter? You sound upset."

"You are not to write to that woman." He positioned himself between me and the door. Standing inches from my face, straining his head to look me in the eyes, breathing heavily, he was suddenly out of control again. "I forbid you to write to her. I will have your mail confiscated. Don't push me David. I've gone far enough for you. You do exactly what I tell you or…"

"Or what?"

"Or I'll have you sent to Shandaken for treatment."

"Is that the day my case folder will be shipped to the archive as well?"

Brauner didn't answer.

"Look, Doctor. I don't know what game you're playing. I don't know why you picked me for this job or why you're putting up with me. It's not like you to be this kind and understanding. You obviously want something from me and you're not going to get it unless you level with me. The truth, Brauner."

He said something totally unexpected, a grudging admission of sorts. "I'm afraid I taught you too well."

I didn't bite. "The truth."

He shook his head. "Not yet. It's not time."

"I'm leaving."

"You can't. I forbid it."

"Try to stop me."

I stalked from the office, leaving Brauner speechless and grim. I made my way to the front door and heard him run after me.

"David. Come back. Come back right this minute."

I flung the front door open. The same guard was still on duty. Again he clicked his heels and saluted. As he did I lunged at him, catching him by surprise. Before he had a chance to react I reached for his holster and grappled for his gun. He clawed at my hand but was too late. I waved the gun in his face.

"On the ground, officer. And you, get back inside." I waved the gun back and forth aimlessly."

As tense as Resurrection had become following Axton's murder, it didn't take long for a small crowd to form on the sidewalk. Anticipation ran high: something was going down.

"David, don't." Brauner stood next to me, pleading and wrestling for the gun. I brushed him aside easily, amazed by his feeble resistance. "Inside. Or I'll blow your head off."

"No. Please don't."

Sirens wailed in the distance, approaching Terwilliger House rapidly from the southern end of Albany Avenue.

"Move it." I released the safety and aimed.

"All right David. You win. I'll tell you whatever you want to know."

I was so relieved by Brauner's capitulation that I started to shake uncontrollably. I couldn't have lasted much longer without cracking. A wave of relief flooded through me. I started to tremble, not noticing when Bruner took the gun from my shaking hand. I offered no resistance. Suddenly I couldn't wait to get rid of the gun.

Brauner handed the gun back to the ashen-faced guard. "Officer Solchnik, is it?"

Officer Solchnik nodded, his face still twitching with terror.

Brauner said, "See, David. I told you he'd handle it with restraint. Well done, Solchnik. I'm proud of you. You handled the situation extremely well. You put my safety ahead of your own. I will personally recommend you to General Amadeus for a commendation. We need more people like you in Resurrection."

Officer Solchnik accepted the gun, slipped it in his holster, and saluted. His expression was one of wide-eyed relief and bewilderment. "Thank you, sir."

Brauner returned the salute. "At ease, Officer."

The crowd disbanded. The siren wailed louder, passed Terwilliger, and continued to race north along Albany Avenue. They had not been called to respond to our confrontation after all.

Brauner took me by the arm and led me back into his office. With the confrontation out of the way he regained his confidence quickly. Only a slight cracking of his voice gave an indication of how upset he had been.

"All right, David. We'll talk. But there is something I have to show you first. Let me get my coat and we'll go."

"Where are we going?"

"To the *House*. To the truth."

Chapter 40

Sometimes one's imagination runs amok. Sometimes conjuring up visions of evil paints a picture in one's mind that far surpasses reality. I had anticipated a surreal house of horrors surrounded by moats filled with murky waters, a gothic nightmare adorned with demonic gargoyles and crowned with ominous turrets, inhabited by satanic cultists who devoured small children and offered their blood in sacrifice to their God. Nothing could have been further from the truth.

The House was squat and ugly, a huge concrete death factory surrounded by a no-man's-land of scorched earth. Smokestacks belched yellow sulfur clouds into a leaden sky. Thus the first sight of *The House* wasn't the building itself, but of an amber ashen pall that shrouded its outline. Only when one came within a few miles of the place did the structure reveal itself. As Brauner maneuvered his car around a hairpin turn on Route 28 and we passed through a mountain gorge *The House* suddenly burst into view. I was struck by its imposing size, but more so by how unlike my expectations it was. It was probably this contrast between abstract and reality that gave it a more sinister appearance than I had had imagined. This wasn't a supernatural creation, it was a death camp built by man. And it occurred to me that its name, ordinary and non-descriptive, was perfect. No adjectives could adequately describe *The House*.

We drove the last mile in silence, Brauner concentrating on the road while I stared at an endless row of cement bollards on either side that resembled cemetery headstones and made off-road driving impossible. Then, as we reached the scorched earth no-man's land, the road narrowed, the bollards were gone, and straight ahead sharp-toothed concertina wire announced our final destination.

Despite being a well known and frequent visitor, Brauner was subjected to the same strict security procedures as I was. Ten minutes after arrival, we were waved on and descended into the *Eerie Canal*. With the engine shut off, we were transported by conveyer, moving slowly from one chamber to the next. Inside each, a crushing sense of confinement increased my feeling of suffocation. Daylight yielded to glaring floodlights. The melody of leaves rustling in the wind was replaced by droning turbines. Hydraulic pumps opened and closed steel doors. Instead of the scent of the countryside, so pronounced in Resurrection City, there was antiseptic, refrigerated air. Instead of life, there was death.

But on Brauner *The House* seemed had an energizing effect. His appearance changed. Once inside the facility and past all check points, after being photographed and fingerprinted and issued a visitor's badge, Brauner walked with stiff-limbed determination, reminiscent of the jerky, exaggerated motions of Axton's security guards. His expression hardened. Miraculously, his skin tightened, emphasizing his bone structure, making his nose appear predatory and his cheekbones more prominent. He was a man on a mission.

I walked a step behind him, growing more apprehensive by the minute, knowing that I was heading into a nightmare. The few people we met along brightly lit halls on our way to the elevator were all cut from the same cloth. Robot-like faces with tightly pinched and unsmiling lips, vacant eyes staring past us, each of them too preoccupied to say hello or nod a greeting.

I tugged Brauner's jacket and he stopped and turned to me.
"Where are we going?"
"To the research lab."
"What for? What's in the lab?"
"The truth."

He resumed his pace and I hurried to keep up with him. As much as I hated him, he was the most comforting sight in *The House*.

*****

At first glance the lab looked like the nerve center of a sophisticated hospital. A glass enclosed circular core was crammed with medical and computer equipment. White-clad men and women hurried about, checking computer terminals and diagnostic monitors, aids wheeled carts filled with medications, doctors congregated in clusters to compare diagnoses in hushed voices. It gave the appearance of efficient care-giving and bestowed a sense of wellbeing. It seemed medicine at its best.

But once outside the lab as I followed Brauner along a hallway that arched around the building's core we were greeted by silence and inactivity. We passed patient room after patient room and any sense of comfort I may have felt came unraveled. Something struck me as odd. I recalled the last time I'd been in Resurrection General to interview a patient. At that time, after obtaining his room number at the nurse's station, I had been overwhelmed by the number of patients in the hospital. They were everywhere. Every room was filled. In the hall, patients holding onto walkers strolled past me, saying hello or chatting with room-mates, aides pushed soiled laundry carts in and out of rooms, and it seemed that every room had a minor emergency that caused nurses and doctors to rush inside. Nothing of the sort was evident here. I didn't see a single patient. Not a single door stood ajar.

I stopped at several of the doors, each of which was fitted with a wire-mesh reinforced window, revealing a slice of uniformly drab interiors. Each room was private and windowless. Single beds were placed strategically alongside the far wall to allow for unobstructed viewing from the hall. Only four of the beds were occupied.

The enormity of what I saw began to sink in. "No. Oh God, no."

Brauner, who was ten feet ahead of me by now, turned and called to me. "Come along now, David. We must hurry."

"NOOO!" I screamed but no sound escaped. This could not be. It must not be. I refused to believe it.

A nameplate next to door twenty-three caught my attention. *Kowalski, P.* I stopped, premonitions of horror churning my guts.

I wanted to pull back but morbid fascination drove me forward. I touched the door.

Brauner was by my side and tried to dislodge me. He tugged at my sleeve, then pulled my arm as hard as he could. I didn't move. I was paralyzed by the scene behind the door. Inside, attached to a maze of tubes and wires, were the remains of Paulette Kowalski. She was merely a torso. Her arms and legs had been amputated. Her limbs were reduced to stumps, each carefully wrapped with bandages. Her hair was shaven. Her mouth was twisted open, revealing toothless gums. Her empty eye sockets were fixed on a gurney that kept her suspended two feet above the bed.

"NOOO!" I became violently ill, retching and crying and screaming simultaneously. "NOOO!"

*****

Brauner's voice and a pinch of smelling salts returned me to consciousness.

"He's back," someone announced.

"Yeah, I see. Okay, nurse, you can leave now. I'll take care of him."

Brauner's face was inches from mine. Second by second his features became clearer, his voice more recognizable.

"David? Can you hear me?"

Second by second my pain grew stronger.

"David, speak to me."

A maelstrom of emotions drowned my sanity. I wanted to give in and go back to sleep but Brauner kept shaking me relentlessly. He slapped my cheek and held smelling salts under my nose again. And all throughout he repeated his hypnotic incantation. "David, speak to me."

I shook my head.

"David. Can you hear me? We must hurry. Come on David. It's time for you to know."

*****

Brauner and I were alone in one of the computer rooms at the core of the lab. Beyond a half-opened door two orderlies cleaned the floor in front of room twenty-three. It took them less than a minute to clean the mess I'd made, splash disinfectant on the floor, and swab it dry with a squeeze mop. Eye-stinging ammonia vapors were the only reminders it hadn't been merely a nightmare.

Logic told me that the world couldn't have gone insane. There had to be a perfectly normal explanation for everything. After all, the universe was ruled by a certain order and that order couldn't be altered by anyone but God. If anything had gone mad it was I. I recalled one of Brauner's earlier lectures, telling me how the human brain was like a traffic cop that kept constant flows of information moving without colliding. Well, in my case it felt like a head-on collision.

I retreated into a reassuring world of make-believe. Beyond the computer room's frosted glass partition I saw shadowy outlines hurrying back and forth in a soothing ritual, attending to patients, nurturing and healing the sick. Once I thought I saw Paulette Kowalski walking past me but before I could call out to her she disappeared from view. I wanted to run after her but my legs were too heavy. I'll catch up with her later, I told myself, as soon as they release me. That's what they did in hospitals, right? Release their patients as soon as they were better. And this was a hospital, wasn't it? It looked like a hospital. It had an unmistakable hospital smell. It had all the right sounds, intercoms summoning doctors, monitors beeping, bells ringing, patients moaning, patients moaning, patients moaning…

Brauner slapped me again. "David."

I regained full consciousness and didn't hear a sound other than Brauner. His hand was on my shoulder and I recoiled.

"Don't touch me. Don't ever touch me again."

"David, you don't understand. You must know everything. You must see the sum of the parts before you judge."

"Oh no. I don't want to see or hear anything." I shook my head. I sat opposite Brauner, gripping my chair's armrests, afraid of falling, shaking violently. "No. No." Again and again.

"There is a purpose. A beautiful purpose."

"No, please."

He slapped me again. To my shock, I saw tears in his eyes. Brauner was crying.

"Yes. You must know, and only then can you judge." He raised his arm in a sweeping gesture from left to right.

"There are fifty rooms here, and most of the time they are all filled. Fifty patients whose only purpose is to contribute to the greater good. They all have something to contribute. Brilliant minds. Intelligence. Bravery. Honesty. Determination. Sensitivity. Whatever it might be, they are the parts that make up the whole."

"No. I won't listen."

"Take the woman in room thirty four. She has an amazing memory. Truly a photographic memory. Or the man in eight. I've never met anyone with such a determination to survive."

"You're mad."

"We take the very best from each. We splice and infuse. We transfer greatness. We can turn a dullard into a genius. And in the end we create a true master race. We…"

"No. Stop it. You're a butcher. It can't be." I wanted to choke him. I wanted to rip the skin off his face and gouge out his eyes.

"Oh yes. It can be. It already is."

His eyes shone with unearthly fanaticism.

"No. I don't want to know anymore. Put me in one of your damn rooms. I don't want to live anymore."

"I can't do that, David. How could I destroy my finest creation?"

*****

I woke to bright lights glaring into my eyes. My arms were tied to the bed. My ankles were shackled. My head felt as if it had been stuffed with cotton balls.

Brauner bent over the bed, penlight in hand, and smiled at me.

"Good morning, David."

"What did you do to me?"

"Oh, don't worry, David. It's nothing more drastic than a sedative. You'll be all right in a few hours."

Hearing him call me David opened the floodgates. "David? How can you call me that? Who's David? Goddamn you Brauner, who the fuck is David? Not me. I don't exist, do I? I'm some monster you created."

"Far from it. You're David all right. It's only your mind we improved. Physically you are the same infant who was brought to Resurrection more than thirty years ago. We never use body parts for our own creations. Those we sell to our clients. How do you think we finance our research? You would be surprised to learn how much the government is willing to pay for organs and limbs. And our revered institutions of higher learning, their appetite is insatiable. Well, let them use what we must ultimately discard. We are much more sophisticated than they are. We use a person's mind. We alter it. We modify behavior. We create what God was never able to create."

I was consumed with hatred. It stemmed from knowing that innocent people have died for me. It was caused by having lost my identity. I didn't know who I was any longer. Most of my hatred came from knowing that I'd never be able to forget.

The only salvation I would ever have was to help those for whom it was not yet too late. It was too late for Justin. Mercifully, it would be too late for Paulette Kowalski. But there were still a number of patients here who could be helped. If I helped them, if I could help just one of them, then perhaps I could die in peace.

Chapter 41

"Nonsense, absolute nonsense," Brauner spluttered. "I won't do it."

We were back in Resurrection City. It was a week after. That's how I referred to my life now. The week after. The day after. Anything after, because the David I'd been was buried deep inside *The House* where he'd been spawned. The new David, who as far as I was concerned didn't deserve to live, showed remarkable mental resiliency. All the talk about dying was just that, talk. I didn't really want to die, I just didn't have the guts to admit it to myself. Instead I made a decision that I might regret for the rest of my life.

I confronted Brauner with it a week after we returned from The House. Back in the isolation of Terwilliger, where life went on as if nothing had changed, and Rachel Firestein still ruled the outer office with an iron fist and a nasty attitude. I shut the door on Firestein and motioned Brauner to have a seat. Surprised by my show of authority, he sat and waited patiently while I worked up my nerve to say what was on my mind.

"I want you to Retool me," I blurted, catching him by surprise.

He raised his eyebrows into two question marks and skipped a breath. "What on earth are you talking about?"

"Just what I said. I want you to Retool me, you know, finish the job. Is that so hard to understand?"

"Finish what?"

"Finish what you started," I said. "You made me into someone whom I can't live with, so the choice is yours. Either make me into the person you wanted me to become or change me back to who I was."

"It's not as easy as that," he objected. "It takes time, years of careful work."

"I've got a lifetime."

Brauner didn't reply but his expression told me that he was carefully weighing the pros and cons of my request. I held my breath. The stakes were high, not only for me but for Resurrection.

After what seemed an eternity Brauner stirred, his mind made up. He looked pained. "I'm not so sure I know what kind of person I want you to be," he admitted. "At one time I thought I knew but life was simpler then. Logic and order dictated our decisions. Nowadays it seems that the human heart has become an equal par of the equation."

Funny, hearing this from a man who probably didn't have a heart. Even funnier, I thought, that he and I would have this conversation, considering that it was my heart that was taking the risk of becoming as heartless as him. To be honest though, wasn't I acting out of selfishness? After all, whatever person he'd ultimately turn me into, I could always blame him.

"Talking about the human heart," I picked up on his comments, "this human heart has one last request."

"What's that?" he asked warily.

"The remaining patients you have in the *House* right now, I want them released. After that I don't give a damn what happens. I'll be whatever you make of me. Take it or leave it."

For a moment I thought Brauner would laugh. "You must be joking," he said. "They're what keeps this place going. They're worth a lot of money, money we need to keep Resurrection running."

"Bastard."

Not surprisingly, seeing his pain made me feel good. It was probably the first time I took joy in hurting someone. Nevertheless it was easy to justify my behavior. If anyone deserved it, it surely was Brauner.

"It's my only offer," I continued. "I'll trade you my life for the thirty or so patients in the *House*. You let them go and I'll do whatever you want."

"All right," Brauner agreed, a little too quickly for my liking, making me feel as if I had played right into his hands. "Under one condition."

"What's the condition."

"You'll take over for me. You become Resurrection's Chief Administrator."

"And what are you going to do?" I asked, incredulous that I, an ex-Disciple, was being offered the highest position in Camp.

Brauner took a moment or two to form his words. When he spoke, I was convinced that he was speaking the truth. "I'm an old man. Seventy-one years of life has taken its toll on me. A wise man is one who knows when to pack it in and I plan to live out the rest of my life as a wise man."

The offer was so unexpected, the burden so enormous, that I was at a loss for words. All I could manage was a feeble, "I wouldn't know where to start. I'm not qualified to take over."

"Who'd be better qualified than you? Think about it, David. You're one of the Camp's children. You are Camp Resurrection, you're its flesh and blood."

"I can't," I said. "I can't do it."

"Then there's no deal. The next shipment goes out as planned."

He sealed his comment with a shot of Wild Turkey and waved for me to leave the office. "Good bye, David. There's nothing more to be discussed."

It took me less than a minute to capitulate. Weighing the pros and cons tipped the scales in his favor. "All right," I said. "You win. I'll do as you say. But all patients in The House must be released."

He shook his head. "It's too late for some of them," he said. "Sixteen have already been processed."

I flinched. Processed: the clinical word for butchery. Limbs and organs packed on ice, ready for shipment. "All right, the sixteen you're talking about will be given a Christian burial. The others must be released."

"That's impossible," Brauner pleaded. "You don't understand the condition they're in. Some are vegetables by now, they don't have the mental capacity to exist. Others would pose a serious security risk. Take John Brothers for example, he still remembers how…"

"Stop," I shouted, covering my ears. "Don't say another word. I don't want to know who's alive and who isn't. I don't want the responsibility of condemning even a single person to death. I don't want to play God, I can't. They have to remain nameless and faceless or I'll go out of my mind."

"There is no God," Brauner scoffed. "But if there were, he'd want them to die. It's the merciful thing to do."

"You're dead wrong," I said. "There must be a God because without God there wouldn't be a devil, and without the devil there wouldn't be someone like you. And so help me God, unless you do as I say I'll blow the whistle on you and everybody else in Resurrection."

Brauner smiled. "I guess I've just witnessed the not so immaculate conception and birth of our Savior," he said. "Welcome to our imperfect world, David."

*****

I accompanied Brauner to the mass burial two days later. Sixteen gaping black holes received sixteen plain wooden coffins. I walked from grave to grave and threw a handful of earth into each, said a quick prayer, and returned to Brauner's side. Sixteen wooden crosses were driven into the ground bearing sixteen John Does. No names. No dates of birth. No dates of death.

Following the funeral we stopped at The House. At my insistence I inspected fifty patient rooms. All name plates had been removed. Each room stood empty. Eye-stinging disinfectant odors permeated each room. Gurneys and wires and tubes dangled from ceiling connections. Fifty monitors, although still connected to a central computer site, stood silent.

In contrast, The House's Recovery and Reconstruction wing buzzed with unusual activity, although I took Brauner's word for it. I refused to take the elevator to sub-basement 2 to observe the work being done on the remaining patients who had been spared. The process was a delicate one as Brauner explained in excruciating detail during our daily 9:00 AM strategy meeting at Terwilliger.

At first I had dreaded hearing about the reconstructive process. Brauner was right. It was too late for some, and they were better off dead. They were removed from their life support systems and allowed to die. Fortunately, twenty-eight remaining patients had a legitimate chance of recovery. The problem however lay in the definition of recovery. As I found out this morning, Brauner's idea of recovery was different from mine.

*****

"Well, we're finished. This is the last one," Brauner stated. He signed a medical chart with a flourish and stamped it *Complete*. He was about to place it on a growing stack of release forms when I stopped him.

"Not so fast," I said. "Let me see the prognosis."

"Help yourself." Brauner sounded annoyed. "If you think you know more than I do then maybe you should take complete charge."

"It's not a matter of knowing more," I said testily. "It's a matter of trying to make sure that these people can function when they're released into society. So I want to know what skills they have, what level of social interaction they've attained, and so forth."

"Who said anything about society," Brauner asked, shaking his head. "They'll never live anywhere but right here in Resurrection."

I guess I should have known but his answer caught me by surprise. "What the hell are you talking about? I thought this whole exercise was to heal them and get them out of here. I mean, I don't understand this voodoo medicine you're practicing. I know you've got all kinds of scientific names for it but to me it's nothing but witchcraft. So why are you doing all of this if the best they can expect is to live the same miserable life they've had in Resurrection?"

With Brauner's professional expertise under attack he turned furious. "Is that what you think I'm doing, voodoo? Witchcraft? How about neural stimulation and genetic engineering? I use the most advanced medical and psychiatric techniques known to man, like splicing, sensory impulse adjustment, memory infusion, and so on. The list goes on and on. I work miracles. I create life. And you have the nerve to denigrate my work. You make me sick, you and your do-good attitude. Well, just remember one thing, I made you. I molded you and breathed life into you. If it weren't for me you'd be just like them, another Disciple whose worth is proportionate to the height and weight of his body, like an animal that's brought to a slaughterhouse."

Brauner jumped out of his chair and swept twenty-eight patient charts off his desk. He stood trembling, hands balled into fists, he kicked the folders, propelling medical forms and computer printouts across the floor. Like a man possessed, he refused to stop, kicking and stomping violently until he ran out of breath. When he stopped he sank to his knees and started to sob, gathering papers and smoothing creased pages. "Look at what you've made me do," he said between sobs and pointed an accusing hand at me. "They're my children, my proudest achievement."

I knelt next to him and helped him retrieve the last of the papers. Feeling a tremendous surge of compassion, I placed my arm around his shoulders and held him until his sobs subsided. "C'mon Bruno," I said. "Let me help you. Let your children live."

*****

Six of his children did live. It took three months to eradicate all traces of the *House* from their minds, a process I took immense interest in. Over time I found Brauner's work increasingly fascinating. Brauner modestly referred to it as vacuuming the brain. It was not an inaccurate description. He used various techniques with varying degrees of success but in the end their experiences in Camp Resurrection were completely erased from memory. This was followed by virtual reality treatments, the crowning achievement that would give them a new identity, realistic experiences of a false life supported by new identification papers, including such items as birth certificates, diplomas, and social security cards. Heavily sedated, they were transported by ambulance to University Medical Center in

Manhattan, where they were to be released over the next two weeks after receiving treatment for amnesia suffered due to accidents.

Case closed. All loose ends tied up. All Ts crossed and Is dotted. A new beginning for six Disciples who had graduated beyond Apostle. Time would tell how successful the new Resurrection would be.

*****

Mt greatest achievement at the helm of the new Resurrection was the transformation of The House, The most sinister reminder of the past had been turned into a hospital. Instead of despair and death it now stood for healing and life. This monumental change came with terrible consequences however. In fact, disaster loomed on the horizon. Brauner made it abundantly clear that in a very real way the new Resurrection was a miserable failure.

"We'll be out of money in less than three months," he stated flatly. His eyes said what he didn't have to tell me, *I told you so.*

"Well, find some money somewhere," I said, not willing to get bogged down in the everyday minutiae of running a vast prison. "There must be a million ways you can raise cash."

"Name one," he said.

"I don't know. What if we sell some land? We've got acres and acres just waiting to be snapped up by real estate developers. We certainly don't have any use for it."

Brauner laughed. "Just like that, huh? I'll just put an ad in the Times. How about something like this, *Prime prison acreage for sale in gated community. Guaranteed right of way through containment perimeter. Call David Koertner to arrange escorted tour.* Look, there's only one way we're going to be self-sufficient. We have to reopen the *House.*"

"Over my dead body," I shouted, shaking my head vehemently. Under my tutelage The House had been turned into a major research hospital unrivaled in upstate New York. I was not willing to return it to its sinister past. Unfortunately, a large portion of the building stood empty. There just weren't enough patients in Resurrection to fill its six thousand beds. The more sinister sections of the *House* had been sealed off. But without the income of a wholesale body-part and organ farm the rest of Resurrection had fallen on hard times. So hard that Brauner's suggestion made financial sense, as repugnant as it was.

"Look, David, we don't have to go back to the past, he pleaded. "Just a limited operation to cover some of our operating expenses."

I shook my head, "I have a better idea," I said. "Blackmail."

Brauner was puzzled and interested at the same time. "Whom?" he asked.

"Senator Kerr," I said. "I hear he's loaded. It wouldn't take a lot of arm-twisting to convince him that an endowment is in his best interest."

"I hate to tell you this but a couple of million, which is probably the most you'll get out of him, wouldn't cover our expenses for more than half a year. Then what?"

"Then I'll worry about it in six months," I closed our conversation.

Kerr proved to be more than cooperative. His net worth was well over three-hundred million. As an expression of my gratitude, I invited Kerr to take up residence in Resurrection. He was less than cooperative but I prevailed. Of course I went to lengths to make sure his new home was appropriate for a man of his stature. He was assigned to room twenty-three the *House*, the very same room once occupied by Paulette Kowalski.

Chapter 42

I THREW MYSELF into my assignments with untiring enthusiasm, viewing them as a chance to make a real difference. And I grudgingly agreed with Brauner's earlier assessment. Who could be better qualified than I to run Camp Resurrection? I also knew that Brauner would be of invaluable help. Whatever I didn't know, and there was a mountain of unknowns, he was at my side, helping, counseling, and teaching.

We remained in our respective offices, he in the impressive, wood-paneled space he'd always called home while I chose to stay in my closet-sized office. I certainly didn't need the trappings of success, and I wanted to show him the respect he deserved. As far as I was concerned, he did command respect. Only now, after having taken over the reigns, did I realize that running Resurrection was an all-consuming job. Actually it was more than a job, it was a lifelong sacrifice.

We disagreed vehemently on some issues but found common ground on many others. Our biggest bone of contention was Resurrection's cottage industry. Never again would I allow another shipment. But even I grudgingly agreed that we might someday resume limited research. After all, research was the backbone of scientific breakthrough, and I had no intention of letting Resurrection become a backwater of modern medicine.

"Okay, as long as it is strictly controlled," I agreed during one of our weekly status meetings. "And as long as we use acceptable medical practices. And as long as we only use patients that are terminally ill."

"Absolutely," Brauner agreed and raised his glass. "To compromise and success."

We clinked glasses. "You know something, Bruno? You were right. This stuff isn't so bad after all."

I sipped my Wild Turkey, a habit I had fallen into easily. The warm glow it produced far outweighed an occasional hangover. As long as I drank moderately there really wasn't any reason to deny myself an occasional indulgence.

"How about that new mission statement you proposed?" Brauner switched to another subject as we put away our glasses and locked up the Bourbon. "Have you made up your mind?"

"Absolutely," I said. "I think our most critical mission is to preserve Resurrection's insularity. If I've learned anything from the past, it's that the outside world must remain just that, an outside world. Who knows how things would have turned out if people like Justin hadn't had an inkling that there was more to life than Resurrection? I'll bet you anything he'd still be alive."

"I agree, but that means we'll have to institute a total news blackout again."

I agreed reluctantly. "Yes. I know it sounds crazy, me being the ex-editor of the Sentinel and all, but we can't take a chance. No more controversial articles in the Sentinel. Let's keep it confined to things like pie-baking contests or Bible-class news. And WREN should probably be limited to nothing but classical music. And I want you to head up a commission to evaluate every book we've got in this place. If there's a hint of controversy, even something as innocuous Rip Van Winkle, I want it out of circulation. You never know when someone puts two and two together, you know, like reading about the Catskill mountains and says, hey, that's where Resurrection is, and so on and so forth. I don't want to go so far as burning books but they need to be locked up in a secure location."

Brauner looked skeptical. "We've got to give our Disciples something in return," he said. "If it's not radio or the Sentinel then we have to replace it with something else."

"Yes and no," I said. Brauner gave me a quizzical look and I explained. "The trick is to keep them physically challenged. What

I'm saying is let them expend their energy working and participating in some sort of athletic activity. Make sure they're so tired that all they want to do is go to sleep. You see what I'm saying, Bruno? A tired mind is dull mind. A tired mind doesn't ask questions."

"I don't know," Brauner said skeptically. "I don't think that's the answer. We need everyone to be happy with their existence. We need more than just strenuous activity."

Brauner was right of course. Reluctantly I gave in to reason. I had to propose the one thing I had vowed to eradicate forever. "Retooling" I said reluctantly. "We have to fine-tune and re-establish Retooling."

"I can't believe what I'm hearing." Brauner was incredulous.

"Yes. If we have to create a nation of sheep, well, so be it."

Brauner didn't say a word. The silence in the office was deafening. Now that I made up my mind I couldn't wait to change the subject. But I felt compelled to defend my proposal "Think about, Bruno. Our Disciples are unfortunate throwaways of society. They're genetically inferior but they aren't modern-day lepers. We can't risk heaping more misery onto these poor souls. If that means suppressing their curiosity to learn, well, so be it. They must never know. After all is said and done they're our responsibility. We have to protect them. We need to give them our never ending love and compassion. They're our children."

"Consider it done."

*****

And so we took a small step backward on the road to reshaping Resurrection. A small price to pay, considering the other changes I instituted over the past year. Some were purely symbolic. Fair Street has been renamed Frederikson Plaza. The overgrown lot where Justin was gunned down was transformed into a beautiful park. A small fountain marked the exact spot where he died. Frederikson Plaza will also be the site of an annual candlelight vigil in his honor. The *Apostle's Lounge* was reopened to all Disciples. So was the John Street library annex, although most books were locked up in a restricted vault. I had insisted on it.

Less visible but far more important was the selection of Colonel Axton's replacement. I was a member of the candidate search committee and cast the deciding vote in favor of Curtis Jacobson, a hard-nosed but decent career prison administrator. Jacobson's tough enforcement of Camp rules was initially greeted with skepticism but he has since become a popular figure in the Camp.

My proudest achievement to date was passage of a new Disciples Dignity Act. Never again would Disciples be treated like second-class citizens. Dorm room doors could now be locked for privacy, curfews were lifted, and the drab Resurrection Rags were abandoned in favor of conventional clothing. Personal preference would dictate fashion, not a trio of Camp administrators. Hard as it was to believe, this provision proved to be the most popular, spawning a massive public burning of the hated Rags by thousands of Disciples attired in the style of the moment, jeans and T-shirts. How easy it was to please these unfortunate children. How blessed they were not knowing of their genetic handicaps. How zealously I had to safeguard their future.

But despite improvements many problems remained. Brauner had hit it right on the head. Senator Kerr's money dried up in the first year. With lucrative government contracts cancelled, I had to rely on federal grants that were being slashed every year. Lately there'd been talk of closing Resurrection and transferring its population to federal penitentiaries across the country. I couldn't let that happen. I couldn't let my children be incarcerated like common criminals. I wracked my brain every day and spent many sleepless nights in search of money. Money.

*****

Money was the topic of discussion this morning as well. Brauner and I waited for the elevator to take us to the Recovery and Reconstruction wing at *The House*. I had become a frequent visitor at the facility, drawn to the once sinister hospital as much by choice as by necessity. Seeing first-hand how the focus had shifted from death to life helped me cope with some of the difficult decisions that had to be made. This morning was no exception.

The doors opened. I followed Brauner into the cab and at the spur of the moment pushed the sub basement button. Brauner looked up quizzically. "I thought we're going to R and R?"

"We will," I answered. "I just want to check up on Kerr."

Brauner shrugged his shoulders and remained silent. It wasn't an unusual request although I had avoided the sub basement during every prior visit. Now, making our way along a deserted corridor, passing by the central lab and seeing forty-nine of its fifty monitors shut off, my anxiety grew with each step.

Forty-nine doors stoop open, revealing stripped down hospital beds and scrubbed floors. Door twenty-three was locked. Behind it Kerr paced like a caged animal. Seeing him was a shock. The once robust senator had deteriorated badly. Matted strands of gray hair hung to his shoulders and he was unshaven. Fever sores covered his lips. His complexion had the pallor of death. Dried food stained his green hospital gown. He seemed to be talking to himself, incessantly babbling the same words over and over. I put my ear against the door but couldn't hear anything. He suddenly looked up as if he'd sensed that someone was on the other side. Our eyes met. His stare bore into me and I recoiled. Then, just as quickly as he had looked up he lowered his eyes and continued pacing.

"How's he doing?" I asked, trying to sound calm.

"Well, that depends," Brauner said. "Physically he's okay. He lost some weight and he's a bit weak from lack of exercise but overall, not too bad. Considering he's been locked up for almost a year he's holding up pretty well. Mentally it's a different story though. He's lost touch with reality. He thinks that he's the second coming of Christ. He spends all day talking to God. Says they're planning for a new kingdom on Earth and that he's in The House to give his life for mankind."

"He may be closer to the truth than he realizes."

"Huh? What the hell are you talking about?"

I ignored Brauner's question, studying Kerr through the reinforced window. "You did say he's in good health," I commented. "I mean there's nothing wrong with him, right?"

"That's what I said. What're you driving at?"

"And we *are* running a huge deficit, right?"

Brauner shot a curious glance in my direction. "That's right."

"Tell me, Bruno, what's the going price nowadays on the black-market for lungs and kidneys and eyes and so on."

"Don't forget hearts," Brauner added.

"I'm not so sure you're going to find one in him but if you do it'll probably pay someone's salary for a couple of years."

We shook hands. In the final analysis, it hadn't been such a difficult decision after all.

Epilogue

I MOVED INTO Brauner's office a week after his death. His was a simple funeral, attended by a handful of friends. I felt strangely moved, as if I'd lost a father, and in a way I had. So what if Brauner had been unscrupulous? So what if he had been the instrument of death for some of our poor Disciples? Because of him thousands lived. Because of him I lived.

Of course I could never fill his shoes. The best I could hope for was to make a small difference, one contribution at a time. But lately my achievements paled in comparison to insurmountable problems. Getting volunteer workers was our most pressing need. With very little money available, we had to rely on volunteers for everything. The list of openings was a mile long. Doctors and nurses and psychiatrists. Teachers. Counselors. Secretaries. Technicians to keep our power plants running. Laborers to patch potholes and pick up garbage, cooks for the mess halls. You name it, we had a job opening for it. Our entire infrastructure was beginning to crumble into terrible disrepair. And our bills kept soaring. Soon my children would be doomed. I simply couldn't let that happen.

*****

There really was no other choice. And like any family, some of my children really didn't deserve to live, But they could help the thousands who deserved to live. The end justified the means, didn't it? And it would be a very limited operation. The shipments would we very small compared to what they had been in the past. 'I'm sure Brauner would have approved.

*****

It had been a particularly bad afternoon. I'd spent the entire day interviewing recruits and hired only two people, a nursery teacher and a computer operator. Only one applicant remained, waiting patiently in the anteroom.

Brauner's medical diploma was prominently displayed behind the desk. Next to it hung my Apostle certificate. A small Christmas tree glittered cheerfully on a credenza. The old visitor's chair that I had occupied so often held the day's completed work, small in comparison to the mountain of papers still on my desk.

Discouraged by my lack of progress I decided to call it quits for the day. I still had to attend a Christmas performance by some of Resurrection's youngest inmates. Although I wasn't in the mood to celebrate, I couldn't possibly let them down. They had practiced for weeks, and their rousing rendition of Handel's *Messiah* was remarkable. Then it was on to a crucial budget meeting. Then an inspection of the local butcher shop, where unsanitary conditions caused an outbreak of salmonella poisoning. Then…

I reached for the Wild Turkey and poured three fingers. A quick drink and I'd be out of here. I drained the bourbon and was tempted to pour another, but the intercom buzzer stopped me before I could refill my glass.

"Mr. Koertner. Your last interview, did you forget?"

"Oh. yes. Sorry Rachel." I capped the bottle and placed it on the top shelf. I'm sure Brauner would have appreciated it. "I'm almost ready. Just give me another minute."

"Yes, sir. And if you don't mind, I'll leave now. I still have to…"

"Go ahead, Rachel. I'll lock up when I'm finished."

*****

I swiveled my chair to face the window and stared at Albany Avenue. For just one moment, before my last interview, I wanted to lose myself in oblivion. Forget. Maybe even die.

A soft knock was followed by muffled footsteps as Rachel Firestein left. I swiveled the chair back to the desk and searched for the remaining applicant's folder.

Another soft knock.

"Come in."

I found myself looking at a tall and thin woman with shoulder length black hair and large brown eyes. She balanced wire-rimmed glasses on the tip of her nose and had a nervous habit of blinking her eyes. But she had the most beautiful and compassionate smile I have ever seen. I couldn't tear my eyes off her.

She appeared nervous and self-conscious. "It's from a car accident."

"I...I'm...I'm not sure what you mean."

"This," she explained matter of fact, her index finger tracing the faint outline of a scar that ran from the corner of her right eye to her mouth. "I was sixteen years old when it happened."

I followed the path of her finger, hypnotized by its slow progress across her cheek. "I'm sorry, I didn't mean to stare. I was just..." I felt stinging heat rising and knew my ears had turned deep red.

"It's okay." A quick smile curled her lips. "It always happens when I meet someone for the first time. No need to apologize."

About the Author

THIS IS JOERG Mueller's first published (and fourth unpublished) novel. Now seventy-nine years old, Mueller started dabbling in creative writing at the tender age of thirteen, beginning on a manual typewriter and finally graduating to a PC. Along the way Mueller attended creative writing courses at Hunter College and the New School for Social Research in New York City, and published his own literary magazine with his college writing buddies.

Writing has been a lifelong passion for Mueller, but life got in the way in the form of a family and work. Now in retirement, he has returned to pursue his lifelong dream and published his first novel. "*It keeps me young*," Mueller claims.

After a lifetime of living in big cities, he now splits his time between the mid-Hudson valley of Upstate New York and the Jersey shore with his wife of fifty-six years.

CPSIA information can be obtained
at www.ICGtesting.com
Printed in the USA
BVHW041015280621
610637BV00002B/309